Also by Ned Calmer

BEYOND THE STREET
WHEN NIGHT DESCENDS
THE STRANGE LAND
ALL THE SUMMER DAYS
THE ANCHORMAN
THE AVIMA AFFAIR
LATE SHOW

Madam Ambassador

Madam Ambassador

❖ ❖ ❖

NED CALMER

1975

Doubleday & Company, Inc., Garden City, New York

ISBN: 0-385-05106-9
LIBRARY OF CONGRESS CATALOG CARD NUMBER: 74-24484
COPYRIGHT © 1975 BY NED CALMER
PRINTED IN THE UNITED STATES OF AMERICA
FIRST EDITION

26493

All of the characters
in this book are fictitious,
and any resemblance to actual persons,
living or dead,
is purely coincidental.

For Gloria

Madam Ambassador

1

Sᴇɪʟᴀ, ᴀ ᴅᴀꜱʜɪɴɢ ɢɪʀʟ (happily married, alas), came to the door of my office and said, "The undersecretary called while you were at lunch and wants to see you immediately, Mr. Paine."

"The hell you say."

I gathered from the deadpan reaction to my remark that Sheila found the expression unsuitable, as I'd expected. Actually the summons wasn't all that surprising—I'm one of the undersecretary's special assistants and I talk with him frequently, though usually by phone. But I can't resist needling the unflappable Sheila. It annoys me that after nearly two years she still won't call me Tyler, even during our most intimate moments, like when she brings ten o'clock coffee and pours it as she leans over my desk. God knows I've encouraged her to be informal. But Sheila is of those who bask in the cold light of dignity, one of several reasons why she fits in well at the Department of State.

"What's it about?" I said, as if Sheila would necessarily know.

"I think you'd better go right now" was her advice.

I thought I'd better. Hurrying through the corridor, I looked at my watch and realized I'd stretched my lunch hour well beyond habitual limits. But it was such a beautiful day—a crime to be indoors. Washington, in the early spring of 1977, was at its loveliest. With a friend from Philadelphia, in town for a few hours on government business, I'd lunched handsomely at the Sans Souci before he headed homeward, and I'd strolled, not to say rambled, reluctantly back to the not very appealing stack of paper work awaiting me and the equally uninviting surroundings I work in.

I was bound for that exclusive area of the building where the most important and most secret matters of our country's international affairs are conducted. As always, the eagle-eyed Miss Saw-yer was on duty behind the reception desk, and as always, she waved me on toward the inner sanctums, down the very private hallway where the brooding eyes of former Secretaries of State stare at you out of their portraits on the walls.

As many times as I've taken this short walk, I never pass these pictures without feeling a couple of ghosts are following me. No place else on the premises has the same atmosphere. People who've seen the rest of the department find it a fairly cheerful place, sort of institutional, if you like, but still cheerful. The inner court, the long corridors, and that sumptuous top floor, with its pleasant dining room and the promenade looking out across the city and the Potomac to the leafy vistas of Virginia—all that can make a most attractive impression. Unfortunately, I spend most of my time in a part of the building which reminds me more of the *old* State Department—that gloomy gray pile across from the White House now used by presidential staff. Being a lover of light, space, and air, I feel somehow stifled and oppressed in these top-echelon offices with their massive leather chairs and dark paneling.

Was the prospect really that dreary, or was it just the spring day that made my current life seem suddenly drab? Friends often think my job is stimulating, even glamorous, working so close to the top in a government rejuvenated by the "New Broom" administration which swept the '76 elections, with its new faces, new ideas, and evident will to give the country a fresh start, domestically and internationally, after the trauma of the previous four years. And it *was* very special at first—scheduling the undersecretary's visitors, managing his correspondence, providing staff backup when he's traveling. I handle his action memorandums, shift through two or three hundred cables every day, bringing only about a dozen to his personal attention. And take care of his visitors—foreign am-bassadors, appointments with delegates of special interest and discussion groups, businessmen, students or teachers, labor or-ganizations. Frequently I sit in, as there may be follow-up neces-sary. And I'm on the phone a lot relaying the undersecretary's thoughts to deputy undersecretaries, desk officers, and others. On occasion I even see the Secretary of State, "Stoneface" himself, as he's not too cordially called by some of my colleagues.

A word about Stoneface. Although in office only a few short months, he was already building a reputation within the department for autocratic behavior toward subordinates and fits of sudden violent temper. He also was partial to arrogating decisions to himself alone, with a taste for secrecy, and would mysteriously drop out of touch for days at a time, so that even the White House and my boss the undersecretary didn't know how to reach him.

Aside from this quirky situation, I manage to keep pretty much abreast of what's going on. I guess what irks is my role as a conduit, rather than having any responsibility of my own for serious decisions. And my overseas experience has left a tantalizing aftertaste of nostalgia, especially when springtime comes around again. At any rate the undersecretary's message was a break in the routine, whatever it was about.

He didn't keep me in suspense. They were expecting me all along the bank of secretaries and I was ushered in without delay.

Silver-haired Mitchell Remington sat alone behind his desk—large, somber, rimless glasses, the perfect portrait of a veteran career man. By contrast to my own desk, there was hardly a paper on his, denoting, of course, our difference in rank. He bade me to a nearby chair and looked upon me with benevolent gravity. "What I have to tell you, Tyler, must remain totally classified until further notice."

That was normal. "Certainly, sir."

"I have a rather special assignment in mind. Let me add that you are perfectly at liberty to decline it, but I'm rather hoping you'll like the idea."

I could feel an unexpected awakening of curiosity. "Press on," I said, and smiled.

"I've been going over your background in France. I assume the information on record is all accurate?"

France. The curiosity yielded to a slight thumping of the heart. Then I remembered to say, "Oh yes indeed."

"Conversant with the language since childhood, speaking and writing? Some schooling in Switzerland and the Sorbonne before

Yale? Three years at the Paris embassy, Cultural Affairs?" He peered a little over his glasses. "Liked it there, did you?"

"Decidedly." The thumping became a warm, spreading glow.

"One other consideration. You'll have to bring me up to date on this. You're not contemplating marriage at the moment?"

I gave him my sunniest grin. "That is correct."

The undersecretary settled in his high-backed chair. "I don't mean to mystify you further with questions, Tyler. The President has decided to nominate Mrs. Mariana Hillman Otis to be ambassador to France. We want someone who can work with her as special assistant—someone from the department who has our confidence, who can serve as her interpreter on public occasions and, in general, make himself useful to the ambassador in whatever capacity may be required. I have suggested to the Secretary that you would qualify in all respects."

I sat there slightly stunned, as much because a woman would be given the Paris post as at the idea of Tyler Paine becoming her assistant. Internationally, we were going through an extremely delicate period. Détente with Russia was the popular theme. By contrast, our relations with France were at their lowest ebb in many months, partly because the previous ambassador had been unpopular but mostly due to fluctuating political conditions in that country. In fact relations with Western Europe in general were poor (always excepting West Germany, a favorite of the Secretary's). The trend in Congress on these issues seemed increasingly irritable—a sign perhaps of that recent development called the New Isolationism. Talk of disengagement, not only from Europe but from our expensive commitments in Asia and the Mideast as well, was becoming more general in Washington, and a lot of people were wondering whether the new President wanted to make it policy.

They would have done better to keep their eyes on the new Secretary of State. From where I sat it was the Secretary, not the President, who seemed to be making foreign policy. Stoneface had the ball, and the question was which way he was going to run with it. The man made me uneasy. I tried to tell myself this was just a case of gut reaction to his personality. After all, we can't like everybody. I had no objection to him on any other grounds. But the feeling persisted.

The undersecretary was saying, "Does the proposal interest you? If it does, I think I can spare you for the job."

"My reaction is entirely favorable, sir. If I seemed to hesitate it was only because I was a bit, well, startled. I mean the President is certainly breaking with tradition, putting a woman in such a major post. Especially at this time."

He almost smiled, in a resigned sort of way, the old department hand who's seen everything in his day. "Ours not to reason why, Tyler. A dynamic administration has come to power. Public attitudes have changed. The President is an innovator, as you've doubtless already observed, and he intends to have his way."

I wondered if Stoneface himself in this case didn't think maybe innovating can go too far. But even the Secretary of State serves at the President's pleasure, and there was certainly no indication he would put his job on the line so soon because of Mariana Otis. I was still curious, though. "I shouldn't have thought that of all people the French would consent to this."

"They were reluctant, no doubt about it. But I suspect they're anxious not to offend the new administration so early in the game. We've just received their approval." He stood up to signify the discussion was ended, and I thought I saw the beginning of a twinkle in his eye. "You feel equal to the task, Tyler?"

"If Mrs. Otis is equal to it, I guess I am. I'll be frank to say I know very little about her other than what everybody reads in the papers. I've never met her."

"We're going to give you that opportunity. Mrs. Otis is expecting you for an interview tomorrow at eleven. She's staying at her father's house on Connecticut Avenue." He paused and took a brown manila envelope out of his desk drawer. "I suggest you look over this biographical material very carefully. It contains just about everything that's ever been published about Mariana Hillman Otis, plus the department's own assessment and including the FBI report—full field investigation. Eyes only."

"Of course." I took the envelope and we shook hands.

"Stop in again tomorrow afternoon, Tyler. We shall want to

keep in touch from now on. And remember, say nothing to anyone."

I paused a moment outside his office to ponder. Why hadn't I seen any hint of this in the undersecretary's cable or letter file? It had to be because the matter was so delicate it was being handled directly by the Secretary and the White House.

I also retained a distinct impression there would be more to my job than I had yet been told.

Waiting to be received by Mrs. Otis in what could only be called a Jamesian drawing room, into which I had been introduced by an impeccably low-keyed manservant, I felt again that little flurry of dazed emotion which persists during unexpected upheavals in the life schedule. On the pale cream walls reaching to the lofty ceiling hung several of Herbert Hillman's collection of celebrated paintings. One was obviously a Manet. Another was most certainly a Renoir. And the wild one had to be Picasso. I couldn't place either of the abstracts but they looked familiar. Prohibitively valuable they undoubtedly were—if Herbert Hillman possessed any piece of art worth less than a hundred thou, I would be highly surprised. As the owner of one small Winslow Homer and a tiny Miró, I sighed in envy. But I resisted the temptation to snoop around for signatures—and be caught looking. It just wasn't that kind of room.

By now, thanks to my cramming on the family background, I knew quite a bit about Herbert Hillman from the moment of his birth in the New York ghetto, son of a Lithuanian immigrant, to his present eminent philanthropic status. And anyone researching the daughter will discover that she's intimately linked with her famous father. Checking through the bio material chronologically, I got the impression that after the mother's death, when Mariana was fifteen, father and daughter grew very close and kept it like that. This apparently was so even after her marriage at only twenty to Clay Otis, a young Maryland aristocrat (they met in college). She bore him a daughter who was ten when Clay was killed in a hunting accident. I kept running across young-married pictures of Clay and Mariana in which his father-in-law appeared more often

16

than seemed necessary, holding tight to Mariana's arm. Later snapshots included Christine, who would now be about seventeen. She had that uncomfortable teen-age look of being photographed. (Our ever-watchful operatives from the Justice Department had certainly done a thorough job of cribbing from newspaper files.)

The background material also showed that Mariana took after her own mother in many ways. She was a national committeewoman from her home state by the time she was thirty, as her mother had been before her. Incidentally I suspected that the "Mariana" came from Mary Ann Gallagher Hillman, who must have almost risen from the grave in pride when a grateful President credited her daughter with devising the strategy that won him wide feminine support in the November election—his naming of outstanding women to high government posts, a pledge on which he made good when elected.

So the appointment to Paris couldn't simply have been a payoff to Herbert, one of the country's richest conglomerate tycoons and very large contributor to the 1976 campaign chest. This was no mere figurehead whose daddy bought her way in. She evidently was as bright an intellectual as the late Mary Ann, with added advantages like Radcliffe, *summa cum laude*, which her mother never had in the Hillmans' early struggling years. Counting off the pluses in her track record, you would have to concede that not since Clare Boothe Luce went to Rome back in the fifties had so likely a female presented herself for a diplomatic post. And Mariana was only thirty-nine. I suppose that's where I came in—to help ward off the boo-boos of diplomatic inexperience. At thirty-eight I was even younger than she was. But maybe they thought we'd relate better this way.

I wondered about Clay Otis—why they ever got married in the first place. He was certainly neither intellectual nor political. She didn't seem to have any great enthusiasm for horses or fox hunts. But there was nothing in all the stuff I'd read to indicate it had been anything but a normal marriage. He'd been a keen amateur photographer, and they both liked to travel—Russia, Africa, the Far East. I guessed it was Mariana who was interested in the history. Clay would have liked the local color and the shooting. But somehow it still seemed like an odd match to me, and there remained the question of why this young and vital woman had not remarried.

My little reverie was interrupted by the appearance in the flesh of the chief subject—accompanied, not surprisingly, by her father, and by a younger, swarthy, rather flashily dressed man introduced to me as Marcus Feld. It wasn't really necessary to have identified Mr. Feld—I recognized him as the high-powered Washington attorney who represented a score of nationally known big shots as well as various Herbert Hillman interests. Mr. Feld thrust out a hand with a lot of gold on it, gave me a piercing once-over, and seemed reluctant to leave, but did so when Mrs. Otis (somewhat pointedly, I thought) bade him good-bye.

As for the two who remained in the room with me, the very first impressions, I'm told, can be the truest, and I quickly sensed that although they both adored each other it was daughter who very subtly dominated. Even in the opening commonplaces, getting seated, taking the glasses of sherry from the silver tray proffered by the gliding manservant (none for Mr. Hillman), it was clear that she was in charge, and that this frail, soft-voiced but rather hard-eyed old man would have it no other way.

How to describe Mariana Hillman Otis? Striking might be the best word. Possibly, in certain dresses and lights, even beautiful. And one other reaction that surprised me—more sexily attractive than her pictures revealed, though I had an impression she tended to hold it back. Most impressive of all was the quality of intelligence she radiated in the challenging gaze, incisive voice. She made me feel at once that practical achievement, success, was all she really cared about in the world.

It was disrespectful of me, and none of my business, but in those first few moments of observation I found myself wondering if Clay Otis had had the same feeling about her in bed.

The interview wasn't at all what I'd expected. For one thing, it was a little unsettling to feel the steady scrutiny of her silent partner. I had come prepared to reassure the neophyte diplomat that being head of an embassy with one thousand employees was not as frightening as it sounded, to fill her in on the basic routines of the job, and to get in return some idea of what she would require in our proposed relationship. Instead I was confronted with the most searching examination of my own personal history, views, and tastes, and assailed by a barrage of penetrating questions, all political, about the situation in France, the current Paris team, the people in the European Bureau at State. A lot of those questions I was unable to answer, and I began to feel as if I'd been the sole interviewee, drained of what knowledge I possessed.

I wasn't sure I liked Mrs. Otis.

But our leave-taking was gracious enough, with a frank handshake, a cool smile, and Papa looking enigmatically on. As the servant opened the front door for me I was nearly knocked down —well, rudely brushed aside, anyhow—by a handsome young girl in blazer and flannel skirt with a school bag in one hand who went loping past and into the hall.

"Cristy!" Mrs. Otis said to her. "I want you to meet Mr. Paine."

The girl was already at the foot of the stairway. She didn't turn around. She didn't acknowledge the remark. The three of us watched her gallop up the stairs and disappear into the floor above.

Her grandfather looked troubled. Her mother just smiled. I could see it wouldn't be necessary to teach Mariana Otis the first rule of *personal* diplomacy—never apologize, never explain.

In the street, walking away, I wondered whether Tyler Paine was acceptable as her special assistant.

I almost hoped he wouldn't be. Much as I was enjoying the prospect of living in Paris again, I almost hoped something would happen to threaten the whole deal and force the President to change his mind about naming a woman to an embassy which now more than ever had become a key post in the touchy international situation.

Something did happen. Or rather, somebody. By name, Wayne Kearsart, Washington's best informed and consequently most feared nationally syndicated columnist.

Mitchell Remington was staring moodily at the newspaper on his desk when I responded to his summons.

"Seen it?" he said.

I shook my head.

He reversed the paper and bade me read the item. It was a long item. Kearsart had broken the story a full two weeks before the White House planned to announce it. And he had more than the projected appointment of Mariana Hillman Otis as ambassador to Paris—he reported friction between the President and the Secretary of State over the wisdom of such a move, and asserted that French Premier Nicollet was incensed.

To what extent all this was true wasn't the point, at the moment. The news was out, the hullabaloo was on, and the media had a field day. I could see from Mitchell Remington's agitated reactions that Stoneface had given him a hard time, having no doubt been given a hard time in turn by the President, quick to blame State for the leak. To the contrary, poor Mitchell told me sadly, it was highly likely the leak occurred at one of the high-flying cocktail parties that were becoming a trademark of the new presidential assistants—smart, savvy, and sometimes reckless young men who rejoiced in their own wit, loved playing practical jokes on one another, and chummed openly with the press and the broadcasters. It was a trend, the undersecretary said, that would cost the President dearly one of these days unless he took steps to cut it back. But the President was an indulgent man toward his own staff. They seemed to amuse rather than alarm him.

Most serious of all, as anyone at State could see, was the effect of Kearsart's item on Bryce Halsted, chairman of the Senate Foreign Relations Committee, who wasted no time politely blowing his top to the reporters. They had reason to run to him—the Senator, a bachelor, was a famed misogynist. Mere mention of a female politico's name was waving the red flag at the bull. The prospective nomination of Mariana Hillman Otis had to be confirmed, of course, by Halsted's committee. He immediately made it clear he'd do his best to block it.

The battle lines were drawn, but the White House, in a characteristic move, did nothing. The President's spokesman commented only that no final choice had been made for a new envoy to France and that the job was being competently handled at the moment by the U.S. chargé d'affaires, Stuyvesant Spaulding, a distinguished career diplomat of long experience. Mrs. Otis was merely one of those under consideration. The report of high-level friction was simply pooh-poohed.

It remained for Brad Lindley, TV's international reporting star —who disclosed in a broadcast from Paris that the French Government had already agreed to the appointment—to galvanize the President's young men into counteraction. Orders went out from the White House to prepare Mrs. Otis for a news conference. At the same time a quiet but assiduous cloakroom campaign was begun to persuade the Senate membership it was in the nation's best interest—and theirs—to confirm the nominee. It would be a test of the new administration's strength.

But the prospects didn't seem too good, and my personal doubts about the whole enterprise increased. They reached a point where I appeared in Mitchell Remington's office to tell him he ought to find another man.

I was surprised at his reaction—he seemed definitely disturbed.

"I had thought you were enthusiastic about the project, Tyler."

"About going back to Paris, yes. But from what I understand—."

"You're still troubled about Wayne Kearsart's piece?" he interrupted. "The Secretary has personally assured Mrs. Otis there's nothing to the story."

"You said yourself Paris is reluctant to accept her."

He tut-tutted it. "Auguste Nicollet would be reluctant to accept *anybody* we proposed at this juncture. He's being difficult about everything—including his own Foreign Minister, I hear. It's just the French, Tyler. In all this talk about the future of Europe they feel insecure. Eventually they'll face up to the realities and get over it."

I shook my head. "I'm not so sure. I have a feeling it wouldn't work out, either for Mrs. Otis or me."

"Come, now. How can you say that when you've barely made her acquaintance? Permit me to predict that this assignment will prove a lot more interesting than you think."

"I wish I could feel that way about it."

He thought a moment, then said, "Do this much for the department, Tyler—stay with the plan a little longer. Give us the benefit of your further reflection. We want you to work with Mrs. Otis on preparations for her news conference and be at her side on that occasion." He was at his most fatherly. "Will you go along to this extent?"

"Of course, sir."

So there I was. But I mistrusted the scheme for the press conference and felt uneasy about the White House tactics. It was suggested that her father be detained by business in San Francisco and daughter Cristy banished to the country house in Middleburg on the big day, so neither would be on hand for the proceedings. There would only be Mrs. Otis, and me, she having declined offers to help from Marcus Feld, the family adviser.

Public interest was intense, judging from the advance play the papers were giving the interview. A horde of reporters besieged the house on Connecticut Avenue an hour before the event. They found two television teams already setting up. Inside the house the phones had clanged all morning with requests from newswomen for individual personality chats—the feminine angle. To these entreaties I responded patiently and politely, "Mrs. Otis will let you know," and noted down name and number.

Since our first interview I'd seen the ambassador-designate only briefly. I couldn't tell how she was bearing up. Wayne Kearsart had upset State's timetable, and further talks between us were cut short. I had some fear, in fact, that at the last minute she might not have the courage to face the pack of wolves awaiting her.

I needn't have worried. Serene and smiling, wearing a simple gray suit with shirtwaist open at the neck, she came down the stairs with a graceful, confident step, gave me a firm handclasp, and said, "The President called me last night, Tyler. We talked for ten minutes. He was very reassuring. Please tell Crawford to let them in."

The mob poured into the drawing room. The TV lights went on. A score of cameras focused on the woman at my side and clicked away until I signaled enough was enough. To myself I was mumbling something I suppose could be called a press agent's silent prayer for his client. Then my client took a step forward and the news conference began.

She was alert, friendly, cheerful, unassuming, and brief. She said nothing of the slightest political consequence. She fielded the questions as if she'd been holding press conferences for years. Without batting an eye she reminded the questioners that she didn't even know whether the President would finally select her for the post, that this meeting was being held at their request, not hers. At the same time, she would feel honored if the President did choose her. She would try to serve the national interest.

She got a friendly laugh on the very first question, from a beady-eyed local newspaperwoman up front. "Do you think being a woman would inhibit your success with French diplomats?"

"It would be fun finding out," said Mrs. Otis with a sexy grin. And after the laugh had subsided, "Seriously, I don't see that it would make any difference whatever."

"Brad Lindley says the French people don't want you," said *Newsweek*.

"I've seen Mr. Lindley on TV. He's very good-looking."

This time it was a guffaw.

"Just in *case* you're appointed, Mrs. Otis"—again a female, with heavy sarcasm—"are you brushing up on your French?"

"Well, I'm taking a course in having my hand kissed."

Another laugh.

"The chairman of the Senate Foreign Relations Committee says he would oppose your nomination," intoned the New York *Times* with some irritation at all this levity.

"I have nothing but admiration for Bryce Halsted, and I speak in all sincerity. The Senator is undoubtedly a better judge of my fitness than I am. If he says I'm no good, I guess I'm no good."

So it went for half an hour. Lots of fun, and highly usable news copy. She kept it all light, parrying the weightier political questions with a skill I hadn't suspected. A cool cookie indeed, and I wholly admired her for the first time.

All the same, the day would come when the problems of an ambassador could no longer be finessed with a shrug and a smile. I hoped she realized it.

We stood facing each other, alone in the silence, after sherry had been consumed all around and we'd sped the mob on their way. Suddenly she sank down as if exhausted on a Louis XV sofa and I saw her hands were trembling. After all, she was a woman.

"Can I pour you another glass of sherry?" I said.

"Sherry, hell!" said Mariana Otis. "Tell Crawford to bring the Jack Daniel's."

I looked at her and grinned. The light in her eyes spelled combat and victory. Maybe she'd make it after all. I guess it was then I decided I would definitely take the job.

2

As it turned out, the boys in the White House had made a cunning move. The news conference revealed Mariana Otis to be human, imperfect, and feminine, and substantially altered the climate for the appointment. I've noticed Americans are funny that way. Media reaction changed from suspicious or contemptuous to something warmer and friendlier. In the press accounts the ambassador-designate came on as intelligent, sensible, and good-humored. The TV image was straightforwardly honest. The women's movement rallied around, and there were even some pleasant comments in the Congress, which as usual awaited public portents before venturing final opinions. The exception, of course, was the chairman of the Senate Foreign Relations Committee. Senator Halsted gave no indication he had changed his views on women in general or the candidate for Paris in particular.

Evidently the President was undeterred by prospects of a tussle. He let things simmer back to normal and then announced he had selected Mariana Hillman Otis to be Ambassador Extraordinary and Minister Plenipotentiary to France.

The market had already discounted the reaction, as they say in Wall Street, so Wayne Kearsart's scoop became official with only a faint echo of the uproar it originally caused. The newspapers were focusing on other matters by now. People said vaguely to one another, "Oh, I thought she'd already been appointed." And Bryce Halsted immediately set a date for confirmation hearings. I could almost see the old boy grunting and rolling up his sleeves.

The same day as the White House announcement I received orders from the undersecretary to turn over my duties to Henry

Perkins and join Mrs. Otis on a permanent basis on the following Monday for her briefing sessions.

Henry will get along beautifully with my Sheila. Made for each other, at least in office hours.

There were two kinds of briefings—Social Usage in the mornings, Political Affairs in the afternoons. Since Mrs. Otis was a VIP of the first water, elaborate attention was paid. A larger conference room than usual was required to accommodate the briefing officers for the morning sessions. They were all women—one from the Office of Protocol, one from the Executive Secretariat, and two from the Wives' Seminar at the Foreign Service Institute. I was the only male present but I might as well have been invisible. Nobody spoke to me or even referred to me the whole time, which was spent going over the rules governing responsibilities of chiefs of mission to their staffs and vice versa, initial activities on arriving at a new post, calling officially on whom and when, returning official visits, entertaining, precedence of introductions, receiving lines, seating plans, toasts, proper attire for official occasions, forms of address, titles, accepted courtesies, and so on. God, when I was at the Paris embassy I must have realized you had to know all this, but somehow I never visualized it written down.

Mariana—of course I don't call her that to her face—took it with patience, though I suspected she was amused at the rigidity of it all, as well as at the faintly patronizing tone of one of the ladies from the institute—a kind of WASP country club condescension in the teaching of manners. I'm afraid my potential ambassador was not a good conformist. I also caught her in a couple of yawns.

How was she to be addressed? Things were going to be a little sticky in that area. The panel attacked the question with solemnity, citing chapter and verse of previous similar situations in Luxembourg, Italy, Bulgaria, Norway, etc. It was my turn to be amused. If I'd surmised anything at all about Mariana Otis, she couldn't care less. The ambassadress? Ms. Ambassador? How would it translate into French? They spent half a morning poring over this one, and for the first time Mme. L'Ambassadrice spoke up with overtones of women's lib.

"Why is it necessary to consider the title either male or female?"

she said sharply. "Am I not simply the representative of the United States of America?"

Of course nobody could get anywhere with that, short of inventing a third language. It was just left hanging. But I knew the reporters would give it a fresh shaking out when the hearings began.

The Political Affairs sessions were a whole other world. Here we male chauvinists outnumbered our protégée (she wouldn't like that extra *e*) by two to one. There was only myself and the briefing officer, Wade Hunnicutt, recently appointed Assistant Secretary of State for European Affairs, and I found it prudent to keep quiet. Mr. Hunnicutt was a fussy. He reminded me very much of my Greek professor in college, somebody I hadn't thought of in years. First he gave his pupil a detailed outline of the French political system, then went into the historic balance of parties up to the present. It was complicated stuff, but not to Mariana, who dutifully took copious notes.

"At this point," Hunnicutt said, speaking slowly and with grave emphasis, rather in the style of an Emergency Limit Distribution dispatch, "I need hardly stress the department's standing instructions to *all* chiefs of mission. You will be expected to follow day-to-day policy directives at all times, without deviation, and to be extremely careful in your official contacts not to divulge those directives, or commit your government, at any time. You are fortunate to have available," he added, "the advice and assistance of one of the ablest career officers in the field, your deputy and the present chargé, Stuyvesant Spaulding, who will take up the briefing where I now leave off." He smiled a kindly professorial smile.

The ambassador-designate made her first comment. "We haven't dealt with pending questions," she said.

Wade Hunnicutt looked uncomfortable. He seemed to be framing his reply very carefully. "Ah yes," he said finally. "Actually there's nothing major, Mrs. Otis. No outstanding problem, nothing under negotiation. At any rate, nothing for you to concern yourself with right now. Hopefully, in a few days you will be in Paris, and Mr. Spaulding will fill you in on current questions far better than I can." Again he smiled. "I think you may always defer safely to his experienced judgment in your future decisions as ambassador."

I glanced at Mariana. She couldn't have been told more clearly that for all intents and purposes the department expected Stuyvesant Spaulding to continue to run the embassy after she arrived at her post. I could see how she might consider this very close to an insult, and I had the impression that behind that mask of cool composure she was struggling to keep her temper. But if that's what it was, she mastered it. She said nothing.

Her silence continued after we left the briefing. Whatever her reactions to Wade Hunnicutt's rather ambiguous attitude, she didn't communicate them to me. For my own part I thought his closing remark crude, stupid, and unnecessary, but if she wasn't going to mention it I didn't think it was for me to revive the subject. I did wonder if she'd felt, as I had, that the briefing officer hadn't given us the whole picture—either was reluctant to do so or was passing the buck, perhaps on instructions. And I also wondered, as I'd been wondering for several days now, how well the new ambassador would get along with her Number Two in Paris. Knowing Snuffy Spaulding as I do, I had my doubts. But I wasn't about to pass them along to my boss. She had enough on her mind as it was. This was a case of knocking on wood and hoping for the best.

I still didn't know whether I liked her.

Oddly enough, Connie asked me that question when I saw her the same night. Connie is one of three girls I've been seeing irregularly since I came to Washington, never quite able to make up my mind which one of them I care the most for—or how much I really care for any of them. But I have to say Connie seems to like *me* better than the others do. She's the only one who cooks for me, as she was doing tonight. And keeps clean shirts and shorts and socks for me in her apartment in case I stay over. And tells me I look a little like Cary Grant.

"I'm going to miss you, Connie."

"In Paris? You're teasing."

"Maybe she won't get confirmed and I'll stay in Washington after all."

"You hope not!"

"Well, I admit I'm psyched up to go, now."

"You'll go. Do you like her, Tyler?"

"Like who?"

"Come on! Mariana Hillman Otis."

"You know, I just haven't made up my mind about that."

"Why not?"

I shrugged. "Something, somehow, puts me off."

"You're scared."

"Scared? No."

She was grinning. "Admit it. Deep down you're scared of *all* the girls."

I didn't answer. But it wasn't the first time the suspicion had occurred to me.

Bryce Halsted is a maverick in politics, which is another way of saying he's a man with a genuine old-fashioned conscience. He is not afraid to buck his constituents if he thinks they're wrong. He does not follow party policy unless he believes it's right. He does not bow to pressure from the White House unless he believes the President is right, in which case the pressure was not necessary, as previous presidents have learned. And he does not make deals—I'll scratch your back if you'll scratch mine. Lobbyists hold him in terror and have long since realized it's useless to try to persuade him to do anything, even grant them an innocuous favor.

Bryce Halsted is chairman of the Senate Foreign Relations Committee because of seniority, not popularity. Inside the Senate and out of it, he is not beloved; he is respected. His reputation for honesty is such that the political cartoonists make jokes about it.

For all these reasons, an administration can't be sure which way Bryce Halsted is going to vote on any given issue. That's why there was uneasiness at State over his reaction to the nomination of Mariana Hillman Otis to a major post in the Foreign Service. With another committee, another chairman, the White House can often feel out sentiment in advance and save time and disillusion for one of its projects. But you couldn't just give Bryce Halsted a ring, or buttonhole him at a party (he never went to parties, anyway) and say frankly, "How do you feel about this, old friend?" Such an approach might have disastrous consequences for your proposal, might lead him, for example, to turn Mariana Hillman Otis down on grounds of improper influence.

As the date for her confirmation hearings drew near, the reporters went through the motions of one more try for reaction. Useless, just as they had known. The Senator gave them the arched white eyebrow and a courtly no-comment.

Meanwhile, State was proceeding on the by no means guaranteed assumption that in the end the committee and the Senate would vote to confirm. Mariana was engrossed in a whole mess of books on French politics, and I was extremely busy with double duty—looking after the ambassador's public relations and making my own personal preparations for departure. I spent a great deal of time dealing with Mariana's correspondence and fending off requests for interviews from radio and TV stations, in between hurried trips to Brooks to get some suitable clothes together. Ms. Ambassador—that was the sobriquet most in favor now—let it be known she would buy half her official wardrobe in Paris, while bringing with her the latest from Seventh Avenue for the other half. I was pleased at this indication of her talent for diplomacy. It was good publicity both at home and abroad. Weekends she joined Cristy at the Middleburg place for some farewell rides. Cristy's only passion, it seemed, was horses. She wasn't a bit happy to be leaving them. Her father had put her on her first pony at the age of two, and trained her thereafter until his death.

I hadn't laid eyes on young Miss Otis since that first day she'd flung herself in the door and up the stairs of the Washington house without acknowledging her introduction. But I was going to see a lot of her in future—Mariana was taking her along and consulted me about her education.

"She can enroll in the French Civilization summer course at the Sorbonne," I told her, "and I'm sure you can find an adequate private school in the fall. What does she think about living in Paris?"

A fleeting sadness crossed her face. "I wish I knew what Cristy really thinks about anything."

"Aren't adolescents supposed to be kind of mysterious anyway?"

"I wonder if it's only that," she said.

"I'm sure it is" was my fatuous remark. What did I know about Cristy? Or her horses, for that matter? At any rate Mariana didn't continue the discussion.

I guess you could say I too had a stable of sorts. Like Cristy, I was bidding good-bye to my friends. I'm afraid I was rudely short with Vivian and Jan, but my farewell with Connie was memorable. As a matter of fact she gave me three farewells. They just seemed to flow into each other.

I was really sorry to say good-bye to that girl. But she's the kind that doesn't repine for long. Blithe.

On the day of the confirmation hearing the atmosphere in the Old Caucus room was calm and relaxed, perhaps deceptively so. Senators of both parties, ranged alongside the stern-faced Bryce Halsted, beamed down indulgently on the slim figure that faced them from the witness chair without a trace of visible tension. In that strong, clear voice she read an opening statement prepared for her by Wade Hunnicutt and read it well. Compared with some ambassadors-designate I'd seen before this same committee, Mariana was superb. And somehow—though I was sure her own statement would have been much more direct—she made it sound as if she'd written every word herself.

Sitting in the row behind her, I suspected the little clucks and nods of approval from the platform might be as much due to the nominee's good looks and smart appearance as to the cogency of her observations. These were couched in the generalities of pure State Departmentese, put together by a master of equivocation, and rang with a verbal sonority that conveyed much more optimism about the world situation than could possibly be warranted. To the Senators, this was an acceptable, indeed welcome, presentation that placed no strain upon anybody. They were fully at home with the same technique themselves in the questioning that followed. On the whole, her answers seemed to satisfy them. At this rate, only one hearing should be enough.

The room seemed extra silent as the ambassador-designate concluded with a passage I felt sure she *had* written herself—a brief summary of the two-hundred-year-old friendship between France and the United States, a relationship that went back to the earliest days of this republic and drew its basic strength from both American and French political philosophers. Then, putting aside her prepared text and looking in turn along the row of senatorial heads above her, she added, "If I am confirmed I shall make the preservation and extension of that friendship the basic aim of my mission in Paris."

It was a sign of the prevailing public mood, I felt, that nobody made reference to Mariana's sex, even humorously. The only examination that could be called at all searching came at the end from the chairman, and this was more a lecture than interrogation.

Senator Halsted, peering down sternly over his half-glasses, was concerned about the Soviet presence so close to the democratic countries of Europe. Senator Halsted also noted the increasing number of Soviet naval units in the Mediterranean Sea. Senator Halsted wanted to know how sincere was this policy of détente the Russians were dangling before the Western governments, and expressed doubt that anybody in Washington knew enough about Russian thinking to tell him. On such unstable terrain he therefore had to fall back on plain old Yankee caution—grin, and keep your powder dry.

Of course he was aware that U.S. ambassadors don't make policy, he said. They'd been reduced to the status of mere messengers, and perhaps that was inevitable in modern diplomacy, but to be regretted because nine times out of ten an ambassador with *experience* could evaluate an international political situation better than anybody in the head office back home. He understood, said the chairman, that one such veteran professional diplomat, Mr. Stuyvesant Spaulding, was doing a very creditable job in Paris providing the evaluations so greatly needed by his superiors in Washington at this tricky time. The White House spokesman, in fact, had made some reference to this just recently. It was reassuring to hear it.

In principle, the Senator favored career Foreign Service officers every time. Occasionally a President selected a really competent envoy as his political appointee, but the Senator was sorry to say he hadn't seen it happen very often. The whole system of political appointments to foreign embassies was wrong, in his opinion, but it's our system and we have to live with it. With minor posts it rarely matters. Who cares who is rewarded with appointment to Loogaboogaboo in southwest central Africa? How much harm can he do, after all? But Moscow, Peking, Tokyo, Bonn, Paris—these were the very hub and center of the diplomatic universe, where decisions were made that would vitally affect the lives and fortunes of all Americans now and beyond the foreseeable future. It was well known that French diplomacy especially could be illogical, even capricious. A steady American presence was required in the French capital.

The chairman had cautioned this President and other presidents before him on the danger of selecting, for domestic political reasons, well-meaning but untrained persons for key responsibilities in the slippery world outside our borders. He wanted to make it quite clear that he was not speaking personally of the present witness, but only of what he regarded as a very risky practice with nothing to recommend it but tradition. Although he had listened carefully to her testimony today and found it commendable as far as it went, he felt obliged to say forthrightly now—and hoped his colleagues on the Foreign Relations Committee would agree with him—that he could not in good conscience vote in favor of confirming this appointment.

The gravelly syllables ceased. The hearing room was silent. The chairman had not asked for comment on his decision and the witness offered none.

It was what we'd feared all along, but when the moment came I wasn't quite able to believe it. I was aware of a slight sick feeling in the pit of my stomach, that was all. I leaned forward then to look at Mariana. She had gone a little pale but was perfectly composed, still sitting ramrod straight, her hands in her lap. And I knew for the first time that everything we'd worked for in these past weeks had meant as much to me as to her, and for her sake, not my own.

Had Bryce Halsted's judgment finished us off?

As it happened, what had been anticipated from the President down as the last and toughest obstacle was in fact the most easily overcome. When the committee vote was taken only two voices were opposed to the nomination—Halsted's and that of the failing Senator Wethers, a rockbound reactionary from a rockbound reactionary state. Confirmation by the full Senate was assured. The diplomatic career of Mariana Hillman Otis was under way.

Was it the witness's personality and conduct that had swung the balance? Partly that and partly, as we later realized, the President's intensive behind-the-scenes lobbying effort.

In the car taking us back to Connecticut Avenue Mariana leaned suddenly toward me and kissed my cheek.

"Now you can pack your bags," she said.

But before we left for Paris, Mitchell Remington called me into his office alone and told me something that changed the whole concept of my assignment.

"It is a matter of department business," said the undersecretary in his most ingratiating tone. "And the paramount issue is confidentiality. Only one other person is aware of what I am asking you to do. At no time must you allow *anybody* else to find out. That most definitely includes Mrs. Otis."

There was a pregnant pause. As I was departing with the ambassador the next day, I'd assumed this meeting was to be merely for the ritual handshake, maybe some minor last-minute odds and ends to be cleaned up, then a cheery godspeed. I'd half expected Mrs. Otis herself to be present, and now found her specifically excluded.

Waiting for him to proceed, I calculated that since Mitchell Remington could keep no departmental secrets from the Secretary of State, the only "one other person" had to be Stoneface himself. So I nodded smugly, as befits an officer privy to such deep, dark undercurrents in the department. At the same time I felt a twinge it was, and my distrust of the Secretary was revived.

Remington proceeded. "I'm sure you've already realized you're going to be in an unusual position at the embassy, Tyler. You will

34

probably be with the ambassador more than anyone else on the staff. This may be resented—."

He paused again. I said boldly, "By Snuffy Spaulding, for instance?"

That nickname goes a long way back and I could see his surprise at my use of it. "Was Spaulding in Paris in your time?"

"No, sir. We've known the family since I was a child. He was at St. Paul's with my father."

He nodded. "I doubt if there will be any friction with Spaulding. I had in mind some of the others. They may feel the arrangement is a little odd. After all, the staff situation is anomalous. The ambassador is a woman. Still young, attractive—."

I said it with a grin. "Are you by any chance cautioning me against getting any romantic ideas about her? If so, I can assure you I—."

He held up both hands. "Of course not, Tyler."

"I was just going to say you needn't have the slightest worry about that. As a matter of fact, I've wondered why Mrs. Otis wouldn't rather have had a woman assistant, anyway."

"She told the President in their first talk that she didn't want a woman private secretary. And here at State, that suited our purposes very well indeed."

I must have looked puzzled. "Purposes, sir?"

"Which brings me"—he nodded—"to the purpose of this conversation. While you are in Paris you will of course be subject to the standard disciplines of all other staff members. Normal communications with which you are involved will strictly follow channels. The ambassador will report to the department in Washington like any other chief of mission. But you, Tyler, will have one responsibility that no one in that embassy but yourself is to know about. You will make periodic and, if necessary, emergency reports *outside the diplomatic pouch* by ordinary airmail to my home address, which you will post in an ordinary mailbox when not observed. The intervals will be up to you. The substance of these reports will be your detailed observations on what the ambassador is doing, and thinking, above and beyond the information available to the department in the normal course of her activities."

In the rather long silence I looked at my superior officer. I saw now that he had sort of sidled up to this, as though wishing to break something to me easily. I also saw why—my first reaction, as his meaning became clear, was something of a shock. But Mitchell Remington looked neither shocked nor uncomfortable at the nature of the proposed arrangement. He had anticipated questions and was waiting for them.

"Am I to understand that Mrs. Otis is under some suspicion? Because if she is, I don't see why the President—."

He cut me off with a wave of the hand. "Nothing like that, Tyler. Nothing at all like that." He smiled slightly. "We don't want you to feel like a counterintelligence agent. All this is just—well, a precautionary gesture, one might call it."

"Because Mariana Otis is a woman?"

He shrugged and the smile widened a little. "Put it that way if you like. But that's only part of it. Mrs. Otis is also inexperienced. She is being placed in a position of high responsibility in a field that is new to her—a vast field, where major and complicated problems arise. You will be close to her. You can observe her, perhaps better than anyone else can, under the stress of these pressures. We will feel more reassured, if at any time reassurance is needed, knowing that a trusted member of the department is supplying us with confidential reports to buttress our own evaluations."

"I didn't realize the President was so concerned," I ventured.

"The department is concerned."

It was as far as he would go, but it confirmed what I wanted to know—that this was the Secretary's project. Stoneface was still doubtful about Mariana Hillman Otis. And I remembered then my feeling on my initial talk with Remington, that there might be more to the assignment than I was told at first.

In a word, I was to be a kind of spy.

"Is there something special going on in France?" I said, just groping. "Or somewhere else involving France?"

Again, as with Hunnicutt's briefing, I had the impression the question made him uncomfortable. He spoke after brief hesitation. "Let me say this much. We've had recent indications of top-level dissension in the French Government. We're not sure what it's about, but it seems to concern decisions on future international policy. Whatever's up, they're keeping it quiet, and so far the press hasn't smoked anything out. Of course it may add up to no more than domestic jockeying for the President's favor in that grab-bag Cabinet they've got. For instance, Premier Nicollet and Foreign Minister Courtailles belong to different political parties —Nicollet's a Left Centrist, Courtailles represents the Center Right. In the present shaky government coalition, no one would want to be the first to rock the boat too hard and bear the onus of bringing down the regime. Under the circumstances, our cue is to tread very cautiously and make no move to exacerbate a tricky situation. You can see," he concluded, "Mrs. Otis may find herself in treacherous waters immediately she arrives at her post."

There was a silence. Mitchell Remington seemed to be waiting for other questions, but I didn't feel like any more sparring. Some kind of evasion was going on. He was holding out on me, and I didn't like it. I saw quite distinctly that if the job no longer appealed to me, this was the last chance to say no thank you.

At the same time, I felt a strong sense of commitment. I couldn't just walk away from it. Mariana Otis was counting on my help.

And there was the matter of duty.

I am a Foreign Service officer. I had my orders.

Despite persistent forebodings that all this would end badly, I decided to comply.

3

It was nostalgic and exhilarating to cross the Atlantic by ship. Hardly anybody does it anymore, which of course is why so few ocean liners are left. But to Mariana Hillman Otis it was the dignified, traditional way for a new ambassador to arrive, and her choice of transportation evoked a ripple of pleased comment in the French press. She had guessed it would appeal to the French and she was right.

The airlines didn't like it a bit.

For me it was a return to the scenes of my childhood. Like most Americans, I'd been flying places so long I'd forgotten there was any other way to go. But when I was a boy the family spent every summer abroad and I was a veteran ocean traveler by the time I was twelve, happily running up and down those decks and companionways, making friends with passengers and crew, finding chums my own age, hiding behind stanchions, exploring the lower depths. It was strange the first day to be aboard as a grown-up, feeling that slow, steady roll under my feet again and smelling the dimly remembered seagoing smells. And then, once more accustomed to it all, succumbing gratefully to the timeless isolation of the voyage.

For these few days, after being with her virtually every day for a month, I was to see Mariana very little. She suggested it would make a nice change for both of us. As befitted her rank, she and Cristy were ensconced in the Royal Suite, A-Deck, took their breakfasts and lunches there and their dinners at the captain's table, and apparently spent the rest of the time in steamer chairs on their private veranda. Here in my own quarters, a single cabin far different in style and location but more than adequate to my taste, I was free to withdraw into myself, contemplate the uncertain future, and flesh out the entries in my private diary.

The one thing I regretted was that in the bustle of departure I hadn't had a chance to talk privately with Mariana since my final meeting with Mitchell Remington. Maybe it was just as well. What could I have offered beyond my suspicions about the department's attitude toward her assignment? And what right had I anyhow to confide my belief that Remington and Hunnicutt were keeping something from the new ambassador, for reasons they weren't talking about to Tyler Paine? Didn't my pledge to send back secret reports put me squarely in their camp? Perhaps Stuyvesant Spaulding would offer a clue to all this mystery when we arrived in Paris. But the answer to that question wouldn't be known until then, and meanwhile, I told myself, there was no use fretting about it. A sea voyage to Europe was for relaxing. The guessing would resume soon enough.

Very quickly I fell back into my old travel habits, the more easily because I knew what to avoid. I took my morning laps in the pool before the crowd woke up, skipped the lectures and the awful entertainment, and kept away from the ritual daily horse races in the main saloon. Most scrupulously of all I resisted the pathetic singles get-together on the second night out. One searching glance through the doorway was enough to confirm my decision—I could only spot three men among at least twenty eager, chattering females, not one of them worth a second look.

I was fairly lucky with my tablemates—only one slob, two widows with the roving eye, unacquainted, a German cutlery exporter and his wife, both adventurous wine-lovers, an aristocratic old French lady with family in New York making her seventy-eighth Atlantic crossing, and Henry Armbruster of Akron.

Henry, a brisk, smiling junior chemicals executive on his way to work for his company in Belgium, deserved special mention because he announced to us on the first day his intention to eat his way through every dish on the immense menu and then start ordering special items (no charge). He proceeded to do so, to the wonder of all with the exception of the slob, who fortunately dropped out of our friendly circle the second day and thereafter

40

was satisfied to take his nourishment in liquids at one or another of the ship's bars.

Young Henry worried Mme. de Meraud, the French lady. "When they eat like that, they die," she confided to me in an awed whisper, but nobody warned him. The maître d'hôtel just beamed. The German couple and I were busy with the sommelier sampling wines. The two widows paired off with steady middle-aged singles at the first dancing session. So Henry had the special orders all to himself, observed warily and sometimes enviously by the rest of us.

What is it about travel abroad by ship that makes a new person of you after only a few days? I guess for one thing it's because you're cut off from the chores of your normal daily life, so you might as well forget them for a while. For another, the whole pace of living is slowed down—nothing you can do about that till you reach land again. You can feel the very rhythms of this pace in the ship's engines somewhere far below you, in the slow swell of summer seas as you walk the deck. There's *time* for everything, playing, loafing, reading, thinking, writing. And oh those afternoon naps you never can take during a working day!

The ship's whole crew is babying you—stewards bring you snacks before lunch, bouillon in the afternoon, cocktails before dinner. Above all, your fellow passengers are relaxed as you are, feeling friendly, open, telling you things they'd never say to strangers under their normal conditions of life. Yet with all this, wrapped against the breezes in a deck chair, you can still be alone with the endless horizon, savoring a lost freedom, a thing of the past for most of us now. A whole generation has grown up without experiencing it.

Traveling by air, a trip to Paris or Rome today is no different from flying from Washington, say, to Los Angeles. With jet lag, it may take days to adjust after flying to a foreign country. But by sea, especially if you travel on a European liner, those days are used for adapting yourself to the atmosphere, the language, the new kind of life that awaits you. This is as it should be. Everything changes you gradually, even the clock, and even the clock is a romantic sound of ship's bells. In my own individual case, of course, this crossing was special indeed. I was returning to what will always be, for me, my real home.

Weatherwise, the voyage was idyllic. The sea was flat calm, the sun shone. I slept a great deal, and the eating was superlative. The captain's table was well removed from mine, but I had a view of it. Ms. Ambassador wore a succession of stunning dinner dresses, and each evening we exchanged bows and smiles at a distance. Cristy didn't seem to know me. As far as I could tell she didn't know anybody at the captain's table, either. From occasional glances I got the impression her tablemates were all trying to converse politely with her, without much success. Even the captain seemed to give up after a while. Like all skippers of big, fashionable liners, charm was part of his personality. Mariana was seated at his right and spent a lot of time matching his vivacity—in which language I couldn't be sure, but her spoken French was still elementary so the captain's English had to be pretty good.

I'll say this—no high school girl grind ever studied French harder than my ambassador. She'd told me early on that she regretted the omission of languages in her schooling. At Radcliffe her main interests were economics and history, with a lot of sociology fieldwork—as you can see, her political instincts were already well developed by the time she finished college. But Mariana couldn't let five minutes go by without learning something, and I now realized she was using the captain mostly to improve her conversational French. I also realized, with a little less amusement at the thought, that as her regular teacher I resented this. Not so much for professional as for emotional reasons. I had to face it—I missed being with her.

Was it a matter of affection or just habit? Sitting in my deck chair, staring out sleepily at the horizon, I now knew the answer to my friend Connie's question: I did like Mariana. There was no longer any doubt about it. And I hoped she liked me. It may have been the little kiss on the cheek in the car on our way home from the Senate hearing that marked the turning away from ambivalence to direct regard. It wasn't a real kiss, of course, just a quick, impulsive gesture born abruptly in that complicated female psyche out of elation, pride, relief, maybe a bit of all three. I don't know just *why* she did it, but I wanted to think I, Tyler Paine as a person, was part of the reason.

Tyler Paine the informer. That was something I *didn't* want to think about, but as the placid hours at sea rolled on I managed to rationalize my role pretty well to my satisfaction. After all, seeing myself as a sinister secret operative was only one way of looking at it. As the department saw it, I'd merely been entrusted with a discreet, quiet function practiced in every business firm. I was a sort of backup man for normal channels. My sub rosa comments would be only confirmatory, I couldn't imagine any situation in which they would be decisive. For all I knew, this had been done with other ambassadors as well. Mariana was no subversive, so how could she go wrong?

No, I refused to further trouble myself with moral musings on the issue. Put it all down to Stoneface and his obsessive preoccupation with security. In the short time since he became Secretary of State that was already well known in the department, and certain to be noticed before long by the press.

What wouldn't Wayne Kearsart give for a tip on the arrangement made behind the back of the new ambassador to France!

Well, there was nothing conceivably interesting for me to report so far. The crossing had proved delightful but uneventful, and now it was almost over. Tomorrow we docked at Le Havre. Tonight was the Captain's Dinner.

And what a dinner! Caviar from the Caspian with Stolichnaya vodka, *consommé double* impregnated with Amontillado, *truite saumonée* to the accompaniment of a delicious Riesling, a noble Corton-Grancey escorting the Charolais beef, Laurent-Perrier champagne to bless the frozen soufflé. Henry Armbruster, pale now but determined, cleaned up as usual.

You don't see its like anymore—the old-fashioned farewell gala at sea. And it's never coming back. Glowing after that tremendous meal, I went to the ship's ballroom to watch. It was a scene out of a 1930s movie, everybody in evening dress, the band pumping out Kern and Gershwin dance tunes, trespassers from tourist class sneaking up from the lower decks to join the spectators on the fringe and smile at the old ones, the older women especially, who were dancing their hearts out as if trying to make it all come true again, those summers of the golden age aboard the *Normandie*, a kind of life that is gone.

I wished I was a dancer myself when I saw Mariana glide out there with the captain. She looked altogether alluring in a white sheath that almost reached the floor, and I followed her whirling progress with half a dozen other partners. The sheer glamour aspect was a side of her I'd hardly had a chance to observe up to now. And standing there watching her, a brandy in my hand, I was a little surprised to realize I was beginning to feel a definite sexual attraction. This came not so much as a discovery as in belated recognition of a feeling I'd had for several days. Was it the confinement and separation of the voyage? Or because of all that wine at dinner? Whatever was making me feel this way, it had its paradoxical side, for at the same time I saw that as my respect for Mariana had grown, I'd gradually ceased to regard her in sexist terms. I no longer thought her competitive or just strange, as the Secretary and Mitchell Remington seemed to do. She had become instead a totally accepted *person*—no different in any primary way from Tyler Paine—whose actions were as familiar and welcome as my own.

These reflections suddenly pleased me so much I felt like celebrating my new leap in understanding with another drink. By the time I came back from the bar, glass in hand, Ms. Ambassador had vanished from the floor.

I must have dozed a little while I was reading in my bunk. When I opened my eyes the book had fallen to the deck. The dance music was still going, dimly heard. I also heard what must have waked me up—an insistent knocking at my state-room door.

"Minute, please—I mean, *un moment!*"

I pulled on my wrapper and opened the door. Cristy Otis stared at me from the corridor. It was so unexpected that I blinked. Then I smiled.

"Hi, young lady. What brings you all the way down here?"

She didn't say anything for a moment. She was wearing a short black dress and earrings that made her look more grown-up than

44

her age, but her hair was still that disheveled mass. Her eyes were excited and troubled.

"Aren't you going to ask me in?" she said, with an edge of sarcasm.

"By all means." I stepped aside and immediately she moved past me into the cabin. She stood there staring around her, then looked back at me in plain disappointment. I had to laugh.

"Quite a comedown, isn't it?" I said. "After all that luxury on A-Deck."

"Isn't there any more to it than this—I mean another room?" she demanded.

"Not unless there's a secret opening or trapdoor in the place. If there is, I haven't found it. Sorry, Cristy."

I thought as she frowned that she may have resented my using her first name. Who knows what silly reactions adolescents suddenly come up with? Was she going to be the ambassador's haughty daughter now and play snooty along with the diplomatic set? We stood there looking at each other and I could see the possibilities in her maturity—the sexy young body already belied the tousled hair and tomboy walk, and there was something passionate in the wide-set green eyes.

But what had she come for? Just a teen-age impulse to go slumming? The sudden appearance was the first time I'd ever really exchanged more than two words with her, but they were enough to reveal antagonism, God knows why. I said, smiling, "Won't you sit down, Miss Otis? There's only the one chair, but I can perch on the bunk."

She shook her head, still holding me with that half-defiant gaze. I shut the state-room door behind me. Instantly she spoke.

"Don't do that."

"Close the door? Really, Cristy! If there's something you want to know, come ahead out with it. But I'm not in the habit of conducting conversations in the hall."

This time the reaction seemed more sensible. The harsh look softened and there was even the suggestion of a smile. The words were arch.

"Don't worry, *Tyler*. I'm not going to tell my mother you made a pass at me."

I laughed. She reminded me irresistibly of a girl playing the grown-up lead in a school play. "I should hope not," I said. "Because she wouldn't believe you if you did."

"Don't be too sure of that."

I was holding down irritation with an effort. "Cristy dear, there must have been some reason why you turned up here tonight. Why don't you just say what's on your mind? It's really quite late, you know."

"There's nothing on my mind, Mr. Paine. And *don't* call me Cristy dear."

"You mean you just dropped in to say hello."

"Exactly."

I grinned and held out my hand. "Hello. I've been looking forward to meeting you. Let's be friends, shall we?"

She seemed to hesitate about extending her own hand, then did, drawing it back quickly after barely touching mine. Her fingers felt cold and slightly damp. She took two steps and opened the door again.

"Is it good night?" I said.

Over her shoulder she threw me a grin, part sardonic, part impish, woman and child in the same moment. She disappeared around the corner of the corridor.

I stood there a moment looking after her. It was only then it occurred to me why she'd come. She was looking for her mother, of course. She thought Mariana was having a tryst with the special assistant. She was going to surprise us.

But if Mariana wasn't in her suite, where did she go after she left the dancing?

It gave me an odd feeling, not pleasant.

Coming back into the state-room, I noticed a very faint scent that hadn't been there before Cristy came. It wasn't perfume. It had to be pot.

There was no opportunity to clear up this little mystery the next day. Because of an unexpected development, we had a public

46

relations problem even before we landed. Nobody had given us advance warning that the pilot boat would bring out a large press contingent, clamoring for an interview in the lounge while the ship was docking. I'd looked forward to a happy half hour topside watching the green bluffs of la belle France hove into view. All I got was a quick glance, but that was quite enough. What had been the pastoral loveliness of the Norman Coast I'd known since I was a child had become in a few years a vast, smoky, noisy commercial harbor full of tugs, cranes, and tankers, hardly distinguishable in the mist from Hoboken or Galveston.

Would Paris itself have changed this much since I'd last seen it? I shuddered to think so, but judging from what I'd heard and read, I feared the worst.

It was Beasley Turner, the embassy's assistant press attaché, who found me standing sadly at the boat-deck rail. A friend in the department had given me a brief but riveting rundown on him. "You'll love Beasley," this fellow grinned. "He's sweet."

There wasn't much chance to observe whether Mr. Turner was all-out gay or just prissy. Right now he was full of the agitated news that the advance party of journalists was already aboard and slavering. The official welcoming ceremony would take place in a reception room on the pier after we tied up. He flashed me an ingratiating smile that took me in from head to foot while announcing that Foreign Minister Courtailles himself would be waiting ashore with Snuffy Spaulding.

"The Foreign Minister? Isn't that a bit irregular?"

"The red carpet, I guess. It's certainly more than protocol requires."

It certainly was.

"Except for the Americans," Beasley breathed as we hurried below to deal with the fourth estate, "the mood is inclined to be antagonistic."

I remembered Mariana's press conference in Washington. "You can relax," I said. "She'll handle them."

The ambassador was waiting calmly for me in her suite, and I caught a glimpse of Cristy lying flat on her back on one of the twin beds in the adjoining room, staring at the ceiling.

47

"It seems the press couldn't wait to get acquainted," I said. "They're assembled in the forward lounge. Your deputy and the French Government delegation will greet you more formally as you step ashore."

She nodded. "Did you tell somebody to give the press a drink?"

"A Mr. Turner from the embassy has them in tow. I assume he's done the necessary."

He had. They were five deep at the bar when we came in at the other end of the room, not immediately spotted. Beasley Turner sped across to us and I introduced him. He had bright, prominent blue eyes.

"Most of them know English," he said, "but if any translation is needed—."

"Tyler will take care of it," the ambassador said.

We stood there in the doorway while Turner filled us in. Present was a large and skeptical cross-section of Europe's media, mostly male, in addition to the American correspondents from the networks, the press associations, and news magazines. It was by no means an exclusively Paris selection—they were there from London, from Bonn, Brussels, Rome, even Luxembourg. Turner pointed out the Paris-based Tass man, one Serge Grolikoff, warning that this was no typical crude Soviet proletarian but a suave Western European Communist with all the graces who could be just as rough. He also indicated the famous Anthony Wardwell of the London *Times*, a portrait of middle-aged urbanity and wisdom in tweeds and Tattersall vest standing off to one side and holding what was undoubtedly a whiskey-and-splash.

"He usually has his dog with him," Turner whispered. "Poopsie must be allergic to the salt air."

Turner had a jittery little laugh. The ambassador seemed to be barely listening. She was watching a tall and still youthful figure detach itself from the mob at the bar and walk toward us, smiling. I recognized Brad Lindley, the broadcaster who had first reported France's hostile reaction to Mariana's appointment.

The others must have been keeping an eye on him for the signal. There was a stampede from the bar into the center of the room, so Lindley had the ambassador to himself for only a moment. But it was long enough for him to extend his hand and say, warmly and cordially, "Welcome to France, ma'am, and good luck!"

His eyes followed her as Turner led us behind a table he'd set up on the starboard side of the lounge. Camera bulbs flashed. Two sailors standing vigilantly nearby touched their caps in salute as we faced the suddenly silent crowd, motionless now except for a bustling little sharp-eyed woman who forced her way into the front row. I'd seen her before, in Washington—it was the re- doubtable Fanny Watkins, at present wielding her catty pen from her syndicate's Paris office.

And it was Fanny Watkins who asked the first question. Jabbing her finger at Mariana's costume, she demanded abruptly, "Bill Blass?"

The ambassador smiled. "You're making it easy," she said, and a little ripple of amusement went around.

But the rest of the questions weren't as quickly disposed of. For one thing, they were mostly in French, which brought awkward pauses while I translated. For another, this group wasn't to be put off with the banter Mariana had used so successfully in her Washington conference. The man from *Le Monde*, obviously annoyed by the Fanny Watkins approach, set the tone by testily expressing hope that no more time would be wasted with trivia. *Le Monde* wanted to know when the United States Government was going to give Western Europe equal consideration with Russia and China in its international dealings. France, he asserted, was deeply resentful of this attitude.

To which Mariana replied she was not aware of such an atti- tude, but if the charge had substance she would make it a cardinal aim of her mission to improve the relationship.

Rome's *Il Tempo* likewise had hurt feelings. He asked if the ambassador knew when the White House would get around to filling the vacant ambassadorial post in Rome—or was Italy be- ing neglected by the new administration as a second-rate power?

She did not feel she could properly offer an evaluation of U.S. policy toward Italy, Mariana answered, but the new administra- tion was reviewing its foreign relations with all possible dispatch

49

and was undoubtedly aware of the importance of a prompt appointment to Rome.

The Italian reporter persisted. "Is it likely the appointee would be a woman?" He cast a mocking glance at his French colleagues. "After all, it was the splendid example set by Madam Luce in Italy that made women ambassadors popular."

Mariana smiled again. "I have no foreknowledge of the President's choice," she said, "but I'm sure it will be made on the basis of ability, not sex."

The Tass man had his opening. "The question of sex has more than one aspect," he remarked silkily. "I am interested to know whether Madame is aware of the significance of her given name in this country?"

I groaned inwardly. It was an angle I'd overlooked in my briefings. Ms. Ambassador had a puzzled expression, as well she might.

"Perhaps," Comrade Grolikoff continued in avuncular fashion, "Her Excellency does not know that the name Marianne symbolizes the spirit of France herself?" He smirked. "And does she not perhaps wonder, this being the case, whether the French people will find the coincidence entirely to their liking?"

"That's poppycock!"

The words exploded from Brad Lindley, in his loudest, clearest television voice. He was glaring at Grolikoff. "I must say it's a pretty poor exhibition when the Soviet correspondent starts baiting the American ambassador even before she's off the boat."

"You are baiting *me!*" cried Grolikoff. "I shall apologize in behalf of all for your manners to Madame Ambassador." He turned and made a sweeping bow in her direction.

Lindley came right back at him. "It's intimidation and you know it!"

The murmurs in the crowd swelled suddenly. In a moment everybody was talking. There was some laughter. Beasley Turner threw out his arms in an imploring gesture but was ignored. It was Mariana herself who quieted the tumult by holding up one hand. She waited for total silence before she spoke, a slight smile at her lips.

"If this is the spirit of détente," she said lightly, "I think some further work needs to be done toward better relations. May I thank *both* you gentlemen for your concern? And may I remind you that one of the greatest diplomats of them all, Talleyrand, recommended against too much zeal?"

The man from *Le Monde* was nodding approval. That was something of a diplomatic triumph in itself.

There was a brief flurry outside the lounge just as the conference ended. I caught a glimpse of a stretcher being borne toward the ship's hospital. The supine occupant was Henry Armbruster, paler than ever but still smiling.

Preceding Mariana down the gangway half an hour later, Cristy beside me, I ruled the ambassador's first encounter with Europe a success despite the flare-up between Russian and American. Comrade Grolikoff, I decided, was just being mischievous, and Brad Lindley had too much sense of the dramatic. The rest of the press conference had gone smoothly. Mariana had handled herself very competently, as I'd been sure she would. But strong anti-American currents, political and emotional, ran beneath the surface of that crowd in the ship's lounge. It was as well she became aware of them right away.

Big as life, black fedora in hand, Stuyvesant Spaulding waited on the pier below. His hair was thinner and I guessed he'd put on a bit of weight since I last saw him. He looked through me without a sign of recognition and past me to the ambassador, which was typical. Later no doubt he would acknowledge my presence, right now he was heavy official.

TV picked up our progress along the red carpet that led to the reception foyer where the French Government delegation awaited us—Mariana and Snuffy side by side, then Cristy and myself, with Beasley Turner as rear guard. The press mob was held back on deck by a local police detachment, much to their indignation. I noticed that Mariana gave Brad Lindley a little smile when we went by. Passing the TV camera on the pier, Cristy snorted unpleasantly and jerked her head away.

The first I saw of Claude Courtailles was an immense bunch of roses that framed out the face above the balloon belly, short legs, and tiny feet. The Foreign Minister held out the bouquet as our little cortege entered the foyer and Madame Ambassador accepted it in commendable French. Sure enough, he kissed her hand. Trays of champagne appeared at once. With Snuffy Spaulding looking on, the Foreign Minister went about the elaborate business of presenting his entourage, one of whom was a young man of striking good looks whose name Beasley gave me as Count Blaise d'Archeval. Like Brad Lindley, this one regarded Mariana with special admiration—or was I just imagining these things?

Cristy and I, standing in the background, were the last to be offered champagne. I was not astonished when Cristy grabbed a glass but I was startled at the speed with which she put the wine away and grabbed another.

The very proper waiter stared, then smiled indulgently. "Hey," I said, "take it easy, girl. We've got a way to go yet."

She looked at me scornfully. "Are you serious? I can handle this stuff better than you can."

I laughed. "Somehow I believe you."

She said in her abrupt way, "You tell my mother I came to your cabin last night?"

"No, should I?"

"I don't care whether you do or not."

"But you wanted to know."

A pause. "Anyway," she said, "I found her. All alone on the top deck—thinking."

I felt a sense of relief. "You see?" I said.

She gave me that sardonic look and tossed the unruly hair back, then yielded to a brief blurted laugh. We turned at Mariana's voice. "Mr. Foreign Minister, may I present my assistant, Tyler Paine? And this is my daughter, Christine."

I looked into a face ravaged by a thousand great dinners and a tank car of Napoleon brandy, into small, wicked, mischievous, appraising black eyes, and at an incongruously delightful smile that made you like the man at once, though you'd never trust him. Even Cristy was momentarily charmed. Responding to his bow, she summoned up her forgotten manners and actually curtsied.

52

The eyes turned back to me. "Assistant?" he said softly, in a way that gave the word every possible connotation.

Mariana replied for me. "Assistant," she said, in a firm voice, and they moved a few feet away.

Despite his bulk the Foreign Minister carried himself very gracefully. I noticed the ambassador had parked her roses in Beasley Turner's arms. The poor fellow couldn't reach for the champagne.

Snuffy Spaulding was deciding the fate of nations with the Foreign Minister's good-looking young aide, but the count kept watching Mariana out of the corner of his eye.

I was very much aware of the ambassador myself, and could listen, without directly staring, to her clearly audible conversation with Courtailles. "Your young daughter likes champagne," he was observing.

Mariana laughed. "So you've noticed that."

"But I notice everything, *chère madame.*"

"I intend to enter her at the Sorbonne in whatever classes are available."

"She will learn more *between* classes," commented the Foreign Minister with the faintest suggestion of a leer in his tone. "The conversation in the student cafés is both stimulating and constructive."

I glanced at the ambassador. She looked as if she might want to pursue that, but Monsieur le Ministre was already launched upon other subjects. These included lamentations over the architectural destruction of Paris and the decline in the art of living well. Everything decent in life was now either hideously overpriced or no longer obtainable. Good eating on the diplomatic circuit also had declined. The standard of cuisine at the British embassy, for one instance, had sagged like an amateur's soufflé.

Madame Ambassador was fortunate in her chef, perhaps she did not know how fortunate. Ah yes, Jean-Paul had formerly worked at the Quai d'Orsay. The man was worth his weight in jewels. One would soon be forced to retreat to the restaurants, and even the best restaurants no longer cared as they used to. Another glass of champagne? He insisted. Alas, not only good food was fading. Drinkable wine was scarcer and scarcer. The best cellars of France were being depleted each year because the new vintages were all bought up by speculators in the wine futures market, like soybeans or hog bellies.

This time I glanced at the speaker, who was joining a shrug with a sigh. A personal tragedy, he went on—his favorite claret, the Lafite-Rothschild 1961, was no longer to be had. There wasn't a drop of it left in Paris, above or under ground.

The tray returned, and Cristy grabbed another glass.

"Now look here—" I began.

"Oh, don't be such a drag," she snapped.

I shrugged. I wasn't a nursemaid, after all. My responsibility was to Mariana Otis, not her daughter. And I looked back to where she stood a little apart with the Foreign Minister, still listening to him with great attention. So far, not a word about politics, which seemed odd.

It came just at the end, and I almost missed it. I had half turned away to join Beasley, still weighed down with all those roses, when I heard the Foreign Minister's parting words as he bent again to kiss the ambassador's hand in *au revoir*.

"I leave Madame with a final word," he was saying, the soft, suave tone unchanged, "and I do not speak it lightly. In Paris, things will not always be what they seem. Madame would be well advised not to believe everything she is told."

The embassy's two limousines drew up just then and I didn't hear Mariana's rejoinder, if any, but I had a few moments with her while Spaulding was bidding formal good-bye to Courtailles. Somewhat to my disappointment, the only reference she made to her conversation with the Foreign Minister was to remark, amusedly, on his nostalgia for that wine.

"Wouldn't it be fun," she said, "if I could find some Lafite '61 and surprise him with it?"

I agreed, and let it go at that.

4

CRISTY OTIS STOOD beside her mother in the courtyard of the U. S. Embassy Residence and stared up at its columned facade, its vast windows and ornamental balconies. The building had anything but a residential look.

"Cozy," commented Cristy. "Is all that necessary?"

Her mother smiled. "To maintain the dignity and prestige of the United States among the great powers, yes."

"Like they all try to keep up with each other this way?"

The ambassador glanced at Mrs. Stuyvesant Spaulding, who was accompanying us, and smiled again. "Just about."

"Reminds me of a bank," said Cristy.

"Well, it used to belong to the Rothschilds," I pointed out.

"No wonder!" Cristy said.

Behind us afternoon traffic beeped and zoomed recklessly through the Rue du Faubourg St. Honoré, past the presidential Palais de l'Elysée, past the Palais Matignon, official home of French prime ministers, past the imposing British embassy down the street. We mounted the massive stone steps and entered the building.

"Where's all the offices?" asked Cristy.

Mrs. Spaulding looked down at her. "This is the Residence, my dear. It's not to be confused with the Chancery on the Place de la Concorde. This is where your mother and you will live."

"What a waste of money for two people!"

I saw Mrs. Spaulding wince a little. As kids sometimes do, Cristy had put her finger on something, though in this instance she'd remarked that the Emperor had too many clothes rather than none at all.

Mrs. Spaulding turned to the ambassador. "I *do* wish people knew the State Department does *not* maintain the American establishment overseas all by itself. Actually the greater part of the costs here in Paris is reimbursed by other agencies, in proportion to the support they offer the mission. Nominally the ambassador is the chief representative of our country in France, my dear"—again looking down at Cristy—"but there are many hundreds of government employees here who are *not* connected with the department, nor are they paid with department funds. I *do* hope these facts are now clear in your mind."

Cristy nodded absently, only half listening. Her mother was regarding the lecturer with a glint of amusement in her eyes. Abigail Spaulding might best be described, in a good old New England expression, as a stick. Devoted to all the Protestant virtues, she was in point of fact a Brahmin of the purest Beacon Hill breed, the daughter and granddaughter of ambassadors, and like her husband an almost perfect example of hereditary diplomatic. In her own country, everything west of Worcester was Indian territory, but abroad she was as much at home in Tokyo or Tehran as anywhere else, since one was always with the right people. Abigail recognized members of the group instantly, of course, and usually had met them somewhere in the world long before. All those outside this category she tended to regard rather as foreigners, even if American, treating them with somewhat frosty *noblesse oblige* and feeling fully serene only when consorting with her own kind, whatever the nationality.

For Abigail Spaulding life was to be lived from beginning to end according to the Rules. She was sincere, humorless, and utterly without charm. In the many years I'd known her nothing had caused her to change, and it was a safe bet nothing would. Yet within her limitations she meant well, and right now she was bending every effort to make the ambassador welcome on the threshold of her new home. But there was constraint in the air, especially after Cristy's candid observations.

Lined up at attention to greet the new lady of the house were seventeen servants, the limit authorized by State's Bureau of European Affairs for the Paris ambassador, ranging from butler and housekeeper down to the humblest kitchen boy, all French. One by one they were presented by Mrs. Spaulding, who knew every name, and each acknowledged the introduction with an austere bow. There is this about the French of all classes and occupations —they will meet you halfway with the best will in the world if your manners are good. Trifle with their dignity as individuals and you've had it with them, no matter how important you are. Respect that French individuality and you will make as loyal a friend as you will ever find.

I saw my little maxim shining from every face, perhaps most of all in Mme. Hanotte, the housekeeper, a small, steel-backed lady who stepped forward now to make the welcoming speech. In a very few unsmiling phrases, deferential but never obsequious, she made it clear that the staff would give its total effort to care for Madame and her daughter—who would be expected, in exchange, to understand that the French do things in the only correct way they can be done: you will safely leave that to us.

She didn't have to be specific. I suspected that even Cristy, who knows less French than her mother, got the message in Mme. Hanotte's firm tone. Abigail then proceeded to show the Otises to their apartment and I left.

Outside, the sinking sun of a late afternoon in April bathed the city I love best. I was free for a few hours to lose myself in my memories. Tomorrow I would discuss housing with the embassy, but this one night at least I would sleep in my old hotel in a room looking down on the Seine around the corner from the Place St. Michel. I'd cabled in advance to make sure that René saved me that particular room. And I'd sent the embassy driver on ahead with my bags.

There was only one way to recover Paris, and that was to walk —slowly, lazily through the Rue de l'Elysée and down the Avenue Gabriel, into the Tuileries Gardens, past the Louvre and across the Pont des Arts, where Anatole France watched the most beautiful sunsets on earth. I lingered on the little footbridge to watch one for myself, until daylight melted into dusk. And to make the picture perfect, a brief Paris shower fell like a woman's veil over the city.

Now I was on the Left Bank, feeling my heartbeats with each step along the river, remembering a hundred times I'd walked these quais as a student, and later, and not alone. The Pont Neuf loomed ahead, beyond it the Cité and the towers of Notre Dame. I stood at last in front of the place that always means home to me in Paris, and looked up at the little fourth-floor balcony of the room that is haunted by the image of Yolande.

How many years had it been? Where was she now? Married without doubt, and with children, and living with a proper French husband in a proper apartment in Neuilly, in Passy. Out of reach, of course, and hardly likely to remember much about Tyler Paine. I'd looked for her in vain during my previous tour of duty. The undoubted fact that she had another name by then didn't make it easier to find her. It was probably just as well. In such a long time she would have all but forgotten me. We were only kids together, after all, and our philosophy, if we had one, was easy come, easy go. Yet it was strange how I couldn't shake her off. I still dreamed about her, now and then.

There's never been anybody quite like Yolande—in my life anyway.

The quick spring night had descended. The streetlights came on. I shrugged, smiled to myself, and went in. And there was René behind the tiny desk in his concierge's coat, expecting me.

I needed a bath after my long day, and when I'd shaved and changed I opened the French windows and stood for a long time on my little balcony staring across at the Palais de Justice. Inspector Maigret's old office was dark, but a haze of yellow light illumined the spire of the Sainte Chapelle, chaste and lovely against a sky of midnight blue. I'm not the type to show much emotion, outwardly at least, but the sight brought back so much there were tears in my eyes and I had to turn away.

A little later, while dining alone at the Balzar, a hangout of my Sorbonne days, I felt again the anti-Americanism so evident today at the news conference aboard ship. Maybe it was shown more nakedly here because they were mostly students sitting around me, but there was no mistaking the jeering hostility in their glances—and they were in no hurry to drop their eyes. Several of them seemed on the verge of challenging me. I know I look definitively American and have no desire to hide it. But if they could only know that I was once one of them, had sat on the same banquettes where they were sitting now, had eaten at these same tables with my French *copains!* And where were the *copains* now? Last time out I hadn't been able to find a single one of them in Paris.

I gorged myself on long-remembered delicacies—the *cervelas rémoulade,* the *pâté en croûte* with salad, a liberal selection from the *plateau des fromages.* (That Muenster, with that bread!) And Kronenbourg beer throughout, of course. By the end of the meal I couldn't have cared less about the stares, the frowns, the supercilious smiles. They were forgiven in advance. I loved them anyway. Departing, I almost told them so, but that would have been dangerous. I reminded myself that as an accredited representative of the United States Government in a foreign country I must preserve dignity and decorum at all costs.

Suddenly I was very tired, but I walked awhile to digest all that dinner—up the Boulevard St. Michel as far as Montparnasse, circling the Luxembourg and back down the Rue Bonaparte to St. Germain des Prés, old stamping grounds every step of the way. I had my coffee on the terrace of the Flore and let the flood of memory wash over me in waves of unashamed tenderness.

I wished Mariana Otis were sitting here with me in the cool, misty night. There was so much I could have told her about the French. She might have even heard a little about me.

Stuyvesant Spaulding received me in his office next morning. I say "received" because that's the most accurate word. He was being gracious, in his way, but the manner implied he was still doing me a favor by having me in. He must leave no doubt as to his rank. Snuffy is a ceremonious fellow, tall and distinguished. He always struck me as a type who'd been in the shell of protocol so long he'd forgotten how to escape from it. The shell seemed to have a tighter fit each year, and he was wearing it now like a suit of mail.

I recall being told of a state occasion when for some reason his chauffeur forgot to jump out and hold the door open for him as he was leaving a reception at the Quai d'Orsay. Did Snuffy reach down and open the car door himself? If you know him, you know he didn't. Although he was holding up a long line of diplomats and limousines he just stood there stiffly and waited, looking straight ahead, coattails flapping in the wind off the river, top hat held correctly against his chest. Somebody, anybody, would have to open that door, but it wouldn't be Stuyvesant Spaulding of the United States embassy.

The driver finally became aware of the situation, grinned like an idiot, and hopped out, saving the day for protocol. But for a while it looked like an impasse in negotiations.

Today Snuffy gave me his chilly smile, offered me his hand, and did not ask me to sit down. "Have you seen the ambassador this morning?" were his first words.

I shook my head. "I assumed you would have some instructions for me."

My assumption pleased him. "I would just like to make clear, Tyler, that you are assigned to the ambassador on full-time duty but otherwise there is nothing, ah, special about your position in the embassy. You are subject to all standard service regulations. Come directly to me whenever you need guidance. As you must have realized, having a lady chief of mission is something that will take a bit of getting used to, for all of us. But I daresay we will soon be taking it in stride." Again the formal smile. "I trust you've experienced no, ah, difficulty so far?"

"Quite the contrary, sir."

"Indeed?" He waited.

I had to smile myself. "I mean Mrs. Otis is very easy to get along with. I think you'll find that to be so."

"She speaks well of you, Tyler."

"That's nice to know."

There was a somehow awkward pause. I had the impression he wanted me to talk about Mariana. Or was he feeling a little uncomfortable about my status in the embassy? It wasn't tidy. He couldn't very well handle me as just another cog in the machine.

If he did feel that way, there wasn't anything I could do about it. I thought I'd prompt him. "Wade Hunnicutt gave us an interesting briefing," I said, "but he left the essential part to you."

"I have already briefed the ambassador."

That was all he said. He wasn't going to brief me, too. Not that I'd expected it. If there were other things he could have told me and didn't, as I'd felt about Remington and Hunnicutt, I could detect no hint of it in the chilly gaze. And if he knew about my private reporting arrangement with the undersecretary, he wasn't letting on. Of course it was always possible, if not likely, he was even more ignorant than I.

I wondered what Stuyvesant Spaulding had told the ambassador, and whether she had confidences now that she was pledged to keep from me.

"Well," he said, rubbing his hands as if to dismiss the matter, "just let me know should you have any problems."

"I need some office space to do my work," I reminded him, "and I need a place to live."

He raised a surprised eyebrow. "I assumed the ambassador had told you. You will have an office directly adjoining hers here, and an apartment in the Residence, so that you will be readily available at all times."

It was my turn to be surprised. "Living quarters in the Residence?"

"That is correct."

He sounded disapproving. He wasn't wildly happy about it, that was for sure. Now he stood up, probably glad to change the subject and turn to the amenities. "I haven't asked you about your dear parents," he went on in quite a different tone. "Both well, I hope?"

"Both thriving, sir. Father's getting a trifle stiff in the joints, I suspect, but he won't admit it."

"Ah yes," said Stuyvesant Spaulding. "Tell him for me he's not the only one."

"That should comfort him," I said, and left the deputy chief of mission not quite certain whether the new special assistant was teasing him a little.

I lost no time inspecting my new office—small but snug, with a door leading directly into the ambassadorial sanctum. The door was ajar and I peeked in.

It was a magnificent room, three vast windows overlooking the Place de la Concorde, two beautiful chandeliers, two fireplaces, and the tasseled Stars and Stripes standing in the corner.

Mariana Hillman Otis, trim and tailored, looked up at me and smiled from behind the massive desk.

"Come in, Tyler. You're just in time to meet the staff."

She dismissed a severe-looking woman stenographer who'd evidently been taking dictation and motioned me to a nearby chair. "Got your land legs back?" she went on cheerily. "Or did you spend your first Paris evening café-sitting?"

"A combination of sitting and walking, ma'am, observing my old haunts on the Left Bank. I hope you and Cristy find your new quarters comfortable."

"They're fine for me, but much too grand for Cristy. She did like dinner, though. Did you know our chef used to cook for Foreign Minister Courtailles?"

I grinned. "That means you'll have to watch your waistline, won't you?"

"As it happens, my predecessor left me a fully equipped exercise room, which should help. I had my first workout this morning. You're welcome to use it too, Tyler. I've given instructions to have an apartment prepared for you in the Residence and you can take your meals there." She paused. "Unless, that is, you'd prefer to live elsewhere."

"Considering the shortage of apartments in Paris, and now that I know your chef cooked for Courtailles, I'd be crazy if I did."

We laughed together. "Courtailles is a delightful man," she said, but made no further reference to the monologue in Le Havre.

"He would be a good friend to have."

"Of course Premier Nicollet would be even better, as Stuyvesant Spaulding points out." She smiled almost mischievously. "I think I startled Mr. Spaulding by summoning him to a seven-thirty breakfast conference. I'm not sure whether he thinks it's unseemly of a lady to entertain a guest at that hour, or just surprised that I'd start work so early. By the way, what's your opinion of his ability?"

The unexpected question threw me for a moment. It was the first time she'd consulted me so directly about anyone in authority, and I hesitated before I answered. "Actually, I've never worked close enough to him to be a proper judge of that, ma'am. He has an excellent reputation, and I believe he enjoys the department's complete confidence."

She gave me a keen glance. "So I've heard. Is that another way of saying he's a yes-man?"

I had to smile. "A Foreign Service officer has the choice of obeying orders or getting out, ma'am. I'm pretty sure Mr. Spaulding is no different from anybody else. He feels his duty is to respect the chain of command."

"He wants to make sure I respect it, too. That's mainly what his briefing was about. In fact," she went on, "I could hardly distinguish it from what Wade Hunnicutt told us in Washington. Particularly the indirect recommendation that I take care of the receptions and dinners and leave the politics to him."

I couldn't help saying it. "You told him you would, of course?"

Her eyes flashed and for a moment I saw a strong facial likeness to Cristy. "I made no such commitment. You think I should have?"

"I spoke ironically, ma'am."

"I'm glad to hear you say so. I told Mr. Spaulding rather bluntly that if he wouldn't or couldn't discuss the French political situation more specifically with me than he did this morning I'd conduct inquiries to my own satisfaction without his help. He very quickly assured me he has every intention of giving me a full breakdown at subsequent meetings."

She didn't pursue the point and I didn't need to press it. She said no more about Spaulding, nor did Abigail rate so much as a mention. Glancing at her watch, she continued pleasantly, "Frankly, I'm relieved you have no objection to living in the Residence, Tyler. I can understand why an attractive and unattached man in Paris might want his own private digs, quite removed from observation by official eyes." She smiled. "Having you accessible has become a habit, I'm afraid. You've spoiled me for any other arrangement."

"It's a habit with me, too."

"Then we'll lean on each other."

The buzzer on her desk sounded and a flat secretarial voice said, "The gentlemen are ready."

"Ask them to come in," said the ambassador, and I rose with her to face the door.

Spaulding entered first, alone. When he saw me he stopped in his tracks and frowned before resuming his sedate step to the ambassador's desk.

"Good morning again!" Mariana said brightly.

The deputy chief of mission acknowledged the greeting with a formal nod and said, "I understood you were to receive the section chiefs at this hour."

"So did I," she smiled. "Has there been a hitch in the schedule?"

"Not at all. They are with me now." He looked at me. "I suggest we wait for Mr. Paine to finish his business and return to his office."

"But Mr. Paine has finished his business," Mariana said. "He's remaining because I want to introduce him to the staff."

There was a moment's silence, then Spaulding said, "It's damned poor protocol."

"Nonsense," said the ambassador. "Show them in."

I saw his color heighten. Then he inclined his head slightly and went back to the door. One by one he brought in the embassy's key personnel to be presented—the economic minister-counselor, the administrative officer, the science officer, the defense attaché, the public affairs officer, the consul-general, and representatives of the Treasury and Justice departments, the Military Assistance Advisory Group, NATO and UNESCO—all new faces to me.

In each case the ambassador turned and said, "Tyler Paine, my special assistant."

Only one of them was introduced simply as Mr. Ralph Hobbs —no title, no rank. He was obviously the CIA chief of station and looked it, though whether the ambassador knew this yet I couldn't tell from the smooth, smiling expression she bestowed equally upon all.

When the handshakings had been duly accomplished and Spaulding's rather pompous tones were silent at last, Mariana made a brief speech. It was one of her minor masterstrokes. Her glance resting in turn on each of her listeners, her voice low and earnest, she professed her ignorance and willingness to learn. She humbly asked for their patience. She greatly needed their help. She stated her admiration for the man who had so ably led the staff as chargé d'affaires and said she was sure that with his counsel, backed by their co-operation, we would all succeed in our immensely important mission in this time of high challenge.

Looking around as she spoke, I realized there wasn't another woman in the room. She could have noted this, and wisely did not. She wanted them to feel that Mariana Hillman Otis was alone and vulnerable without their strong, steady, experienced, masculine support, and I could see them feeling it, and liking the feeling.

Only one of them caught my wandering eye. Mr. Ralph Hobbs shot me a hard glance out of his weatherbeaten face—neither friendly nor unfriendly, just searching. In a sense we were comrades in arms, but I doubted if he was aware of it.

On the other hand, he might be.

The buzzer on my desk sounded shortly after ten next morning, summoning me to the ambassador's office. Without a word she handed me a message she'd just received from Premier Auguste Nicollet, inviting her to call on him at the Palais Matignon at her earliest convenience.

She looked puzzled. "What do you make of it?" she said.

"I'll say this, ma'am—it's damned poor protocol."

I hadn't intended to put it in quite those words but it just came out. Momentarily we laughed together over Stuyvesant Spaulding's attitude. Yet he hadn't intended to be rude, I was sure of that. It's just the way he was, with sometimes ridiculous results.

As for what I'd said about poor protocol, I wasn't merely joking. Normally the Foreign Minister, not the Premier, conducts relations with foreign ambassadors. If Claude Courtailles hadn't taken it into his head to go personally to Le Havre to meet the new American envoy, he could have properly waited until the day she presented her letters of credence to the President in the formal ceremony at the Elysée palace. The Premier normally wouldn't meet her until some time after that.

Yet here he was knocking on the door even before Mariana had presented her credentials to his government.

I explained this background to the ambassador, adding that the vagaries of French behavior in high places were baffling at times.

"Could it be," she said, "Monsieur Nicollet is just trying to catch up because Courtailles stole a march on him by coming to the ship?"

"Ma'am," I replied, "you can see now why the French favor the shrug in confronting mysteries like this."

"In any case I intend to see the Premier at once. Does he speak English, Tyler?"

"Very little, according to Beasley Turner."

"Then you will come with me, of course."

I smiled. "I'm pretty sure Mr. Spaulding will prefer to do that."

She shook her head. "That won't be necessary. I'll tell him I won't need him."

Like the two Frenchmen, I thought with admiration, the ambassador wasn't losing any time. But Snuffy would be steaming.

Whichever of us accompanied her, I hoped Nicollet would be more to the point than the brief meeting with Courtailles on the French Line pier. Except for that closing caution, it had been strictly a performance, a gracious first impression, very evidently designed to win the ambassador's liking with his Gallic charm. And maybe even his parting shot had just been more of the same. At least Mariana seemed to have taken it as such.

I was not privy to the scene where she told Spaulding she wouldn't need him. But whatever was said between them, she prevailed, and he said nothing more about it to me.

Although the Premier's residence is just down the street from the embassy, we journeyed there by official limousine much as though we were embarking on a three-hour drive. More protocol.

66

The ambassador was handed in and out at each terminus of the five-minute trip with all the solicitude accorded a weary traveler.

The Matignon is a building of somewhat frosty elegance, and the interview with Monsieur le Président du Conseil reflected the same spirit. A rather forbidding type, slender and ascetic-looking, with the utmost politeness of manner, he omitted to utter a single word in English throughout, so I was kept busy interpreting everything he said. He certainly knew how to toss off complicated sentences. Only the original French text could properly demonstrate the Nicollet speaking style. At moments when he turned his pale gray eyes in my direction I was almost sure he was deliberately trying to give me a hard time, but whether he was really able to test my translations I had no way of knowing. He looked like the kind of cultural chauvinist who stubbornly refused to recognize the English language and is proud of it.

As to what came out of all those tortuous sentences, delivered as they were so gracefully, large areas of meaning just seemed to evaporate when rendered into our plainer tongue, like air escaping slowly from a balloon. It was a discourse that old De Gaulle himself would have appreciated, and indeed could have been the model for—full of ambiguous references to French destiny and grandeur.

Auguste Nicollet was not telling the new ambassador anything his government had not been declaring for years while blandly ignoring the inherent contradictions. We are opposed, he said in effect, to a condominium of U.S. and Soviet power that would leave Western Europe and France, its natural leader, out in the cold. A permanent peace is a worthy goal, but under the cloak of détente and disarmament Europe must not allow its autonomy to be sacrificed and its future mortgaged. And although France, of course, must continue to refuse to participate directly in the Atlantic military alliance, America must never withdraw its armed forces and their nuclear deterrents from its European bases (always excluding French soil).

All this in the serene tone of a Supreme Court justice setting out the precepts of the law.

It was prudent of the ambassador, I thought, not to challenge the Premier's logic. After all, she was here to listen. He didn't ask her for her own observations and she didn't offer any. In its own way, this was as much an impromptu preliminary as the Foreign Minister's sly dockside caution the day of her arrival, even though Nicollet had turned it into something like a lecture. I couldn't help comparing the two styles—both were pragmatists and cynics, Courtailles warm, witty, and playful, Nicollet haughty, pedantic, and dry, embodying between them most aspects of the French character.

On our way back in the car it was my turn to ask, "What did you make of it?"

"Spaulding told me more or less what to expect."

I grinned. "I see you've already learned to shrug."

"These French gentlemen," she said, "will have to tell me something new if I'm expected to report it to Washington. I can't send a shrug by cable."

I was remembering Mitchell Remington's rundown of the French situation. Courtailles had never mentioned Nicollet, and today Nicollet never mentioned Courtailles. If they were feuding they certainly were keeping it quiet. Or was Auguste Nicollet the target of his Foreign Minister's little advisory to the ambassador at Le Havre?

Again I decided not to bring my reaction to Mariana's attention. She had enough on her mind already, including a final ceremony of introduction. There now remained only the formal call upon the President of France, and she would be fully accredited as Ambassador Extraordinary and Minister Plenipotentiary from the United States.

5

IT WAS QUITE an occasion. Precisely at the appointed hour two cars arrived from the palace accompanied by motorcycle escort, although the presidential residence is almost next door to the embassy. Escorted by the gallant Count Blaise d'Archeval, the ambassador (looking queenly, I thought, in gray) entered the first car while Stuyvesant Spaulding and I climbed into the second. Snuffy was faultless, of course, in his formal clothes. I felt uncomfortable in mine but hoped it didn't show.

Mariana had decided she wanted to be picked up at the Residence rather than the Chancery because there would be less display of pomp on the trip to and from the Elysée, so our little cortege was seen only briefly by the public. Like true Parisians, pedestrians in the sunny Faubourg St. Honoré gave us scarcely more than a blasé glance as we passed. But we couldn't avoid the pageantry in the palace courtyard—a company of infantry drawn up to receive us presented arms amid ruffles and flourishes from bugles and drums.

Waiting on the palace steps were the chief of protocol and military commander of the Elysée. Solemnly they took over the escort from the count and solemnly we all paraded through a lane of plumed, brass-helmeted, knee-booted guards of honor up to the second floor (or as the French number it, the first floor) where the President of France awaited us standing in the middle of his office, flanked by Foreign Minister Claude Courtailles and a uniformed entourage.

I hadn't seen this President in the flesh before, though of course his pictures were familiar throughout the world. He wasn't a tall man, but somehow the shock of stiff gray hair, the intensity of look and austerity of manner made him stand out among all others in the room. The marks left by wartime Nazi torture still scarred both jaws. Cabinets could come and go, men like Nicollet and Courtailles could be replaced a dozen times, but during his presidential term this man was the real repository of power in France. And he was famous for keeping his own counsel on all issues until the moment he decided to speak out. Even the highest officials of his government were reputed to have trouble learning the President's thoughts until he was ready to tell them. No Auvergnat peasant could be more taciturn, more watchful.

I'd never seen a picture of him smiling, and today on what should certainly be regarded as a pleasant occasion the President's face was bleak. At this point in the ceremony Mariana had to remember not to follow her natural impulse to shake hands or even bow—strictly forbidden by protocol. Instead she placed herself carefully in front of the President, with her back to the windows giving on the green and lovely palace gardens. Messrs. Spaulding and Paine, also according to strict protocol, carefully placed themselves behind and to the right of the ambassador and we were ready to proceed.

With all the aplomb of royalty, speaking in clear, cool, pleasant tones, Mariana then delivered her remarks (limited by tradition to three minutes and sent ahead to the President's office in writing). This was followed by similarly vague, gracious, and respectful comments from the President, whereupon Mariana smiled, stepped forward, offered him her hand, bowed to Claude Courtailles, was presented to presidential staff members, and, in turn, introduced Spaulding and Paine to the President, who never cracked a smile the whole time.

Next a grave-faced photographer entered and the requisite official picture was taken—the President in the middle, Mariana on his right, Courtailles on his left, after which protocol called for the President and his visitor to retire together to the end of the room to exchange a few of the formal phrases that pass for friendly chitchat suitable to the occasion, such as, "I shall be pleased, Madam Ambassador, if you will convey my most cordial good wishes to your President," and, "Monsieur le Président, I shall not fail to do so." It was also the moment for me, as interpreter, to follow them across the room and take part in the dialogue, as needed. In the interim, Claude Courtailles stepped up to engage Stuyvesant Spaulding in conversation, while Blaise d'Archeval, at his shoulder as always, good-humoredly gave me a wink that clearly said, "Sorry there's nothing to drink at this one."

The whole bit couldn't have been more like a carefully rehearsed scene from a play, everybody speaking memorized lines, right down to the exchange of compliments between chiefs of state.

Except that the President of France dropped a final remark to the ambassador that wasn't included in the script.

"I understand," he said quietly, "that you have already had meetings with the Premier and the Foreign Minister at their instigation. I have no knowledge of what either said to you, and no need to be told. But I would remind you that neither can say the final word for France."

Just that, and nothing more. As I translated I saw Mariana's pleasant look stiffen in surprise. She had no time to respond even if she'd wanted to. Still deadpan, the President quickly bent forward over her hand, straightened and stalked back across to his group of aides.

It was over. My collar was wilting in sweat. We retired with the same solemnity as before—same ruffles and flourishes from bugles and drums, same motorcycle escort. In the car ahead I could see Count Blaise sounding off gaily as he leaned toward the ambassador. Snuffy Spaulding, sitting silently beside me, had no apparent interest in the substance of the President's conversation. Doubtless he counted on Mariana to inform him in due course. As for his reaction when he heard about that closing comment, I suppose he'd consider it damned poor protocol.

Or would he sense, as I did, it was a lot more than that?

In the brief time since the ambassador arrived in France, she'd received three successive and enigmatic warnings from the nation's highest officials . . . first the Foreign Minister, later the Premier, now the President. They could all be coincidence, and then again they could be twists in a skein whose pattern was still to be woven.

I wrote my first confidential report to Washington three days after the meeting with the President. By that time I was settled in the Residence in two very comfortable rooms and a small foyer on the third floor rear, overlooking the garden. These were on the same floor as Mariana's living quarters, which I hadn't yet seen but which opened into the same central hallway as my own. Between the two apartments was a spacious study, intact with two desks, typewriters, telephones, filing cabinets, dictating equipment, and other office paraphernalia. The study had been used by Mariana's predecessor as an office for his social secretary and freshly wallpapered and painted for the new ambassador. An inside extension connected the study with the ambassadorial apartment, and I discovered that the new incumbent had immediately ordered this private line connected to the phone in my bedroom.

All very snug, efficient, and thoughtful of the new incumbent. I didn't know whether she'd mentioned it to Stuyvesant Spaulding and I didn't ask her, but I was fairly sure the knowledge would raise his eyebrow an extra notch. No doubt my presence in the Residence would be a cause of gossip throughout the mission as the news permeated the various levels, but to the ambassador the arrangement apparently seemed the most natural thing in the world and she obviously hadn't thought twice about it.

Mariana's discreet attitude toward all issues was the underlying theme of my first report to Mitchell Remington. It seemed to be what he was hoping for. I tried to give the undersecretary the emotional background of her shipboard news conference, which had been only routinely covered in the American press, but I omitted such personal sidelights as Cristy's nocturnal visit to my stateroom during the voyage. Foreign Minister Courtailles, I noted, had given us an almost excessively cordial welcome, though it had not been echoed by the French press as a whole, and Premier Nicollet, in his own fashion, had signaled special interest in her arrival. The ambassador herself, of course, would report her colloquy with the President, but I did detail her introductory speech to the staff section chiefs and offered my own impression that her intra-embassy relations were off to a good start. Regarding our dual setup in the Residence, I described it as though it were perfectly usual, and made no mention of the volatile Spaulding eyebrow in this or any other situation.

As secret reports go, the curtain-raiser certainly was no hair-raiser. I had to laugh a little, posting the letter in an ordinary mailbox during an after-dark stroll along the Champs Elysées. It made me feel like a character in a movie. Had I been followed? Was Ralph Hobbs already on my trail? And what would be the rest of the scenario? I guess I should have worn a slouch hat and glanced furtively over my shoulder before I dropped the envelope in.

At any rate Ralph Hobbs was no longer a mystery to either of us. Referring casually to the fact that he didn't seem to be on the personnel list, I took occasion to ask the ambassador what his function was. "CIA," she replied without hesitation. Spaulding would have told her at one of the briefings at which he was bringing her up to date politically.

From what Mariana told me about these briefings I gathered French-American diplomatic relations were more or less static at the moment, with no recent signs of policy changes due at any early date. Ongoing treaty arrangements, customs conventions, and so forth were being observed as usual, but no political negotiations were in progress between Paris and Washington. The French continued to offer oblique resistance to American influence on the European Economic Community—they accepted us as friends but not as partners. As Nicollet had made clear to the ambassador, they saw no contradiction in their refusal to contribute their share of troops to the NATO organization while enjoying the protection of American military might. And they still regarded themselves as the spearhead of a West European Third Force, existing in proud independence between the two superpowers.

As to internal French politics, Spaulding believed the coalition Cabinet was holding together pretty well, considering its motley makeup and partisan squabbles. (The latest rumor in diplomatic circles about the Courtailles-Nicollet feud had the Premier upbraiding his Foreign Minister for arriving late and half-drunk at a cabinet meeting, but like so much other gossip the story lacked confirmation.) No one party controlled Parliament. Even if the current government should fall, the same old game of musical chairs would bring the same old faces back into office, swapping portfolios among themselves.

Plus ça change. . . . It had been true of France when I was a student, and it was true now.

My day with Mariana began at half-past eight, in the Residence study, and was usually only a brief consultation—we'd go over the morning papers together and review her schedule as to whether I'd be needed to accompany her somewhere or interpret for her at the Chancery. There was no time for political analysis in depth, and the ambassador's reactions to the situation as they reflected her political convictions were still unclear to me, maybe because she herself hadn't made up her mind and was keeping her thoughts to herself until she did.

Apart from translating her speeches into French for such occasions as French was required, the main burden of my daily routine was to translate into English all shades of French opinion as set forth in the press—newspapers, magazines, excerpts from significant new books on politics—and collect them each afternoon in a loose-leaf folder for the ambassador's perusal. Together, with some suggestions from Wade Hunnicutt, we'd devised this method of putting her abreast of what the country was thinking while she struggled to attain command of written French.

It made a full day's work for me, and sometimes an evening's work as well, although Mariana was often too busy with the ceremonial and social activities which take up so much of an ambassador's time to digest the ceaseless flow of information I shoveled onto her desk. But I must say she worked at it doggedly, taking my translations back to the Residence with her to catch up on what she'd missed. This meant a very long day for her, which in turn meant a short night's sleep, yet she'd nearly always be at her desk by nine after a brisk walk from the Residence, alone. Since I was rarely required to appear until later, I could take my time over Jean-Paul's Brazilian coffee and exquisite croissants, served to me in my apartment. Usually I was still there when Cristy hurried by on the way to her French lesson at the Institut Phonétique.

The embassy staff very quickly found out that their new boss was in action early and their deputy chief even earlier. According to Beasley Turner—who was cultivating me assiduously, dropping in when he was "just passing by" several times a day—an unaccustomed vitality now prevailed throughout the staff. I was undecided for a while whether the fluttery eyelashes and faintly girlish laugh put Beasley definitively in the gay column, but came to the conclusion he was just a very refined rich boy, of whom there are still quite a few in the Foreign Service, engaged in a gentleman's occupation at a plushy post.

I was curious, though, whether Snuffy might be indirectly using Mr. Turner to keep an eye on me and bring back occasional tidbits of gossip about the ambassador not otherwise available. One of these times, when I got to know Beasley well enough, I could just ask him if this was so. The difficulty was, did I want to get to know Beasley that well?

In due course I was invited to lunch with the Spauldings at their vast apartment in the 16th Arrondissement. (Everybody who was anybody at the embassy lived in either the 16th or 17th, and in my previous tour of duty my affection for the Left Bank had been regarded as definitely odd.) At lunch the Spauldings seemed to expect me to speak freely about Mrs. Otis, but I had to disappoint them. Despite Snuffy's rather autocratic signals in that direction, and Abigail's transparent effort to draw me out by praising Mariana's "intellect," I managed to keep the talk almost entirely on the subject of my parents. So it was just a bore for all three of us.

The ambassador would simply have been amused, I'm sure, at some of these thoughts, but I wasn't about to confide them to her. I didn't want to break the confident rhythm of these first weeks of her tenure with such petty observations. She had plunged into the required round of formal first diplomatic calls and get-acquainted dinner parties at the invitation of the British and other neighboring ambassadors, and was obviously savoring every minute of it. She also managed to shop the great couture houses, to find a hairdresser who came to the embassy twice a week, and to enter Cristy in a couple of courses about to begin at the Sorbonne. And at least once a week she wrote at length to her father, who recipro-cated in kind.

Despite all this activity, we were getting better acquainted all the time. Some evenings, if she didn't get back from her dinner parties too late, my phone would ring and Mariana would say something airy like: "If you're decent, meet me in the study." I suppose she needed someone to slack off with, lower the pressure from that amazing wellspring of energy. I'd sit there listening to her go on for an hour, maybe just a little high on the wine, cer-tainly very stimulated and talkative, about this or that character she'd met at such and such an embassy.

She had been struck by the lack of stereotyping. The German ambassador, for instance, wasn't fat, the Britisher had a middle-class accent, the Chinese didn't grin, the Japanese was big and burly, the Italian blond. Only the Russian, Krubitsyn, looked the part.

"Have you had a chance to chat with Comrade Krubitsyn?"

"He doesn't chat, Tyler. He looms, squeezes my hand hard in a bear's paw, stages a big smile, wags a warning finger, always makes the same speech, and then lumbers off without waiting for com-ment."

"And what's the speech about?"

She gave an astonishing imitation of male guttural Russian, replete with harsh sibilants and liquid *l*'s, clumsily expressing pleasure at the progress of détente, praise for the new American President, and good wishes to his representative in France.

She also disclosed that Brad Lindley had been pestering her with phone calls proposing a TV interview in depth, and asked me what I thought of the idea.

"Too early in the game, ma'am."

She agreed, and added: "Still, I don't want to snub him. Per-haps I ought to have all the American media people in for a cock-tail?"

I couldn't quarrel with that.

She seemed happier about Cristy, who was riding in the Bois every morning and rode with her mother on weekends. If Cristy knew about our talks in the study she evidently didn't resent it.

Passing her in the hall occasionally, I'd get a guarded grin. She definitely was looking more cheerful, in some new French clothes. Maybe a big change was what the kid had needed all along.

But had Cristy changed that much? I began to wonder again when Mariana, during one of our late evening chats in the study, told me Cristy had heard a Frenchman's suave voice in Mariana's bedroom late the previous night and had burst wildly into the room—to find her mother sitting up in bed listening to her Linguaphone lesson.

"She had the strangest look on her face, Tyler. Then just as suddenly she turned around and stalked out again. She didn't say a word."

"She didn't have to, did she?"

Ms. Ambassador smiled with a hint of sadness, put her hand on my hand for a moment, and said quietly, "How well you understand."

I suppose I could have told her about Cristy's visit to me on the ship, but what would that have added? She probably had been aware of the girl's jealous suspicions for a long time. Couldn't she have done something about it by now? Cristy's trauma had its roots somewhere. For both their sakes, widowed mother and child, I wished I knew where. Maybe then I could help, somehow.

The little scene in the bedroom only emphasized the paradox I had sensed repeatedly since we left Washington, most recently in Mariana's first encounter with the embassy staff, and now in these vivacious night meetings in the study. For all the authority and glamour of her position, the ceaseless round of official actions and contacts with eminent people, at the close of the day she was a woman alone, and lonely.

The cocktail party for American media representatives was held in the White and Gold Room, one of five reception and entertainment salons giving on the Residence garden. Mariana chose it as the most intimate setting available, if intimate can be said to describe any part of the palatial ground-floor setup. She had vetoed Beasley Turner's suggestion of the garden, sensibly pointing out to him that in so much space her guests would tend to scatter.

She wanted this gathering to be nose-to-nose because then, she told me, laughing, she could hear what everybody was saying simultaneously. As it happened it was raining heavily the afternoon of the party, as it frequently does in Paris in May, so the garden was out anyway.

There were twenty-seven in all—bureau chiefs and special correspondents—with half a dozen women among them, including the formidable Fanny Watkins. Those who were making their first visit to the Residence looked suitably impressed as they clicked past the wall fountain across the black, white, and pink marble floor of the entrance hall and stared up at the monumental white stone staircase soaring two stories high in the stairwell. Amid the Louis XVI elegance of the White and Gold Room the first arrival, the man from *Time*, immediately pulled out pad and pencil to record the architectural details.

The ambassador herself—fresh and radiant in spite of an even busier day than usual—obliged him. "One of the workmen who was about to repaint the walls," she said, "discovered the original gold leaf decors under an ancient coat of paint. Notice the gilded moldings—aren't they lovely?"

"Of course this wasn't the first building on the site," she went on. "In 1720 the Chancellor d'Aguesseau built a house that passed to other families after the Revolution. Over a century later the Baronne de Pontalba tore down the original place and built the present mansion. She was an American, by the way."

"American?" He scribbled. "Didn't know that."

"Born in New Orleans and married into an old Louisiana family. Later, the Rothschilds . . ."

"Ah!"

"Baron Edmond and Baron Maurice, his son, lived here during the Third Republic. It was the social and artistic center of Paris. In World War II the Nazis turned it into a Luftwaffe club, then the British made it a Royal Air Force club. Congress allocated a million nine hundred thousand dollars to buy it in 1948."

"Is it true your predecessor left you his wine cellar?"

"I understand so, but I haven't had time to inspect it yet."

Time bowed his admiring appreciation and moved on toward

the drinks. Mariana saw I'd been listening in and winked. "How'm I doing?" she murmured as she went past.

Fanny Watkins arrived and took over. This time she couldn't guess the dress, so Mariana had to tell her. (It was by Grés.) Miss Watkins (she refused adamantly to tolerate Ms.) was also interested, as I learned later, in Mariana's activities in Paris society. Not the diplomatic treadmill—that was automatic—but what Fanny called *real* society. Actually there were two categories, she kindly pointed out to the ambassador: the international jet set and the old aristocracy. Fanny tended to ignore the former—too fast for her, maybe. She felt more comfortable with the latter. How was Mrs. Otis rated in the Faubourg St. Germain? Had the La Rochefoucaulds yet invited her to tea, the Rohans to dinner? No? Pity. She gave the ambassador to understand that in Paris, until that happened, you weren't really here.

Half an hour after the appointed time for the party the dialogue was eyeball-to-eyeball, the sound was high in the decibel range, the smoke haze was thickening, and Mariana was taking on all comers with great good humor. Beasley Turner, tied into his third martini, had just come up to engage me in small talk when I felt a friendly hand on my shoulder and heard the Voice of TV hearty and cheerful behind me. I wheeled to behold Brad Lindley, fashionably late, addressing me as an old pal.

"This was a great idea, Tyler. I assume it was the ambassador herself who thought of it?"

"Let's see," I said perversely. "Wasn't it you, Beasley? I can't remember."

Turner just grinned, glad to take the credit. My uneasy feeling about Brad Lindley had returned. It was foolish of me, but there it was. He ignored Beasley and kept the famous gaze on me.

"I'm glad to have this chance to chat with you, old man. We'll probably be seeing a lot of each other."

"Glad to be of any help I can."

"Good! I happen to need help right now." He had a boyish smile. "I've been trying to persuade your boss to give me a video interview for my 'Spoken Portrait' series, but she keeps saying no. She won't even let me come and talk her into it."

"Sounds to me," I said, "as if she means what she says."

"You didn't know about it? *Come on*—I understand Tyler Paine knows more about her than anybody on this side of the Atlantic. That right, Beasley?"

Turner shrugged and fluttered his eyelashes. I wished he'd go away. Brad Lindley kept after me.

"How's she getting along with Spaulding? Or is it oil and water?"

"From everything I've observed," I said, "they're an excellent team."

He laughed. "I suppose I'll have to accept that, coming from the horse's mouth."

My turn to smile. "You flatter me."

Turner had drifted off, no doubt in quest of a fourth martini. The TV correspondent looked restlessly over the crowd and saw Mariana on the far side of the room, surrounded by half a dozen people. "There she is," he remarked, "and looking smashing, too. Tyler, I think I'll just whip over and break that up. Nice to have seen you. We'll talk again."

He headed in her direction, evidently convinced he wasn't going to get anything provocative out of me for now. These were just preliminary soundings. He would try again, of course. I couldn't blame him, it was his job. And in spite of the too-familiar approach and the brash questions, there was something disarmingly honest about Brad Lindley I was ready to like, if I could forget my instinctive impulse to regard him as a rival.

I enjoyed certain advantages at a party like this. I could devote myself to observing. I didn't have any official work to do because no interpreting was needed. I wasn't a celebrity. I was an assistant celebrity, true, but most of this crowd didn't know that yet. I wasn't a press attaché, so I had no obligations to the guests. Actually I was a guest myself—a rare sensation. A guest of the bright and lovely lady in the Grés cocktail dress toward whom my glances kept wandering, especially now. Yes, my colleague guest from TV had broken it up, just as he'd predicted. He had the hostess backed into an elegant Louis XVI corner under the original gold leaf decors and not protesting at all. I was too proud to go over there and eavesdrop but I wanted very much to know what they were talking about so earnestly. It was the first time Mariana had looked *genuinely* earnest since the party began.

Beasley Turner rejoined me at this point. He was beginning to weave a little and knew it, so he suggested we both quietly repair for some dinner to a bistro he'd been boasting to me about in the Rue Duphot.

"Don't you have responsibilities with these people?" I demurred.

"Hell with it, they're on their own now."

Just the way I felt at the moment about Mariana, although I probably wouldn't have expressed it quite as baldly.

At the bistro a really good cassoulet, accompanied by a delicious though very expensive Musigny and followed by the cheese tray, seemed to sober Beasley up considerably. The gift of second wind must be a godsend in public relations work. I was beginning to feel more respect for my friend's capacities. He also insisted on picking up the tab, another estimable trait. He decided he would walk home and appeared well able to, so we parted outside the restaurant and went our separate ways in opposite directions, having talked hardly at all throughout dinner.

I was glad of that. Tonight I didn't want to listen to anybody but Mariana Otis, and sure enough my private phone rang not ten minutes after I got back to the Residence.

What had she been talking about so earnestly with Brad Lindley? During a half-hour recital of her party impressions in the study she told me without my having to ask. In fact she wrote it down before the conversation began and handed it to me on a piece of copy paper.

We must be extremely careful what we say, she had written in her firm, graceful hand. *Brad Lindley has it from an outside source that the Residence is bugged.*

The Residence bugged? But by whom, and why? In this study alone there were a hundred places listening devices could be concealed—in walls, ceiling, floor, telephones, typewriters. You'd practically have to tear the place down to locate them. Electronic surveillance was now so sophisticated the mechanisms could be almost microscopic, the whole system controlled by radio waves. While we talked, trying not to sound guarded or self-conscious, we both looked uneasily around the room, wondering what kind of malevolent machine was eavesdropping on us and where, but mere guessing was useless. We didn't know where to begin.

In the hallway, returning to our own apartments, Mariana said casually, "Oh, about the protocol list, let's discuss it on the way to the Chancery in the morning."

It was the first time I'd walked to the office with the ambassador. This way, at least, we knew we couldn't be overheard. The marine guard saluted smartly as we left together, following Mariana's favorite route down the Avenue Gabriel. The sun was shining, temporarily anyhow, and Paris was a glory in green. From time to time I glanced at my distinguished companion, forcing a little to keep up with her buoyant step. She strode along like a young girl—clear-eyed, exuberant, still glowing from the session in her gym, one of these women who never really will look old, in the conventional sense, no matter how long they live.

She didn't tackle the bugging problem right away. She wanted to tell me about today's breakfast conference with Stuyvesant Spaulding. "I suspect," she said, "he was piqued that I didn't invite him to meet the press yesterday."

"Snuffy? That surprises me. He wouldn't think of meeting with them himself, unless specifically instructed by Washington."

"*Snuffy!*" It made her laugh. "I hadn't heard that."

"It goes all the way back to prep school. He was always sniffling into his handkerchief."

"*Stuffy* would suit him better."

We walked in silence a few moments. "Naturally," she went on, "I couldn't talk to him about the bugging. That will have to wait till I see him later. And if it's true we'll have to check out the Chancery, too."

"But who's doing it?"

"Brad doesn't know that. So far he's only had a veiled hint."

"From a good source?"

"From a wartime friend he knew in the Resistance."

"I'm surprised he hasn't broadcast the story."

"He promised his source he wouldn't. And I promised Brad I wouldn't divulge my own source."

She was already calling him Brad. It annoyed me. But didn't everybody call him Brad? A million people he'd never met called him Brad. After all he was in their houses practically every evening. During our brief conversation last night I'd almost called him Brad myself.

I said, "What's his guess? Are the French doing it? The Russians?" I hesitated before I added, "Some devious arrangement backed by the CIA?"

She gave a little shrug. "Ralph Hobbs will be present at my meeting with Spaulding. I'll give him a good long look when I tell them."

"Incidentally, Lindley asked me some questions of his own last night. Like whether you're getting along with Stuyvesant Spaulding."

"And what did you tell him?"

"I said you made a pretty good team."

"Bravo, Tyler."

"I thought I'd better say it whether it's so or not."

Her little laugh sounded a trifle grim. "We'll straighten things out. Then once this bugging mystery is solved I can settle down to work."

I couldn't help saying, "How can you possibly work any harder than you're doing right now, ma'am?"

"Tyler," she said, and gave me her conspiratorial wink, "you ain't seen nothin' yet."

We had reached the Chancery gate. Standing stiffly beneath the American Eagles atop the gateposts, the marine sentry came to a smart salute as we went past into the courtyard. I caught his glance and smiled. He looked as if he was thinking the same thing I was: This was quite a woman.

6

I WAS NOT present when the ambassador called in Stuyvesant Spaulding and Ralph Hobbs to disclose her suspicions that the Residence was bugged, but afterward she told me Hobbs was either genuinely startled or did a good job of feigning it. Although he pressed her for a source, she replied merely that she'd heard occasional clicking sounds on the phone, and wondered whether listening devices might have been installed at the time her living apartment and the study were being done over by decorators in anticipation of her arrival from Washington.

The following morning at half-past eight, while the ambassador and Hobbs and I all stood watching, two experts from the Embassy General Services office took everything apart on the entire floor and, sure enough, found what they were looking for, hidden with extraordinary skill in seven separate locations, including Mariana's bedroom and mine.

By the time they got through, the study and living area looked quite a lot as if the San Andreas Fault ran under the Faubourg St. Honoré.

Before we left this mess for the Chancery, Ralph Hobbs swore me solemnly to secrecy, and I solemnly assured him I would say nothing to anyone. During that exchange I avoided looking at Mariana for fear we both might just break up.

The little ironies of the scene hadn't escaped me. If Hobbs was a double agent at this moment—knowing all along that the bugs were there but not telling the ambassador—so were Mariana and I for not bringing Brad Lindley into it. Actually I was more insidious than any of them. Not only was I playing ignorant on Lindley and the wiretapping to Hobbs, I was writing secret reports behind Mariana's back. And if neither the embassy nor the CIA knew about those reports, that made me a quadruple agent. Or something of the sort.

I didn't feel devilish, though, just uncomfortable. I suddenly wished I was back in Washington with Sheila on the seventh floor of the State Department, comparatively tranquil and safe.

Still unanswered was the question of who were the spooks? Who installed the bugs and why? Neither Hobbs nor Spaulding offered a theory. Hobbs said he was taking up the trail immediately, beginning with the reputable French electrical firm of Rousselot Fils, which did all the embassy's installations, and the equally trustworthy Maison Firmat, which had done the redecorating job in the Residence.

For his part in the inquiry, Spaulding would set up discreet soundings among his pals in the diplomatic corps without actually disclosing the secret. Of course he got together with the ambassador immediately on a report to Washington, and they also instituted a check on the Chancery's entire communications system, which turned out to be in the clear.

As for the ambassador, she took forthright action of her own. The day after the Residence was pronounced clear of bugs and restored to its normal appearance, she called me into her office at the Chancery and said, "Tyler, for all we know a fresh set of bugs was slipped into place while they were ostensibly cleaning out the old ones. I don't trust Ralph Hobbs, as a matter of principle. I don't trust anybody—except you." Her sudden warm smile made me glow. "From now on we'll keep to small talk and routine matters in the study. Anything sensitive can be discussed at this desk or at night in the garden."

"I'm in favor, ma'am."

That little conversation resolved my doubts about my next secret report to the department. I'd pondered whether to name Brad Lindley as the source of the bugging revelation, but now I knew that if Mariana was protecting her source, so must I. Official duty notwithstanding, I felt a strong moral obligation. More and more, Mariana was showing her faith in me. As my superior officer and her friend, I owed her the same.

86

There had been no response from the undersecretary to my previous report, at which I felt relieved rather than disappointed. Except in dire emergencies, I probably wouldn't be hearing from him in the future. Considering the innocent nature of what I'd recounted so far, Washington had no cause for alarm about anything in the ambassador's private life, and that made me feel glad indeed. As to my latest report, it was hardly less innocent.

Since Remington had seemed most interested in the personal side, I took occasion to comment at some length about young Cristy Otis, pointing out that the daughter seemed to be adjusting well to living in Paris. Her mother, I said, was pleased at Cristy's interest in her work at the Sorbonne. (It occurred to me as I wrote that we were seeing less of Cristy around the house lately, and I smiled remembering the Foreign Minister's prediction that she would learn more in the cafés than in the classroom. I knew something about that from personal experience, and once again the delicious shadow of Yolande flitted across my mind.)

I also described the cocktail party for the American news people in my report, and here I dropped a hint that it wasn't the sort of friendly gesture the press had been used to before the ambassador came to Paris. The undersecretary must already have noticed, I added, the cordial stories in *Time* and *Newsweek,* as well as New York and Washington papers and Brad Lindley's enthusiastic endorsement on the air (Beasley Turner had brought me word of that). This reaction would seem to indicate the ambassador had made a smart move and was starting to build a favorable public relations image as an accessible and pleasant person.

I made no further reference to Lindley. Generally speaking, he was a subject I felt reluctant to dwell on, and I was relieved to learn from Beasley that he was off on assignment in Cairo.

Nor did I mention my own growing awareness that members of the embassy staff above a certain rank were shying away from any too-chummy relationship with Tyler Paine. There's always an undercurrent of jealousy and backbiting in a large embassy, with its strict official and social hierarchy, but the reason for this attitude toward me seemed to be twofold: my colleagues both resented my closeness to the ambassador and affected to show me they were indifferent to it. Since the undersecretary had mentioned that the situation would probably develop along these lines I saw no reason to go into it further in my report. That would just sound like grousing, and I wasn't grousing. The only exception to this cool-shouldering was good old Beasley, and as I've said I was never sure he wasn't working as a petty informer. So what? My allegiance, my interest, and my affection were solidly attached to Mariana now.

(But I would have felt so much better if I weren't writing these damned reports to Washington!)

A curious repercussion from the ambassador's friendly attitude toward Foreign Minister Courtailles came very close to home, right here in the Residence. I was in the midst of my usual morning conference with Mariana in the study before she left for the Chancery when we were interrupted by a knock on the door.

It was Mme. Hanotte, the housekeeper.

Mme. Hanotte was still mostly unknown territory to me. She was small, trim, somber, and obviously the kind of person you kept a certain distance from, as she did from you. She was not ungracious, just terribly businesslike, in her traditional French way. She reminded me of Gertrude Stein's characterization of the three kinds of French—the commercial French, the funereal French, and the good old French. Mme. Hanotte had more than her share of the first two. You admired the intelligence she brought to her job of making the Residence tick. And you had to respect her dignity. But you couldn't imagine telling her a joke.

Mariana indicated once or twice she had approximately the same feeling about Mme. Hanotte as I did. Of course as a woman she could understand her much better. Still, I think I sensed very soon that there were reservations in their relationship. Mme. Hanotte had never served a female ambassador, and had not wholly accepted this one.

Now as she advanced with calm, determined steps across the room I suspected a lecture was coming. It was the first time I had heard her speak English—pretty well, too. "Mme. Ambassador will excuse me," she said, respectfully but to the point, "if I interrupt a moment her work."

"But of course," Mariana smiled.

"Just now I have spoken with the *chef de cuisine*. There is a case of wine to be delivered to M. Courtailles at his home."

"Quite correct," said Mariana. "You need the address?"

"The *chef de cuisine*," Mme. Hanotte went on, not answering the question, "informed me that there is to be sent the Château Lafite-Rothschild of 1961. Mme. Ambassador may not be aware that this is now already a very rare vintage. It is perhaps the most valuable wine in the cellar of the embassy. I have consulted the inventory, and I wish to suggest a *Mouton*-Rothschild to be sent to M. Courtailles. This is an excellent wine of the same year."

"Do you bring this suggestion from Jean-Paul?"

"The *chef de cuisine* has not an opinion, Mme. Ambassador."

Mariana was still smiling. "You will send the Lafite."

Motionless, the two women faced each other in silence for a moment. The housekeeper's mouth tightened imperceptibly before she spoke again. "As Mme. Ambassador wishes," she said coldly, and withdrew.

Mariana looked at me after the door closed. "She's been building up to something like this, Tyler. We had to have our little showdown."

I grinned. "Mme. Hanotte scares me. It might have been safer to give in. After all, she was still keeping your gift in the Rothschild family."

Mme. Ambassador shook her head. "I couldn't possibly send Mouton. Mouton's the family black sheep."

She seemed to enjoy her little pun as much as I did.

It was just three days after what Mariana and I called the Hanotte Incident that the ambassador received a visit from André Perpidan, chief of the Service de Documentation Exterieure et Contre-Espionage at the Sûreté, investigating the bugging at the Residence. As so often happens, he looked highly unlike the fictional image of a key official in the French secret police—I would have tagged him for a smug Swiss banker or maybe a stolid Dutch lawyer. His approach was mild, deferential, and leisurely. M. Perpidan was obviously a man who took his time.

Spaulding and of course Hobbs were both present on this occasion. As a matter of fact, in view of Snuffy's seeming tendency to keep me in my place, I was surprised I'd been invited to sit in, until Mariana told me Perpidan insisted I was essential to the discussion. But there was little I could add beyond confirming the ambassador's statement in all respects.

Hobbs, it appeared, had drawn a blank in questioning the two firms who did the embassy's regular electrical and decorating work. If Spaulding's soundings among the diplomatic corps were any more fruitful, he didn't tell M. Perpidan. And Mariana, true to the pledge she'd given Brad Lindley, stuck to her story of strange buzzings and clickings on the line which first aroused her suspicion.

"I'm afraid that's all there is to tell," she concluded.

The Frenchman nodded. "We will wish to examine the equipment, with Your Excellency's permission."

"Certainly," said the ambassador.

"That won't be necessary," Ralph Hobbs said. "I've checked it out myself."

M. Perpidan smiled gently. "A matter of routine, M. Hobbs. If you do not object—."

"By all means," said Mariana. "Go right ahead."

Hobbs didn't look too appreciative, but he'd been overruled and that was it.

It was Spaulding's turn to address M. Perpidan. "What," he said, "is your theory about this dirty business?"

"Perhaps you have a theory of your own, M. Spaulding?"

"Absolutely none. Neither here in the embassy nor in Washington."

The inevitable shrug. "My office is making the usual inquiries. It is a fairly common situation. Perhaps we will turn something up, perhaps not. There are the normal possibilities, one as likely as the next. Of course, I am in the dark as to an immediate political background." He looked blandly at Ralph Hobbs. "If there were some indication of a motive . . ."

Hobbs said stiffly, "We are as much in the dark as you, sir. I was hoping your government might have given you a lead."

M. Perpidan shook his head. "Nothing," he said.

That's the way it was left. The same afternoon a team of experts from the Rue des Saussaies looked over the setup in the Residence, under the personal surveillance of Hobbs and one of his assistants, but were politely turned down when they proposed examining the communications system in the Chancery as well.

"Hobbs predicts that's the last we'll ever hear of it," the ambassador told me later. "Unless," she added, "Brad Lindley's source comes up with something more."

"Any chance of that?"

"Let's hope so. But we won't know anything until Brad comes back from Cairo. Meanwhile, I refuse to worry further about it."

"An excellent idea, ma'am."

But I still resented her calling him Brad.

We were enjoying one of the longest periods without rain in my memory of Paris. Each day was lovelier than the last. The Tuileries were in full bloom and gardeners had decked out the vast Place du Carrousel with brilliant floral designs. It was as though the whole city had taken a deep breath of renewal and started life afresh.

So had Mariana Hillman Otis. Her fledgling diplomatic preliminaries over, she really took hold of the job. The formal accreditation at the Elysée Palace had been a kind of watershed. Now she was fully in the swing, an equal among equals. You could see that in her very manner at the Chancery, the poise and bearing of a leader conscious of power and position. The men who worked with her sensed it, too, and perhaps rather ruefully contrasted it with that humble little speech she'd made to them on the first day.

She had more than their sympathy now, she commanded their respect.

I marveled at how much this woman could accomplish with her time. She would have made a first-rate corporation executive—she knew how to categorize the problems, outline the work methods, and delegate the authority—and I began to see the reasons for her success as a political campaign organizer.

One of her first decisions after arriving at her post was to call Herbert Hillman in Washington, stipulate certain furnishings she wanted for her suite in the Residence, and ask her father to lend her a number of his paintings. These had now arrived, and with great care, under Mariana's hawk-eyed supervision, were hung in the downstairs salons. I gasped when I saw them—two magnificent Monets to vie with the blue crystal chandelier in the Gallery, a Renoir and a Pissaro looking down on the two Waterford candelabras in the Samuel Bernard Room, a Gauguin and a Manet for the White and Gold Room. Upstairs in the house guest area a set of Degas dancers were hung in the less formal Blue Salon. Altogether, a staggering collection of masterpieces whose market value I didn't even want to think about.

Her Excellency was making psychological changes as well. She spiced the official entertaining of diplomatic guests by discarding the long-table setup in the state dining room, where the portraits of General Lafayette and Admiral Rochambeau now looked down on dinner parties at small round tables enlivened by attractive younger embassy people, chosen regardless of rank. This was exactly the sort of thing Abigail Spaulding and the senior embassy wives could be expected to resent, but the ambassador had taken care to disarm Mrs. Spaulding in advance by asking her to serve as her appointments adviser, a move that pleased Abigail and removed one of Mariana's most irksome chores. Under her mentor's guidance she made cordial personal contact with the dean of the American Cathedral and heads of other American colony institutions, patronized American Guild charity functions, opened deserving art exhibits, visited the Ecole de Puériculture, and dutifully accepted the right invitations to speak—such as addressing the France–Etats-Unis organization—while politely ducking the wrong ones.

Similarly the chore of social correspondence, an endless job, was turned over to Honora de Chapdelaine, a multilingual embassy employee with extensive diplomatic connections who also dealt with the innumerable appeals from individuals for financial aid from the ambassador. (It had rapidly become known that Mrs. Otis was the daughter of a great American tycoon.) These appeals came not only from the French but from countries all over Western Europe. Honora was an expert at sympathetic rejection. I even got a few such letters myself, piteously imploring me to intercede with the ambassador. Beasley Turner advised me they were the work of professional beggars and to ignore them.

Mariana gave Honora free rein in all correspondence, but still made it a point to copy the more important thank-you notes in her own hand, usually going out of her way to add a graceful personal comment—another example of the thoroughness with which she was doing her job. She also kept an eye on significant incoming mail, and in at least one case received a note that was definitely worth keeping.

This was the Foreign Minister's prompt acknowledgement of that case of Château Lafite-Rothschild '61. It was ornamentally handwritten on the personal stationery of Claude Courtailles with the address of his town house on the Quai d'Anjou, and it ended with a typical flourish of his lofty, old-fashioned style (here I translate): "*I shall never forget this noble gesture of the ambassadrice, so eloquent in both feeling and taste, which I refuse obstinately to regard merely as official; just as I shall never forgive her if at some future time to be agreed upon she declines my wholly unofficial invitation, herewith tendered, to share her precious gift at my own table, incognita, under my own rooftree. Accept, dear madame, the assurance of my humblest gratitude and highest admiration.*"

Mariana called me into her office at the Chancery to show me the note and giggled a little, like a schoolgirl excited by her first invitation to a dance, while I stood there reading it.

"It looks as though you've made another conquest" was my remark as I handed it back.

She had no rejoinder to that, but I'm sure the Foreign Minister's note was an added fillip to her feeling of self-confidence recently so evident.

Cristy too, when I very occasionally saw her, seemed to be maturing fast. The youthful intensity was still there but I had the impression it was less erratic now, more focused. Obviously the Sorbonne had become the center of her interests. She was spending more and more of her time in the Quarter, sometimes not returning to the Residence until nine or ten at night, and she'd taken to tart, slangy comments to the servants which betrayed an aptitude for French argot that was quite remarkable. A couple of the cracks I overheard would have startled her mother into a blush, I'm certain, but Mariana didn't seem aware of this sudden blossoming, if you could call it that. She always looked in on Cristy at the end of her long ambassadorial day and usually found her already in bed and asleep.

As if the ambassador's morning exercise in her little gym wasn't enough to keep her in top shape, she added Tuesday and Thursday visits to the Racing Club for tennis with the pro and a swim. With all this, she still found occasional moments to extend her interest in the domestic problems of the Residence staff. She was on relaxed terms with everybody from the butler, Maurice, all the way down the line to the maids and footmen, and she didn't forget to pop into the kitchen for a word with Jean-Paul and a nod to his staff. On one not-to-be-forgotten afternoon she appeared without warning in the servants' dining room as they were finishing lunch and asked if she might take coffee with them, much to their astonishment.

She even got interested in table arrangements and worked with the gardener on decorative flower schemes.

Only the relationship with Mme. Hanotte failed to warm up. I got the impression they both were steering clear of each other. Since their little showdown in the study over the gift of wine, word seemed to have spread through the Residence that the ambassador was a woman who knew exactly what she wanted and saw to it that it was done her way.

This was evident in a chat I had with Jean-Paul. He appeared one evening in the second-floor dining room where I was repaying Beasley Turner for that meal in the Rue Duphot bistro. Garbed in apron and tall toque, the chef inquired cordially as to whether we found his *aiguillette de boeuf* satisfactory and urged me, as he had before, to let me know in advance what I liked in food and drink. It would give him pleasure to suit my taste.

"My favorite wine," I said solemnly, "is Lafite-Rothschild '61. I should not be satisfied with the Mouton."

It was the first time I'd heard the dignified Jean-Paul laugh and possibly would be the last. There was nobody else listening except Turner—Mariana was out for the evening and Cristy always had a tray brought to her room. So Jean-Paul just let go. I could see I'd given him material for a week's sniggering in the kitchen.

"Don't you think," my guest said when the chef had retired, still chuckling, "you might let me in on the gag?"

"Sorry, Beasley. Private reference. You wouldn't think it was funny."

He blinked those long lashes. "I suppose there's a lot goes on around here that's not for public distribution."

"Not at all. We're eminently respectable in the Residence. In fact, dull."

"Is that why you stick so close to home?" he grinned. "Most guys would be having an occasional date on the town by now."

"Beasley," I said, "I've been considering taking action along those lines. Care to offer a helpful suggestion?"

"Gee, I don't happen to have my address book with me. But I'll get back to you on it."

"Wish you would."

Actually I didn't expect him to. Not Beasley. But my dining companion had touched a tender spot. I'm not, like some of my bachelor acquaintances in Washington, more or less constantly on the make. Connie, and sometimes Jan or Vivian, had taken care of that. (Vivian, by the way, required an effort more elaborate than the end result was usually worth. It was a full-scale production. If pressed, I didn't recommend Vivian, although she is a hell of a good-looking girl.) Still I am, I believe, a healthy male, and I'd been in France nearly six weeks now. So it was perfectly natural that I was beginning to feel somewhat inclined. I'm not used to going that long. The trouble was I didn't have any contacts. Females in the embassy were out of the question, of course—not that I'd seen anything very exciting. And prowling the Grands Boulevards through a maze of middle-aged whores didn't fascinate me, never has. There again, I'd had Yolande to comfort me. (But it was more than that, we comforted each other.) Yet I knew I could never duplicate the wonder of that affair, at my age, even in Paris.

Maybe it was the haunting memory of Yolande that sent me wandering, a few nights later, among the scenes of my salad days in the Quarter. Things didn't look quite the same, of course. As Claude Courtailles had put it, the new buildings were destroying Paris. And even in the leisure of a soft summer night the people I passed, especially the older people, had a hurried, harassed look, as if they knew they had to keep up with the changed tempos of life but resented it to the depths of their Parisian souls. Only after I left the neon-garish Boulevard St. Michel and walked into the narrower, quieter streets behind the Pantheon did I begin to get the old feeling. Just the street names were helping—Rue de l'Estrapade, Place de la Contrescarpe, Rue du Pot de Fer . . . it was all student territory, the little bar and restaurant hangouts casting their glow onto the dim sidewalks, the bursts of strident talk or laughter reaching out to clutch my heart as I passed. Could this ever be different? No, the students hadn't changed. My old *quartier* was still here. And Yolande beckoned from every shadow. *Oh les fraises et les framboises, les bons vins que nous avons bu* . . . How easy it was to believe I could find Yolande Vannier again, here, tonight! still eighteen and flawless, bare-armed and bare-legged, copper hair to her shoulders, still see the urchin smile of loving mockery. And how hard to realize that the boy she knew had vanished, a ghost in the streets like his girl of long ago.

Moonlight was flooding the facade of Ste. Geneviève as I walked back toward the river. In a tiny café on the Rue Descartes a group of four or five kids hunched over coffee at a sidewalk table were listening raptly to the low, passionate discourse of a very blond boy well this side of twenty. I couldn't catch what he was saying but had a close-up glimpse of them all under the streetlamp as I went past. Cristy Otis was one of his listeners.

I don't think she would have heard me even if I'd called her name.

7

MY PHONE RANG unexpectedly. It was nearly midnight and I was getting ready for bed. This was the first time Mariana had used our private line at such a late hour.

She sounded troubled.

"Are you decent?" she said, as she always did.

"I can be, with a slight delay."

"It's such a beautiful night, Tyler. I thought I'd take a turn around the garden, but I don't want to go down alone at this hour."

"Quite right. I'll meet you on the terrace in ten minutes."

She was wearing a sort of sari shawl over her evening dress that shimmered in the moonlight. The air still carried the faint chill of early summer. Without a word she took my arm and we walked slowly toward the far end of the garden. I waited for her to break the silence. Usually she was ebullient, but not tonight. I could sense her mood and it worried me.

Finally it was I who spoke, trying to sound casual. "Another one of those deadly protocol evenings?"

"Quite the contrary, Tyler." The words came low and muted.

I knew she had been at a reception and formal dinner tonight at the Cercle Interalliée for the U.N. Secretary-General, but it was hardly an occasion at which surprises might be expected. No country of importance pays the United Nations more than lip service when it comes to the crunch, unless it seems politically profitable to use it for selfish ends, and nobody knows this better than the Secretary-General himself.

"Did the guest of honor get out of line?" I asked.

She made a small, impatient gesture. "Of course not. Anyway, they barely listened."

Again there was a long pause. This time I waited for her to speak. We had come to the hedge and stopped before she said anything more, then, "Claude Courtailles came up to me as I was leaving. He suggested rather insistently that he drop me off in his car, that it was the only way he could talk privately. So I dismissed my car. We were observed, of course."

I smiled. "The Foreign Minister and the lady ambassador leaving together? A nice little morsel of gossip on tomorrow's circuit."

"I don't give a damn about that, and I don't think he does either. He said it was something I ought to know at once."

"And was it?"

She didn't answer immediately. Where we stood at the far end of the garden we were quite isolated, her arm still linked with mine, but she glanced around us before she spoke again in a voice weighted with shock and humiliation.

"I've been had, Tyler. I know now what it is they held back from me in Washington. So far, only a few top-level people are in on it. Courtailles found out only this afternoon in a personal message from his ambassador in Moscow." She gave a brief, bitter laugh. "We sat outside the Residence in his car until he finished. I thanked him and he said good night."

I waited, not sure whether this was the end of our conversation or if she was going to tell me what it was all about. She seemed deeply disturbed by what she was thinking, almost as if she'd forgotten I was with her. I broke the silence again. "Courtailles must have had his reasons for telling you."

"I'm sure he had. He didn't say what they were, but he was as upset as I was." Suddenly her hand tightened on my arm and she looked up at me in the shadows. "We've opened negotiations with the Russians on a plan for basic reorganization of Europe's security structure. From what Courtailles knows so far, Washington and Moscow are considering proposing that France and Britain join them in a treaty renouncing the use of nuclear weapons in any future European conflict. But Courtailles indicated there's much more than he's been told as yet."

I was stunned. "And this embassy hasn't been informed."

"Not a hint. Unless," she added in the same bitter tone, "Spaulding knows about it. Courtailles says the plan originated with the West Germans several months ago but they presented it in Washington only last week. He believes the Russians knew earlier but sat on it."

"Maybe we knew earlier, too. Maybe the White House didn't know till last week." Hush-hush Stoneface and his German friends . . .

"Perhaps," she said, "the Secretary is up to his old game of not letting his own government know what he's doing."

A ray of moonlight fell across her head and shoulders. For a moment, despite the grimness of what she was saying, I thought irrelevantly I'd never seen her as beautiful.

I said, "Will you tell Spaulding?"

"Not until morning. I'm going to the study now to write a dispatch for immediate transmission. I may need your help with some of the language."

"Of course."

She turned and we started back to the Residence, walking with little steps. "And I'm not going to mince words, Tyler. I want to know why this has been kept from me and I want to know from the Secretary himself."

"You've told *me*," I said. "That makes me feel rather proud."

She stopped and looked at me. "But I wanted you to know," she said simply.

On impulse I leaned forward, took her hand, and kissed her fingers. She held my hand a moment before releasing it, then I saw her lips part. It was almost a smile. She could have said, "Now what's *that* for?" or any number of other things, I suppose, but she didn't speak at all. I straightened up stiffly with a suddenly hot face.

I didn't say anything either.

Following her into the house, I glanced up at the rear facade in the moonlight and saw the figure of Mme. Hanotte looking down at us from a third-floor hallway window. Abruptly the housekeeper drew back out of sight.

It was like a scene from a movie made from one of those Gothic romances. I didn't really take Mme. Hanotte very seriously.

All the same, going up the stairs, I wondered about it.

The ambassador finished the dispatch in an hour and marked it NIACT for night action. I took it to the Chancery myself and stood by while it was coded and transmitted. In Washington, State was through for the day. They'd have to track down the Secretary at a dinner party if he wasn't at home in Chevy Chase.

The tone was level, the language controlled. But there could be no mistaking the personal resentment underlying Mariana's report. She made no mention of her source, not even to say the information had been given her in confidence. Nor did she ask why the embassy had not been informed. She simply restated everything Claude Courtailles had told her and asked whether it was an accurate account of what was happening.

If it was, either wholly or in part, she said, the embassy would expect immediate instructions. If it was not, she expected an immediate answer to that effect.

She hadn't really needed my help. She drafted her dispatch like a professional. When she checked it with me afterward I couldn't find a syllable to change. But I knew she had wanted me with her in the study, whether to give her confidence or just keep her company. It didn't matter which, I was grateful to be there.

Grateful and disturbed, because it was the first time I had seen Mariana Otis angry.

There was more to the anger than the humiliation she felt. She was profoundly uneasy at what Claude Courtailles had told her, and well she might be.

I thought about it walking back from the Chancery. Darkness was claiming the city. The lights on the Champs Elysées were beginning to wink out. Even here, in the middle of the tourist area, Paris was an early-to-bed town. All the rest of it except for little enclaves on Montmartre and the Left Bank lay already asleep.

On the face of it, the projected treaty Courtailles had described could only mean good for Europe and the world—another step toward permanent peace. The great question, as Mariana had seen at once, was whether the signatories of such a pact would live up to their pledge of mutual trust—and by this she meant, of course, the Russians. And what were the other provisions, so far only hinted at, that had so alarmed the Foreign Minister? The secrecy in which negotiations were being conducted—so typical of Stoneface, as Mariana had learned to her hurt—was far from reassuring. Was the Senate Foreign Relations Committee aware these talks had been launched, or was Stoneface contemptuously withholding the information from Bryce Halsted and his colleagues as he was from his own diplomatic missions in the countries involved?

If he was nothing else, the Secretary was a realist. He must, and so must the White House, have gauged the prospects for approval by Congress and acceptance by public opinion. Pourparlers with the Soviets must have been held some time ago, perhaps even during a secret visit by the Secretary to Russia, where the American ambassador, like Mariana Otis, may have been kept in the dark until after the fact.

And certainly the majority mood of the American people, as I'd judged it myself since the presidential election, seemed by and large favorable to a firmly anchored peace in Europe, if for no other reason than most Americans were just plain sick of it all— the years of threatened nuclear holocaust, the cynical mistrust underlying negotiations between the two superpowers, the futile efforts to halt the spiraling arms race, and a growing belief that the Russians might be as tired of it as ourselves, that Moscow was at last ready—genuinely, this time—to make an agreement, and to keep it.

Assuming all this to be true, if Stoneface now had assurances from the Russians that such a treaty were indeed possible and could count on West Germany's and an obedient Britain's backing, where did the rest of Western Europe stand? Above all the French, without whose participation the whole project was doomed? From Mariana's description of their Foreign Minister's reaction, there were rough waters ahead at the very least. But did his alarm necessarily mirror the feelings of others in the government, primarily Auguste Nicollet and the President? Had Nicollet's briefing been a sincere policy statement, or double-talk? And what of the Parliament, a hodgepodge of divided splinter parties obstinately upholding the French tradition of independence and individuality at all costs, representing the unpredictable divisions among the French people themselves?

I think it was Washington's failure to consult its Paris ambassador on France's attitude that had wounded Mariana the most. Could it be that the department had been in touch with Stuyvesant Spaulding privately, instructing him to keep the whole matter to himself?

We weren't long in finding out.

I was standing at Mariana's desk at half-past eight next morning, after sleeping as restlessly as I'm sure the ambassador did, when Spaulding pushed aside the half-open door and strode in, uninvited, a paper in his hand and a look of outrage on his face.

"The duty officer called me about your dispatch," he said, tight-lipped, brandishing the paper accusingly and ignoring my presence.

The ambassador nodded. "Evidently you've already read it. Or did you know all about the contents beforehand?"

"I knew nothing!"

I studied him. A diplomat is a gentleman who lies for his country, but Snuffy Spaulding is no actor. It was obvious he was telling the truth.

"Very well," Mariana was saying, "then we will discuss it."

"Alone!" For the first time he switched his glare to me.

"As you wish," she said. She looked up with a small smile. "We'll resume later, Tyler."

I bowed and retired to my office, making sure I closed the door tight.

It was hard to concentrate on anything else while their discussion lasted. The door was soundproof, so there was no hint of what was being said on either side, but I was sure Spaulding was as surprised by the Foreign Minister's news as he was hurt that Mariana hadn't shown him the dispatch before she sent it. I didn't feel a bit sorry for him.

Meanwhile I checked every morning and afternoon newspaper for any reference to the subject. Not an inkling. Whatever the reaction of the Nicollet government, it was being handled with complete discretion. But that couldn't last. This was Paris, and leaks to the press were inevitable sooner or later, even more so than in Washington.

At midday Beasley Turner came by and suggested lunch at the Crillon grill. I declined, wishing to remain handy in case Mariana called me in. Walking down the hall with him as far as the men's room, I noticed the door to the ambassador's inner office was closed, which meant she was still at her desk. I glanced at my watch. She was due at the American Women's Club at one—or had she canceled that?

Betsy Grant, who helped out on letters when I needed her, brought me coffee and a ham sandwich from the Chancery cafeteria.

Just afterward the buzzer summoned me to the ambassador.

She was alone in the immense room, seated behind her desk, her face expressionless. Without a word she handed me the decoded reply to her dispatch. It was addressed directly to the ambassador, eyes only, but unsigned.

> 1. INFORMATION FORWARDED IN YOUR CABLE THIS DATE NOT REPEAT NOT TO BE RELEASED IN SUBSTANCE OR SLIGHTEST DETAIL OR DISCUSSED ANYONE REPEAT ANYONE EXCEPT DEPUTY CHIEF MISSION TO WHOM SEPARATE MESSAGE FULLER INSTRUCTIONS BEING TRANSMITTED DUE COURSE.
> 2. EMPHASIZE EXTREMELY GRAVE REPERCUSSIONS LIKELY SHOULD U S MISSION BECOME INVOLVED EXCHANGES ANY FRENCH GOVERNMENT DEPARTMENT THIS SUBJECT EVEN MOST CASUAL CONVERSATION.
> 3. AMBASSADOR WILL CONSULT DEPUTY CHIEF MISSION ALL FUTURE DEVELOPMENTS THIS AREA AND ADHERE CLOSELY HIS COUNSEL ALL RESPECTS.

I handed the cable back to Mariana in silence. What was there to say? The response from Washington had been direct, terse, and crushing. The ambassador had been told to stay out of it. More, she had been instructed to take any future cues from her subordinate in what might well become the most crucial diplomatic negotiations of her term of service, over an issue vital to the future of the world.

Our eyes met. Mariana was managing a tiny smile, but when she spoke the bitter irony in her voice was unmistakable.

"Well, Tyler, I can't say I wasn't warned. All the way back to Wade Hunnicutt, in fact. And I can't deny I was aware that career Foreign Service officers take over from fly-by-night amateurs when the heat is on."

"You're no amateur, ma'am. You've already proved that."

"My dear friend, I could serve in this post five years and they still wouldn't call me a pro. Because I'm a woman."

I shook my head. "You underrate your abilities. It's the Secretary—."

"I can see him dictating it," she said. "The mean little mouth. His chance to put me in my place. He did dictate it, didn't he?"

"It sounds like him, yes."

She glanced at the cable in her hand. "Not a word of acknowledgement. Just a scolding. And the implication, of course, that I'm incapable of handling anything of importance on my own."

"With some exceptions, that's the usual attitude in the department toward political appointees at major posts."

She gave a weary little shrug. "Not that he didn't make his objections quite clear to the White House before my appointment was announced. I wonder if he's deliberately keeping this snub from the President."

"He might be tempted to, considering the President's preoccupation with domestic problems at the moment. But it would be vindictive and petty, hardly becoming to a man in high office."

"I may be new to diplomacy" was her answer to that, "but I've seen enough of men in high office to know just how vindictive and petty some of them can be. More so than a lot of women of my acquaintance." She added, "I would not include the President in that category, of course."

"From what I hear of him, I wouldn't either."

"He may have faults, Tyler, but pettiness isn't one of them."

Something in the way she said it suddenly made me wonder for a moment whether the President's relationship with Mariana Hillman Otis had its source entirely in the business of government. But I wasn't going to get into that. I said, "Has Spaulding seen this cable yet?"

She spoke with icy calm. "No. And I don't intend to discuss it with him. I shall seal it in an envelope when I leave tonight and put it in interoffice mail."

"So it won't reach his desk till after he's left for the day."

"Exactly."

"He'll be upset, especially if he gets his message from Washington first."

"I shouldn't wonder."

"As a matter of fact he looked pretty upset when he barged into your office this morning."

"Naturally. I'd defied the policy that requires me to go running to him every time I hear anything of importance. He also knew you knew it before he did, which didn't help. For all I know, he phoned Washington this morning to be sure I was reprimanded for sending a report without showing it to him first."

"Reprimanded for doing your job?"

"What else? At any rate, they all know now how I feel about it."

Looking at her, I saw the hurt pride in her face and wished again I could do something to assuage her very human reaction.

I needn't have been concerned any longer. With an abrupt gesture and a brilliant smile that seemed to dismiss the whole subject, she suddenly got up from her desk and walked to the window. Below her in afternoon sunshine lay the matchless panorama of the Place de la Concorde, the bridge across the Seine, the Assemblée Nationale, and the Quai d'Orsay. Beyond, the fair land of France stretched limitlessly away. She stood there with her back to me as if lost in thought while I waited beside her desk in silence. Then she turned, and now her smile was almost mischievously gay.

"Young man," she said, "what is it they call that famous French bicycle race—the one that goes all around the country?"

"The Tour de France?"

"Exactly. That's what's prescribed for you and me, Tyler—a *tour de France*. Obviously we won't be missed around here."

I blinked.

"I want to find out what the French people think about all this," she said. "And there's only one way—to ask them, face to face."

8

So began the American ambassador's whirlwind first trip outside the Paris area, all of it new to her, some of it new to me. The objective was just what she had told me in her office—to meet the French of all classes and occupations and learn their hopes for the future of their country and Europe. The plans were laid in secrecy in the Residence study between the hours of six o'clock and midnight the same day she received the cable from Washington which had motivated her sudden decision. Mariana was in a fever of anticipation, and like two avid tourists we put the itinerary together with the aid of a road map, the Guide Michelin, and the list of U.S. consulates in France.

We managed to keep our secret until the last moment before departure. When Cristy came in shortly after ten that night she was told her mother would phone her every morning, wherever we were, and to my astonishment she failed to show the slightest objection to the fact we were going away together. Not even Pascal, the Number One embassy chauffeur, knew our destination when he drew up as ordered in front of the Residence at seven-thirty the next morning in his long black limousine.

If the butler was startled he gave no sign. Imperturbable as always, he loaded the ambassador's three bags and my single suitcase into the luggage compartment and opened the car door. We took our places in the back seat and only then did Mariana hand him an envelope.

"Please see that this is delivered to M. Spaulding's office this morning, Maurice."

"*Certainement,* madame."

From behind the wheel Pascal, also imperturbable, looked around at me.

"La route de Meaux," I said.

"*Bien,* monsieur."

And we were off on the first leg of our own *tour de France*.

It was a project conceived by Mariana Otis in a mood of exasperation and protest as a gesture that could not fail to be noted by her department colleagues in Paris and Washington. Impetuous, yes, but like all her gestures, whether pleased or displeased, as I was learning, it was masked in the same appearance of reason and calm. It's not unusual for an ambassador to undertake systematic visits to the whole of the country where he's stationed, and Mariana had chosen this tactical moment to begin hers—with a difference.

The difference was that she informed no one anywhere in advance, an unheard-of breach in the normal way of doing things. The whole trip was to be a trailblazing exercise in informality—a continuous interview-in-the-street across the length and breadth of France. Her casual note to Spaulding—she'd shown it to me before sealing the envelope—simply asked him to take over her appointments and told him she would keep in touch with the embassy each day during her absence, but didn't say how long she would be gone. (I could see Snuffy's face when he read it.) By this method she'd avoided nuisance pursuit by the media, and by declining to enclose her itinerary she hoped she could prevent Spaulding's communicating with either American consulates or local French authorities in advance, as she preferred to descend on them without notice and thus avoid time-wasting ceremonies.

Perhaps most disturbing of all from the protocol point of view, aside from the official discourtesy of failing to notify the French locals, would be the fact that the ambassador was making the journey accompanied only by a young (well, reasonably young) male assistant, setting up a surefire target for leers in the scandal press.

I mentioned this jokingly as we sped eastward through the misty summer morning.

Her reply was prompt. "You're forgetting Pascal. Could you think of a more ideal chaperone?"

Rheims had been selected as our logical first stop on a roughly circular route that would cover most of the country. Once past Meaux, we avoided the main highway in favor of the side roads. The morning's drive took us through an area of historic significance to Americans, across battlefields where the doughboys fought in World War I—Château Thierry and the Argonne. At a U.S. war cemetery, where we roused an astonished custodian from his nap, the ambassador left the car to stand in silent tribute before the rows of crosses. The simple sincerity of this act was very moving to me. The custodian, however, expressed regret there was no cameraman present to take pictures. He was more used to that.

In each village along the way, wherever we saw a likely shop or even a single person cycling or walking through the countryside, Mariana called a halt and hopped out for a little chat, her interpreter at her heels. Occasionally I was needed, but I quickly realized what extraordinary progress she'd made in her French. Her vocabulary was still limited, but its very simplicity imposed a directness and clarity that helped both sides of the exchange. Above all it was her down-to-earth manner that drew out even the most taciturn types. And as they talked, she took notes like a reporter at a press conference.

Without exception, they reacted to her identity with dignity and poise, seeming to understand immediately the purpose of what she was doing.

At the Hôtel du Lion d'Or in Rheims, where we registered in early afternoon, a beaming management recognized the distinguished guest at once and found us handsome accommodations —the ambassador in a suite, which they insisted on, Tyler and Pascal in separate rooms down the hall, the ambassador having in turn insisted on first-class sleeping quarters for her chauffeur.

There was to be no slackening of pace. Within half an hour the mayor of Rheims bustled around to the hotel, accompanied by two of his municipal councillors, and an impromptu *vin d'honneur* was offered in Mariana's suite—champagne, naturally. At least

I'd warned her in advance. Rheims is headquarters for one of France's noblest contributions to civilization, the champagne industry, and could not be ignored by an American ambassador who was anywhere in the vicinity. And of course the official greeting had to be followed by a series of ritual calls at the champagne companies, but not before we paid our respects to the beautiful cathedral where Jeanne d'Arc crowned the Dauphin and Napoleon crowned himself.

I suppose the number of American tourists who've been through the tasting routine in Rheims is in the millions by now. We were taken to just one cellar (if you've seen one you've seen them all) and the rest of the time was spent talking with industry executives in their offices, where of course a *vin d'honneur* from each firm's private stock could not be refused. As the afternoon wore on I noticed the ambassador tended to steady herself on my arm as we moved from place to place, but I'd never seen her as vivacious or heard her pose sharper questions. It was inevitable that the mayor, in concert with several company big shots, finally overcame Mariana's resistance to their invitation to "a small dinner, just for a few of the champagne families"—the Heidsiecks, Polignacs, etc.

The ambassador looked at me and sighed, but happily.

I was feeling pretty good, too, by this time.

The faithful Pascal, waiting for us as we left to return to the Lion d'Or, admitted when pressed that he'd had an occasional sniff of the grape himself during the afternoon. He was forgiven.

A crowd of reporters and photographers were clustered by the hotel elevators. In the provinces, word gets around fast. A very young man disengaged himself from them and came forward with a bright smile. "I'm from UPI," he announced in good American.

Did I detect a momentary shadow of disappointment on Mariana's face that it wasn't a certain Brad Lindley, or was it my jealous imagination, as usual? Anyway she was charming to them all. The UPI kid didn't pursue his interrogation beyond the conventional queries but when he asked about our next stop the ambassador firmly shook her head.

"Wherever it is," she said, "I don't wish to be followed."

Five different kinds of sparkling and still champagne, one with each course, were served at the "family" dinner party at La Chaumière. I'd known, and Mariana found out, that once you've drunk enough champagne you can go on indefinitely, especially with wines like these. Obviously the families had reached very deep into their cellars for them. Looking back on it after we returned to the hotel, my favorite was the one that accompanied the *feuilleté d'escargots*.

Was that the second course or the fourth? To this day I can't be sure. But I do remember that the conversation, by turns light and serious, was the most interesting I'd heard since we got off the boat, sometimes in French, sometimes in English, sometimes in Franglais. Nothing brings out the best in a Frenchman like the combination of good food and pretty women. The ambassador, looking great in a trim little outfit by Ungaro (I believe it was), better than held her own in all departments, though I must admit some of the other ladies were strong competition. I never did catch the last name of the princesse I was seated next to. She said to call her Sizi.

It was Pascal who knocked on my door next morning to inform me the time was after ten o'clock and the ambassador was anxious to be on her way. My little traveling clock had failed me for the not surprising reason that I'd forgotten to set the alarm. Mariana seemed amused when I explained.

"No apologies necessary," she said. "I was skunk drunk myself."

Somehow, salty comments from that dignified presence always made me laugh, especially today in my woozy state.

We took off for Nancy after an elaborate *au revoir* from the mayor and several of the champagne boys, who presented an enormous bouquet of pink roses with their farewells. Minutes later we noticed the UPI man was following in a rickety old Citroën, but he didn't follow for long. Pascal kept an eye on him in the rearview mirror and reported shortly thereafter the car had either broken down or run out of gas half a mile behind us.

Mariana chuckled and settled back beside me. It was the first chance I'd had to talk with her alone since we reached Rheims. "Did you remember to call Paris?" I said.

"Paris called me. As soon as Spaulding saw the morning papers. He was furious, of course."

"I can hear him now."

"He said our project is unwise and dangerous, especially in the light of Washington's instructions, and insisted we return to Paris immediately."

I glanced at Pascal, who was bowling along at a steady eighty kilometers an hour in the opposite direction from Paris. "You seem to have rejected the suggestion."

"I'm afraid I did. He then declared he'd send us an embassy political officer to keep us out of trouble."

"Likewise rejected?"

"With thanks." She smiled. "I told him I was already sufficiently well staffed."

I think we both noticed the inadvertent double entendre in her phrase at the same instant. Anyway we both laughed. "He'll never forgive me for taking part in this," I said. "He considers himself my ultimate boss."

"I see it differently," said Mariana.

"I'm glad you do, ma'am."

"Don't you think," she said, "it's time you stopped calling me ma'am? Somehow it doesn't sound right anymore."

"Except in public."

"Yes, I suppose you're right about that."

We rode in silence while Mariana reread her interview notes. I closed my eyes and nursed my hangover.

"Tyler?"

"Present."

"I called Cristy after I finished with Spaulding—rather abruptly, I'm afraid, and without giving him our itinerary. Cristy sounded very proud to be on her own, which is probably the best thing for her right now. Have you noticed she's become more serious-minded lately? She's growing up fast."

Maybe a little too fast, I thought, remembering the intensity of the scene around the little café table that night in the Rue Descartes. I hoped my uneasy feeling was unjustified.

We stopped in Châlons to buy the morning papers and saw pictures of the ambassador, sometimes with me at her side, plastered all over the front pages. The articles were friendly on the whole and seemed amused at Mariana's flouting of protocol procedures, with only one rather snide allusion to her "traveling companion, M. Taylor Paine." There were few references to political issues. The stories in the regional press, as I'd expected, made more of the female ambassador angle than the Paris papers. In many ways provincial France is a different country, far more conservative in its life-style than the capital. I was glad Mariana was seeing that.

At least so far, none of the reports had noted the ambassador's roadside interview method, since in Rheims she'd seen only officials and business people.

"But give them another day or two," I said, "and you'll be hounded by reporters no matter where we go."

"How about American TV?" said Mariana.

Brad Lindley again? "Well, they have to cart around a lot of equipment. I suppose they could send a correspondent to talk with you and then go back to Paris to do his broadcast."

"It wouldn't be very effective without pictures, would it? Anyway, what I'm doing isn't news in America."

"*You* are news in America."

"Bad news, to the Secretary of State."

To take her mind off it I returned to the Voice of TV. "How long will Lindley stay in the Middle East?"

"I've no idea. But I hope he can clear up the bugging mystery when he comes back."

We took to the side roads again after Vitry-le-François and spent a solid three hours shaking hands and asking questions before and after Nancy, historic seat of the Dukes of Lorraine, where I showed the ambassador the noble Place Stanislas and we lunched on a memorable quiche complemented by the local *vin gris*. As may have become apparent by now, I have a major weakness for food. This trip was obviously going to be hard-core gastronomy all the way, and why not, weren't we in France? The restaurant must have notified the mayor, because he bustled in while we were still at lunch and gave Mariana a rundown on local and regional politics over a balloon glass of excellent brandy. However, we did manage to get out of town before the press rallied round.

In Strasbourg the ambassador made her first contact with an American official. Before checking in at a hotel we drove directly to the U.S. Consulate and caught the consul-general just as he was leaving for the day. The gentleman was not exactly startled. He told us Stuyvesant Spaulding had called him earlier to warn him to keep an eye out for us just in case. The ambassador said she would be delighted if the consul-general and his wife would dine with us at the restaurant of his choice.

"I'll be talking with Mr. Spaulding in the morning," added Mariana sweetly, "so it won't be necessary for you to call him tonight."

When we entered *chez* Aubette at seven not only the consul and his wife awaited us, the place was full of leading citizens, including the mayor and *his* wife, alerted no doubt by the hotel, and they all stood up as we came in. The result was that our dinner party for four was constantly interrupted by impromptu toasts from the mayor's table, then from other tables, and the welcoming speeches were practically nonstop.

Nonetheless the ambassador managed to get a full briefing from the consul on the operation of his office in this region, and I managed to put away hot foie gras, Vosges salmon and an exquisite Gewurztraminer. By the time we'd finished dinner the local reporters were on the scene, happily sipping free *framboise d'Alsace*, and Mariana consented to an informal press conference at which she explained that she wanted to meet the French people as a friend, not an official, and had come to the provinces to listen, not to make speeches. She smilingly declined to divulge the next stop on our itinerary, even to the consul-general.

Spontaneous applause and popping flashbulbs followed her departure from the salon where she spoke, as it had from the restaurant. The consul-general was obviously charmed, and his wife had been given an evening she could talk about for years. I must say that the ambassador, despite her long day's work, too much eating, and too much drinking, looked fresh as a daisy.

But I was exhausted.

Another unpleasant conversation with Spaulding next morning before we headed southward. As Mariana recounted it in the car, he had received a long cable from Washington to supplement the message to the ambassador, but naturally couldn't reveal its contents on the telephone. Once again he asked that we return to Paris immediately, but Mariana told him she intended to complete her inquiry first.

"Was he trying to tempt you with the cable?" I asked.

"He doesn't need me there, Tyler. He's just afraid I'll embarrass him in some way while I'm where he can't control me. The truth is our Mr. Spaulding is only really happy when he's bossing the embassy himself. And checking his weekly staff efficiency reports."

The UPI correspondent, still doggedly on the trail, caught up with us at lunch in Belfort (quail with a Kaefferkopf wine) and the ambassador took pity on him and his battered car. She invited him to join us at our table, but then quizzed him closely about his work all the way through the meal. She kept the poor fellow so busy he hardly had time to chew, let alone ask questions.

Her vitality really astonished me. I began to wonder whether she was maintaining the pace on sheer nerve. Before saying good night at the Chapeau Rouge in Dijon, after her first dinner in Burgundy (creamed Morvan ham with morels, accompanied by a Côte de Beaune), I asked my incredible boss how long she thought she could hold up under the strain.

She smiled and for a moment put a cool hand against my cheek. "Dear Tyler," she said, "I believe you really care about me."

"Don't you know that by now?"

If she'd stayed so near me another instant I think I would have put my arms around her, but almost as if she sensed that might happen she suddenly turned and went into her room.

"Good night, Tyler," she said, in a way she'd never said it before, and softly closed the door.

She was her businesslike self again at breakfast, but she looked tired and for the first time I bluntly told her so. She finally consented, with some give and take, to postpone our departure on the next lap for a few hours of just sitting in the sunshine, but on condition we devote the time to summarizing the interviews we'd obtained so far on the trip. It was only after we'd made out an over-all chart, classifying the subjects, that we could study the priorities in opinion at the various levels of French life. And the farther down in the social scale we went, the less concern was expressed about political problems.

Our ordinary voters knew the word détente, but often not in its current significance. The European Economic Community? The Atlantic Alliance? A politically united Western Europe? Communism? These weren't questions they thought about much. It was prices, scarcities, inflation, that troubled them most. And, to a surprising extent, especially in the industrial areas we'd checked, pollution of the environment and their drab, mechanical existence. Party affiliation? That was for the politicians. They were increasingly doubtful about politicians. Maybe the previous generation had thought of them as leaders, but France was different now, there were new problems, and the "leaders" didn't seem able to understand them, much less deal with them.

It was only at higher levels—in executive offices or at that dinner party in the champagne country, for instance—that we'd heard argument on larger international issues. And even here the talk was colored by a tired sort of cynical wit, no longer the healthy skepticism, the good-natured willingness to argue both sides of any question just for the fun of it that I remembered from my earlier years in France. The natural gay insouciance once so typical seemed burdened now with a fatalistic resignation, resentful at the core, together with a deeply buried uneasiness about the nuclear future. And there was always, of course, a latent and sometimes outspoken anti-Americanism, a mixture of jealousy, intellectual contempt, materialistic envy—the United States seen as too powerful, too rich, imperialist, hypocritical, vulgar. Added to this was a growing belief that France and Western Europe didn't need the Atlantic Alliance anymore, a revival of nationalist sentiment always just under the surface in this independent-minded country, and—especially among students—no fear of war because the new generation simply didn't know what war is in the only way that war can really be known, by experiencing it firsthand.

Our survey offered a dismaying prospect. Mariana was silent

and perhaps a bit depressed as we resumed our journey, but it wasn't long before her spirits rose again to something more normal, and with good reason.

The Wine Trail through the Burgundy countryside is a lovely drive, and it took all my willpower to resist recommending a turn-off every time we passed one of those glamorous signposts on our way south—Gevrey-Chambertin, Chambolle-Musigny, Nuits-St. Georges. We did stop briefly so the ambassador could see the Hospices de Beaune, surely one of the most beautiful buildings in Europe, where we gave a solemn promise to return to witness the celebrated wine auction in November. But awaiting us was our biggest city so far and we had to keep moving despite all these temptations.

As it turned out, Lyon took two days, what with street interviews, visits to textile factories, a reception at the Hôtel de Ville absolutely insisted upon by the mayor, and, of course, the eating. The greatest of the three major meals we had there (but is any meal in Lyon minor?) was *chez* Paul Bocuse, as expected, where the ambassador feasted on *mousse de truite* and *poulet de Bresse*, though I must say La Mère Brazier ran a close second with its pike soufflé. On the advice of the American consul, a wine fancier of some experience, we eschewed sampling the more famous labels and made the acquaintance of the lesser known but worthy Morgon and Juliénas.

Time was passing quickly, yet Rheims and the beginning of our trip seemed a month ago. We were working hard and long each day, but somehow it all seemed like a happy vacation. The record high point in gastronomy was reached after we headed south once more through the Rhône Valley and stopped for lunch at, naturally, the Pyramide. Not that I was surprised. As we bade Mme. Point good-bye, the ambassador told her it was, simply, the most perfect meal of her life.

To which Mme. Point replied, just as simply, "Your Excellency, we try."

And that evening in the lobby of the Grand Hotel on the Canebière in Marseille, Brad Lindley stood waiting with a big smile on his face.

Actually it was a coincidence. As he told us during dinner at the Calypso (*bouillabaisse*, what else? then grilled lobster flambé in Armagnac, with the white wine of Cassis), New York had phoned him in Cairo with a tip on a dope-smuggling story just as he was leaving for Paris. A camera team had been sent to meet him in Marseille and he was starting work in the morning. Oh, sure—with that winning smile—he knew all about our *tour de France*, had been following each lap in the Paris *Herald Tribune*, and in fact had picked up Madam Ambassador's Lyon doings on his arrival at Marignane airport this afternoon. So he'd not been in the least startled to see us disembarking on the Canebière.

"Europe," he intoned casually, "is pretty much a small town, as you can see."

He congratulated the ambassador on her meet-the-people initiative and I saw with relief that she gave him no reason to suspect she had a special motivation for making the trip.

Unless I deceived myself, there was an extra sparkle in her eyes while she listened, fascinated, to Brad's analysis of the Middle East situation. We were both calling him Brad now. Informed that our custom was to have all bills forwarded to the ambassador in Paris, the celebrated voice rumbled "Not this one," and proceeded to pay the very large dinner check himself. It was a generous gesture (even if his network was good for the tab) but I felt a certain dismay. Brad Lindley was taking over the party. He included me in with an occasional smiling glance, but everything he had to say was directed to Mariana, of course.

It was only after he finished his report on the Middle East that he brought up the bugging of the Residence. He didn't seem surprised when Mariana told him no clues had been found.

"I'll check my contact as soon as I get back to Paris," Brad said, "but whether he'll give with any more I just don't know."

I was hoping he would elaborate, but I was disappointed. And Mariana didn't press him.

Later, speaking in low tones over *fine à l'eau* in a colorful little dive he knew on the Vieux Port, he told us New York had passed him word of corruption in the French Government narcotics squad permitting entry of a huge new shipment of opium that was now being refined for the illicit drug traffic in the Marseille area and would eventually end up in America.

"As you know, ma'am, the French work in co-operation with the U. S. Bureau of Narcotics in the Paris embassy, so perhaps you're already aware of this?"

The ambassador shook her head and I saw her lips tighten. Here was something else they might be keeping from her.

"Then," Lindley said, "wouldn't this be an opportunity for you to look over the headquarters operation here? That is, if you're not too busy."

"I can certainly postpone any other activities."

"I'm dropping in there tomorrow about ten. Informally. I'd be honored if you came with me."

"I look forward to it," said Mariana.

He turned to me again. "It won't be necessary for you to tag along, old man. We mustn't look like an official delegation."

"Oh, quite," I said.

If I'd been more alert I think I would have added that I felt immediate misgivings about the project. But it was obviously out of my hands now.

So it was that the unscheduled and unannounced visit of the United States ambassador to the startled headquarters of the French Government narcotics organization in Marseille took place exactly as Brad planned it, under the eyes of an American television camera which photographed their arrival and departure. I could see the account in next week's *Time: Hatless, trench-coated Foreign Correspondent Lindley, a grim look on his handsome face and our lady ambassador on his arm, scored another news coup last week by exposing . . .*

It was too late now to stave off the consequences.

9

BRAD LINDLEY'S NEWS report from Marseille, transmitted via satellite to New York, was broadcast coast to coast on his network program and picked up by French Government TV, the BBC, and all major stations in Western Europe.

The political repercussions were immediate and severe.

In Paris Premier Nicollet issued a statement quoting the narcotics squad as completely denying Lindley's story, and followed up with a formal protest to the American embassy over what he called the impropriety of the U.S. ambassador in associating herself with it. The entire Paris press joined him in angrily expressing its resentment. Foreign Minister Courtailles was silent.

In Washington the State Department declined public comment but privately communicated at once with its Paris embassy to demand a full account of what happened and how. The White House referred inquiries back to State. American newspapers had something of a field day with the incident, featuring UPI's report from its own correspondent on the scene.

Lindley and his camera crew had left Marseille on the first available flight after the visit to narcotics squad headquarters and were in seclusion in Paris.

Stuyvesant Spaulding was on the phone to the ambassador before she retired that night. Their conversation lasted half an hour, during which it was decided we would return next morning to the capital aboard an embassy plane sent to pick us up, leaving Pascal to bring the car back to Paris alone. We would have to strike the Nice and Bordeaux consulates from our itinerary.

The *tour de France* was over.

On the flight from Marseille we sat side by side in the cabin without saying much. The air force attendant discreetly left us alone and joined the crew in the cockpit. Mariana was composed as always but a little pale, immaculately gloved hands folded in her lap and a slight, rueful smile playing at her lips.

"Tyler," she said suddenly at one point, "I've been a fool."

I wanted so much to reassure her. "It's really not all that important. It'll be forgotten in a few days. This kind of thing happens to every ambassador, one time or another. It's really my fault more than yours."

"Just why do you say that?"

"Because I should have spoken up in the café when Lindley suggested it. I know the French well enough to have realized they'd get on your back if you visited any official area without advance notice. And this narcotics thing is very touchy with them. They've done their best to break up the drug traffic into Marseille."

She sighed. "I knew too, the minute we walked in on them. Of course they denied everything Brad suggested. But I think most of all they were just dreadfully, well, embarrassed because I was there. I'm sure they would have thrown Brad out immediately if I hadn't been with him."

Was she thinking what I was thinking—that perhaps she'd just been used? It was mean of me, but I also had a sneaky feeling of satisfaction, amid all this disaster, that maybe friend Brad would suffer a setback now in Mariana's trusting affections. I wasn't proud of myself for the thought, but I'm only human.

I steered away from it. "Was Snuffy pretty upset?"

"He'll never forgive me, Tyler. He was polite, of course, but he said the undersecretary was clamoring for an immediate report, obviously because the Secretary and perhaps even the White House wants to know exactly what went on. And he couldn't help implying that if I'd consulted him about our trip this never would have happened."

With a silent groan I remembered I owed the undersecretary a report, too. I said, "I blame myself for letting it happen."

She smiled warmly and for a moment put her gloved hand on my knee. "Stop talking that way. That's an order. The blame is mine. For forgetting who I am, what I represent." She added dolefully, "I'm afraid I have the instincts of a news reporter, Tyler."

"What could be more essential to your job as an ambassador?"

"Ambassadors aren't what they once were. Especially women ambassadors. Washington requires a figurehead. The staff does the work. Snuffy is right, Tyler—it's all protocol."

I wondered if she'd really learned that lesson or was just saying it. "I still think the *tour de France* was the right thing at the right moment, if I may say so."

"You know you may say so. You know I expect you to say so, at all times."

"Okay," I said, "right now I wish I had a drink."

"I never want to see another glass of wine!"

She didn't mean it, of course, but her laugh was more like the Mariana I knew.

The homecoming, though, was anything but gay. Ironically, the immediacy of the unfortunate climax to the ambassador's *tour de France* overshadowed the far graver issue which had caused her to undertake her journey in the first place. We found on our return that the iron lid was still down tight on any Washington-Moscow talks for a new European security pact, the press on both sides of the Atlantic remained in the dark, and no further proffers of inside information were to come from Foreign Minister Courtailles.

Stuyvesant Spaulding greeted his chief with a brackish smile and a determined effort to look friendly, but he couldn't quite conceal the profound disappointment he felt in both of us. Knowing him, I knew it would rankle for a very long time.

Within a few days, of course, the furore over the Marseille incident subsided, but I was wrong in my prediction that it soon would be forgotten. In our own country it might have been, but the French don't easily forget, and who can say they don't have a right to a long memory? It was clear the Paris press would remember, and for quite a while—especially the leftist papers which in the main supported Auguste Nicollet's policies. Normally the exception there was the Communist press. It rarely agreed with any opinion without Soviet sanction, but in this case it went along with the others in expressing disapprobation of Madam Ambassador and suspicion of what she might do next. With the rightist crowd, of course, mistrust was traditional. Most distressing of all to Mariana as she went through the clippings was the thread of smug innuendo that the bad official judgment she showed in *l'incident de Marseille* was only what could be expected of a woman.

And of course the gossip magazines and the satirical journals had themselves a ball playing around with such fantasies as a sex triangle pitting me against Lindley in a struggle for the ambassador's personal favors. *Le Canard Enchaîné*, the most widely read of all, printed a very witty piece (I admit it made me laugh) lampooning Mariana's earnest encounters with provincial notables. A Marseille paper carried a cartoon showing the ambassador, wearing a cowboy hat and boots and holding a six-shooter in each hand, chasing the dope smugglers out of the city.

Another consequence was inevitable: Brad Lindley, already jealously envied by his European colleagues for the money he earned in his glamorous job, had become the most unpopular member of his profession in Paris. (Beasley Turner remarked to me that even the American reporters were shying away from him.) All French papers carried the narcotics squad denials of Lindley's story without, apparently, bothering to investigate it themselves. Young Mr. UPI jumped on the bandwagon and discredited the report. But neither Lindley nor his network disavowed anything he'd said on the air, nor did the U. S. Bureau of Narcotics spokesman join the French in their official denial.

At the embassy the Narcotics Bureau's regional director, Nick Yannos, was called in for a conference with the ambassador and her deputy, which followed a much longer conference between Mariana and Spaulding alone. It was finally decided there would be no public statement but that Spaulding would privately and verbally offer his regrets to Premier Nicollet for Madam Ambassador's inadvertent connection with the episode.

Would this satisfy the department in Washington? Whether it did or not was beside the point after Mariana received a brief note, personal and confidential, from the Oval Office in the White House. It was handwritten and said simply:

> *Dear Mrs. Otis,*
>
> *Beware the Devil in the guise of attractive newsmen, but don't let this psych you out!*
>
> *With all good wishes for the continued success of your mission. . . .*

It was signed with the famous indecipherable scrawl.

She called me to her desk to show it to me with a grave little smile.

"That should make you feel better" was my reaction.

"But even the President," said Mariana, "had to draw the sexual inference."

There was a silence. It gave me the opportunity to ask a question I'd had on my mind since we returned to Paris. "Has Lindley been in touch with you?"

"This morning," she said quietly. "He called me. He was very apologetic. I told him there was nothing to apologize for. It was my fault, not his."

The new warmth in her voice echoed in my ears. "Is that all?" I said.

"If you mean was it intentional on his part, I've come to the conclusion it wasn't. Thoughtless perhaps, but not intentional. After all, he was concentrating on his job."

I felt a slight sinking sensation. Well, that was that. Whatever Mariana may have thought at first, Brad Lindley was forgiven now.

I still half suspected she'd been had, but I wasn't about to tarnish her evident faith in the man by saying so. I changed the subject, slightly.

"Nobody seems to be backing up his charges of corruption in the narcotics squad."

"As nearly as Yannos knows right now, there may be some truth in the story, but our team isn't sure enough yet to confirm it."

A new silence. Mariana was looking past me at the wall. Was she thinking about Brad Lindley?

Her desk buzzer rang.

"Congressman and Mrs. Coyle, Madam Ambassador. They're in the anteroom."

She straightened up as if to dismiss our conversation from her mind and showed me that grave smile again. " 'Tis the season to be jolly," she said. "The annual invasion has begun."

It had indeed. By every plane and train the summer tourists were flooding into Paris. More significantly for the embassy, each day brought its quota of official visitors—junketing Senators and Representatives and their wives (in some cases girl friends), vacationing cabinet members and government agency officials, state governors, the high military and their staffs on "inspection" tours. Expenses borne by the taxpayer, of course. They all wanted to meet the ambassador, especially the wives, and they all had to be entertained.

It was that time of year when obscure shirt-sleeved tourists hung with cameras, trailing wives and two or three children, wandered in off the street looking for a telephone, a bathroom, or just a casual chat with the ambassador on the simple American assumption that it was their telephone, their bathroom, and their ambassador. The season of letters from Radcliffe classmates not too subtly suggesting that they be invited to stay at the embassy. (Mariana said to me about one of them, "When I was in college she snubbed me completely because I was half Jewish. Now it turns out we were intimate friends.")

I also saw a letter from Marcus Feld, the Hillman family adviser I remembered from my first meeting with Mariana in Washington, remarking it wouldn't be at all inconvenient for him to slip over to Paris during a forthcoming stay in London, just in case he could be of assistance of any kind.

He was thanked and turned down, rather coolly, I thought.

The Residence went into high gear. Scarcely a day passed without a triple schedule of VIP luncheons, teas, and dinners. I was on the periphery, thank God. No interpreting was needed for visiting American officials, and I kept out of the way. Mariana had my sympathy, but there was one aspect to all this that amused me in spite of my compassion for the hostess. In most cases what these gentlemen callers were really looking for in Paris was fun—food, drinks, night spots, luxury, maybe a little dalliance on the side—using the embassy as a kind of private club, message center, and bar. What they *didn't* expect—and didn't much care for—was that the ambassador took an entirely different view of their visits, turning the table talk into relentless pursuit of political topics, incessantly questioning her distinguished guests, and simply ignoring, or just barely noticing, other females present.

I had occasion to sit in as an emergency "extra man" at a couple of these parties, and found they weren't really parties at all, usually to the evident dismay of those invited. They were more like panel discussions, with Mariana as chief interviewer. She gave little attention to American domestic issues, on which she'd been something of an authority during the election campaign. Instead, she hammered away at the international situation and most particularly the state of opinion on détente with Russia versus armed vigilance in Europe. She wanted insistently to know how Americans in every section of the country, at every level in every field of activity, felt about that issue, even more the federal Executive's and congressional reactions to public opinion and what they were going to do about it.

As a result of this all-out initiative, Mariana's guests were inclined to leave the premises sooner than they'd planned, especially the Senators. ("Senators tire easily," the ambassador observed to me one night while on her way to an early bed.) Although the hostess was sometimes disappointed that the evening's conversations didn't last longer, I was pleased for her sake that she was getting a little more sleep. The *tour de France* and its emotional consequences had tired her out, although she wouldn't admit it. I suspected one reason she flung herself so recklessly into this new interrogatory phase lay in the effort to forget her Marseille experience. But beyond an indirect rebuke from the department, passed along respectfully and gently by Spaulding, there was no further complaint from Washington about the episode. Presumably the Secretary was now aware of the President's indulgent view.

In a way it made my next confidential report much easier to

prepare. I had no difficulty in any case praising my boss's trail-blazing tour of the provinces, on which she herself had reported at length to Washington. I pointed out she'd acquired a considerable fund of valuable knowledge about French public opinion, current business and industrial activity, and made new friends for her country by her informal approach (thus confirming French views that this was what a typical American was like and charming them in the bargain).

On the subject of Brad Lindley and Marseille I made it clear beyond equivocation there was no sexual attraction involved, simply by describing the incident as though the possibility never occurred to any of us. The ambassador, I said, was carried away by the successful momentum of her trip and took advantage of an opportunity to study the drug traffic problem at first hand, unfortunately running into resistance from the bureaucratic mind.

I took my ritual late evening walk along the Champs Elysées to post the letter to Remington, and just after I got back to the embassy the trouble with Cristy began.

The feverish pace of recent entertainment activity had somewhat disrupted the ambassador's routine, and she'd omitted dropping in on her daughter to say good night as regularly as before. Tonight, realizing she'd neglected this for several days, she made a note to be sure to resume their little bedside chats. Downstairs, the postprandial political session had surprisingly lasted later than usual (the only Senator among the guests had grumpily retired to his hotel shortly after dinner) so by the time Mariana was free to retire herself, she assumed Cristy would be sound asleep. Nevertheless she knocked softly at her daughter's door and peeked in. Not only was Cristy not asleep. The bed was empty. She wasn't there.

Mariana waited awhile, as she told me later, just sitting on the edge of the bed. Then she found a cigarette in an ashtray on the table and lit up. It was three or four minutes before, in her innocence, she discovered she wasn't smoking any ordinary tobacco. Still holding the peculiar cigarette, she went back to her bedroom and called me.

I was half asleep when the phone rang. This time she said, "I don't care if you're decent, can you come to the study?"

I whipped on a bathrobe and slippers and found her waiting for me, a little pale but perfectly calm. She too was in a dressing gown, but much better groomed than I was, for which I apologized.

"How absurd," she said, and handed me the cigarette. "First, taste this. It was in Cristy's room."

Even with my limited experience I recognized it in a few puffs —stronger, richer than marijuana. And I remembered the only time I'd ever tried the stuff, one crazy night at Jan's. There was no mistaking it. This was hash.

I told Mariana.

She was paler. "Cristy's not home yet. I doubt if she'd want to let the guards know by coming back this late, in case I found out, so I suspect she's out for the night. And if she's staying out tonight, I have an idea she's done it before, once she realized she could get away with it."

"While you were out of Paris?"

"And even since I've been back."

In the pause I debated whether to remind her that Cristy was playing with college kids now and that things had changed quite a bit for her age since Mariana Hillman was in Radcliffe—possibly changed even more in Paris than in Cambridge, Mass.

She was speaking again, quietly. "While I was sitting in her room, Tyler, it occurred to me that I know literally nothing about the life Cristy leads on the Left Bank. I don't know her friends. I don't know her teachers. She doesn't talk about them in the little time we have together. It was the same in Washington. She talked more freely to her grandfather than she did to me. Now, the more I coax her, the less she tells me."

She hesitated, then went on softly, "Sometimes I wish more than anything her father were alive. She adored Clay. She obeyed him. They were great pals. They were riding together the last day of his life—."

Again she stopped and her eyes misted over, as if the memory of that day, even after the years between, was too painful to endure.

"Maybe," I began, "if you told Cristy her father wouldn't have approved of her attitude—."

She shook her head. "Cristy won't talk about her father. She never has, since his death. Has she talked to you, Tyler? Do you know anything about her classmates?"

"It happens I've seen some of her friends. I don't know if they were classmates—one, at least, looked several years older than Cristy." And I told her of my night walk through the Quarter and the little band of students around that table in the Rue Descartes.

"They were all very intense, listening to the older boy who was even more intense, but I didn't catch what he was saying."

"Did they look like kids on drugs? That was my great worry about her in Washington. Somehow, I don't know how, she got started there, but her grandfather scared her out of it. At least I thought he had."

She spoke so wistfully, she looked suddenly so forlorn, I had that impulse again to put my arms around her, reassure her, comfort her, somehow. Instead I went back to the beginning and told her about Cristy's night visit to me on the ship seeking her mother.

"Perhaps I should have told you then," I said.

"I wish you had. But it wouldn't have surprised me. She's been suspicious about my behavior ever since—since Clay died. She was so very young then, but so strangely aware."

We sat there facing each other in silence. I could see she didn't want to talk about it any longer, and after a few minutes she got up and went back to her apartment. Her guess was right—Cristy didn't come home until the next evening, and in the meantime Mariana got it out of the upstairs maids that this had happened three or four times while we were on our *tour de France*, though she was always back home to receive her mother's morning phone call.

There was a heated meeting between mother and daughter as soon as Cristy reappeared at the Residence, but I didn't hear about it till next morning. Mariana looked troubled and pale, as if she hadn't slept well. She didn't mention the subject, however, till after we'd checked her day's appointments and dealt with the other business-as-usual chores. Then she closed her little red book with a snap and looked across the desk at me. "I've had it out with Cristy," she said.

I nodded and waited.

"I told her it wasn't the staying out all night. She's old enough to know what she's doing, as long as she tells me she's going to do it. But deliberately deceiving me while I was away, and now even when I'm here—I said that was unacceptable and unworthy of her."

"And was Cristy properly contrite?"

"The reaction was total defiance. She offered no explanation of why she'd stayed out or where she spent the night. She told me she's perfectly capable of taking care of her own life from now on and advised me not to concern myself. When I brought up the smoking she just laughed at me. I—I'm afraid I lost patience with her at that point."

"It's not surprising."

She said in a kind of wonder, "I couldn't believe what was happening between us. I didn't recognize my own daughter. I didn't recognize myself. I was actually crying, Tyler. I haven't cried for years. She just stood there watching me, like a stranger on the street. And then when she started on you and Brad Lindley—."

I stared.

"I don't know who's been filling her head with it, but she repeated every low insinuation that's been in the newspapers since Marseille, and that wasn't enough—she said everybody knows what went on between you and me during our trip and I was a hypocrite to criticize her behavior."

There was a silence before she rose abruptly and gathered up her papers. The conference was over. I wished I could say or do something to help, but it was so obviously Mariana's own problem to deal with, any counsel would have been superfluous.

I was not prepared for the next development. Four or five minutes after the ambassador left for the Chancery a single sharp knock sounded on the study door and Cristy Otis didn't wait to be invited in. She swung the door open and marched across to my desk, her eyes blazing, her body taut and trembling.

"I hear you've been spying on me" were the first words. "That was a pretty lousy thing to do!"

"Just what are you talking about, Cristy?"

"You know damn well what I'm talking about. You were prowling around the Quartier trying to make trouble for me and get in good with my mother."

"Slow down, girl. I happened to see you quite by accident. I only mentioned it to your mother because she asked me if I knew any of your friends."

She almost hissed the words. "You *don't* know any of my friends. You never will. They wouldn't even speak to you, or anyone like you!"

"Cristy," I said, "your mother feels you're treating her like a stranger. Do you really think she deserves that? She hasn't had a very easy time lately. She'd be much happier, I know she would, if you'd simply let her know you know she loves you, confide in her, tell her the truth—."

"Confide in her! There's nothing to confide. And what truth? There's nothing to hide, either. If I want to sleep in someone else's bed besides my own I'll do it any time I want, and I told her so. She's got enough friends—too many! She doesn't need me. I've got my own friends, the first real friends I ever had, and nobody's going to interfere in their life, either, so just keep your nose out of it. That's what I came in here to warn you, don't look for trouble or you'll find it!"

She turned and started toward the door.

"Let me tell you one thing you may have forgotten, young lady."

Something in my tone must have stopped her. Instantly she wheeled to face me again. "I'm listening."

"And I'm not warning you. I'm just advising you, although I have no authority to do either. I'm glad you've found some real friends, Cristy. Believe this or not, I want you to be happy just as much as your mother does. But there's something you must remember. You are not just a girl who likes her new life. You are the daughter of an ambassador in a foreign country. And whether you want it or not, at your age you still have a special responsibility, not only to your family but, in these circumstances, to your country as well. You may not have learned this yet, but you're going to have to. The way things are, you can't escape from that position."

She didn't reply for a moment, but when she did it was in a low, level tone, with all her mother's poise, each word spaced, distinct, and full of bitterness. "Thanks for the wisdom, *Mister* Paine. You've wasted your time. I have no family. I have no position. I'm myself, and that's what I intend to be from here on in. All this other crap you're laying out is just that—*bullshit!*"

She spat the last word. The door slammed behind her.

10

I KNEW I MUST tell Mariana about Cristy's astonishing outburst, but I didn't get to see her right away. By the time I arrived at the Chancery she was involved in a staff meeting, then with two types from the Public Affairs section. When at last she was free she had just ten minutes before her next appointment, and I slipped in three steps ahead of Abigail Spaulding, who wanted to grab the same ten minutes and withdrew somewhat haughtily at Mariana's request that she wait in the anteroom.

"I'm interrupting," I said.

"You don't have to tell me it's serious, Tyler. I can see that in your face."

"Cristy came to the study just after you left this morning. I thought you'd better know what was said."

She tensed a little. "Please."

I recounted the exchange as nearly word for word as I could. After I'd finished the ambassador sat there looking steadily at me without speaking. Finally she said, "Thank you. You've confirmed my own feeling about this—something positive will have to be done, and as quickly as possible."

It was. Within half an hour she was on the phone to Washington and Marcus Feld, who located Herbert Hillman in an airplane between Tulsa and Dallas and was able to report back that her father would be on his way to Paris tonight.

Mr. Herbert Hillman was the first house guest the embassy had welcomed since Mariana's predecessor returned home. His arrival obviously pleased the servants, even though it gave them a little more work to do. They seemed to feel the ambassador might now have an excuse to enjoy at least a semblance of a family life which

Cristy, with her more and more frequent absences, had made impossible. Cristy Otis, in fact, was not popular with the Residence staff. In the beginning they'd wanted to like her, to coddle her a bit, I was sure of that, but the girl's abrupt manner and lack of politeness, so very un-French, put them off. After a time even the patient Jean-Paul gave up trying to spoil her with special dishes she didn't appreciate. And once or twice I saw the usually inscrutaable Mme. Hanotte look at Cristy with the unmistakable inclination to give her a hard slap—the French solution to adolescent petulance.

It might have helped, at that.

Le grand-père was the antithesis of Cristy. The staff took to him at once, without overdoing it, of course. Here was a slender, elegant, gracious old man with the manners but not the arrogance of a European aristocrat, who spoke kindly to one and all and never forgot to say *merci*. He was as tickled as a kid to be allowed to sleep in the same bed Charles Lindbergh slept in after flying the Atlantic in 1927. He was also manifestly proud of his daughter's eminence and fascinated by the history and architecture of the Residence to which the loan of his own paintings had contributed so much.

In addition—and this was plainly evident in the servants' eyes—Herbert Hillman was rich as only an American magnate could be rich, that is beyond the dreams of even a Frenchman's avarice. Altogether an almost ideal guest, to be outshone perhaps only by a president or prince of the blood.

But the real reason he was here, known only to the ambassador, her father, and me, was his wayward granddaughter. I say wayward for want of a better word. Perhaps, later, we would all learn more about her. For now it was more than sufficient to know she'd been giving her mother a hard time and Herbert Hillman had been summoned to help.

With the ambassador, Cristy greeted him at the airport and consented to cancel her Sorbonne classes for the day, just as Mariana had reduced her own heavy schedule at the Chancery. On arrival at the Residence the three withdrew into privacy for a family conference even before Mr. Hillman was shown to the VIP suite on the second floor. What was said at this meeting I didn't know, but it inaugurated a new kind of concentration for the ambassador. Ordering Abigail Spaulding to ease up on her social appointments and confiding political affairs temporarily to the ministrations of her deputy, Mariana set aside mornings during the next few days for strictly family activities. In effect, for those hours (and it was so like her to have devised this sort of plan) she transformed herself into a purely private citizen for the sake of her father and daughter and accompanied them on the typical tourist's round of Paris sight-seeing.

Well, not exactly the typical tourist. Even incognito, an ambassador gets privileged treatment. Thus they visited the Louvre under personal escort of the curator, received similar attentions at Versailles, and in restaurants where they lunched Mariana was immediately recognized and given the best accommodation—a hijacked table if necessary. From what I gathered about all these excursions in Mariana's occasional brief references (when I saw her, which was little) Cristy was amenable, but silent. Her relaxed, voluble relationship with her grandfather had suddenly become a thing of the past. She turned aside all invitations to talk about herself. But neither the ambassador nor Mr. Hillman was giving up easily. An outing of sand and sea at Deauville was scheduled for immediately after the July Fourth party at the Residence.

Each evening all three dined together at home. Fortunately Mariana had no major diplomatic dinners requiring her presence. Jean-Paul was delighted at being able to show off his specialties to the old man, who, as the chef told me later, had a good deal of gourmet wisdom. I made it a point to take my meals these evenings in my own apartment, judging, correctly as it turned out, that Mariana hadn't asked me to join them because she feared it would upset Cristy. Anyway I was glad of the respite, especially in the daytime, since I was working on translations of three speeches to be delivered in French before the end of July.

However my nights were not as free as I'd expected. Quite late on the third evening of his stay, Mr. Hillman surprised me by knocking on my door and suggesting I join him for a game of chess in the second-floor library. Luckily I enjoy chess, though I'm hardly an expert player, and maybe this would be a chance to learn more not only about Herbert Hillman himself but Mariana and Cristy as well. Alas, the gentleman disappointed me in that respect by responding equivocally or hardly at all to my polite sallies. It wasn't because he was tired, as he should have been at his age after a day spent traipsing around the city with his indefatigable daughter. His mind was alert and clear as a bell, and he proved it by disposing of me with ease on the chessboard. I was the tired one when we finished, and I left him that night rather relieved that he wouldn't be challenging me again at least for the next few days.

But the Deauville weekend never took place.

America's Independence Day is celebrated in U.S. embassies all over the world as an immutable tradition affected only by wars, revolutions, or earthquakes, and sometimes observed even then. On July 4, more than any other day on the calendar, the embassy becomes the gathering place for American citizens of all persuasions, resident and transient. The latter species is particularly evident in the great tourist capitals—London, Paris, Rome—where provision must be made to receive guests by the hundreds, in addition to those from the permanent American colony who may be even more numerous.

In Paris, Ambassador Mariana Hillman Otis was determined that her Fourth of July reception should be surpassed by none, either in personal cordiality or lavish outlay of funds—Mariana's funds, of course, for in this as with so many other ambassadorial expenditures the State Department's Bureau of European Affairs sets strict limits to official expense allowances. It goes without saying that except in the rarest situation you have to be rich to be ambassador to France, and this ambassador's orders to her staff were to spare no expense to give our compatriots a truly glorious Fourth. Everybody, but everybody, was to be admitted.

"Fortunately you didn't have the responsibility for last year's party," said Abigail Spaulding to Her Excellency as they stood together in hot morning sunshine on the terrace, surveying final preparations in the Residence gardens. "It was the biggest event of the Bicentennial—but an utterly *exhausting* experience." She gave a high, fluting sigh. "Of course it wasn't *all* drudgery. There were special compensations—the Descendants came."

"The Descendants?" said Mariana politely. She was watching the workmen finish erecting a second striped marquee.

"Of the Revolutionary families—the Lafayettes, and so on. They were quite familiar with the house, knew it in the Rothschild days. Several asked about the missing balustrade, *such* a beautiful thing." Another sigh.

"The balustrade?"

"It was just here, where you're standing, my dear. You knew, I'm sure, that the owners stripped the house of its most valuable decorations *after* they sold it to us."

She sounded as if her own family had been tricked out of its most precious heirloom, and in a way that's how she felt. Mariana glanced at me and almost smiled.

Mme. Hanotte made an appearance, correct and cool as always, bearing another of her checklists. I stood a little apart while the three women bent over it and was glad my own assignment today was merely to stick around and make myself useful in emergencies. I didn't envy them their jobs. The business of setting up a party for perhaps as many as a thousand persons, who in a few hours would spill through the Residence like an invading army, had been nothing short of staggering.

First, the Residence staff was augmented by caterers from half a dozen Paris firms, personnel from the Chancery were pressed into service, the full complement of marine guards were summoned for special duty, Jean-Paul's kitchen staff was reinforced to three times its size, extra waiters and bartenders were enlisted for the afternoon from the diplomatic employment agencies and even private homes, including all five of Abigail Spaulding's servants.

For two days I'd been staying out of the way as much as I could, while huge quantities of American picnic stuff were carted in from the embassy commissary—frankfurters, hamburgers, cheese slices, rolls, mustard, ketchup, Cokes, ginger ale—along with the paper plates to hold them and the glasses to drink them out of. Endless supplies of French eatables flowed in from Fauchon at the Madeleine and a dozen other Paris food shops—delicate little ham, chicken and watercress sandwiches, pâtés, tiny éclairs, every variety of cakes and cookies known to the French, who know them all, and with this cases of beer, wine for the punchbowls (hard liquor was firmly out), and more pitchers, cups, glasses of all shapes and sizes.

All over the Residence, on every floor, people I'd never seen before were bustling past. Doors were opening and banging shut, cabinets unlocked and locked again. At one point when Mme. Hanotte went by I would have sworn she had a hundred and fifty keys on a chain around her waist. None of the ambassador's personal silver or china was used, of course, and the best table service reserved for diplomatic dinners was put safely away. On this morning of the big day guards in civilian clothes were stationed unobtrusively near the Hillman paintings, and uniformed marines stood ready to repel intruders who might be curious to see the upper floors.

"*They'll steal anything that isn't nailed down,*" warned the ambassador's predecessor in a charming advisory she received from him a week before the Fourth. He advised setting up "travel lanes," as he had done, which would ferry all arrivals through the ground floor into the garden, and Mariana gratefully adopted his plan. Guests would be permitted to sight-see briefly in the salons and then invited to partake of food and drink outdoors, where, instead of the more usual stuffy band music, Mariana had smartly engaged three wandering accordionists and an American dance combo from the New Jimmy's.

In short, the scene was set for a great occasion. And by late afternoon I could stand at the corner of the terrace and look out across one of the largest, loudest, liveliest crowds I'd ever seen at a party anywhere. The diplomatic corps had come and gone—Mariana arranged two sets of invitations so as to keep out the main mass until the most important guests were received. Watching the "first sitting," as she'd called it, I had a look at some of the characters described so vividly at our night meetings in the study and recognized them at once. Only today the Chinese ambassador was true to stereotype—grinning like Charlie Chan.

It was Claude Courtailles who wore the mask of inscrutability. He arrived, drank one cup of punch, and left murmuring pleasantries, nothing more.

Now the second sitting was under way. The sun was still shining, and beneath the nearest marquee a radiant Mariana, wearing a huge filmy hat, was conducting a handshaking marathon for which the mob had formed a line fifty yards into the garden. Her father stood at her side, looking benign in a morning coat. The embassy ladies under Abigail Spaulding's stern supervision wove dexterously in and out of the throng, making sure everybody felt welcome. Gaily decorated refreshment stands were placed at convenient intervals. Balloons in bright colors were handed to the kiddies. The band blared away on its raised platform at the foot of the garden but failed to daunt the strolling accordionists, one of whom was delighting a swarm of tourist children with "Yankee Doodle" just below where I stood.

The crowd was coming in so fast now I could no longer check out each face as I'd tried to do from the start. They were all the familiar categories, dressed to the nines for the occasion, plus a few you couldn't imagine unless you'd seen them, including a peg-legged black man in shorts striped red, white, and blue and a group of big-bellied Hawaiian tourists wearing Mother Hubbards or wild shirts, each with a little American flag in hand. The babble of talk and music and laughter rose into the soft summer air.

"The things you see when you haven't got your gun!"

The voice at my ear startled me. It was a voice I knew, and so did a lot of other people who were looking in this direction. I turned to find Brad Lindley smiling the celebrated smile at me.

"Hello, stranger" was all I could think of to say.

"I almost didn't come," he grinned, "but I thought it was time to raise my profile again."

"That's nice," I said.

"Any more news on the bugging inquiry?"

"Not since Perpidan was here. We still don't know who did the installation. Do you?"

"Tyler!" he said in mock reproach. "You know I'll tell you as soon as I find out."

"Seen your informative friend?"

"He's away on a job." He was looking restlessly over the crowd. "Ah, there she is! My God, what a hat! Guess I'm going to have a long wait to wish her a happy Fourth."

"Just go to the head of the line, Brad."

He glanced at me a little suspiciously, then laughed. At the same moment the sky above us suddenly darkened. We both looked up and saw the black cloud blotting out the sun. There was a frightening clap of thunder.

"In five minutes," Brad Lindley said, "it'll be raining like hell." He dodged into the crowd toward Mariana, followed by admiring stares.

He was wrong about the rain. It came sooner than that—one of those summer cloudbursts that strike Paris almost without warning. And when it came, it came in sheets, drenching everybody and everything out of doors. A great wail went up from the garden as they all stampeded for the house, pushing those of us on the terrace helplessly back inside. I found myself still moving backward through the salon and into the entrance hall, where I ducked off to one side and stood mopping my face at the foot of the stairway.

The marine guard smiled. "We can't keep 'em outside now, sir."

They were flooding into the salons, pushing and laughing. It wasn't the way Mariana had wanted it to end. No arrangements had been made to entertain inside the Residence. Well, she'd gambled on the weather and lost.

I saw the guard stiffen and followed his look up the stairway. It took me a moment to grasp the meaning of what I was seeing. Cristy Otis, in a dirty shirt, ragged dungarees, and sneakers, was coming down from the second floor carrying a heavy suitcase. Beside her, holding her arm with his free hand and carrying some books, was one of the boys I'd seen with her that night at the café in the Rue Descartes, the blond one they all were listening to so intently.

She recognized me at the same time and included me in the contemptuous little smile she flung at the people milling around in the hall. As they reached the bottom step she said, "Don't bother to run to my mother with this one, Paine—I've left my grandfather a note."

"Cristy—wait!" I put my hand on her arm but she jerked fiercely away, hurrying on. I got a swift, expressionless stare from the boy over his shoulder as they walked to the front entrance and went down the steps into the courtyard, impervious to the teeming rain.

It looked as if the ambassador had lost again.

Mariana showed me Cristy's note late in the evening. It was the first time in quite a while we'd met in the study, as we did so often in the early days. After the tumult of the party the Residence seemed cavernously quiet. But it had taken hours to get rid of the crowd because the rain fell without a break through the rest of the afternoon, finally stopping just after dark as suddenly as it began. By then nearly everybody still in the house was anxious to leave. The hardy ones had braved the downpour earlier, sloshing across the courtyard and signaling frantically and vainly for taxis in the street. Too often, finding an empty cab in Paris is difficult even in fair weather, but in rain as heavy as this it was impossible. Yet even after the skies cleared a few unidentified souls hung drearily on, wandering through the ground floor salons and, who knows, maybe hoping to be invited to dinner.

But the ambassador had long since gone upstairs, leaving Abigail Spaulding to shoo the last guests on their way, and Mme. Hanotte's cleanup crew had already taken over, dismantling the dripping structures in the garden and mopping and dusting the indoors. Perhaps I should have gone to Mr. Hillman the moment Cristy and her friend left, to tell him there was a note awaiting him, but I hesitated to add one more complication to the confusion brought on by the tropical deluge. Nothing could be done immediately anyway. Cristy was gone.

With Snuffy Spaulding holding one arm and Brad Lindley the other, the laughing ambassador ran for the house along with everybody else when the storm broke. Once inside she went right back to handshaking, this time in the Samuel Bernard Room. Her diaphanous hat was ruined but her smile was broader than ever.

I suppose I could have told her then what I was sure was bad news, but somehow the lovely look of her against the background of light blue and creamy gray walls, facing her garden party disaster with such insouciance, made me hesitate again. She would know soon enough. At that point Brad Lindley drew her into a corner—his usual monopoly tactics—despite Abigail's disapproving glare. Whatever he was saying to her couldn't have been very serious. She looked highly amused.

It was Herbert Hillman who interrupted them. At my last glimpse of him he was proceeding sedately through the cloudburst, undisturbed by the panicky crush around him and probably headed for his room and a dry jacket. But he was a long time coming back downstairs, perhaps because he, too, hesitated to take Mariana away from her reception. Now, at last, he appeared again, stepped past Abigail with a courtly little bow, and went to his daughter. Where I was standing with Beasley Turner I couldn't hear what he said, it was a very few words, but she immediately excused herself to Lindley, still smiling, and followed her father into the hall and up the staircase.

Brad immediately attached himself to me and hung around until almost the last guest had gone, obviously expecting the ambassador to come back downstairs. Something was going on, he seemed sure of that, but he didn't know what and I didn't help him. For my own part I tried to get some more information out of him about the source of the Residence bugging, but he didn't help me, either.

"If you're waiting for the ambassador," I said finally, "I'd guess she's lying down. And I don't blame her. Don't you think we've all had enough for one afternoon?"

He agreed then and departed, much to Abigail's relief.

But Mariana didn't appear for dinner and neither did Mr. Hillman. Presumably they were dining in the ambassador's suite, but I didn't query the waiter about it. At eleven o'clock, in my room, I did something I hadn't done before at night—I rang her apartment on the private line and told her about seeing Cristy leave. Five minutes later, gravely facing me across her desk in the study, she handed me Cristy's note without a word.

It said:

Dear Herbert,

*I stayed around as long as I could for your visit. Tell my
mother I have gone to live with friends in another part of
Paris. I will be all right. Do not try to find me. I just want to
be left alone.*

Christine

The schoolgirl handwriting was clear and forceful, the unaccustomed name signed with a defiant little flourish. I looked back at Mariana.

"Do you want me to try to bring her back?"

She shook her head. "I've discussed it at length with my father, Tyler. He feels we should give Cristy her head and let her get over this on her own."

"Do you feel that way?"

The words came low and troubled. "My father is a very wise man. I've decided to take his advice."

"But she'll need money, won't she?"

"There was a hundred dollars in her bed-table drawer that her grandfather gave her just yesterday. It's not there now, so she must have taken it with her."

In the long silence I waited for her to say something more, marveling at her self-control after the day she'd gone through and was still going through. Finally she spoke again. "Can you tell me anything about the boy?"

"Two or three years older than Cristy, not more. Not bad-looking. Very determined, even grim." I remembered something I'd thought earlier tonight. "He definitely doesn't look like he's on drugs."

"I think," she said, "I'll sleep a little easier for knowing that."

"It's about time you had some sleep, Mariana."

The name came out before I could catch myself. I'd never said it to her before. As if in answer, she leaned across the desk, put her hands on my shoulders, and gave me a warm, lingering kiss on the cheek.

"You too, dear Tyler."

I watched the door close softly behind her.

11

W ORD GOT AROUND the embassy fast that Cristy had departed against her mother's wishes. But the staff saw no outward
sign of sadness or anxiety in the ambassador. She rejected all expressions of sympathy with a bright smile and a manner that said
plainly: Let's get on with the job. Which she certainly did, plung-
ing back into her round of official activities with fresh vigor. It was
clear that in following Herbert Hillman's advice she was determined to put aside any thought of her daughter and prove to the
people around her that private problems would not affect her public life.

Mr. Hillman also lost no time in returning to his own affairs
in America. Within twenty-four hours after the ill-fated garden
party he was on his way, but not before bidding friendly farewell
to each member of the staff who had served him (and dispensing
a generous tip) together with expressions of hope he would see
them all again soon.

To me he said in his quiet fashion, smiling his faintly enigmatic
smile, "It's good to know we can count on you, Tyler"—the first
time he'd ever called me anything but Mr. Paine—but he left me
wondering what exactly Mariana had said to him about her feelings toward me.

I was very pleasurably haunted by the memory of that night in
the study, could still feel the touch of her lips against my face, and
two or three times caught myself pressing the spot with my finger,
that age-old theatrical cliché!

One result of the new situation was a specially happy one for
me. My late-evening meetings with the ambassador in the study
were resumed with some regularity, and with a new frankness and

warmth. Sometimes I even called her Mariana, everything seemed so natural. The subject of Cristy wasn't mentioned, nor did I try to bring it up, but there was plenty else to talk about. Normally, the summer political lull should have by now settled over the Western world, but the scene was suddenly enlivened by the unexpected visit of Premier Nicollet to Moscow.

The French Government explained its purpose was the signing of long-pending addenda to the Soviet-French trade pact—an event originally scheduled to occur some time in the fall. From what we knew, it seemed more likely Nicollet wanted face-to-face information from the Kremlin about the status of its secret negotiations with Washington on the proposal for a new European security structure. Significant fact: Nicollet was not accompanied on his Moscow trip by Foreign Minister Courtailles, described as temporarily incapacitated by something resembling gout. Newspapers seized on this at once, contending that the rumored rift between the Premier and Courtailles was now fully in the open and heading toward a public showdown. Instant denials came from both the Matignon and the Quai d'Orsay, prompting the general belief in diplomatic circles that the story must therefore be true.

But how to pin it down? The American ambassador was doing her best, discreetly, to find out what was going on. Toward this end she gave a series of intimate dinners, held not in the State Dining Room on the ground floor but in the more private quarters on the floor above used for smaller-scale entertainment. Her invitation to Claude Courtailles to be the honored guest at the first of these little parties was regretfully declined, in English, on the stationery of his home address—*as you know, dear friend, I am not yet capable to move about freely*—an excuse which Mariana told me she didn't believe for a moment. The Soviet ambassador had been next on the list, but he was called to Moscow for the Nicollet meetings. So the series started off with a dinner for the British envoy, Sir Harold Phillips, described as a purely social affair with Lady Phillips and a number of nonpolitical persons among those present. A few nights later the honored guest was West German Ambassador Erwin Lutziger (no problem in acceptance there) and after that came a similar dinner for Italy's Alberto

Morozzi, who was of course simply delighted to attend and give his government's views—for what they were worth.

But all of this, Mariana confided to me, added up to nothing. Sir Harold was as inscrutable as Courtailles, Herr Lutziger was *seeking* information, not imparting it, and the man from Rome, as usual, had nothing but opinions to offer. It had been difficult to draw the ambassadors aside at the dinners, even if they'd been willing to say something in confidence. The small talk was a bore, and the women kept getting in the way. To make things even more frustrating, said Mariana, Stuyvesant Spaulding was discouraging her efforts. He kept an eye on her at the dinner parties. He said the Secretary would not be pleased by too much ambassadorial zeal in the current state of international relations. The word from the department was sit tight unless otherwise instructed.

"And where *is* the Secretary?" Mariana demanded rhetorically, pacing the study floor after the dinner for Morozzi. "Taking a month off in Maine! And the President? Relaxing at his favorite new vacation spot—the Hawaiian island of Niihau!"

"That's about as far away as the President can get and still stay in the United States," I observed. "Has either of them thought of looking things over in Europe?"

"They don't *care* about Europe! Except as a piece in the jigsaw puzzle of power they're trying to construct with the Russians."

I'd never heard her quite so nervously vehement. She was champing like a thoroughbred filly before the big race. I felt an absurd urge to jump up and pop a lump of sugar into her mouth and stroke her back. But I knew there were deeper reasons for her tension than just exasperation. Hidden underneath was a fear for Cristy Otis, missing and still silent, wherever she was.

"I wonder if your colleagues in London and Bonn are also sitting tight," I said.

Abruptly she stopped pacing and stared at me. "You've given me an idea," she said. "I should have communicated with them before. Maybe I ought to go *see* them!"

"Over Snuffy Spaulding's dead body."

Suddenly she laughed and reached for a cigarette on her desk.

"You're right, it's out of the question. But I'm going to write to them. Tomorrow. Without saying a word about it to Spaulding. I want them to know how I feel. I want to see all this as it looks to them. Perhaps, if we speak with one voice, Washington will listen to us in the time ahead. . . ."

I nodded. What else could I say? I didn't want to tell her this just wasn't the way things were done. The Department of State wasn't about to hand over the reins to Mariana Hillman Otis. At the same time I admired tremendously her *caring*, the way she bucked the traditional procedures that bound us all, from Mitchell Remington and Stuyvesant Spaulding down to the clerks in the code room.

I also admired the way she looked right now, leaning toward me in the shimmering low-cut gown, her eyes alight, her white skin flushed with emotion. She said, more quietly: "Thank you, Tyler. You're always so patient about letting me get things off my chest."

In the moment I wished I could tell her what I was feeling about that same chest. But of course I didn't.

Whether it was a mark of new favor to me I didn't know, but I found myself a guest at Mariana's next dinner party. Like the others it was a comparatively small affair. In the upstairs dining room the mahogany Sheraton table extends for as many as thirty-six persons, but the ambassador had limited her recent dinners here to sixteen and there were only twelve places set tonight. Until I entered the room I had no idea who else had been invited.

It turned out to be quite a surprise.

Five or six male guests were already in the room, grouped around Mariana under the historic *America* tapestry (on loan to the embassy from the *Four Continents* series at the National Gallery in Washington) and with her uncanny knack for blending with the decor, wherever she was, the ambassador's simple, sack-like dinner dress somehow managed to look eighteenth-century Flemish. Almost immediately I guessed what was to make this evening a true original—it would be a stag party. Except for the hostess, of course. Something like mischief flickering in the ambassador's eyes as she greeted me seemed to bear me out, and by the time we were all assembled I had my confirmation.

It was a curious mixture—some diplomats including Blaise d'Archeval from the Quai d'Orsay, some embassy people including myself and Beasley Turner (acting press attaché in the absence of his immediate boss, on leave), and some news people, including Brad Lindley and the recently arrived Paris correspondent of the Washington *Post*. One thing I noticed when we checked our place cards and sat down was that nobody present was over the age of about forty. Another was that the Count d'Archeval had been put at the head of the table facing the ambassador at the other end, while Brad Lindley and I faced each other in the exact center.

I caught Mariana's sparkling eye as I glanced around the table at the guests one by one and followed her look to Lindley, who was doing the same thing I was. He didn't seem too happy about the seating arrangement, and I wondered if that was what was perversely amusing the hostess, who had the good-looking third secretary of the Danish embassy in the place of honor on her right, and the Washington *Post* man on her left. Whatever plan, or whim, had occasioned this little get-together, it was soon clear the ambassador was bent on having a rousing good time tonight, and on taking care that her guests had one, too.

Conspiratorial collaboration with Jean-Paul's kitchen was evident. The fare, set before us on Mariana's newly purchased Limoges china, was sturdy masculine throughout, from the fish soup *à la marseillaise* (a sly salute in honor of the recent past?) to the Charolais beef *béarnaise* accompanied by an asparagus quiche, by way of hot foie gras *en brioche*, all topped off with a dozen varieties of cheese and an imposing dessert called *banane flambée Rothschild*. Professional intelligence had seen to the wine, too—a lusty white Châteauneuf-du-Pape with the fish, Gevrey-Chambertin with the beef and cheese, vintage Pol Roger *brut* with the dessert. Dinner had begun in a circumspect, almost cautious atmosphere, with politely subdued conversation limited to immediate neighbors, but by the time we reached the champagne the talk was general and the decibels had risen dangerously toward the level of a bachelor's farewell to his pals.

What was talked about at that table? The amount of wine I consumed had a considerable effect on my memory of it, but I do recall trying to explain baseball to the Yugoslav press attaché on my right, eagerly awaiting his transfer to Washington, and listening to the Belgian economics officer on my left outline the engineering problems of the Channel tunnel.

But I held one part of my brain open so I could keep asking myself a persistent question: Since Mariana always had a constructive purpose, what was the underlying reason for this party and how had she selected the guests? Why was she not taking over, as I'd known her to do, and directing the discussion to the political issues of the hour?

Well, I came to the conclusion that my ambassador, throwing protocol to the winds and ignoring diplomatic seniority, had chosen her guests with no idea in mind but to defy convention and bring together a group of attractive, amusing, and still youthful men, to dine, drink, and have fun with them all by herself. And that for once she was deliberately avoiding the weighty exchange of political views in favor of an evening of lighthearted relaxation, let the Spauldings fall where they may.

Judging from where I sat, it was all working out very well. In fact when Blaise d'Archeval rose to offer the traditional toast he gave his opinion that it was the best damn party of the year and asked why hadn't other ambassadors thought of hosting a dinner for women only?

The roar of laughter and prolonged applause ceased only when Mariana got up to thank the count for his sentiments, to express qualms that she had set an example for the diplomatic corps only slightly less scandalous than her behavior in Marseille (cries of "No! Impossible!"), and to recommend that we all proceed to the Blue Salon for coffee and brandy.

It was in the Blue Salon that Beasley Turner reminded the ambassador the winter fashions openings were about to get under way and suggested she might want to consider giving a cocktail party for the American buyers now in Paris.

It was also in the Blue Salon that I overheard Brad Lindley laughingly protest not being seated at the ambassador's right hand at dinner and, more seriously, disclose to her that he was making a study of a new wave of student unrest at the Sorbonne, "still under the surface but threatening to break into violence."

My next confidential report to Washington was overdue, and once again I was facing a problem as I sat down to write it. The problem was Cristy, of course. Her story had to be covered because Stuyvesant Spaulding had undoubtedly mentioned it to the undersecretary by now. The question was, how much of it should I tell? It was just the kind of thing the man in Washington expected me to know about.

I cursed this backstairs espionage and hated it more with each report.

At least I knew Mariana had told no more than the barest outline to anyone, just as she was reluctant to speak of it even to me. That much was obvious from the fact that both the Spauldings had tried to quiz me about details—Snuffy in his indirect, dignified fashion, Abigail more crafty (she thought) and cajoling, especially about the identity of the boy who took Cristy away. I followed the ambassador's lead in this as everything else, and neither got anything more out of me. But they both seemed to feel I was withholding something from them—they couldn't believe, for instance, that we didn't even know the boy's name. On Herbert Hillman's advice Mariana had made no contact with the Sorbonne authorities. We had to take it on good faith that Cristy was still attending her classes. The whole objective was to keep the matter away from the media and let her stormy mood run its course.

So in the end I decided to classify the Cristy story in my report as more or less a footnote to the ambassador's social life, commenting casually that this gifted adolescent (highly intelligent like her mother and grandmother before her) had responded to her first taste of college by desiring more personal independence, and had therefore chosen to live at least for a time as a typical Sorbonne student, among her own kind. The ambassador, I indicated, didn't encourage Cristy's move but saw no harm in it, feeling that anyhow her daughter would soon return from digs on the bohemian Left Bank to her considerably more comfortable existence in the Faubourg St. Honoré. I took care to stress the ambassador's intention was to avoid publicity in the matter and therefore she was saying as little about Cristy as possible to her embassy associates.

As for the rest of the report, beyond noting that she had given several informal dinners for friends in the diplomatic corps, I made it clear I had no way of knowing what was discussed there, since I felt sure Spaulding was keeping the department informed. (Naturally I said nothing about what Mariana told me at our night meetings in the study.) I did admit, in the same casual way I referred to the Cristy affair, that I'd been a guest at the stag dinner, which was now the subject of amused general gossip in Washington. But I described it as a party to reciprocate for personal kindnesses extended to the ambassador within and outside diplomatic circles—another example of her painstaking care in making and keeping friends for America, at all levels.

Reading it over, I wondered whether either Mitchell Remington or his boss could possibly find anything of essential value in this or my previous reports. Maybe, I thought, they'll just decide to discontinue the process. But I wasn't really hopeful. At any rate, as long as Claude Courtailles continued to play coy it looked as if the ambassador was stymied in her efforts to analyze the motives of French policy, whether Washington cared to hear about them or not. And she was ready to admit it.

I realized this at our very next meeting in the study. Mariana didn't even mention politics. With her ability to lay aside unfruitful undertakings and plunge into new projects, she was all enthusiasm tonight about Beasley Turner's suggestion of a party for the American fashion buyers. Did I think it could be arranged quickly enough? There were less than ten days before the showings were over.

For a moment I blinked. I'd forgotten about the idea. Then I said, "Why not? I'll see Beasley in the morning and we'll put a plan together. Honora will help."

The extraordinary Mlle. de Chapdelaine did indeed help. She got in touch immediately with something called the Chambre Syndicale de la Haute Couture and obtained the official buyers' list. Turner, with the aid of the *Herald Tribune,* produced the buyers' hotel addresses. The best suggestion of all not surprisingly came from Mariana herself. She summoned me to her desk and said, "The Americans are only half of it. Let's invite the French, too."

"Great!"

"And the clothes," she said.

I blinked again.

"The heads of all the fashion houses, and have them bring along their top models and star new outfits. As the climax of the showings we can have our own Academy Awards ceremony." She smiled at my expression. "You like that, eh? Especially the models."

"But where would you put all these people?"

"In the Music Room, of course. There's a stage at one end and space for a hundred and twenty guests."

I looked at her. "If you ever decide to give up your diplomatic career, ma'am, they'll always have a job for you on Seventh Avenue."

"There you go, calling me ma'am again."

"Maybe it's this office. I don't know why, but you're a different person at the Residence."

"So? Then let's keep it that way."

We laughed together and she pushed a piece of paper across her desk to me. The names written on it were Dior, Givenchy, Corrèges, Laroche, St. Laurent, Grés. "Those are the ones I know personally," the ambassador said. "There are more. Make sure Honora includes them." She paused. "Does Beasley want to invite the press?"

I shrugged. "There won't be many seats left after the buyers are taken care of. I suppose we could fit in the news agencies."

"And let's make room for TV cameras along the back wall. We have to keep everybody happy, Tyler."

"Very well," I said, and saw her watching me with a small, knowing smile.

"Am I mistaken," she asked, "or do I detect a note of resentment?"

"Resentment?" I lied. "Of TV? Certainly not."

Since the stag party I'd hoped her interest in Brad Lindley was leveling off, but obviously it wasn't.

"One more thing. Tell Honora I want at least a dozen of the best-dressed women in the American colony."

"Yes, ma'am."

Now the smile was lovely and wide and warm. She shook her head. "Somehow," she said, "that *ma'am* doesn't sound right even in this office."

She probably just said it to make me feel better. And I did, immediately.

The fashion show cocktail party was to be the biggest indoor gathering the Residence had seen since the ambassador's arrival, and another first. But a surprise development interrupted Mariana's planning and suddenly turned her mind back to weightier concerns.

It was an unexpected invitation to a "small luncheon" at the Chinese embassy that broke the pattern of her fruitless diplomatic soundings and filled her with fresh anticipation.

Coming simultaneously with the French Premier's visit to Moscow, it seemed to promise that this time she might actually learn something substantially new. It also led Stuyvesant Spaulding to suggest that perhaps the ambassador should plead previous engagement, or else accept and then suffer "indisposition" on the fateful day.

Needless to say, Mariana rejected the advice, though she told me she'd listened patiently to his cautionary counsels.

"What's worrying him now?" I asked.

"He thinks they're trying to find out what Nicollet is being told in Moscow, and he's afraid I'll repeat what Courtailles said about secret Soviet negotiations with Washington. In other words, he doesn't trust a woman to keep her mouth shut." A teasing smile. "Do you, Tyler?"

"I'd trust this woman."

156

"Even in an opium den like the Chinese embassy?"

"Even if they put you to the water torture."

She gave a little mock shudder and laughed. "It wouldn't surprise Spaulding if they did."

What made the Chinese invitation so stimulating was the apparent change in attitude of Wai Chun, the ambassador, who on his few prior social encounters with Mariana—except for that one big grin on July 4—had never dropped his careful reserve to give a sign of real friendliness. Snuffy Spaulding saw nothing but oriental cunning behind this attitude. I should have thought Spaulding of all people would disdain that worn-out cliché, since in earlier years he'd served a tour of duty with the Chiang Kai-sheks on Taiwan, but not so. Mariana said he'd got along fine with the Gissimo and Madam but evidently learned from them to regard all *Communist* Chinese with deep suspicion, like people of another race.

The way things are going, maybe they eventually will be.

At any rate the ambassador departed for her luncheon date with avid expectancy. I wished I were accompanying her—I'd like to have listened in on this one. By the time she returned, after three o'clock, my curiosity was highly aroused. But she was immediately claimed by Spaulding and other duties for the rest of the afternoon, so I didn't hear the story till she summoned me to the study after dinner.

She was wearing a white silk Mao-type jacket with little green figures on it and smiling inscrutably.

"You even *look* Chinese tonight," I couldn't help saying.

"I thought you'd like the outfit. I considered slanting my eyes but decided that was going too far."

"And I like the smile. But I'm dying to hear the words."

"Tyler," she said, "the food was as nearly heaven as anything I've tasted in France."

"Never mind the food. Just tell me who ate it besides yourself."

"A *very* interesting group. Exactly six of us, and the only other non-Chinese was Clément Marot. Incognito, of course."

"Well, well!" But not so remarkable after all, considering that young Marot was a maverick in the French Communist party, and said to be covertly anti-Soviet and pro-Peking. They'd almost read him out a couple of times, but he emerged from the crises with nothing more than admonition, probably because he had a fanatical and growing following among young people, particularly students.

"I was fascinated to meet him," Mariana was saying. "He spoke English English and beautifully, too." Her eyes were somber for a moment. "Somehow I kept thinking he was that boy Cristy went away with, fifteen years from now. It frightened me. Especially when he mentioned Cristy."

I felt a little chill myself. "How would he know anything about Cristy? And what did he say?"

"It was just a passing reference to her living in the Latin Quarter. As though it's a fact known to everybody. But there was something menacing in the way he said it, Tyler. A warning in his look. Indefinable, but I felt it."

"You think Wai Chun had you over just to meet the indefinable Clément Marot?"

"Oh, no. The ambassador and I did most of the talking. The other Chinese said hardly a word the whole time, including the woman. Did I mention her? Obviously one of the embassy functionaries, and absolutely deadpan like the three men."

"She's probably the real boss."

"She could be. Why do such women make me feel shivery? They're like machines, Tyler—totally concentrated, totally dedicated, not a trace of gentleness left in them. She watched me every moment. She'd have shot me, if the order was given, without the slightest change of expression."

I had to laugh at that. "You must have had quite an experience. And was Snuffy right? Did Wai Chun quiz you about Nicollet in Moscow?"

She shook her head. "The ambassador was interested in my recent travels in France. You know how some people can take notes without writing anything down? That's what he was doing while I told him about our interviews. Marot, too."

"And tonight they're reading all about it in Peking."

She shrugged. "If they are, they're showing more interest than my own government in what I learn here."

"I hope you asked a few questions yourself."

"I certainly did. And what better way to do it than by bringing up the subject Spaulding expected them to ask *me* about? I was careful, of course, feigning wide-eyed amateur innocence—although I doubt whether the ambassador was fooled by it. I'm sure *she* wasn't. All these rumors about Nicollet and Courtailles feuding, I said—perhaps the ambassador could put a friendly colleague straight."

"And he did."

"Of course. It's typical of the lack of political discipline in the so-called democratic governments, he explained, making it very clear such dissension wouldn't be permitted for one instant in his own country. But as long as the people tolerate it, jealous bickering at the top is inevitable."

"He said nothing about the reasons for the dispute?"

"I told him their differences must be pretty grave, whatever they were, if Nicollet didn't take his Foreign Minister to Moscow with him. And at the first mention of Moscow his mind snapped closed. I could distinctly hear the click."

"That was all?"

"Marot moved in at that point. He said China would have no reason to be interested in Soviet relations with France unless the Kremlin was trying to make a deal to neutralize Western Europe, which would enable the Russians to build up their Far East frontier forces and eventually attack China."

"And did Wai Chun enlarge on that little theory?"

She shook her head. "He made an utterly beguiling transition from the differences between politicians to the differences between French and Chinese food—both eminent cuisines but with characters of their own."

"In other words, the subject was dismissed."

"So far as the ambassador was concerned, yes. Later I tried again with Marot. I asked him as a Frenchman to give an ignorant foreigner some idea of the background of the feud. He just made a joke out of it, remarking with a little shrug that the answers to such questions were for Frenchmen to know and for ignorant foreigners to find out. I told him I was serious, and he replied he was never serious so early in the day. When it became evident he was not disarming me with his most disarming grin, the ambassador came in on cue and suggested we go out on the terrace for a liqueur." She gave a small vexed laugh. "They work very smoothly together, those two."

"There's an old saying, Mariana—the French are the Chinese of the West."

In the silence I saw the frustration and discouragement in her face. To Mariana the luncheon was another failure on her part, and I wanted to tell her to cheer up, her job was a game like any other game, with good days and bad days, runs of luck and periods of drought, and that was the only way to look at it.

"Your career friends in the department are right," she said then. "Fancy ambassadors should stick to their social life and leave the serious business to the pros." She picked up a pad from her desk. "Shall we check out this list of visiting buyers?"

12

I T W A S A great party, especially for me. As will presently become evident.

Snuffy Spaulding felt it undignified, though he was probably relieved that no political implications could be drawn. At any rate he descended to the occasion with true grit. Abigail was thrilled. She was beginning to get used to Mariana's "daring" departures from tradition, especially when they turned out to be successful. Like the ambassador, Abigail knew the importance—in fact the necessity—of chic in Paris diplomatic circles. In addition to the clothes horses Honora had culled from among the American colony she'd added the most fashion-conscious of the foreign diplomatic wives, with emphasis on the gay Latinos, as rich as they were pretty, so it was a glamorous crowd that settled between the carved oak woodwork walls with their curtains of flame-colored velvet to watch the parade of models on the stage.

Once again Mariana displayed her showmanship. She made her little welcoming speech wearing an Oscar de la Renta, who could pass as half European. More than showmanship—it was international diplomacy. And it pleased everybody, even including the French. Coming back down off the stage and taking her seat, the ambassador walked like a model—and got more applause than any of them.

Cocktails were served after the showing to a mob that overflowed two salons, the Gallery, and even spilled out into the entrance hall. The crowd in the Music Room had been preponderantly female, of course, and anticipating that situation Mariana had invited the husbands of all those present to come in afterward for drinks. Though there were many temptations, particularly the models and those South Americans, I stayed as usual pretty much to myself, drifting with a glass in my hand and keeping a jealous eye on my boss, the center of a noisy group that inevitably included Brad Lindley. I was standing alone, in fact, when Honora de Chapdelaine brought up someone for me to meet.

At first I thought Honora was just taking care of a shy man. Then I recognized Yolande.

The same Yolande, *my* Yolande, but also someone I'd never met before. She just stood there, her smile breaking through the mists of sixteen years, while the babel of voices died around us and I could find no words to break our separate spell.

Being a female, Honora sensed very quickly that something unforeseen was happening and moved away from us into the crowd. The female facing me, handling it all much better than I (it's a special talent they have in spellbound situations), looked more amused than anything else.

Then she said, "Hello, Tyler," and gave me her hand.

"I can't believe this." I heard myself speak like another man speaking, but I was the one who was holding her hand with both my hands, I made sure of that.

"Why not, Tyler?"

I shook my head, speechless. "Can I just look at you a minute?"

Her little low laugh that I'd never forgotten. She withdrew her hand, put it on top of her head, and revolved slowly before me. "*Eh bien,*" she said, "*regardez-moi!*"

She was beginning to come into focus. She would be about thirty-four now and looked ten years younger. She was almost as tall as I, slim, olive-skinned with a layer of suntan, poised, elegant, and from *boucles d'oreille* to *chaussures, tout à fait parisienne.* (Already she had me thinking in French again.)

But Yolande was back to English—very French English, and smiling impudently. "Well? Are you satisfied, monsieur?"

"It's you, all right. May I tell you something? There's hardly a day since I came back to Paris I haven't thought of you and wondered where you were."

"I did not have to wonder about you, Tyler." The smile was

mischievous now. "You are perhaps the most famous American in France—after Madame Otis."

Was I flushing a little? "Come on, you're grown up enough not to believe everything you read in the papers, Yolande."

"Grown up, yes. But what they said—is it true?"

We laughed together. "I won't dignify that with an answer. What I want to know is why you didn't call me if you knew I was in Paris?"

She still sounded amused. "I was busy getting divorced, monsieur. Does this reply to your question?"

Somehow it came as a bit of a shock. Not so much the divorce as learning that she'd been married, though God knows I'd expected it. I must have shown my reaction because Yolande said, smiling with a touch of mockery, "You are surprised?"

"Nothing about you has ever surprised me, Yolande."

"I prefer to accept that as a compliment."

"It's simply the truth." Just talking to her I could feel waves of pleasure rising in me. "Now tell me how many children you have."

"No children." She said it in the same lighthearted way she said everything else. In the moment I wondered if she was going to ask me if I'd been married or divorced but she was waiting, it was my turn again.

"Then you live alone?"

"Quite alone, now."

"And what do you do with your time?"

"But that is why I am here, Tyler! I work for the Chambre Syndicale."

"Doing what?"

"I suppose you would call it public relations."

"You should have been modeling up there on the platform today."

"Ah, I used to do that."

"I wish I could have seen you then."

"I was not so different than I am now."

I had to know right away and hoped I didn't show her I was

nervous when I asked. "So the Chambre Syndicale takes care of your days. What about your evenings?"

Once more the mocking little smile. "*Ça dépend*," she said.

"You mean you're free sometimes?"

Laughing, she opened her eyes wide. "Why not?"

I wanted to ask her if there was somebody new in her life but realized how clumsy it would sound to this totally sophisticated French girl. Suddenly I felt like a man being shown a jewel so incredibly delicate he's almost afraid to take it in his hands. Yolande, another Yolande, beautiful and strange, had returned—was here, now, in this place, and I was almost afraid she would vanish if I touched her, if I said one wrong word. And what was she feeling about me, if anything? Could she remember our time together as I was remembering it now as clearly, as freshly, as if I'd left her just this morning, asleep in her little room in the Rue des Ecoles?

"Then I can see you—anywhere out of here?"

"Of course, Tyler."

"Dinner tonight?"

Her little nod of acceptance lifted a load somewhere in the vicinity of my heart. It was my own voice I was hearing again, not someone else's. Reality had resumed and settled down around us. We weren't alone, we were surrounded by babbling people at a cocktail party in the American embassy in Paris.

"Do you know how happy I am right now?" I said because I couldn't help it.

Again the gay little nod, but her eyes were saying: *Not too fast, not here.*

"We'll get away as soon as you can leave, Yolande."

Touching my hand an instant, "First, will you take me to meet your ambassador?"

How quick women are. In the days that followed I kept recalling that first meeting between Yolande and Mariana. We couldn't have stood in the circle surrounding the ambassador for more than a couple of minutes, in fact we rather rudely interrupted a bald, middle-aged buyer who was himself rather rudely trying to monopolize the conversation. But the brief introduction was enough for me to see Mariana's reaction—even more immediate than Honora's had been.

She beamed her most winning smile at Yolande and for an instant looked away at me. And her swift glance told me that my face must have been shining with childish joy. I also saw that though I'd never mentioned Yolande to her, she knew.

Brad Lindley gave my companion an appreciative eye. Then the liquored-up buyer broke in again. "Anyway, to make a long story short," he boomed—giving me the chance to take Yolande's arm and withdraw. We were out of there in five minutes and into her little red Renault.

She drove through the Paris gloaming like the French, which is to say dangerously but steering with great talent. I said, "I guess you know Raquin's is still there. It would be wonderful to go back together tonight."

"In these clothes? They would throw us out of it."

"Not Raquin. He'd *remember*, Yolande."

"No, not Raquin. I mean the students dining there."

"But why?"

"Oh, Tyler! Because you are obviously American, and I would look like a *poule de luxe*."

"Are relations that bad?"

She shrugged. I remembered the shrug from long ago and loved it all over again.

We had reached the Champs Elysées. "How about Ermenonville?" I said. And damn the cost.

That husky little laugh. "Ermenonville! *Oh, là-là!* Remember when we used to walk past *chez* Renard without a sou, Tyler, dreaming of being rich so we could eat there someday? And one night you leaned through the hedge and sniffed the *bisque d'homard* on somebody's table and they tried to get you arrested?" She laughed and looked at me, just missing knocking down a woman trying to cross the street. "Tonight I want to dine with you on the *terrasse* of Renard and devour a huge bowl of *bisque d'homard*."

"Yolande, you are inspired. But promise we'll go to Raquin's another night, in disguise."

A gloved hand came off the wheel and patted my knee in reassurance. "It is a must."

I was enchanted by her fluent English and asked her where she got it.

"From the buyers, dolling, where else?"

"Did you have a dinner date with one of them tonight?"

"It does not matter. We all go in a bunch to Lasserre. I hate it." She giggled. "But there is safety in numbers."

"It's the little dinners for two that are dangerous, right?"

"Not dangerous. Sometimes *désagréable*."

Better to stay off that general subject despite my intense curiosity about her husband. Perhaps later.

I felt suddenly empty. "Hungry, Yolande?"

"Famished, I don't know why."

"You're remembering how hungry we used to get."

"God! You remember that, Tyler?"

The *chasseur* parked the car for us. Getting out, the first thing we both did was look up at the fourth-floor balcony of the old hotel. Neither of us said a word. Then I took her hand and we walked, still silent, along the quai to the Place St. Michel and found a table on the terrace looking straight across at Notre Dame.

No nationalist hatreds here. They were glad to have us. Neighboring male diners ogled Yolande politely. We sat side by side, one of the French customs I like most, and consumed lobster bisque, with seconds, accompanied by a Muscadet. They were mildly astonished when we skipped meat or fowl and leaped all the way to the cheese tray, this too in honor of ancient nights when our dinner consisted solely of a Brie or a Camembert, a crusty *baguette*, and a bottle of Côtes du Rhône, during intimate conversational exchanges on the edge of a bed. Tonight, having finished off the Muscadet we celebrated history with a half bottle of the Rhône.

Not that we needed the wine to unlock our tongues. We talked, how we talked—sometimes both at once, as starved for each other's words as for the food we were eating. Everything forgotten had come back to me from that long-ago time—her laugh, her pout, the conflict of doubt and reason in the lovely hazel eyes, the way

166

she squeezed off little pieces of bread and popped them into her mouth between gulps of her *potage*. Yet in all this flood of reminiscence we weren't really talking about *us*. We were reviving the memory of a boy and girl long dead or vanished. The two people sitting side by side on this terrace by the Seine tonight were strangers just getting acquainted.

And if Tyler and Yolande were to be what they once were to each other, they would have to begin it all over again.

I guess it was like me to comprehend this slowly, while Yolande knew it already in her woman wisdom, perhaps even before she felt free to look me up again. I could hear it in what she said, in what I said—that edge of reticence or shyness replacing the first eager flush of our coming together. Now, talking of the present and speaking English made her sound somehow almost formal.

"Your ambassador is charming. And a little frightening."

"That's just diplomatic dignity, Yolande. She's quite different when the public pressure is off."

"Is it true you live in the embassy?"

"Quite true. And I want you to come to dinner with me there."

"You take your meals there, too?"

"Of course. In the private dining room upstairs."

"And you dine there with the ambassador?"

"Very seldom. If I do, it's by coincidence."

"She is curious about you and me, Tyler."

"You think so?"

"Have you ever told her about your early years in Paris?"

"Not a word."

"You never spoke about me?"

"No reason to, was there?"

"Yet, tonight, I felt she *knew* about us."

"She could probably see I was very happy to have found you again."

"Madame Otis is a very intelligent person, Tyler. I saw that." She paused and then went on, "I recognized the journalist, Brad Lindley."

"I noticed he recognized you, too."

"No, we have not met before tonight. I think I have seen him at one or two parties, not this year. Sometimes he is on French television."

"And you like his looks."

"I like his looks? Not especially. Tonight I wondered—is he a close friend of Madame Otis?"

"He'd like to be."

Another pause. "She is *veuve*, right?"

"Yes, a widow."

"Then who is her *ami*? Someone in America? Someone here?"

"No one that I know of."

She looked at me so skeptically that I laughed. For the first time since we sat down I took her hand and held it. "Yolande *chérie*, don't you think it's my turn to ask some questions?"

Smiling, "That sounds so strange when you say *chérie*. What do you wish to ask me, Tyler?" As if she didn't know.

"Well, about your husband, for one thing—your ex-husband whom you haven't mentioned. And why you're divorced."

She sipped her demitasse before she answered, looking at me with suddenly solemn eyes. "Have you had a wife?"

I shook my head.

"Then you cannot understand how difficult it is, to explain *why* a divorce. There are so many reasons. Perhaps one or two big reasons, and many, many little reasons. It is not all his fault, certainly."

"And were you married long?"

"It would be five years this year." She made a small funny grimace. "Who would think I could endure that long! He wanted me to do *nothing*, Tyler. Just to be a wife." Her shrug. "I tried. It was such a bore!"

"Will you see him now? I mean are you friendly?"

"I think it would prolong a disaster to be friends. It is finished."

"But you have other friends. Other men friends."

"Not really," she said.

It was what I wanted her to say.

The rest of it was a dream relived, in a dream setting. By the time we finished dinner, at lingering last, the sky over the Cité was the special cobalt blue that says *Paris-la-nuit*. Silent again, we walked slowly arm in arm up the boulevard, past the Rue Monsieur-le-Prince and the café where we first met, breasting the student crowds—white, black, yellow, all chattering in a cacophony of tongues, whose faces were reflections of our former selves—and finally, out of the crush and into the quiet, along the edge of the Luxembourg, toward Montparnasse. Just once she gave a little laugh and shook her head.

"What are you thinking, Yolande?"

"How different this, from my evening with the buyers!"

"They're wondering about you right now."

"Oh, not any longer. Everybody is well drunk by now. They all have left Lasserre for the Crazy Horse, and after that they all will go to Jimmy's to dance. They love to dance."

"And what do they talk about?"

"Shop, Tyler! Each other's clothes. What else? What else do they care about? What else do they know? They come to Paris once or twice in a year but they are not in Paris, Paris is just Seventh Avenue for a little while, Lasserre is Seventh Avenue, Maxim is Seventh Avenue. They bring it with them, and then take it away again, after they say good-bye to Paris in their hotel room, at the Georges Cinq or the Plaza-Athénée, maybe with a very expensive girl they have arranged for the last night."

"You don't like them, Yolande."

"*C'est vrai,* I don't like them. Maybe I should not say this. They are very kind. But they are so loud! So loud in everything."

I smiled. "You're just like all the rest of the French, you don't like Americans."

"I will not speak for the rest of the French. Some don't like Americans, that is so. But I like *some* Americans, Tyler." And she very lightly pressed my arm and laughed again.

We had come to the top of the Petit Lucot and stopped a moment. The park stretched below us in soft darkness. Across from where we stood, beyond the Carpeaux fountain, the Closerie des Lilas sparkled with strings of light, and I remembered a long-gone time when I sat with my arm around Yolande on the café terrace listening to a shabby little man play Neapolitan tunes on his fiddle for sous.

"The Closerie?" I said.

"*Je veux bien.*"

We drank Armagnac there because in the old days we could only afford beer. And after the Closerie, stops at the Sélect—still just as we'd known it—and the tiny never forgotten *bar-tabac* on the Place St. Sulpice on our way back to the Quarter to pick up the Renault. This was where we used to come to get away from all the others, to be alone, but the face on the far side of the bar belonged to a stranger now, and we were strangers to him.

"You haven't come here—since?" I said to Yolande.

She shook her head in a solemn, smiling way. "Of course not." It made me feel very glad.

We asked some questions across the *zinc* while we sipped our beer. Yes, he'd heard about Monsieur Charles, but all that was years ago, you understand. The *maison* had changed hands several times since then. No, he had no idea where Monsieur Charles might be found. Was he dead? He shrugged: if he wasn't, maybe it was about time. Perhaps the current *patron* could tell us, but as we left, the *patron* was deep in a game of poker dice with a couple of workmen in the back, and we let it go.

It was after midnight. Our footsteps echoed sharply in the narrow burnished streets. The last stop was at the corner of Rue Bonaparte and the quai for *café noir*, while I finished telling Yolande about Cristy Otis and her mother's distress. She listened with the utmost sympathy.

"Madame Otis doesn't even know the boy's name?"

"She feels she shouldn't interfere, but I know she's deeply worried."

"If you wish, I can make some little inquiries, with total discretion. I still have contacts in the *faculté*."

"You are a darling. Mariana would appreciate it."

She smiled. "Ah, Mariana, is it?"

"You know us Americans. Very informal."

We laughed together and walked back to her car. Yolande insisted on dropping me off at the embassy on her way home, though that meant backtracking to her Left Bank apartment.

I protested only mildly. We had plenty of time, now. Saying

good night, she kissed me French-fashion, first one cheek, then the other. And her warm, firm handclasp gave me all the assurance I needed that my enchanted evening had ended with a beginning.

It wasn't until I walked down the embassy hallway to my own apartment that I learned the evening hadn't ended after all. Brad Lindley was standing outside the ambassador's door and Mariana was withdrawing slowly from his embrace.

Sitting in the study with me a few minutes later, she seemed to have fully recovered herself after the momentary embarrassment of that little scene in the hall (not to mention my own conflicting emotions at what I'd inadvertently witnessed). But the high color, the still glowing eyes, couldn't be concealed by makeup. It wasn't just cocktails and wine, either. I saw a kind of happy relief there, so different from her tensions of these recent days.

It was Mariana who'd come to my door and asked to talk to me just after I heard her say good night to her guest. Was it because she felt in some strange way she ought to apologize, explain? I hadn't tried to analyze that. I was too preoccupied with my own reactions, and with very simple questions in my mind such as whether Brad Lindley was leaving *after* he'd been in her apartment or just seeing her to her door.

Such as the irony of finding Yolande again on this same evening.

And I thought these coincidences only happened in fiction!

Mariana lit a cigarette, smiled a little, and then baffled me by simply remaining silent.

I said, "Was it a late party?"

"Not for the French. But our countrymen never seem to know when to go home, Tyler."

"Especially Brad Lindley?"

It just came out. I hadn't intended to make any reference to him at all.

"Were you surprised?" she said quietly.

I shook my head and thought of Noah Webster's famous definition. "*You* were surprised. I was astonished."

171

That made her laugh. "You had a right to be. I think I was a little astonished myself."

"But there it is."

She nodded, serious now. She was looking past me, beyond me.

"Let's hope you don't read about it in next week's *Time*," I went on. "At least he didn't have his camera crew with him."

There was another silence. Then, "You said that in such an odd, bitter way, Tyler."

"Did I? I'm sorry. I don't feel bitter. Why should I feel bitter?"

In the moment I didn't know what I felt—annoyance, jealousy, even anger, maybe something of each all mixed together. At the same time I reproached myself for being anything but glad, for Mariana's sake.

"I think it's time you realized I'm as human as anybody else," she was saying. "It might have been you, Tyler, instead of Brad Lindley."

"Me!"

She gave me her most ravishing smile. "You're a very attractive man, you know. Hasn't anyone ever told you you look like Cary Grant? Don't you think there've been nights these past weeks when I had to resist just walking down the hall and climbing into bed with you?"

"If I'd known that—" I began, and Mariana said, "Shush!" still smiling, "I want to hear about Yolande Vannier. You two should have stayed on tonight. When we finally got rid of the stragglers Jean-Paul gave us a marvelous supper."

"You remembered her name," I said.

"Of course I did. And what romantic spot did *you* choose for dinner?"

"A terrace by the Seine, facing Notre Dame."

"*Oh, là-là!*"

My turn to smile. For a moment she'd sounded as French as Yolande.

"An old friend?" she was saying.

"We were students together."

"I liked her instantly, Tyler. Will you bring her to dinner here? Brad will make the fourth."

"She would feel greatly honored."

"Pish-tush. You forgot to say ma'am."

"I don't know whether I did the right thing, but I asked Yolande tonight to inquire about Cristy. Indirectly and quietly, of course. She has friends on the Sorbonne teaching staff. Specifically Cristy's whereabouts, and the identity of the boy."

"I shall be grateful for any news," she said.

In the long pause a weariness settled over her face. I said, "Mariana, what's bothering Cristy? What's behind all this? I haven't asked you to talk about it before, but I keep feeling I could do something, something to help you both, if I knew, if *somebody* knew what's going on *inside* the child."

"Yes," she said tonelessly, "it would seem such a simple thing. I suppose it is, really. But guessing at the cause doesn't guarantee the cure. I tried psychiatrists for Cristy. She wouldn't begin to co-operate with them. But they all agreed on the reasons for her behavior."

I waited. She gave a deep sigh.

"It goes back such a long way, Tyler. All the way back to her father's death. And I've tried to keep it out of my mind. I've tried to evade it, hoping it would just dwindle and be forgotten. But of course it won't, it never will, how could it? It's always there. It's buried so deep in Cristy she'll never get it out now. That day he—the day Clay was thrown I was in Washington. I never knew anything about it until nearly four hours after it happened. All that time he was unconscious, lying there beside the jagged stone wall where the horse shied—."

She stopped, then went on with difficulty. "And all through the afternoon that little girl, she was barely ten, sat holding his head in her lap and talking to him, trying to get him to answer her, afraid to leave him alone to go for the nearest help six miles away, afraid he would die if she did, and wondering why I wasn't there, I who should have been riding with them, I who had promised her I would, and then I'd been called to Washington, promising, again, I'd be home in time for Clay's birthday dinner."

Once more she stopped. Large tears stood in her eyes. She spoke very slowly now, looking away from me. "Cristy finally wandered out to the highway and a car took her to the Warrenton hospital. They came to get him in an ambulance, but Clay never recovered consciousness. And by the time I'd been called, by the time my mother and I got there from Washington, he was already gone. Cristy refused to obey the doctors and lie down. She fought them off when they tried to inject sedation. I found her sitting beside his bed, still holding his hand. She wasn't crying. She just wouldn't look at me. During the night she developed a cold and a raging fever. Afterward, after she'd been in bed for a week, still not crying, she began to feel stronger. We'd spared her the funeral. I don't know what it would have done to her if she'd been able to go. When at last she was up and around again, the only person she'd talk to was her grandfather. She never spoke to me about her father again."

Mariana looked back to me. "Herbert was wonderful with her, Tyler. He still is. Much better than I seem able to be. He was the only one of us who could console her at all. Cristy—." Her voice broke slightly. "She'd knitted Clay a white scarf as a birthday surprise. All the time she was ill she wouldn't let it out of her sight. She's kept it near her ever since. She brought it with her to Paris."

We sat facing each other in new silence. I could hear the chimes of St. Philippe du Roule distantly striking the quarter hour across the night.

"But eventually your relationship must have improved," I said finally. "In Washington Cristy struck me as a little abrupt, but no more so than any girl going through her difficult age. And here in Paris, at least at first, she seemed quite happy and normal. What was it at the Sorbonne that dropped her off the deep end?"

She sighed again. "With Cristy one never knows. She's awfully good at making a normal appearance if she wants to. When we first found out about the marijuana in Washington, she'd already been smoking it since she was fourteen. Two girls were expelled from her school. We're still not sure where they got it." She hesitated, as if making a decision, then straightened and faced me more directly. "Unfortunately, by that time there was something else to trouble her. The psychiatrists seized on it right away as a contributory factor. She was twelve when it happened. For about a year, I'd been seeing Marcus Feld, but only in Washington, I made sure of that. He wanted very much to marry me. I was lonely, Tyler. I almost gave in to the idea, but it would have been a grave mistake, I know that now. One Saturday Marcus came down to Middleburg on some urgent business about Clay's estate and I gave him lunch. Cristy was supposed to be riding in a horse show in Charlottesville. We had no idea she was anywhere near the house. She walked into the living room and saw him kissing me."

"She reacted violently?"

"She turned very white and bolted out again without saying anything. But it was strange—her reaction effectively ended any temptation I might have had to marry Marcus. He took it badly. In fact he's never really given up. Of course Cristy won't stay in the same room with him."

She made a rueful little grimace, as if remembering things better left unsaid, and reached for another cigarette.

"May I ask a question?"

"Please do, Tyler."

"Before he—before your husband's accident, was Cristy un-happy with her parents' marriage? I mean, were you and Clay getting along well?"

Slowly she shook her head. "Until the day he died, we never gave anyone, most of all Cristy, the slightest reason to think we were unhappy together." And after a moment, "Why do you ask this?"

"It was just an idea I had—when I was reading through your biographical material in Washington—that somehow it seemed an unusual match, you and Clay."

She smiled. "I think I can answer you very briefly, and I think you will understand. I was just twenty-one when I met Clay, in Cambridge. I felt shy and awkward and out of place, definitely not the pretty-girl type, definitely not the social establishment. Clay was everything I thought I needed, then—elegant, amusing, a top-level WASP! And he said he loved me."

"Didn't he?"

"As much as he could ever love anybody—with what he could

spare from his horses and the place in Virginia. Of course he needed *me*, too, to keep all that going. I guess we each decided we had a good thing and better grab it before it got away." Then with a little laugh, dismissing it: "Poor Tyler! Why am I telling you all this ancient history?"

"Because I asked about your daughter."

"My daughter, yes, but not my love life."

"I suspect you've had a pretty innocent love life, Mariana."

"Less innocent than you think, perhaps. After all, I'm physically normal, and I'm not a nun."

"And I'm not a monk, but I've been living like one lately for too long."

"It ain't much fun, is it?" she said. "Maybe Yolande can help."

"Lucky Brad."

We both laughed. She was the Mariana I knew again.

13

Ju l y w a s w a n i n g toward muggy August, when the French nation would take off for its annual month's holiday. *"Tout Paris"* had already deserted the capital. There was no sign of urgency anywhere on the diplomatic horizon. Premier Nicollet, back from Moscow, was disdainfully silent. What, if anything, he'd talked about during his visit to sign the trade agreement remained unknown. Aside from Nicollet's trip the international political scene was in the midsummer doldrums. Even the superactive Stoneface had extended his Maine vacation, to the relief of old-timers in the department. And to Mariana's relief, Stuyvesant and Abigail Spaulding departed for a brief sojourn in Biarritz, from where the deputy chief of mission kept in fussy telephonic touch with the embassy every day.

Yet beneath the appearance of desultory calm an undertone could be detected, however faint and elusive—a sense of expectation, of slightly nervous anxiety perhaps, of restless waiting. In Washington Bryce Halsted, who never took vacations and rarely visited his home state, prowled the Senate corridors like an old watchdog, betraying his annoyance, according to columnist Wayne Kearsart, "with what he calls the administration's bland acceptance of mounting Soviet military superiority." The American ambassador to France was scarcely less impatient, as I could observe at first hand, though powerless to affect the course of events she suspected were moving secretly and inevitably toward climax.

But she had no further word on developments from Claude Courtailles, and judged that his present situation was too delicate to risk pressing him. Nor was she getting any comfort from her ambassadorial colleagues in Bonn and London. In replies to her letter which seemed almost to have been written by one and the same person, these two gentlemen steered safely clear of involvement in what must have appeared to them an imprudent and presumptuous request from the lady envoy in Paris for their personal —as opposed to their official—political views.

If there was anything to console Mariana in this difficult period, Brad Lindley was supplying it. During the week following the fashion show party he dined alone with the ambassador three times at the Residence. On each of those evenings, as it happened, I was out with Yolande. By the time I returned to the embassy Brad, presumably, had left. No calls came from Mariana that week for impromptu night meetings in the study, and when I saw her in the Chancery she merely mentioned that Brad had spent the evening. Obviously they couldn't be seen in public together, because of the Marseille incident. Newspaper gossip about the ambassador's personal relationships had mercifully died down, and she knew how important it was to avoid reviving it. Most of all, she hoped Cristy's name could be kept clear of any scandal.

I was now able to reassure her about that, at least for the moment.

Yolande provided the information over châteaubriants *chez* Allard, but I waited until our morning conference to pass it along.

"I have some news about Cristy, Mariana."

She drew a quick breath, put down the papers she was holding, and looked at me. "Is she all right?"

"She's all right. The boy's name is Yves Lannuc. He's a Breton. Cristy has been in Brittany with him recently. They're probably still there."

"Visiting his family?"

I shook my head. "Apparently he's not on very good terms with his family. According to one of their friends, Yves rented a couple of bicycles and they left together on a trip. Sleeping in tent hostels, I suppose."

"But what about her classes?"

"In recess. So at least she's not in trouble with the school. Incidentally, Yolande said there's no indication the Lannuc crowd is on hard drugs."

There was more. On leaving the embassy Cristy had moved in with Yves in a hotel somewhere in the Quarter. Yolande couldn't find out just where and didn't want to appear too curious. Young Lannuc was indeed active in student underground politics, as I'd suspected, formerly in the Breton independence campaign, now leading a small group with the somewhat menacing name of Guerre des Jeunes—aims hazy, but heavily radical. There seemed to be no broad general university movement at present, nothing like the revolutionary fervor that led to the violence of '68, possibly in part because student activists were divided into so many splinter factions, all of them in disagreement, some, incidentally, with mysterious sources of financial support. Quite a few girl students were participating, but Yolande had remarked skeptically she was sure most of them were in it because they were in love with the boys.

"That may or may not be true of Cristy," Mariana said. "A flair for politics seems to run in the family, although I can't say she showed any signs of it before she came to Paris. She's still awfully young. That's what I'm afraid of most of all."

I was remembering the last occasion I'd seen Cristy, marching defiantly down the Residence staircase with Yves Lannuc during the July Fourth party and spraying scorn on the people around her. "I wouldn't worry, Mariana. She's become a remarkably self-possessed person in a very short time."

"Too short, Tyler. And I don't like her getting involved with a bunch of young political fanatics. Brad says the Maoist group over there is really dangerous. Brad's researching the Sorbonne for a documentary, you know. He'll be interested to hear what Yolande told you. Incidentally," she added lightly, "if you two can tear yourselves away from each other for a couple of hours, when are we going to have that dinner for four?"

"Any time you feel you can tear yourself away from Mr. Lindley, ma'am."

She laughed, but I'd sounded spiteful and shouldn't have said it. I also realized I'd been subconsciously resisting the dinner idea since Mariana first brought it up. I wished I could be sure why I felt like this.

The one thing I did know was that for the first time in my life I was deeply concerned with two women in the same way.

I hadn't thought much about my relationship with Mariana these first times with Yolande again. That week after the fashion show party I hardly saw the ambassador outside the Chancery, and for good reason—I was with Yolande as often as she could pry herself away from her job. French working hours being what they are in her field, she was rarely free until eight or later, and this being the climax of her current season she looked harassed and tired by the time we met. I was satisfied just to be with her, and to help her relax. At least the American buyers had vanished, so we could have dinner together when she got away from her bosses.

She had a small, delightfully furnished apartment in the Rue de Bellechasse and after she'd freshened up we breezed out to dine at one or another of her favorite restaurants. She was especially fond of the Méditerranée terrace, which occupies one of the loveliest sites in Paris on the Place de l'Odéon and is moderately priced (comparatively speaking). It distressed her that we couldn't do these places on expense account, like the buyers, and another night I had to beg her to let me take her to the Vert Galant on the Cité, which is much more expensive. But once there she succumbed to the magic of the outdoor setting, the Seine flowing silently nearby, the noble lines of the Pont Neuf blurring in the gathering dark.

By contrast to the torrent of talk at our first meeting, we spoke little on these occasions. She seemed to want it this way, and I took the cue that was never put into words. It was as if she were telling me with her eyes that words, between us, were not necessary. Somehow this brought me closer to knowing Yolande again than any words could have done, and I knew I was right when more than once she reached for my hand with both her hands and held it on her lap under the table in silence. Her dresses were very thin and her body was very near, but there were no entreaties.

And later, saying good night at her door, the smiling cousin's kiss on both cheeks, no more than that, was part of the same unspoken understanding.

Walking home across Paris after leaving Yolande one night, I thought suddenly of Connie, back in Washington. For all Connie's loyal affection and sweet generosity, the American girl seemed now as far in the past as someone I'd known in a previous incarnation.

I resolved then and there to write her a letter, but I knew I'd never get to it.

It wasn't until the weekend that Yolande's remembered self revived and reappeared. We were off to Barbizon, where we'd spent some memorable days in the long ago. Driving southward in brilliant sunshine toward Fontainebleau Forest, we reminisced amid bursts of laughter and abrupt, nostalgic pauses.

"Do you remember our breakfasts on the little balcony of the Bonsort, Tyler? No more Bonsort, *hélas!*"

"What d'you suppose they did with that wonderful bathtub? Biggest bathtub I ever saw."

"There was never a bathtub."

"Yolande, how can you *say* it? After what went on in that tub."

"I deny it. I deny everything."

"Come on! The day we took off our clothes and ran around naked in the forest?"

"It was not me, Tyler. You remember some other girl."

"There was no other girl and you know it."

She said after a moment, "Naturally you have told all these things to Mme. Otis."

"Naturally I have not."

It occurred to me this was the first time in a week either of us had mentioned Mariana.

"And also you have told your friend Brad Lindley."

"He's not my friend, *chérie*. He's the ambassador's friend."

"Ah! So now we know at last who is the ambassador's friend!"

I almost told her about surprising them together in the Residence hallway, but if we had our private business, they had a right to theirs. I said instead, "Incidentally, Mariana wants us to come to dinner with her and Brad."

She was obviously delighted. "Just the four?"

"Yes. Are you sure you want to do it?"

Her swift glance away from the wheel. "Why not, Tyler? Don't you?"

"Don't be silly. Of course I do."

But she knew I'd hesitated.

Sometimes I wish women weren't so keen.

Jean-Paul, thrilled by the unusual intimacy of the occasion, provided what he called a *menu classique français*. We sat at a round table. With our cold *velouté de blé vert* we were served a Sercial Madeira, the *crevettes en gelée* were accompanied by a perfectly chilled Meursault-Genevrières, the chef himself came from his kitchen to supervise the serving of the *fricassée de coquelets* (a gesture of obeisance, he explained, somewhat irrelevantly, to the state of Maryland) and to watch Maurice pour the *Mouton*-Rothschild '61 with an expression of almost mock solemnity he hoped was not lost on the ambassador (it wasn't)—all this crowned with a sumptuous *poire cardinal* escorted by a Blanc de Blancs d'Avize and followed by *prunelle d'Alsace*, to even things out with the Burgundy and Bordeaux.

Mariana had decreed no dressing up for the men but she and Yolande were both in long dinner gowns. Candles and flowers from the garden graced the table. I'd never seen the upstairs dining room look so attractive, nor the ambassador herself seemingly so carefree. Tonight she would forget about Cristy, about Stoneface, Spaulding, and company! Actually it was the first time I'd been at table with her in such familial surroundings—facing her directly, in fact, while Yolande faced Lindley. The arrangement obviated placing either Brad or Tyler on the ambassador's right, and as there were no place cards I wondered whether she'd thought of it or if Maurice, who thinks of everything, had just seated us that way.

I doubt if Brad Lindley even noticed this little nicety, since by the third wine he was taking over the party anyway. There was a subtle change in his attitude toward Mariana, as well there might have been. But was he even aware of it? Yolande, of course, was perfectly aware of it, and cast an amused glance in my direction once or twice when he took it upon himself to instruct his hostess in the ways of the world.

Mariana herself seemed pleased to be bossed a little. Maybe she wanted to feel like a wife tonight, just for a change. And I thought of Marcus Feld, another take-charge personality. She'd been Feld's mistress, no question of that, and she'd implied there were other men, too. Had it really surprised me? *I'm not a nun*, as she'd put it. Even with Yolande present, I felt again the little pang of jealous desire. If, that night in Dijon, at the door of her room in the Chapeau Rouge, I'd insisted . . .

Brad Lindley would have, of course. It was something his kind of man did instinctively. It was the way to win. I watched him now, listened to him expatiating on the Sorbonne student body to Yolande, contrasting Paris with the American scene, booming along to Kent State, to the attitude of the black student in the South—and I envied Brad Lindley his cocksure confidence, his easy command. By dessert time he was talking more to Yolande than to the ambassador, affectionately, almost possessively, but if Mariana felt neglected she gave no sign. Once she raised her little liqueur glass to me as if in toast, and her eyes followed through, serene and indulgent as her smile. I was sure they were saying, let the boy chatter, he loves it, he does it well.

Yolande was playing the good listener. She did that well, too. She had taste, tact, and intelligence to go with her beautiful manners and her stunning looks, and the unmistakable European poise that set her apart even from Mariana. Small wonder Brad was centering his attention on her. And I could sense there was more to it than that—the intensely competitive Mr. Lindley was also challenging me, as he was accustomed to challenge any male he found with a desirable female. This was as much a part of him as the authoritative voice, the consciously engaging grin. He just couldn't help it. He was made that way. But like Mariana, I felt no uneasiness about my partner. There was a moment toward the end of dinner, lulled by great food and wine, when I felt all four of us were attuned to a harmony we might never recapture. For even perfection has its flaw—so delicate a balance couldn't hold. There had to be trouble ahead for this relationship.

Or at the least, confusion. Naturally enough, Brad and Yolande departed together. But *of course* she would drop him off on her way home! Nothing was more logical, since the red Renault awaited her and he had no car. That left Mariana and me standing just a little unsteadily side by side at the top of the staircase, merrily calling good night like a husband and wife to our guests for the evening. Suddenly the roles were reversed. I was both sorry and glad.

Was the ambassador feeling something of the same thing? On our way to our separate apartments, still playing the part, she took my arm comfortably and said, "Snuffy and Abigail will be back from Biarritz tomorrow. I'll be under surveillance again, and I need your help."

I smiled. "Is it that bad?"

"It's Mme. Hanotte. I want you to have a little conspiracy with me, Tyler."

"Command me."

"In future Brad will be coming to the Residence occasionally, quite late in the evening, as your guest. Dates and times can be arranged at your mutual convenience. You can take him to the study and, after a few minutes, leave him there. On his way out, if there's a light under your door, he'll stop in for a moment to say good night. But there's no need to wait up for him."

She paused. We had stopped outside my door. Then she said, "Will you do that, Tyler? For us?"

I said after a moment, "Of course," and that was all.

But I couldn't sleep. I lay there in the dark, thinking about Mariana and Yolande, first one, then the other. The wine still sang in my head and my brain felt fuzzy. Only my emotions were clear and strong. And I knew I didn't want to think about Brad Lindley. Several times I tossed over on my other side, trying physically to keep him out of my mind. But I couldn't keep out the image of Mariana in his arms as I'd seen them together in the hallway the night of the fashion party.

And tonight he'd left with Yolande. But did they go straight home or was he still with her? Were they smiling at each other over a table at Fouquet's right now? Or dancing in some night-club? Worse, had she stopped off at his place for another drink? Or invited him up to her apartment for a nightcap?

Was I so sure of Yolande, after all?

There was only one way to make certain.

I swayed a little getting back into my clothes. I was sweating. If I wasn't drunk I was very near it. Who wouldn't be, after what we'd had tonight? If the ambassador hadn't been off the beam herself, would she have so calmly proposed her "little conspiracy" to me? And Brad Lindley, red-faced, was talking semi-nonsense and laughing too much in the salon after dinner. Of all of us, only my French girl was in full control, watching us with amused detachment, the bibulous Americans, half-civilized as usual! Not much better than her buyers, after all.

The guard gave me a sleepy nod as I left the embassy and turned right along the Faubourg St. Honoré. There was a night taxi stand on the Rue Royale but my luck was better than that—I caught a cab almost immediately and gave him Yolande's address in the Rue de Bellechasse. The driver was either drunker than I was or even more anxious to get there, taking crazy turns around the Concorde and hitting the bridge at about sixty. The man wasn't to be believed—until I got a look at his parchment face under the faded old beret and heard him mumbling in his beard. He wasn't drunk, he was just Russian—must have been one of the very last of the World War I refugees who once made up half the cabdriver population of Paris.

Nothing to do now but pray, so I pulled down both windows, closed my eyes, and prayed. The night air laved my face like a refreshing damp cloth. By the time we drew up with a lurch before the house I was feeling more sober and sighing with relief that I was still in one piece.

Two, three, four times I had to pull the old-fashioned bell before the concierge woke up and released the door. I could hear her grumbling somewhere in the black recesses of her loge as I went past, my footsteps muffled on the carpeted stairs. At the second landing I stopped, caught my breath, and knocked cautiously. No response. Again I knocked, but there was only silence within and the feeling like dread returned.

I was also beginning slowly to realize that in the morning my behavior was going to look pretty silly in retrospect if I woke her out of a sound sleep.

I just might not mention this to Yolande at all.

For another two or three minutes I waited and listened. No sound. I was turning away to go back down the stairs when Yolande said softly through the door, "Tyler?"

I jumped. "That's right."

The heavy bolt slid back and the door opened. I could very faintly see her, a dim white wraith in the dark.

"I'm sorry, Yolande. I just—."

She put warm bare arms around me and spoke in half a whisper. "I knew that you would come," she said.

14

F OR THE FIRST time Stuyvesant Spaulding had yielded far enough to anxiety to question me about activities in the Residence. He invited me to observe one of his staff efficiency meetings and I was slightly startled when he asked me to stay afterward.

His effort to maintain the casual approach was obvious.

"Well!"—this spoken with a genial smile as he resumed his position behind his desk and I sat on the big leather chair reserved for his high-level colleagues. "Well, Tyler, it's nice to have a moment to chat without a lot of people around, don't you think?"

I said I thought. And wondered uneasily to myself what would come next.

"As a matter of fact this sort of contact between us is salutary on both sides. That should have been evident when you first arrived." Again the affable smile. "I'm afraid it's my fault, Tyler. Just plain too many other things to attend to. Fortunately the pace will be a bit easier for a while now."

I murmured that I knew how busy he'd been.

"Perhaps you felt—and I certainly wouldn't blame you—that I might not be too warmly receptive to the ideas of a younger officer. Or that your special relationship to the ambassador put you in a rather awkward position vis-à-vis the deputy chief."

Stuffy Snuffy. I wanted to smile. I protested instead that no such thought had entered my head at any time.

"I'm very pleased to hear it. Because you know, Tyler, I'm always very sympathetic to the problems of *all* the staff, right down the line, whenever they may arise."

I told him I was sure of that, and that if I'd had any problems I would have consulted him about them.

He nodded cordially. "Then all goes well with you? I shouldn't want you to feel the need for advice from persons, shall we say, outside the embassy cadres."

I agreed: that would never do. And suddenly I saw the light—news of Yolande was getting around.

Right on the nose. He said, "I know your assignments with the ambassador keep you pretty fully occupied, but still, I hope you've been able to enjoy some pleasant social relationships during the current lull." Again I anticipated him, and almost laughed when he actually said it: "All work and no play makes Tyler a very dull boy, eh? Of course," he went on, "it's advisable to show a modicum of care in selecting one's companions. For instance, I've learned the hard way to be cautious in what I say to the news people."

So it wasn't Yolande and me—it was Brad Lindley and Mariana! I should have spotted that right away. I looked at him innocently and said, "The only contact I've made in that area is the TV correspondent Brad Lindley, sir. We have dinner occasionally *chez* Lipp, and sometimes I ask him back for a drink in my apartment. Beasley Turner is a Lindley fan. Beasley introduced us."

I couldn't resist the little Turner shot, but all I got was a bland smile and a murmured "Oh, really?"

This had to be Turner gossiping to him, and maybe quizzing Mme. Hanotte. Or had Washington suggested he inquire a bit? Anyway I said, just as if it were the gospel truth, "Brad Lindley seems to be chiefly interested in major league baseball. At least that's what we talk about most of the time. Naturally I wouldn't think of discussing embassy matters with him."

"Naturally."

How easy it is to lie, once you get the habit! He was waiting for me to say more, maybe expecting a vignette of that dinner party for four? But I wasn't about to oblige him, and after we politely exchanged a few remarks about my parents I was excused with a final reminder to come to the deputy chief if I felt perplexed about anything at all.

I promised, but had the feeling I left the deputy chief somewhat disappointed in me, behind his mask of cordiality, for not coming across with more substance.

I did make sure to tell Mariana, that same afternoon. She held off another appointment while she listened with keen attention. Like me, she figured it was a combination of Mme. Hanotte and Beasley Turner, and in any case not to be taken seriously. Then she dismissed me with that warm, relaxed smile I'd seen so often since the three of us began to act out our little scenario at the Residence.

Lucky for me this period had coincided with the new happy state of affairs in the Rue de Bellechasse. Being deeply, intimately involved as I now was with Yolande made it easier to keep that painful subject out of my mind. It was also helpful to look at it from the impersonal point of view. There was a definite comic opera flavor to the business of solemnly arranging for Brad Lindley to conduct his romance amid the stately surroundings of the ambassador's official domicile under cover of discussing major league baseball with me. Especially on nights I was waiting to hurry out right after he arrived so I could join Yolande, not to return to the Residence until the next evening. It was just a little like those swinging bedroom door plays the French are so good at.

I didn't reveal the conspiracy to Yolande, though. In fact we hadn't seriously discussed either Brad or Mariana since the night of the dinner party. Was Yolande avoiding the subject, as well as I? Whatever her reasons, she didn't ask further questions about Lindley's relations with the ambassador, and I forbore to ask Yolande whether he made a pass at her after they left the embassy together.

But I wouldn't have bet he didn't.

Stuyvesant Spaulding's unexpected overtures decided me it was time to send my next report to the undersecretary. If Washington indeed had suggested that Spaulding look into recent doings at the Residence, including my relations with Brad Lindley, either Stoneface was becoming inordinately suspicious of the Paris mission or Remington was double-checking on his confidential informant. At any rate I thought it best to surface again, as I'd written nothing since before the ambassador's fashion party.

That event was as good a takeoff point as any. I noted the favorable publicity it had received not only in France but in the American press, and said it had also served to cement the ambassador's relations with a highly influential section of the French establishment. One must not underestimate the importance these people attach to the influence of France as world leader in fashion, I pointed out. They are as proud of it as they are of their wine, their cuisine, and other symbols of civilized progress evocative of French culture.

I also noted that the ambassador was still showing considerable concern over the bugging of the Residence, particularly as we had heard nothing from the French secret police since they launched their investigation. It was clear she had no intention of letting this matter drop and was determined to discover the culprit. As the department had doubtless already been informed, I remarked, inquiries by Messrs. Spaulding and Hobbs had run into a blank wall. (This, just in case these two gentlemen had found it expedient to paint a more optimistic picture for Washington.)

The ambassador's daughter, I reported, seemed happy in her more independent life at the Sorbonne, was enjoying new friendships among the student body, and had no plans to move back to the Residence at any early date. I made no mention of Yves Lannuc or the political angle, although it occurred to me after I'd mailed my report that one of these days Brad Lindley's documentary on the student underground movement would appear on TV and just might start Remington wondering about Cristy Otis again.

What to say about Lindley, if anything, was a problem. With Spaulding sniffing around, not mentioning Brad at all in my report might seem odd. I finally decided to refer to him in passing as the most knowledgeable American correspondent in Europe whom I (and only indirectly the ambassador) was cultivating as a source of valuable background information on the French political scene. It seemed important to make it clear that we were using Lindley, not Lindley us.

As to my own personal life, I'd be damned if I was going to introduce Yolande into these shady communications to the undersecretary, just as I was keeping her out of the comic opera plot at the Residence. She was one person utterly uninvolved with the embassy and I intended to keep it that way. Our own story was my property—mine and hers, and not to be affected by official obligations. The most beautiful thing about it was our total lack of responsibility to anyone but ourselves.

And while it lasted, it was a lovely time—a release, at least for Yolande and me, of something in both of us neither had expected ever to experience again, let alone share with each other. A time that belongs to youth, lucky and selfish and careless, consumed by each day's simple joy, heedless of tomorrow. And we had recaptured it, in the same incomparable setting where it was born.

Youth, yes, but children no longer. I'd returned from France after that earlier time with Yolande persuaded that I'd won my spurs in sex, a self-satisfied bachelor come to maturity who believed in his smug Anglo-Saxon fashion that the affair with Connie, for instance, was where the thing began and ended. Now I saw that Connie and I were kids playing with matches compared to the sexual bonfire of this new relationship with a Yolande grown from child into woman. I didn't know how much she'd been taught by other men (her husband's pictures looked placid enough) and I didn't raise the question. I only knew she was teaching *me*, so gently, sweetly, masterfully that at first I marveled unsuspecting at my own new powers.

But it was she who led, in deep and subtle consummations, who guided us together toward countries never on any map of mine.

How can you lose yourself and still find the way? Yolande knew. Even in blindness her eyes could hold my face.

The hardest thing was keeping it secret. I couldn't altogether hide this feeling that threatened sometimes to bubble over in sheer exuberance, but I somehow managed to control it during working hours, although there were moments at Mariana's desk when suddenly she would look up at me with so much understanding I had to turn away, resisting an urge to drop everything we were doing and just talk to her. It wasn't a sense of duty to our official relationship that held me back, of course. It was Brad Lindley, who stood now between us.

It was also Brad Lindley who brought to the ambassador the single kernel of gossip from the Quai d'Orsay that within a few days was to explode through the protective husk of the French political organism and provide this country with a full-blown international incident.

It sounded harmless enough—more like a brief and trivial outburst of ill-feeling than the precursor of a cabinet crisis that in the end would gravely involve the United States ambassador as well as Brad Lindley himself. The rumor was, according to one of Lindley's "impeccable sources," that an unannounced and stormy meeting of government ministers presided over by Auguste Nicollet had culminated in an act of physical violence more suited to the ways of nineteenth-century duelists than to the suave maneuvering of contemporary politics.

In a word, Foreign Minister Claude Courtailles had risen from the conference table in the heat of argument and slapped his Premier in the face.

Lindley was cautious. He wasn't about to risk expulsion from France by putting a story like this on the air until he had official confirmation. He didn't have to wait long. Within twenty-four hours Courtailles himself confirmed the fact to Agence France-Presse, and Nicollet declined to deny it.

But that was all. Neither man would say what the argument was about. Reportedly on strict orders from the Elysée palace, total secrecy was immediately clamped down. All editorial speculation about the Cabinet's discussion was discouraged. The other ministers present at the incident refused to throw further light on it. The diplomatic corps was agog—and baffled. And Brad Lindley found his impeccable sources suddenly silent.

As it happened, I'd been in the ambassador's office when Brad telephoned her with the original rumor. The following afternoon, when it was clear no more information could be obtained, Mariana called me back to her desk.

She was holding an envelope, her personal stationery. Her smile was taut. She said, "Tyler, do you remember the Foreign Minister's private invitation to me to dine with him at home?"

"I certainly do."

"I've decided to accept it. Tonight, after dark, I want you to take this note to the Île St. Louis and make sure it gets into his hands."

"I'll do my best."

I could have added I was used to toting confidential letters after dark.

"Something big is going on, Tyler. I intend to find out what it is. Claude Courtailles won't tell anybody else, but I have a hunch, given the right circumstances, I can get him to tell me."

"I'm sure you can. I think it's a great idea."

"Give the credit to Brad. He just called me."

"All right. I'll give the credit to Brad."

I took the letter, perhaps a little abruptly, and started back to my office. At the door Mariana spoke again.

"Tyler—. One more thing."

"Yes, ma'am?" I turned.

Her look had softened. Now her smile was almost wistful. "How is Yolande?"

"Oh. In top form. I'll tell her you asked."

The ambassador sighed. "Haven't we all had a beautiful vacation?" she said. "But I guess it's time to get back to the job."

With the lid on by order of the President, the slapping episode quickly died out of the French press. Even the satiric weeklies kept their hands off, although *Le Canard Enchaîné* made some very funny allusions by double entendre to a duel at dawn on the Champ de Mars. But nobody believed the story was over. The long-rumored smoldering enmity between Nicollet and Courtailles was now dramatically confirmed, and while there was no immediate consequence evident, the expectation was it wouldn't be long in coming.

One thing was sure—there would be no duel.

As an experienced cloak-and-dagger man in the service of Mitchell Remington, I tried to anticipate all possible obstacles to delivering the ambassador's letter. It turned out to be a breeze. The Quai d'Anjou was a placid poem in the summer night. No secret policeman, not even an ordinary cop, was on hand to block my entrance. I felt a distinct letdown. The traditional concierge grumpily waved me on upstairs, and none other than Blaise d'Archeval opened the salon door to me.

For once Blaise was not his smiling self. He looked a trifle nervous and definitely unhappy. I didn't see Courtailles, but I knew he was nearby because I heard his voice raised querulously in the background. Tonight there was no pleasant chatting with the count. He didn't even entrust me with a graceful compliment for the ambassador. He simply looked at the envelope, gave me a somber nod, and we wished each other a polite good night.

It was a house of gloom, and going back down the stairs, on my way now to the Rue de Bellechasse, I felt doubt that in this atmosphere Courtailles would be in a mood to entertain a lady for dinner.

I was wrong. Shortly after noon next day Mariana summoned me to her desk, a gleam of excitement in her eyes. Count d'Archeval had just called to ask if tomorrow evening would be satisfactory.

"I hope he was more cheerful than he looked last night," I said.

"He was charming as always, Tyler. But he sounded as if he were in a public phone booth somewhere."

"That's logical. Right now they'd have to be very hush-hush."

"So will we. I've decided not to tell Spaulding."

"That's wise. He'd hit the ceiling."

"Blaise suggested I come in a taxi rather than an embassy car. I'll be the Foreign Minister's only guest. And he warned me not to expect an elaborate menu."

"What, no Lafite '61?"

She laughed with elation in her voice. "If there isn't, I'm going to demand it!" Then serious again, "I have a feeling Claude Courtailles wants to unburden himself, Tyler."

"I'll keep my fingers crossed."

She paused a moment. "You haven't told Yolande about any of this?"

"I haven't told anybody."

"I'd like to talk to Brad after I come back tomorrow night. Would you ask him to drop in to see you, late? I can join you both in the study."

"It shall be done."

That meant breaking up my evening with Yolande again, but we could have dinner together and I'd rejoin her later. I felt disappointed that the ambassador had even considered I might talk out of turn to Yolande. At the same time I resented the inference that Yolande was not to be trusted. For that matter, was Brad Lindley to be trusted? But if I doubted it, I wouldn't take it upon myself to say so to Mariana.

Back in my own office I thought about him for a moment. I knew two Brad Lindleys. The man on the air I admired. The lover of Mariana Otis I could never like.

Then I picked up the phone, called his office, and issued the usual cordial invitation.

"You're a good man, Paine!"

"I'll have the baseball scores," I said, and hung up.

It was more difficult to interrupt my evening with Yolande than I'd expected. She had a surprise for me—for the first time she gave me dinner at her apartment. Up to now the only meal we'd taken there together was breakfast.

She heard my key in the lock and hurried out to greet me, adorably flushed from her labors in the tiny kitchen and wearing an apron.

"But the apron's in back instead of in front," I pointed out.

"*Chéri*, that is intentional. It means I am receptive."

She surveyed me calmly while I broke up. When I was mostly recovered she said, "I don't object to you laughing at me, Tyler. This is the first time I have heard you laugh in three days, do you know that? Something is worrying you. Can you tell me what it is?"

"It's nothing, Yolande."

"Is it me?"

"How could it be? You're an angel."

She shrugged. "Very well, lie. Perhaps you are obliged to lie. It is something at the embassy."

"Really, I'm not worried about a thing. I've never been happier in my life. Believe me, if I could make a deal to stay as happy as I am at this moment I think I'd sell my soul, Yolande."

"*L'affaire Nicollet-Courtailles?*" she said.

"How could that worry me? I know nothing about it. You probably know more about it than I do."

"I know only what I hear at the Chambre Syndicale."

"And that is?"

"Nicollet is a conceited ass. Courtailles is a clown. Who cares? They deserve each other."

"Is that all?"

The shrug again. "What does Mr. Brad Lindley say? He knows everything, does he not? He knows more about the French Government than the French Government."

"They say that at the Chambre Syndicale?"

"*I* say that." Suddenly she shrieked. "My oven!"

She ran back into the kitchen to save the dinner. It turned out to be well worth saving. Her own version of steak Diane, perfectly timed *pommes frites*, fresh flageolets, a Tavel like the breath of spring reborn, and *fraises de bois* with yellow, thick Normandy cream.

"We should do this more often, Yolande," I said over the demitasse, and saw a flash of the urchin grin of long ago.

"Many things we should do more often, *chéri.*"

"You and that apron are making it very tough for me to say I have to go back to the embassy for a little while."

She made a face, not in the least surprised. "You see?"

"I'll be gone a very, very short time. Will you wait for me?"

"No. Mariana is waiting. She is in love with you."

"I won't even see Mariana. I'll be working in the code room."

"Ah, the code room! You see?"

At the door I patted the apron tenderly and asked the wearer to forgive my shortcomings.

The wearer agreed with some reluctance to think about it.

It was raining lightly in the street and a pale mist was sifting down over the river. I wondered if that other little dinner party on the Quai d'Anjou had also ended, and what the host had said.

15

THERE WAS JUST time to put a drink in Brad Lindley's hands and walk with him to the study before Mariana returned to the Residence. She was a little pale and a little out of breath. As she came into the room in her long black strapless dinner dress, her shoulders gleaming white, her hair piled high, I thought she looked like one of those Sargent portraits of a turn-of-the-century Boston beauty.

Brad had a cigarette all ready for her. I watched them smile their special greeting to each other, wife and husband again. I said, "If that's all, ma'am—."

"Tyler!" She spoke sharply and I turned back at the door. "Where are you going? I'll need you here."

"Oh. Sorry." I came back and took a seat at my desk. Lindley's look of surprise amused me. This wasn't the usual way we did it, but then I guess tonight was something else again.

For a moment nobody said anything more. I knew Mariana was still collecting her thoughts. Then Brad spoke. "Well, my dear, how did it go?"

"Outwardly, just what you would expect. The setting very eighteenth-century. The house is full of books. Toward the end of dinner—I think it was the best dinner I've had since I came to France—Claude read me three of his poems."

She looked at me and smiled. "Yes, Tyler, true to his word, he did serve the Lafite '61. I wished you were there to share it with us. Claude still has six bottles left, so he must be hoarding it."

Brad stirred a little impatiently in his chair. "How is he reacting to the Nicollet business?"

"I'd never have known he was disturbed about anything, until after we went into the salon for coffee. Up until that moment he was just the way Tyler and I saw him the day we arrived at Le Havre—courtly, genial, amusing, touching on every subject under the sun except politics. And of course that witty way of complaining about everything, from his concierge's manners to Rimbaud's behavior toward Verlaine. What an education the man is!"

She paused. "Count d'Archeval was nowhere to be seen, by the way. Claude didn't mention him at all. I asked about him, and the way he brushed aside the question made me feel, I don't know why, that there's been some kind of row there. Of course I could be quite mistaken. But d'Archeval had seemed so faithful, somehow. And Claude seemed so fond of him—just my impression that first day, of course." Mariana looked at me. "After all, he did call me only yesterday to fix the date for dinner. And Tyler saw him at the house only the day before."

"He didn't look very happy, ma'am."

Brad cut in. "The hell with the count. I want to hear what Courtailles said to you after dinner."

The ambassador didn't continue immediately. When she resumed she was looking at Lindley. She spoke very quietly and firmly.

"That," she said, "must be reserved for the dispatch I am sending in code to the Secretary of State tonight, eyes only."

He stared. She was refusing to tell him what he wanted to know and he was having difficulty comprehending it. I waited. Mariana was waiting too. Finally he said, "Is this teasing? If so, I don't like it. You never would have thought of going to Courtailles if I hadn't given you the idea! And now you—."

He almost spluttered, then stopped. He still couldn't believe it. The ambassador said softly, "Brad dear, surely you appreciate this is a matter of confidentiality. Much as I might want to share everything I know with you, there are some official matters outside my personal control. Please understand."

"You don't trust me. After what I've done to help you—."

"Of course I trust you. But in this case I've given assurance that what was said between the Foreign Minister and myself will remain undisclosed except to the highest department level in Washington. He spoke to me on that basis only. Would you ask me to break my word?"

But he had stood up. He was really angry. For a moment his eyes went to me in a look very close to rage. Then he said, "Have fun!" and turned and left.

In the long silence the ambassador stared at the door he had shut behind him. The harsh echo of his words still lingered in the room. At last she reached impassively for her evening bag and took out a tiny leather notebook.

"I jotted down some reminders in the taxi, Tyler. I'll dictate the first draft to you."

PARIS

EMERGENCY

SEC STATE
WASHINGTON

HAVE JUST COMPLETED LONG DISCUSSION WITH COURTAILLES OCCASIONED BY SLAPPING INCIDENT. ALTHOUGH SOME ELEMENTS OF SITUATION STILL MURKY AM CONVINCED VERACITY HIS STATEMENTS WHICH JUSTIFY YOUR PERSONAL CONSIDERATION UTMOST URGENCY. FRENCH CABINET DISCUSSION WHICH PRECIPITATED FISTICUFFS INVOLVED POSSIBILITY FUNDAMENTAL CHANGE FRANCES POLICY TOWARD NATO ALLIANCE AND FUTURE OF EUROPEAN SECURITY. ACCORDING COURTAILLES NICOLLET IS BACKING PLAN FOR DISSOLUTION NATO AND WITHDRAWAL ALL US FORCES FROM EUROPE TOGETHER WITH NUCLEAR ARSENAL. USSR WOULD ORDER RECIPROCAL DISSOLUTION WARSAW PACT AND WITHDRAWAL ALL SOVIET FORCES FROM EASTERN EUROPE. COURTAILLES BELIEVES MOSCOW SECRETLY GAVE PLEDGE NICOLLET DURING RECENT VISIT SUPPORT JOINT FRENCH WEST GERMAN PUBLIC DECLARATION THIS EFFECT WHILE DOUBLE–TALKING WASHINGTON. ANGRY EXCHANGE AT

CABINET MEETING RESULTED FROM COURTAILLES
CHARGE THAT NICOLLET BETRAYING FRENCH
INTERESTS AND AMERICAN FRIENDSHIP WITH
NICOLLET TAUNTING COURTAILLES AS QUOTE SU-
PERANNUATED VOLUPTUARY UNQUOTE. CABINET
APPARENTLY DIVIDED ON PROPOSALS AND AS OF TO-
NIGHT ISSUE UNRESOLVED BUT COURTAILLES
BELIEVES BLOWUP INEVITABLE SOON WITH CONSE-
QUENT PUBLIC DISCLOSURES. YOUR PARIS EMBASSY
AWAITS COMMENT AND INSTRUCTIONS.

OTIS

I didn't get back to the Rue de Bellechasse. By the time I was
free to phone Yolande I was sure she'd be asleep by now. But after returning to the Residence from the code room I thought it
would be wiser to call anyway.

I was glad I did. In a voice softly husky with sleep she forgave
me for waking her up, then accepted without questions my necessarily vague explanation of why I couldn't make it back and why
it was essential for me to be on hand very early in case I was
needed.

I apologized again for spoiling our evening. "Dinner tonight,
chérie?"

"I can't wait," she said. "You were sweet to call."

That made me feel a whole lot better, but I wasn't ready
to sleep myself, and no wonder. Tormenting questions kept me
awake. At the very least, assuming Claude Courtailles's story was
accurate, big things were going on behind the scenes—some of
them almost mind-boggling. Reciprocal dissolution of NATO and
the Warsaw Pact. Withdrawal of all American and Soviet forces
in Europe within the borders of their own countries. Removal of
U.S. nuclear weapons from Europe. The possibilities in all this
for international political change were staggering.

Certainly these proposals, if they came into being, would fatally
divide the Right and Left not only here in France but throughout
the Western alliance. The Right would fear Soviet treachery and
loss of the NATO shield. The Left would shout good riddance to

NATO and embrace the Communists. And the moderates, as usual, would face the agonizing dilemma of making up their minds on the central point: whether to trust Moscow and solder détente with an ironclad mutual pledge.

But the Foreign Minister's story might be looked at another way—could he be trying to smoke out Washington's current intentions by inventing a critical situation and tearfully laying it before the lady ambassador? If so, she'd taken the bait. Or was Courtailles merely trying to use Mariana to further his own cryptic purposes in his internal political feud with Nicollet? And where did the French President stand on the issue?

Most important of all, where did my own President stand? What had his Secretary of State been up to, in his shifty, secretive fashion, since the new administration took over? How well aware was the White House of what Stoneface was doing, with its grave implications for the American future? Was there any suspicion in Congress, especially Bryce Halsted, that revolutionary changes might be in the offing?

And what about the Kremlin's secret pledge, according to Courtailles, to double-deal with the French and West Germans by approving their "independent" declaration while negotiating toward the same end with Stoneface? Would this be disturbing news to the Secretary?

We should know something more in the morning, when almost certainly there would be a response from Washington to the ambassador's message.

Meanwhile there was the question of Brad Lindley.

I'd never seen him so upset as when he stormed out of the study, furious at having been excluded by the ambassador. And that baleful glare at me as he departed . . . there was something ominous in his frustration, a look of revenge, as though any of this were my doing! The ambassador, quite the opposite, serenely kept her cool. She might have been dismissing an embassy clerk from the room. But now Brad Lindley was more than an inquisitive newsman to her, he was her lover, and to Brad Lindley she was no longer the ambassador, she was Mariana, to be possessed.

But she'd put him totally out of her mind as she drafted her radio message. She was all concentration. And she said nothing to me about Brad as I left her to walk to the Chancery with her report to Washington. Maybe this had just been a typical scene from their intimate life together. For all I knew these spats were common between them and he'd get over it quickly to reappear in twenty-four hours as his bluff and casual self.

But somehow I doubted this time it would pass so easily.

The extraordinary thing about the Chancery when I arrived for work in the morning was its normal atmosphere of summer calm. Mariana had skipped our usual meeting in the study to get to her office early, and I'd confidently expected to find an outraged Stuyvesant Spaulding standing at her desk upbraiding her for failing to consult him. Instead, when I listened at the door I heard nothing, so I knocked and opened it slightly.

"Come in, Tyler."

Immaculately clad in white linen, she sat behind the big desk with the morning newspapers spread out before her. She motioned me to a nearby chair. "Squat," she said cheerfully, but there was strain and fatigue behind her eyes.

I smiled. "Just thought I'd check in. Can you find anything in the papers? I couldn't."

She shook her head.

"No reply from Washington?"

"Not yet. Unless they've been on the phone with Spaulding, of course."

"You haven't seen him this morning?"

"He hasn't been near me. Which could either mean he hasn't seen my report or he's already talked to Washington."

"He must have seen it. The duty officer—."

Her buzzer interrupted me. "Mr. Spaulding is here," the voice said.

"Have him come in."

I awaited the worst. But today Snuffy wore his smoothest diplomatic smile. To my surprise it included both of us. In fact when I stood up at once to leave the room he said, "That won't be necessary, Tyler," and waved me cordially back to my chair.

"You've seen my report?" the ambassador said.

He nodded. "Interesting."

"Is that the sum total of your reaction?"

He gave the slightest suggestion of a shrug. Plainly he was unwilling to amplify.

"There's been no response from Washington as yet."

He nodded again. "I shouldn't wonder if there won't be," he said.

And I knew then Washington had called him.

Mariana wasn't letting it go at that. "As you must have noticed," she said crisply, "I asked the Secretary for comment and instructions. Are you saying the request will be ignored?"

Once more the faint shrug. "It is a possibility."

"And the situation the Foreign Minister describes—you feel that's only a possibility, too?"

"I would prefer to see the story confirmed in other quarters." He paused and went on without enthusiasm, "At any rate you are to be commended for your initiative, of course. Did you receive Monsieur Courtailles at the Residence?"

"I dined with him last night in his own house."

The instant look of alarm would have been funny in less serious circumstances. Spaulding opened his mouth to speak, then shut it, finally said in a strained voice, "Ah yes."

The ambassador half smiled. "You seem to disapprove, Mr. Spaulding."

"I think it was perhaps a little unwise."

"Damned poor protocol?"

He flushed. "Well, just at this time—."

I listened fascinated. Mariana was going after him now.

"What time? Judging from your reaction to my report, this is a time like any other," she said. "You didn't seem to find the Courtailles story very remarkable."

"I said it just might be true."

"It doesn't seem to have excited Washington. You say yourself the Secretary may not even reply."

"That is only my guess."

"You haven't talked with Mitchell Remington since I sent that message last night? Or with the Secretary himself?"

In the pause he seemed to lose assurance. He said finally, "Yes, the undersecretary called me this morning."

"And you haven't found it necessary to inform this office?"

His voice wobbled a little. "There was actually—. It was not that important."

"What was it about, Mr. Spaulding? Or were you instructed not to tell me?"

The flushed face had gradually gone paler. "Believe me, it was routine business—technical details having to do with Foreign Service rankings, in point of fact."

"And for that the undersecretary called you after midnight Washington time?"

He was silent. Very evidently he'd decided the best course was to say no more.

"May I ask," the ambassador said after a moment, "why you wished to see me just now?"

The deputy chief of mission made a vague gesture. "Just routine matters that can wait for another occasion."

"It wasn't to find out the circumstances of my talk with the Foreign Minister? And to warn me that the Secretary is displeased?"

For a moment the look of exasperated patience returned. "I have tried to make clear from the beginning of your mission," he said, "that it is better for all concerned if you consult with your deputy before undertaking major contacts with French officials. You have seen fit, despite specific admonition from Washington, to continue to do so. In respect to this latest incident your visit to the Foreign Minister's private address might well cause dangerous complications if it should become known. I would certainly have advised you against it."

The ambassador said, "Thank you, Mr. Spaulding. That will be all for the present."

He bowed stiffly and left without looking at me again.

Mariana said only, "Tyler, sooner or later I'm going to get to the bottom of all this, if I have to go to the President of the United States."

Dinner with Yolande. A little place with four tables on the terrace in the Grenelle quarter, Chez Lafon, that we'd become specially attached to. A quiet street, one of the few left in Paris not cluttered with cars day and night. Across the way, under an open skylight on the top floor, a radio playing a *bal musette* tune—the haunting accordion sound that always says so much to me of what I've lived in this city, and now again celebrating the present as it evoked the past. Over all, the blue-gold summer twilight, unmatched anywhere I've been in the world.

At Lafon we sit facing each other, the tables being too small for *côte à côte* dining. "You are tired, poor Tyler," Yolande said.

"Not too tired to eat." I'd consumed an entire platter of charcuterie—truffled Lyon sausage, terrines, confit of duck and goose, much to the proprietor's satisfaction.

Now he poured us more Beaujolais and planted a fat hand on my shoulder. Would we like to sample some fresh peaches in champagne? Yolande was for it. To me, such a dessert will always seem such sinful luxury that I hesitate to accept, like the good puritan I was brought up to be. Of course I ate it, and afterward sat half somnolent over the *filtre*, happy to look at the beautiful young woman opposite. Already the events of last night and this morning had the quality of a dream. International diplomatic issues and top secret political jockeying slowly dissolved in the languorous air, like vast clouds drifting toward a distant sunset, forming momentarily a huge craggy profile of Stuyvesant Spaulding in their changing shapes.

I sighed and smiled. In this mood it was impossible for me to relate to any of it.

Yolande said, "*Now* what are you thinking of?"

"Too hazy to explain, my dear. Must I?"

In answer she put her long fingers over my hand on the table and smiled back at me, ever so slightly shaking her head. I reflected that if there weren't a dozen other reasons, I'd still adore this girl for her discretion. Loving is not having to ask the wrong questions.

"I have almost forgotten to tell you this," she said. "Your Beasley Turner telephoned me to ask a date."

I stirred a little.

"He's not *my* Beasley Turner. You turned him down, of course."

Faintly willful tone. "I said, some other time, dear Beasley."

"You did, did you? So he's dear Beasley."

"Tyler! I have known him a year before you came back to Paris. He's very nice, you will admit that."

"One of your cocktail acquaintances?"

"Where else? He gets around, that boy." She was pleased with her American phrase.

"So do you, I gather."

She laughed. "No more. Really I am a home girl, Tyler."

"Somehow I can't see you in that role."

"Try me out." Her eyes held me, merry, mocking.

"How about tonight?" I said.

Walking slowly back to the Rue de Bellechasse, an arm around her waist, I returned to the subject of Turner.

"I haven't chatted much with dear Beasley lately, Yolande. What did he have to say?"

"Only one odd thing. He asked if I go out now with Brad Lindley." She giggled.

"And do you?"

She leaned swiftly and touched her lips to the side of my head. "I go out with Tyler Paine. Do you know him?"

"Is he the one you wear the apron for?"

"The same one."

"Will you wear it tonight?"

"We will not have time for that," she said.

After that, she spoke only in French. At first she talked to me. Later, I wasn't sure.

16

IT WAS OUR most beautiful night together. If Yolande hadn't had an early appointment at the Chambre Syndicale I doubt if I would have made it to my office before noon, if at all. As it was I was still in a dreamlike state, utterly relaxed, utterly satisfied with myself—*floating* is the best word.

And altogether unprepared to face what had happened since I left the day before.

Beasley Turner informed me. It didn't come out right away, because he naturally assumed I already knew. But evidently he'd been hanging around to get my reaction, possibly on orders, and he caught me just as I arrived, before I saw the newspapers or the ambassador or anybody else.

He gave me his most disarming grin and invited himself to a chair opposite my desk. "Well!" he said, sounding a lot like Snuffy Spaulding trying to be friendly.

"Morning, Beasley."

"*You're* looking pretty smug, considering."

"Considering I had an excellent night's sleep, why not?"

I noticed his puzzled look. "You're fooling."

For a moment I wondered if he'd gone so far as to trail me to Yolande's last night, but it wasn't a leer, it was genuine surprise. I was the one who was surprised by what came next.

"Have you talked to him yet?"

"Have I talked to who, Beasley?"

"Come off it, Tyler! To your pal Brad Lindley."

"He's not exactly my pal, but we'll let that pass. He's a nice guy, anyway."

"A *nice guy!*" Now the look was something like amazement. "After what he did to the ambassador last night?"

That jolted me out of my lovely stupor, but I had enough poise to finesse it without comment, on grounds I was too busy to talk.

"This I can understand," grinned Mr. Turner, and reluctantly permitted himself to be shooed out of the office.

I turned at once to the newspapers on my desk and there, of course, was the story staring me in the face. On his network's evening news program broadcast nationally from New York, Brad Lindley had revealed the American ambassador's secret visit to the French Foreign Minister.

The Paris *Herald Tribune* front-paged the text, quoting Lindley as saying the ambassador's clandestine demarche was directly connected with the dispute between Courtailles and Premier Nicollet. While details of this highly private and unconventional rendezvous were not revealed, Lindley said, it was thought Ambassador Otis was playing the role of mediator in an attempt to head off a French political crisis—the gesture of a friendly ally interested in preserving the status quo in Western Europe.

He was way off the beam, as I knew. Pure guesswork. His real aim must have been to force the true story into the open, and to hell with the side effects on Mariana Otis. Quickly I scanned the French papers. Nothing in the morning editions, but by midday the afternooners would be on the streets and we could expect the worst.

Poor Mariana!

I got up and put my ear to the door of her office. I couldn't make out the words, but just barely heard voices within, at least two besides the ambassador's. One was Stuyvesant Spaulding's, the other unidentifiable. No expletive fireworks—just subdued, unhappy discussion, mostly male, with an undertone of grave anticipation, not quite dread. The door to the anteroom was opened, Mariana's voice sounded across the room, then silence.

My buzzer rang, summoning me to the ambassador's desk.

As always she was composed and immaculately groomed. By contrast, I must have looked so distressed she almost smiled.

"Please don't cry, Tyler dear. I couldn't bear it."

"I'm sorry. I only just found out. Can I be of some help?"

She shook her head. "Spaulding and Hobbs have already taken over."

"Hobbs? What's the CIA got to do with it?"

A shrug. "He's concerned about my security."

"And what's Spaulding doing about it?"

"He doesn't know. He's waiting to hear from Washington."

"There's an old department adage—when in doubt, do nothing."

This time she smiled. "That's where I part company with the department. As you know."

"The Foreign Minister must have seen the *Herald Tribune* by now."

"More than that, Tyler. He's probably already heard from the Premier, or the President, or both."

"He hasn't called you?"

"Courtailles? I doubt if he'll ever speak a civil word to me again. I promised him this would be kept secret."

"At least our broadcaster friend didn't tell the real story."

Her lips tightened. "Only because he doesn't know it."

"Beasley Turner asked me whether he'd called me. Did he call you?"

"The operators have been told not to connect him with my office."

She spoke calmly, without audible rancor, but I knew the hurt she must be hiding. Perhaps, later, she would talk to me. This was not the time to dwell on it. All the same, I couldn't repress a deep-down feeling of satisfaction at their breakup, mixed with sympathy for Mariana and anger at his using her this way. I was a little surprised at myself for caring even this much about it. A month ago, yes, but now? Now I had Yolande.

Everybody ran true to form. The events of that day and most of the day following could have been predicted almost to the letter. The noon editions of the Paris press reprinted Brad Lindley's broadcast and used their blackest headlines to assail the ambassador as with one voice—it looked to me, in fact, as if the attack were being orchestrated from Premier Nicollet's office.

But a curious dichotomy could be detected. The papers took it easy on the U. S. Administration—it was Ambassador Otis personally who was blamed for interference in France's internal affairs, not her bosses in Washington. And the popular press bore down heavily likewise on Foreign Minister Courtailles, charging him with dangerous indiscretion in conducting the affairs of his office.

Most significant, perhaps, was a Soviet Tass News Agency dispatch, datelined Paris and undoubtedly written by the same Serge Grolikoff who'd jousted with Brad Lindley the day we arrived at Le Havre. Recalling the Marseille narcotics office incident, it suggested the possibility that Ambassador Otis might now be recalled by her government and replaced. Brad Lindley, Grolikoff went on, was either working closely with the ambassador or had proved to be a nefarious influence on her, and Lindley's own network would be well advised to consider the wisdom of transferring him to some other country to avoid future trouble or dismissing him outright.

Bad as this was, I was relieved to note that neither Grolikoff nor his French press colleagues insinuated there might be a romantic connection between Lindley and the ambassador, as some reporters had done in my case during our *tour de France*. Fortunately it didn't seem to occur to any of the editorialists to link the ambassador with Courtailles in the same way, perhaps in deference to his lofty position in the French hierarchy. By the time the evening papers were on the street the rightist organs had come loyally to his defense, scoffing at the furore over a simple social visit and brushing off the Lindley broadcast as ill-informed and irresponsible. But by then the damage was done.

Although Stuyvesant Spaulding had predicted there would be a formal or at least informal rebuke to the embassy from Nicollet, none was forthcoming. What the Premier or the President felt about Courtailles, however, was another matter. The next day both Nicollet and his Foreign Minister were summoned to the Elysée for a long discussion. They arrived and left separately, neither would make any comment afterward, and no communiqué was issued by the presidential office. The uproar in the press subsided as suddenly as it began.

Lindley meanwhile, according to Beasley Turner, had once again withdrawn to the seclusion of his apartment as he had after the Marseille incident and was not to be seen in his customary drinking or dining haunts—Chez Francis or Lucas Carton.

"Every American reporter in Paris is pestering me for a press conference with the ambassador to try to clear this thing up," Beasley told me.

"There's nothing to clear up," I said, "so there's nothing for her to comment on."

He grinned that sly little grin. "You can tell *me*, Tyler."

"Out!" I grinned back, shuffling my papers. "I've got work to do."

He wouldn't get it from me, but sooner or later, like most of the embassy staff, Beasley was going to learn via the grapevine of at least one result of Mariana's visit to the Île St. Louis: a personal letter to the ambassador from the Secretary of State, rebuking her for her latest initiative and directing her to clear all future contacts with French officials *in advance* with Undersecretary Mitchell Remington in Washington.

I didn't see the text of this letter. Mariana reported its substance at our next morning meeting in the Residence study. We agreed that Spaulding had probably taken advantage of the Courtailles visit to tell Washington the ambassador was out of control.

"If they expect an answer to their letter," she said, "they're going to have a long wait. What they'd really like now is to goad me into resigning."

"I hope you're not giving the idea the slightest consideration."

She looked at me and said quietly, "I was appointed to this job by the President of the United States. I intend to keep it as long as he lets me stay here."

"Amen to that."

"The President is a decent man, Tyler, but events may force him to change his mind about me. He can't afford to keep an unpopular ambassador in Paris or anywhere else, especially if Bryce Halsted starts needling the White House about me as a result of the Courtailles business."

"But the French people *like* you."

She shook her head a little sadly. "Hobbs says I must have a plainclothes escort on all public occasions from now on."

"That's absurd. I can't believe you're in any personal danger."

"There's something else," she said. "There's Cristy. She's without protection and living in a fanatical student milieu. Brad said—."

She stopped and her color rose. She hadn't meant to mention him. I was sure she didn't even want to think about him. But I remembered Lindley's warning of student underground unrest possibly breaking out in violence. Now she continued, "Hobbs thinks Cristy ought to come back to the Residence for safety's sake. I didn't tell him that was easier said than done. He's not aware we don't even know her address."

"I'm pretty certain I can get it, Mariana. Through Yolande."

She looked at me helplessly. "But what good would it do? She won't come home."

"You could write to her. Or I could see her myself, if you want me to."

She hesitated. "Perhaps if she'd agree to talk with me—."

"We can try. Maybe she's just waiting to be asked back."

After a silence she said softly, "If you and Yolande could do something, I'd be forever grateful."

It was one of those shabby small hotels with a peeling facade which dot the maze of streets around the Sorbonne—much less numerous now than in my time, before new building crowded them out—with a fly-by-night student tenancy and a foreign proprietor, usually a refugee type from central Europe well accustomed to answering questions from the police. This one had what sounded like a Polish accent. A shriveled little man, collarless and unshaven, he threw me a squinting half-suspicious glance across the worn wooden counter inside the door. The dingy foyer was dim after the sunshine outside.

"Yves Lannuc?" I said.

"He went out a few minutes ago."

"Nobody in?"

"The girl is there."

"Which room?"

"Third floor, end of the hall." He'd already turned his back, no longer interested in who I was or what I wanted.

The staircase smelled of cats and one-burner cooking in the rooms. Under the tattered carpet the floor creaked to my footsteps. The back of the hotel was eerily quiet, the sounds of the street distant. Outside the last door I stood a moment, listening, before I knocked.

"*Entrez,*" Cristy's drowsy voice said.

She was lying on the gray sheets of the unmade bed, propped against pillows, a book on her lap. Newspapers were stacked on the floor. In the half-light of the hall she didn't immediately recognize me. Then she spoke with a dry little laugh.

"For Chrissake if it isn't faithful old Tyler."

"Hello, Cristy. May I come in?"

"You're here, aren't you?"

She stirred, stretched her arms, and swung her bare feet to the floor. The faded wrapper she was wearing fell open. She was naked underneath, but made no effort to pull it back around her body, standing there as if defiantly flaunting her nudity. The schoolgirl I'd first seen in Washington had come a long way fast.

"What I want to know is how did you find your way?" she was saying.

I wasn't about to bring Yolande into it. I said, "It's okay, Cristy, I won't tell anybody but your mother."

"And she'll send the Marines, right?"

"Nothing like that."

There was a moth-eaten armchair by the single window that opened on some sort of courtyard. "May I sit down a minute?"

She shrugged and lit herself a cigarette from a pack on the bed table—an ordinary cigarette, thank God—then perched on the bed again and crossed her knees. "And so?" she inquired.

"You may be in some danger, Cristy."

"Danger?" Once more the little laugh. "From what?"

"You read the attacks on your mother in the papers?"

"What's that got to do with it?"

"They may have inflamed some segments of public opinion

against the American ambassador, to the extent that some damn fool might try a physical assault on her. From now on she's under armed protection whenever she appears in public."

"So why would that affect me?"

"You're the ambassador's daughter, remember? I explained that to you once before, but you didn't seem to grasp it. Regardless of how you may feel, you can't escape from that special position of responsibility." I looked around the wretched little room. "I don't know what your life is at the moment, Cristy, and I don't know your friends, or your enemies, but the embassy security people are quite right in warning you that you're exposed to the same risks as the ambassador herself—possibly more so, over here on the Left Bank."

She gave me an insolent grin. "How about if I carry a gun? Will that satisfy them?"

"I'm talking seriously. In spite of yourself, you're a person of importance in the eyes of the French authorities as well as your own embassy. Your safety is a necessary consideration to both governments, particularly at the present time."

She spoke sharply. "Just what does that mean—at the present time?"

"You've seen the papers. You're mature enough to draw your own conclusions."

"And what are *your* conclusions, Mister Paine?"

"Never mind about me. I'm speaking for your mother. You know she'd be here herself, if she could. She's appealing to you to come back to the Residence where you'll be safe. She misses you very much indeed—you should know better than I how much she misses you. And right now she needs you, not only because she needs to stop worrying about your safety but because she also needs you near her, every day. She loves you, Cristy. She needs your friendship."

There was a long silence. I sat back in the armchair and waited. The half-naked girl sitting opposite me frowned, as if thinking hard, leaned over, and ground out the cigarette in a broken ashtray. Finally she looked back at me and spoke.

"And that's the message?"

I put my hand in my pocket and took out Mariana's letter. "Your mother asked me to bring you this." I stood up and handed it to her.

"Does it say anything different from what you've just said?"

"I haven't read it."

"Okay, I'll read it after you go." She tossed the letter negligently onto the bed table.

"If you wish," I said, "I'll wait while you read it. Perhaps you'll want me to take your answer back to her."

She gave me a long deliberate look and then stood up, facing me, letting her wrapper fall wide open again, like a gesture of total indifference to my presence.

"I can give you the answer right now, Mister Paine. I wouldn't want to keep you from the affairs of state. Just inform my mother I feel a hell of a lot safer where I am than over there with that bunch of pigs in the embassy. And remind her that if she needs company, like she says, she's got Brad Lindley and you, right? If she needs more than that, there's always Marcus Feld. He'll be glad to hop over from Washington on the first plane out."

She turned and reached for another cigarette, and I left without saying good-bye.

The ambassador had already returned to the Residence by the time I made it back to the Chancery. I knew she was expecting word about Cristy and I intended to lose no time clearing my desk and joining her.

Awaiting me in the In basket was an airmail special delivery with a Washington postmark on private stationery.

I don't know why I should have been surprised. I'd been expecting that letter. In my opinion it was long overdue. And I certainly couldn't blame Mitchell Remington for writing it, in view of Mariana's most recent actions. What I read was a small masterpiece of ambiguity and indirect allusion. It wasn't a long letter —just a page of business-size onionskin unobtrusively signed MR in the tiny, meticulous hand I'd recognized on the envelope. Aside from those initials and the "Dear Tyler" at the top, a nosy stranger couldn't have got to first base with it. The ambassador was identified by neither name nor title. The tone was mild and courteous, but the thrust was all too clear.

In effect he said he couldn't understand why none of my previous communications to him had foreshadowed the subject's extraordinary behavior. He found it difficult to believe such omission had been deliberate. On the other hand it was equally hard to see how anyone so close to the situation could have failed to furnish at least an inkling of what might be expected.

That was all. Reproach, rebuke, or just friendly observation—whatever it was I found it ominous, especially as it concluded without instructions for the future of our arrangement. Most of all it made me realize I'd have to face up to a question that had been troubling me for longer than I wanted to admit.

I folded the letter carefully and put it in my wallet.

As I was leaving, Ralph Hobbs stopped me in the hall, eyes hard and voice brittle.

"I've been waiting for you, Paine. Where you been all afternoon?"

I was feeling tired and frustrated and the tone suddenly irritated me. "You mean you guys don't know *everything?* Just doing errands. With all this excitement lately I'm behind in my personal life."

"We can check that, you know."

"Easily. You can pick up my spoor at Sulka's, track it to Brentano's, and run me to earth at the Ritz Bar, where I hid the documents under the banquette." I grinned without much mirth. "Next time put a tail on me, it's simpler."

I think my asperity had startled him. "You're in a snappy mood," he said.

"All right, I'll make a clean breast of it—I had a long, delicious rendezvous with a couple of my mistresses at my Number Three pied-à-terre in the wilds of Montparnasse. Too bad you weren't with us. You would have had fun."

His face didn't change. "I'll ignore the cracks. Incidentally, my information is you have only one mistress. Rue de Bellechasse, isn't it? We could be wrong about that, of course, but never mind.

We're not interested in that address. We're looking for Miss Cristy Otis. Do you know where she lives?"

"Have you tried asking her mother? That might be a good ploy."

"The ambassador doesn't know. She's looking for her, too."

"I wish you both well," I said.

In the silence he studied me. "Look, friend, let's drop the sarcasm. We're all working out of the same boat here. I need any help I can get. Little Miss Otis is going to have to give up her present way of life and get back here where we can keep an eye on her. Things could happen. She's in bad company."

"Who told you that, Brad Lindley?"

His turn to grin, also without mirth. "Brad Lindley's in a spot of trouble, too. One of these days he'll get himself booted across the border and that's the last we'll hear of him for some time." He frowned. "Lindley knows where Cristy is?"

"I only mentioned him because he's been researching a TV show on the Sorbonne."

"The Education Ministry doesn't like people stirring things up over there. I'd guess they'll call him off it."

"Why don't you suggest it to them?" I said. "Well, it's been a stimulating conversation, Mr. Hobbs, but I have to go now."

He stood aside and said as I went down the hall, "Let me know what you can find out."

"I surely will, yes, sir!" I called over my shoulder. "And meanwhile I hope *you'll* find out who tampered with my telephone."

I was still sore about it when I reached the Residence, not only his cheap and easy reference to Yolande (that would be Beasley Turner, of course) but the whole atmosphere of festering suspicion and resentment inspired by Spaulding in Paris, by Remington and Hunnicutt in Washington, which now seemed to be coming to a head. It was clear that from the beginning it had all stemmed from the Secretary himself, and something in the way the French press had laid off the Washington brass while attacking the ambassador personally seemed to indicate a possible understanding between Stoneface and the highest level in France.

Mariana was waiting for my call. We met immediately in the study. She listened without interruption to my word-for-word account of the visit to Cristy's hotel and was not in the least surprised by any of it.

"Is that all?" she said afterward.

"I'm afraid it is." I didn't mention the nudity act.

She took a deep breath and gave me a sad little smile. "Thank you, Tyler. And thank Yolande for me. I thought it would be like this, but we had to try."

"I have a hunch she'll write you a different answer after she's thought things over."

She shook her head. "I know you want to cheer me up, but by now I think you must understand Cristy as well as I do. As well as anybody does." And she added softly, "I hope the Lannuc boy won't end by hurting her."

"It might be a good thing if he did. Then she'd come back to you."

"I wonder if anything would bring her back, now. It sounds to me like they've done a brainwashing job on her."

"I thought that, too. But she can survive it. She'll come back, Mariana. But she'll do it her way, in her own time. We can't force it." And I told her about my little encounter with Hobbs. "I didn't tell him I'd seen Cristy. The CIA thinks it can get away with anything, and he might just try to kidnap her out of there. That would be the most dangerous thing that could happen, from everybody's point of view. I don't believe Hobbs knows what kind of dynamite he's dealing with in the student area." I added, "You just might warn Spaulding to restrain our Mr. Hobbs, in case he gets out of hand."

"Our Mr. Spaulding is lying low, Tyler. He's waiting for instructions, as usual. But from now on I'm not worrying about Spaulding or anybody else, here or in Washington." She spoke with quiet determination. "Ever since we came back from our trip through France, one single idea has been growing in my head. I know, now, what I must do. I have my own plan for dealing with this whole situation, and I'm not going to wait any longer."

As it happened, the next move came from Claude Courtailles. A few hours after my conversation with Mariana, he resigned as France's Foreign Minister.

17

THERE WERE TWO versions. The newspapers made the most they could of both. Nicollet's office announced curtly that the resignation had been requested by the Premier, and gave no further explanation. Courtailles issued a short statement of denial, declaring he was leaving the government voluntarily because he could no longer co-operate with the present regime and would give his views at the appropriate time.

Neither principal would consent to interviews that might have thrown some light on the issues in the dispute and possibly illuminated Mariana's role, if any.

Within forty-eight hours Pierre Bloire, a veteran parliamentary wheelhorse and member of Nicollet's party, was sworn in as Foreign Minister, and the coalition Cabinet proclaimed its continued support of the Premier's leadership.

At the Elysée, the President was silent.

International comment didn't appear particularly excited by the change, regarding it as typical of the frequent shuffles and reshuffles in French politics and playing down Mariana's role as catalyst. The *Times* of London made mild allusion to the volatile Latin temperament, while the *Times* of New York, disposing of more space and thus able to deal with the move at greater length, saw it mainly as the hand of the President asserting control. In Paris, only *Le Monde* seemed aware that spectacular possibilities might lie in the offing. It vaguely linked this development with others to come in other countries, times and places not specified.

Just how U.S. and Soviet policy might figure in the situation was not mentioned, even speculatively. It was the guessing game, as usual.

But Mariana knew, if what Courtailles had told her was true, and now Washington knew that she knew. If, as the Frenchman had said, there was a vast secret deal in the making, Stoneface had failed to keep knowledge of it from his ambassador in Paris. All the Secretary could do about that had already been done—Mariana was under strictest injunction to take no official action by word or deed before consultation with her superiors. But she'd disregarded such admonitions more than once in the past. Messrs. Remington and Hunnicutt, among others, must be wondering if this time—under conditions affecting the highest levels of international relations—she might risk the grave consequences of repeating the offense.

"I know, now, what I must do," she had told me. *"I have my own plan, and I'm not going to wait any longer. . . ."*

Just what her intentions were she was keeping to herself. Not even "faithful old Tyler," as Cristy so contemptuously dubbed me, was privy to the ambassador's thoughts in the days following the Courtailles resignation. I wondered if she was missing Brad Lindley's counsel, or if she would ever ask it again. But so far as I knew nothing had been heard from him. Beasley Turner, who monitored his broadcasts, said they stuck meticulously to the few facts available in the situation and contained no explosive new conjectures.

I passed along Beasley's comment, but Mariana received it in silence. Brad Lindley's name had not once crossed her lips since she inadvertently mentioned him during our talk about Cristy. No word from Cristy, either—written or spoken—nor was there any further discussion of her. Our night and morning conferences in the study were suspended, at least for the present, and outwardly the embassy resumed its normal placid life. Evenings the ambassador simply withdrew to her Residence suite. She had no social engagements—"everybody, but everybody," to quote Honora de Chapdelaine, had fled the tourists and the heat in their annual escape to the countryside. Even Ralph Hobbs could relax. No public appearance was scheduled for the ambassador until after the weekend, when she was to address a luncheon meeting of the American Club of Paris.

Mariana's abrupt withdrawal from our regular routine worried me a little. Was she grieving over Brad Lindley? Was she working on her "plan"? I tried a couple of times to sound her out but she didn't respond. She was perfectly friendly when we had business in her office, but that was our only contact. Of course this gave me the opportunity to be with Yolande each evening. Still, I felt uneasy about being away from the Residence for too long, in case the ambassador might need me in some ticklish new emergency, so for the first time I resisted the opportunity to stay all night in the Rue de Bellechasse.

It was Yolande's unexpected reaction to this that made me realize how sharply and how suddenly her attitude had changed.

Maybe because of my concern over Mariana's current situation, I hadn't been observing Yolande as attentively as before. Perhaps I now felt so warmly familiar and secure with her, especially since our wonderful night after the dinner at Lafon, that I was taking her too much for granted. And perhaps I was tending to forget she was French, after all—quite a different matter from my relationships with the American girls I'd been recently used to. I may have been further confused by the way she herself played American when we were together.

Whatever it was, I was unprepared for her vehement response after she'd insisted on serving me dinner at home for the second straight evening and I protested that she'd been working all day and deserved to be waited on in a restaurant.

"A restaurant?" She wiped a smudge of pastry flour off her chin and regarded me with wide, reproachful eyes. "You didn't like what I cook? You don't prefer to be here, alone together, than to sit in some public place?"

I smiled. "Of course I'd rather be here with you. But you're tired, *chérie*. You shouldn't have had to go to work all over again."

It was an insult. "Do I look tired? Naturally, I don't have a coiffeuse to come to dress my hair, like your lady ambassador—."

"Yolande, for heaven's sake. You know I only wanted you to take it easy. Isn't one job a day enough?"

"Job! What do I care about my job? I don't care if I would never go back to them again."

"I know. Sometimes I feel exactly that way myself."

She gave me a scornful little look. "How do you know what way a woman can feel? You are a man!"

I laughed and put my arms around her. "What's going on here? Have I said something terrible?"

Suddenly she clung hard. "Don't talk, just hold me," she whispered.

For a long moment we stood there motionless and close, until I felt a shuddering go through her body and heard the sigh like relief as she withdrew from my arms and smiled up at me with glistening eyes. She had her voice back. "Yes, you are a man, Tyler. You certainly are a man. Now come with me . . ."

We had our *filtre* and cognac sitting in silence side by side on the settee under the big studio window. "What are you thinking about?" she said at last, half turning to face me.

"It was a lovely dinner. Yolande made love like an angel. Things like that."

"I don't believe you. Something is worrying you, Tyler."

"No more than usual."

"Is it the ambassador? Of course it is the ambassador! But it's not your fault if she has trouble now. She makes the trouble for herself, isn't that so? You know that is so, Tyler."

"She's in a tough spot. She's all alone, Yolande. She hasn't even got Cristy anymore."

"Brad Lindley has not come back to her? He will come back, you will see."

"If he does, she won't have him."

"How do you know that? Has she said it to you?"

"No. But after what he did—."

Her eyes were solemn. "He did well. It is right to tell the people what she has done. Mme. Otis has meddled in French affairs. She is a bad influence, Tyler. And don't stare at me that way, you know I am right. Oh, she is quite a person, yes. I admire her. You know I admire her. But you can't see her like the rest of us, like the French. You are too close to her."

I must have shown my astonishment. "Are you serious, Yolande?"

"Of course I am serious."

"I didn't know you felt this way. She thinks of you as a friend."

"It is not a personal thing. I *like* her, but not as ambassador."

This wasn't the Yolande I knew, not the Yolande of even a few days ago. Somehow, subtly, she had changed. I said, "We'll have to disagree about that. She happens to be a very good ambassador. Maybe it's just because she's a woman that you feel doubtful of her ability?"

"A very *attractive* woman. Perhaps too attractive to be an ambassador."

I grinned. "You've been reading the newspapers again."

"I don't need newspapers to know what I can see for myself. It is you who don't see, *mon cher* Tyler."

We were getting nowhere with this. And the concentration on Mariana was making it all the harder for me to say what I had to say—that I wouldn't feel right about spending the night again tonight. She hadn't questioned it before, not really objected, had understood, up to now, even though she pretended not to. But tonight she was different, tonight she meant it, as if she knew already what I felt I must do and had deliberately brought up the subject to make it more difficult for me. If she had gone to a restaurant with me it would have been that much easier for me to say good night at her door. She knew that, too.

It was right there in her eyes, her new eyes, impatiently waiting for me to discover it—the clinging tenderness, the jealousy, the pride of possession I hadn't seen before. Only then, suddenly looking back over the past few days, did I realize how slow I'd been to understand what had happened to Yolande. And it had begun precisely on that night we'd had dinner at Lafon. Yolande had fallen in love.

But she spared me the scene I thought would follow. She must have been satisfied that now I knew. She spoke with a melancholy little smile.

"Well," she said, "what are you waiting for? You don't have to ask permission."

I looked at her. "You're uncanny."

She shrugged.

"You know I'd stay tonight if I could, Yolande. I can't let the ambassador down just at this time."

But it was another hour before I left. Maybe longer. We lost track.

My watch showed nearly eleven by the time I got back to the Residence. Once again there was no call from Mariana, although I delayed undressing till after midnight in case she summoned me to the study. When I finally turned out the lights and went to bed I lay there uneasily in the dark, tired out physically and emotionally by the evening with Yolande yet still worried about Mariana's uncharacteristic retreat into seclusion. It might have been two o'clock before I slept, but restlessly, with vague, amorphous dreams, waking up several times in the night with a sense of impending trouble I couldn't shake off. I must have been still asleep when the ambassador left for the Chancery, because I didn't hear her light, hurried step in the corridor at the usual time.

But when I took my first look at the papers over breakfast I knew that from now on in my life I'd be a true believer in premonition.

Claude Courtailles, in his first interview since quitting the government, was accusing Premier Nicollet of selling out his country in a conspiracy to give the United States and Russia undisputed hegemony over Europe and the world.

In the rightist *L'Aurore*, chosen by Courtailles as his mouthpiece, he charged the two superpowers with trying to build a global political organization with the strength of their combined military and economic predominance. Under this condominium, he declared, a Western Europe now striving for unity and independence would be humiliated and treated like a nonperson, its individual nations divided, its Common Market broken up, and its trading system shattered. West Germany, he predicted, would desert the Atlantic Alliance and joyously reunite with its Communist East German brother, while Britain just as quickly would

return to the American fold, leaving France high, dry, and friend-
less, having no alternative but to accept the new order. And with
Europe thus neutralized and the Middle East firmly under joint
control, Russia would be free to deal with the Chinese threat
to her borders as meantime U.S. and Japanese imperialism carved
out complementary zones of influence in South America and
Asia.

Coffee forgotten, I sat staring at the newspaper. Despite his
warnings of approaching doom, Courtailles in effect was simply
outlining a theoretical situation, at least in this opening salvo. He
was still confining himself to general terms. Nowhere did he al-
lude to current talks between Washington and Moscow. No mention was made of either Soviet or American principals in such
negotiations, nor was Auguste Nicollet cited by name or office—
the reference throughout was to "present government." But the
thrust was unmistakable. The Nicollet regime was now on notice
to defend itself against a major political offensive spearheaded
by the country's most eloquent Conservative spokesman. Likewise
the challenge had been thrown down to both Russia and the
United States, and inevitably the Paris spotlight once more was
squarely on the ex-Foreign Minister's relations with the American ambassador.

This time I didn't wait to be called before I saw Mariana. But I
couldn't get to her right away—as I might have expected, Spaulding was already with her when I reached the Chancery. The
whole embassy was in ferment. It was one of those days when discussions spilled out into the halls, when the international teleprinters worked without a lunch break and, of course, Beasley
Turner came around for a special chat.

He was bright-eyed and bushy-tailed. "What's the inside dope,
Tyler?"

"You'll have to ask one of the inside dopes. I'm outside in the
dark."

"Come on!" he wailed.

"You tell me, Beasley."

His gaze was determinedly guileless. "But I don't know anything. What can I ever find out except from guys like you?"

Of course I could have said I hadn't had a real talk with the ambassador for days, but even that would be telling him too much, so I pleaded busy and ran him out of there.

My buzzer rang, at last. The ambassador sat very straight behind the big desk, very grave and very calm.

"I'm sorry I couldn't see you till now, Tyler." I sensed the tension behind her formal tone.

"I'm grateful you're able to see me at all, today." I hesitated. "Mariana—."

"Yes?"

"I guess I just wanted to say, I've been standing by for anything I can do to help. Anything at all."

Her little fleeting smile was more like herself. "Dear Tyler. I never doubt that, but it's comforting to hear you say it anyway. Just be patient with me, will you? I've needed to be alone these past few days but, believe me, I'll call on you when the time comes."

"That comforts me, too."

"We're both going to look back on it all and be glad we lived it, Tyler."

"Of course we are."

Impulsively I took her hand and kissed it, as I had that night in the garden after the U.N. dinner. It was an awkward gesture but I didn't know I was doing it till after I'd done it. She understood, as always.

"Don't be too concerned," she said softly. "And give my very best to Yolande."

Every day has its ironies, but that last remark was one of the big ones.

"No comment" was the comment from the Palais Matignon, the Quai d'Orsay, and the Elysée. The strategy of silence was still in force. The Courtailles challenge was not even worth the government's disdain.

But with the Russians it was different. It sometimes takes up to a week before Soviet press reaction to an event of importance finds its way into print. This, of course, is because no Soviet editor dares print anything, or put anything on the air, until the form and content of the reaction have been decided on at the summit—and the summit is sometimes too busy with other matters to get around to it immediately.

Not so with the Courtailles blast in *L'Aurore*. The summit lost no time in blasting right back—first with Serge Grolikoff's outraged report to Tass, released in Moscow within twenty-four hours, then with Soviet radio (as monitored by our Voice of America listening posts and heard by major West European stations). Finally, a few hours later, with analysis and evaluation, euphemisms for the official line as handed down from the top. As often as not it comes as a total surprise to the ordinary Soviet citizen, who has been kept ignorant of earlier developments that would give him the background for understanding what all the fuss is about.

Today it was clear the top people were angry. And this time their wrath descended not only on the former French Foreign Minister but indirectly made reference to Ambassador Otis (sparing her only the use of her name) as his supporter.

Novosti fulminated: "One can hardly be astonished at the Soviet public's sharp reaction to provocative acts against détente by the mouthpieces of French and American right-wing extremists, the transatlantic military-industrial complex, and anti-Soviet activists of every stripe, possessed by hatred for Socialism and a desire to maintain the destructive arms race at all costs. The aim of these circles is to harpoon the development of peaceful relations between the U.S.S.R. and the West, though this harms only the French and American peoples themselves.

"Détente is opposed by economic forces whose aims are incompatible with it, by special-interest groups like counterrevolutionary émigrés from the Socialist countries, and by those diplomats, bureaucrats, journalists, and social scientists who rose to prominence because of the cold war and are only able to think or act within its categories.

"Some discredited French politicians are now talking in ways that seek to undermine the special Soviet-French relationship first fostered by De Gaulle. France would be well advised to beware of such machinations with their threat to the future of détente just as its horizons begin to open out with promise for all of Europe."

Et cetera. Et cetera. For the next several days my translating duties kept me so busy with the swelling volume of French press comment I had to put everything else out of my mind, working from early morning till late at night. I could only follow the highlights of what was being said in other countries, most notably my own. Neither the White House nor the State Department issued public statements, although their off-the-record advisories to news correspondents suggested soft-pedaling the story as a passing flurry. We were nearing the end of August and both the President and the Secretary of State were back from their vacations. The word passed on to the Paris embassy—as I finally got it—was to refuse all comment and keep the U.S. profile as low as possible until the excitement died down.

But it was obvious the "passing flurry" was not going to pass. British and West German papers were giving the confrontation full play. The smaller countries of the Western alliance gave signs of deep uneasiness. Repercussions were being heard as far away as China, whose official news agency quoted Courtailles at length and again made known its mistrust of Russia's intentions. It soon became evident a serious political situation had developed in France that could only be clarified when the National Assembly reconvened in September.

In the midst of all this I realized with a sudden pang of shame I hadn't talked with Yolande for two days, nor had she called me at the Chancery as she usually did at least once every afternoon.

Her assistant at the Chambre Syndicale recognized my voice and greeted me with some surprise. But Mme. Vannier was not in, M. Paine. The girl sounded as if I should know that at least as well as she did. Mme. Vannier had gone to the country for a few days. Where in the country? *Je regrette*, M. Paine, Mme. Vannier hadn't left an address—should she leave word that I'd called?

By all means.

Je ne manquerai pas, M. Paine. She wouldn't fail to do so.

But it was I who had failed Yolande. I hung up and sat there hopelessly looking out over the Concorde toward the Rue de

Bellechasse. The only conclusion was that Yolande was deeply hurt and making sure I knew it. Of all times for this to happen!

I'd been inexcusably clumsy. But what could I do about it except wait till she returned and beg forgiveness?

What mattered right now was to get on with my work.

18

THIS WAS TO be the ambassador's first appearance before the
venerable American Club of Paris (stag membership) whose
weekly luncheons with celebrity guest speakers had been a feature
of life in the American colony literally for generations. I didn't
see Mariana before she left for the restaurant with Stuyvesant
Spaulding as escort and, presumably, a couple of security men
close behind. She was busy with visitors in her office all morning,
and she hadn't called me to the study either last night or today
before she left the Residence. Thanks to Beasley Turner I'd
wangled a seat at the club's press table, although I was only a
guest and for once I'd had no hand in preparing the ambassador's
speech. Naturally the embassy was represented in full strength for
today's event, with Spaulding seated at the head table and other
senior officers scattered through the restaurant at the invitation
of members, most of whom were with American businesses in
Paris.

I also saw Blaise d'Archeval, bland and smiling, seated next to
one of the club officers. It was the first time I'd laid eyes on him
since the night I brought the ambassador's letter to Courtailles.
The rumor, not denied, was that the count had broken with his
ex-boss and thereby contrived to keep his job in the Foreign Ministry under Nicollet's new appointee, Pierre Bloire (Monsieur
Blah in embassy chatter). I didn't expect any public recognition
from d'Archeval, however. In the present situation it would be
definitely unwise for him to be seen chumming with the American ambassador's special assistant.

"The joint is jumping," said Beasley as I sat down beside him.
"The club hasn't had such a sellout since Princess Grace. And,"

he added like a snickering schoolboy, "all that stuff in the papers about her and Courtailles hasn't hurt, either."

Beasley would have appreciated some firsthand comment on the latter angle but I wasn't about to oblige him.

"I'd be interested to hear the lady's own reaction, especially to the sexy piece in *Paris Match*," he persisted.

"So would I, Beasley."

"Maybe she'll bring it up today," he suggested hopefully.

"Hi there, Tyler Paine!" sang out a sudden strident female voice from the other end of the table, and I turned to confront the gimlet gaze and professional smile of Fanny Watkins, the only other woman present at the luncheon—doubtless by virtue of her journalistic credentials. "When you going to persuade the ambassador to give me that interview, Tyler?" she shrilled.

I was spared a response by the distinguished-looking gent sitting next to Miss Watkins.

"I'm sure quite a few people are besieging Mr. Paine with the same question," he said, and I recognized Anthony Wardwell of the London *Times*, another personality not often seen at American Club luncheons. Wardwell looked mildly at Newspaperwoman Watkins. "Has it occurred to you that Mr. Paine may be without influence in the matter?"

There were smiles and appraising glances toward me at Fanny's snort of skeptical laughter. "Who shall I ask—Brad Lindley?" she chortled. "Incidentally, he doesn't seem to be here."

If this was the media's idea of having fun I didn't care for it and certainly didn't know how to hand it back to them. I was conscious of flushing and wished now I hadn't come. But the arrival of food cut short further general discussion, and by the time the press had hungrily finished their free lunch the club president was on his feet to introduce various prominent guests of members and reel off a series of announcements about current club activities. Except for the plushy surroundings, fancy cuisine, and French-speaking waiters, was all this any different from the weekly Rotary Club luncheon in any American town? Including the toastmaster, who pretty much looked and spoke model back-home-in-Indiana?

But there was no mistaking the warmth of his welcome to the guest speaker, and when Mariana rose the capacity audience stood up with her, offering prolonged waves of applause that shook the big windows, and even a few folksy cheers—the more aroused, I was sure, because of "all that stuff in the papers."

She was wearing a bright blue outfit topped off by a little hat that perched like a coronet above her brow, and although I knew the strain she'd been under, she looked youthful, smiling, and perfectly composed as she waited for the applause to subside and her hosts to settle back in their chairs with their cigars. I wasn't concerned about Mariana's poise under any circumstances. Natural politician that she was, she knew just how to respond in its own terms to this open show of typical affection and support. Undoubtedly there were those in the audience who had their misgivings about her involvement in recent political events and even her original appointment. But right or wrong, male or female, she was an American among her fellow countrymen in a foreign land —and a damned good-looking woman to boot, as could be observed in their appreciative stares.

She began on her most cherished theme—the two hundred years of friendship between France and the United States. How many ambassadors before Mariana Otis had covered this well-worn ground with a transparent carpet of clichés? Every last one of them, of course, using the complete library of platitudes. But today was made different by Mariana's unique gift of sincerity. Somehow she transformed the tired old words into something fresh and glowing and personal—not a speech, not even a talk, but a one-on-one *conversation* between herself and each man in that room, direct and warm as a serious exchange of ideas between trusted associates devoted to the same cause. It was a simple and somehow very moving reminder of a relationship "never more deeply needed than today," she said, "in this year when the world waits and hopes for decisions that will define the future of us all.

"For not only in America and France but in every country," she went on, "the common man and woman in our more and more industrialized society are confronting that still unpredictable future with a growing apprehension, with bewilderment, with fear even, because their leaders have yet to offer solutions to the agonizing problems that loom ahead—world hunger, impossible inflation, pollution of the environment, the monotony of the assembly line or the slow death of unemployment, most fearfully of all the threat of annihilation in the ultimate nuclear war.

"Very recently," the ambassador said, "I made it my business to visit personally with a broad spectrum of citizens of this country, to find out in face-to-face encounters what most typically affects their lives, and perhaps by extension the lives of millions of other West Europeans as well. Everywhere I found this gnawing malaise, sometimes flatly expressed, in others only sensed uneasily, that underlies the everyday uncertainties of their daily existence, most often in their thoughts of the children—a longing for some kind of reassurance, confidence, security, a détente of the spirit.

"But I also found," she said, "that the great majority of those I talked with no longer feel politicians have the answer—that détente in the *political* sense is an unfamiliar or vaguely ominous term to them. Yet that single word 'détente,' which has come to dominate the international political scene, is now regarded by governments, political parties, and press alike as the key to Europe's salvation and world peace."

I looked around at the listening faces—concerned, respectful, proud to be present on the occasion. At this point, however, they didn't know what was coming. Neither did I, but perhaps I caught on more readily than most. It quickly became apparent that what Mariana had said so far had been only prefatory to an outright attack on U.S. and Soviet policy.

In total defiance of her instructions, Ambassador Otis was speaking out. Worse, she was taking sides against what she feared to be the plans of her own Secretary of State. But like Claude Courtailles she made no slightest reference to secret negotiations between Washington and Moscow, nor did she mention the personalities involved. I felt my heart thumping and watched Stuyvesant Spaulding's face gradually go pale, then turn to deeper red. The room was beginning to get it now. The comfortable stirring and shifting ceased. The silence was almost audible.

It was not a direct assault. She spoke without script, but the careful couching of her words made me realize how long and how intensively she'd worked on this speech and then memorized it during those hours alone in the Residence, trusting no one, not even Tyler Paine, who might have felt it a duty to expose her purpose. Could I blame her for that? In this moment I only felt proud of her courage, and stricken that she was inevitably taking the last step before her recall.

"Détente," she was saying. "The word is easy to comprehend. It is one of those words that cannot be quarreled with. Détente— of course, *détente!* Who would not wish it well, with its purport of hope and peace? Unfortunately, from purport to achievement is a long step, and we have an obligation to think hard before we take it. There is a discrepancy here—between Russia's public proclamation of peaceful aims and the unproclaimed buildup of her military power—particularly, as concerns us, the offensive strengthening of her land forces in Europe.

"There is also our obligation to remember, for our own survival, that treaty undertakings no matter how solemnly made can be abrogated or swept aside overnight. How many times since the end of World War I have we seen this done—and by whom! Have we not the right at least to ask ourselves whether détente may not be the latest strategic move in the ultimate policy of communism since Lenin—rule of the world by one means or another?"

She paused. A murmur of whispers went over the room. Stuyvesant Spaulding looked as if he was having trouble breathing. Then the calm, clear voice of the speaker resumed.

"Let me quote to you from memory the words of a distinguished American political thinker. 'A government that cuts its people off from objective contact with the outside world, a government that becomes the prisoner of its own propaganda, cannot pursue a foreign policy that can be relied upon to respect the moral limitations imposed by a viable balance of power.' That is a clear warning to all of us to reflect very deeply before relaxing our own vigilance in the détente era. Let us look closely at the vital risks involved before we consider reducing the strength of the NATO alliance

—or, even more fearful to contemplate, the dissolution of NATO itself in exchange for dissolution of the Warsaw Pact.

"It is my belief that American nuclear weapons and American ground forces now in Europe provide the crucial base of this continent's military and political stability. They must not be withdrawn. Withdrawal of Soviet troops within Russia's boundaries would leave them still poised and ready to overrun the West. Withdrawal of American forces across the Atlantic would leave Western Europe defenseless against overwhelming Soviet power.

"These are evident facts. Yet the military necessities in such a situation are only the surface signs of America's responsibility. We must never lose sight of Europe's spiritual right to exist as a proud and independent entity in a world that must not be dominated by two superpowers. But in the ultimate sense this is something that cannot be achieved simply with American help. If they are to survive, the nations of Europe themselves must achieve true and full unity. And the country to which I have the honor to be accredited must play a leading part in helping them do so."

In spellbound silence the ambassador sat down. The speech was over. She had spoken less than twenty minutes. Then, all at once, the room burst into deafening applause. As with one mind they rose to their feet and cheered. And among them, Stuyvesant Spaulding, grim with anger but automatically clapping with the rest. Beside me Beasley Turner shivered and said, "Oh boy oh boy oh boy!"

I squeezed his arm in thanks, slipped away from the table, and headed for the door. As I did I tripped over a large, drowsy English bulldog, leashed to a table leg. It lay there amid all the noise staring morosely up at me with drooping bloodshot eyes. This had to be the famous Poopsie, Anthony Wardwell's pet. Poopsie went everywhere.

Poopsie had certainly been somewhere today.

I escaped from the restaurant into the hot sunshine of the Champs Elysées with a feeling of intense relief, mingled with a sense of disloyalty at leaving Mariana to face the reporters who right now must be clustering around her. But there was nothing

I could do to help. Spaulding would have to bear the brunt this time. I hoped she wouldn't let herself be drawn into adding to her speech, which was bombshell enough for one day.

Walking back to the Chancery, I pictured Mariana's return trip with her escort and was glad I wasn't present. During the last part of the ambassador's speech her deputy looked as nearly apoplectic as I'd ever seen him. If he said anything at all to her in the car on the way back, which I doubted he would, it had to be the most difficult conversation he'd faced since Mariana came to France.

Ultimately it didn't matter about Spaulding. Washington was where her trouble was now. I looked at my watch. It was midmorning there and Stoneface would be sitting sulkily at his desk in that big, dark-paneled office where within the next hour Mitchell Remington and possibly one or two others would receive sudden and unexpected commands to join him—the news would be out, in a race between Stuyvesant Spaulding on the phone and AP, UPI, and Reuters on the wires with the first bulletin. The noon broadcasts would have it on radio and TV, and by then the press rooms in Congress and the White House would be in action, pestering the presidential news secretary and Bryce Halsted as their top sources of reaction, trying with less hope for a State Department comment, and following up with just about anybody willing to be quoted.

At this end, Blaise d'Archeval would spread the news through Paris. Already the phones were starting to ring at the Quai d'Orsay, the Matignon, and the Elysée. Late editions of the afternoon papers would have the story in both capitals, and I could see the headline in the Washington *Star*: MARIANA OTIS CHALLENGES DÉTENTE. I turned in at the Chancery with dread.

It seemed much longer than half an hour before I heard her voice through my office door. She was on the phone to somebody, but only for a minute or two. Then my buzzer rang. She was standing calmly by her desk when I went in.

"I know what you're going to say, Tyler. Spaulding has already said it. I've just committed career suicide."

"I wasn't going to say that at all."

Her smile was brief and crisp. "You will, when I tell you what

237

I'm going to do now. I'll have to ask you to keep it totally to your-self."

"You know you can count on me for that."

"And *you* know," she said, "how much your loyalty has meant to me, from the beginning."

I thought of my letters to Mitchell Remington and knew that I must tell her. But not yet. This was Mariana's moment.

"I've told the secretaries I'm receiving no calls or visitors for the rest of the day," she said. "I suggest you do the same. Of course you can't keep Spaulding or the others from storming your office. Just say you can't help them."

"They won't believe me."

"By that time it won't matter."

In low, hurried tones she told me what she intended to do. I listened in stunned silence. Then, without another word, she leaned forward, kissed my cheek, and was gone. I heard the door of my office open and close as she went out that way.

And again, as I'd done before, I raised my hand to my face and touched it where her lips had been.

The morning newspapers were spread out on my desk but today I didn't read them. By comparison to what they would say tomor-row, they were years old. I was waiting. The buzzer on my desk was silent, and it was strange to hear no voices or movement in the ambassador's office beyond the wall. An air of unreality had hung over everything since I left the American Club luncheon. I relived the little scene with Mariana now like a third person watching two actors in a drama that carried all three fatefully to-ward predestined climax. The traffic in the Place de la Concorde below my window was a sound track heard remotely under their dialogue.

But the sudden sharp rapping on my door blinked the image away. The first of my expected visitors would be all too real. Beas-ley Turner would never hazard so peremptory a knock. Was it Ralph Hobbs maybe?

He didn't give me time to say come in. The deputy chief of mission swung the door open and stood there glowering, all amenities forgotten.

"Where is the ambassador?"

I glanced at the other door and stood up. "Isn't she in her office?"

"She is *not* in her office. She is obviously not in *this* office. Is she with someone else in the Chancery?"

"Possibly, sir."

"Possibly! I thought your principal assignment, Mr. Paine, was to know what the ambassador is doing at all times."

It sounded so absurd under the circumstances of Mariana's recent private life I almost laughed. And that "Mr. Paine". . . . Snuffy was really off balance. But the urge to mirth helped restore my own equilibrium. "As I understand my instructions," I said as pompously as I could, "they don't extend quite that far."

"When did you last *see* the ambassador?"

"Just after she came back from the luncheon."

"And she gave no indication of her afternoon schedule?"

"None. Have you tried the Residence?"

"Of course I have tried the Residence. She doesn't answer."

I shrugged. "I'll see if I can find her, but I don't know where to begin to look. Is there a message?"

"Just tell the ambassador," he said while turning on his heel, "that the Secretary of State wishes her to communicate with him at once." He stopped and glared back over his shoulder. "And wishes me to be a party to her call," he added.

"Very good, Mr. Spaulding."

Something in the way I said it must have nicked him. He almost stopped again, but thought better of it and proceeded stiffly down the hall.

The vanishing ambassador. I could hear him trying to explain that to Stoneface.

The afternoon wore on, somehow. I couldn't concentrate on anything until the evening editions were brought to my desk, and there was the story on the front pages. As yet, no reaction from Premier Nicollet or his Foreign Minister. Apparently the reporters hadn't been able to get to Claude Courtailles in time for his comment, if any. I'd just finished checking the papers when Beasley Turner stopped by, his hands full of copy from the teleprinters in the Public Affairs section.

"I'll swap you, Tyler!"

"What are you offering?"

Exuberantly he filled me in on the Washington news angles. Stoneface was closeted with the President, and State was promising a communiqué. Bryce Halsted had called in key members of the Foreign Relations Committee. The American Committee on United States–Soviet Relations announced it would combat the anti-détente views of Ambassador Mariana Otis "and others" with an immediate information campaign directed at public opinion.

"And now, Tyler, where's the ambassador?"

"It's a funny thing, Beasley—Stuyvesant Spaulding asked me the very same question not two hours ago. And if I didn't know for him, how could I know for you?"

He had to go away satisfied with that. I looked at my watch—time to get back to the Residence, and wait.

I waited.

The Louis XVI clock on my bureau ticked remorselessly against the silence. It was after nine, and I was still sitting at the little escritoire, staring at Mitchell Remington's letter.

For nearly two weeks I'd been putting off a reply, debating with myself whether a reply was even required, quietly agonizing over the deeper issue of conviction involved, again and again avoiding the decision I knew I'd have to make in the end, and tonight was no different from others. Just out of habit I'd taken a sheaf of untranslated clippings back to the Residence with me, but I could have predicted I wouldn't work on them. Even if I did there was a good chance the ambassador would never read them now. The events of recent days had overwhelmed any certainties of the future, hers or mine.

For the first time the clippings seemed only vaguely familiar, like the pages of dusty schoolbooks I'd struggled through in the dim past of childhood. Ironically, it was a question whether the ambassador's latest and most dramatic action, now in progress, would be publicly chronicled at all. But this letter in front of me was as real and alive as the present hour. It had to be dealt with for my own sake, whatever the consequences to my relationship with Mariana, indeed it symbolized the fate of that relationship. I'd known for a long time, almost since the ship crossing began, that my deal with Remington had been a moral mistake. There had been a moment, at some point during the voyage, when suddenly and clearly I saw what would happen: my duty to the department and my feelings toward the ambassador as a human being would meet in irrevocable conflict, and I would have to choose.

I didn't want to believe this. I'd fooled myself into dismissing the thought from my mind. But it went deeper than that. Brad Lindley made me understand how deep it went.

Until Yolande. Yolande who relieved the hidden strain by bringing a joyous new dimension to my life. Yet hadn't I known, that night we four were at dinner together in the Residence, it was all too easy to last? How short a time ago, and already the pattern was broken—no Brad for Mariana, now in her deepest trouble, and Yolande gone as if we'd never found each other again, my calls to her apartment unanswered, her office blandly repeating that she hadn't yet returned. . . .

I pressed my fingers over my eyes and felt the weariness mount through my body. Too much tension on this climactic day, too much excitement, too many complications. I couldn't think about any of it anymore. I needed to get out of this silent house and walk, breathe fresh air, clear my head. Then maybe I could hear my conscience again, and act.

Never had Paris looked so lovely in its diamond-studded mantle of darkness. As soon as I'd left the Residence and turned down the Rue de l'Elysée I began to feel better. The cool breeze from the river was like a consolation, and I yielded my frustrating thoughts to pure sensation in the beauty of the summer night. Savoring each step, I strolled along the Avenue Dutuit to the Cours la Reine. To my right loomed the Pont Alexandre III, its Napoleonic splendor wreathed in filaments of mist. Halfway across the bridge I stopped and looked down into the Seine. The black waters mirrored distorted reflections of the Foreign Ministry so recently ruled by Claude Courtailles, bathed in the golden light of its own illumination, and beyond it the National Assembly where in a few days France's deputies would gather for a session that could be fateful for all Europe.

I thrust the thought away and moved on. Here on the Left Bank the streets were virtually empty. A solitary sentry on duty before the Palais Bourbon stared blankly across at me as I walked along the quai, headed down the boulevard for St. Germain des Prés and a glass of beer *chez* Lipp. At the corner of the Rue de Bellechasse I halted suddenly and stood stock-still. The image of Yolande was so near, so overpowering, I had to fight an almost irresistible desire simply to walk down to her building and stand under the dark, shuttered windows of her apartment.

Maybe it was better for both of us that she was still away. Mariana came first, for now. And tomorrow, if all went as planned, I would see Mariana again.

19

B Y   M O R N I N G   T H E   American ambassador's speech was the talk of political Europe, surpassing even the furore over Claude Courtailles. For all their far-reaching implications, the Courtailles charges had been seen mainly within the context of French domestic politics, but now the voice of a superpower had spoken. The issue was joined on an international scale. I woke before seven and switched on my bedside radio even before I saw the papers. Already it was pouring out excited reactions from London, from Bonn, Brussels, Amsterdam, Rome. Nothing yet from Moscow, for the usual reasons, but Radio Luxembourg was carrying Washington reports on the President conferring with his Secretary of State, on Bryce Halsted's Foreign Relations subcommittee meeting and the start of what appeared to be a nationwide debate pro and con over détente.

No word yet from the Halsted deliberations, but the State Department had issued its promised communiqué late in the evening after the White House meeting—the old familiar cop-out I'd heard so many times before. It said the President and the Secretary had discussed "a broad range" of foreign affairs problems currently confronting the United States but would have no comment at the present time on the Paris ambassador's address to the American Club.

Reading this one between the lines was easy: Stoneface, in cold fury, probably had proposed that Mariana be asked for her immediate resignation. I had little doubt his proposal would be promptly accepted.

The French press almost unanimously saw it the same way. From Communist Left to Right Center the cry went up for the ambassador's recall. There was no statement by the Nicollet government. Only the friends of Courtailles, ranged along the rest of the spectrum, gave support to Mariana's position, but several editorials seemed to be leaning over backward to make clear there was no collusion between the ex-Foreign Minister and the U.S. envoy. Warmest commendation came, as expected, from *L'Aurore*, the primary Courtailles mouthpiece in his anti-détente campaign, which quoted him as hailing Mme. Otis as a courageous diplomat and true friend of France and Europe.

To my surprise Jean-Paul himself appeared with my coffee and croissants, the first time I'd been accorded this special honor. He did no more than wish me a very pleasant day, but he looked troubled and I'm sure he was trying to tell me the whole staff was aware of the situation and sympathetic to the ambassador. Well, maybe not the whole staff—it occurred to me that Mme. Hanotte might privately be feeling considerable satisfaction lately.

The chef had only just departed when my phone rang.

"Spaulding here!" He sounded irate, baffled, and ready to hit the ceiling.

"Good morning, sir."

"I'm trying to reach the ambassador."

"Yes, sir."

"She's not with you?"

"No, sir. Might her phone be out of order?"

"The housekeeper has checked the study and her apartment. She's not there, Paine. She left the house to go for a walk and hasn't been seen by the servants since. Did you give her my message last night?"

"I haven't seen her either, Mr. Spaulding."

The cable broke. He was almost tearful. "Tyler, where *is* the woman?"

"If I knew, I'd tell you. I have no idea."

"But you're her confidential assistant!"

"I'm afraid that's not part of my title, sir."

"But can't you suggest where we could find her? Washington will be back on the wire this morning and I have to have an answer for them."

"I've been racking my brains, Mr. Spaulding. If I come up with anything I'll call you at once."

Desperately, "Would she be with some friend? Lindley?"

"I'd consider that highly unlikely, but I'll ask him if you wish."

"Get on to it, Tyler! *Please* get on to it. Let me know if Lindley has any thoughts so we can follow through there. Hobbs is standing by to help. You are doubtless aware this matter is of extreme importance."

"Yes, sir, I am."

He rang off abruptly. I could see the poor guy haggard and quivering, trying to pull himself together to face his staff and the day ahead.

I had no intention whatever of calling Brad Lindley or anybody else, of course.

Later, at the Chancery, I was pestered repeatedly by Beasley Turner for news of the ambassador's whereabouts. I finally had to tell him off pretty sharply on grounds I couldn't get anywhere with my inquiries if he kept bothering me. It hurt his feelings but he retired at last with good grace.

At that point, if it hadn't been so serious for everybody concerned, I think I would have yielded to a sudden irresponsible urge to just laugh. At least it would have relieved the tension.

I didn't see Snuffy again until after lunch, which I took alone, in leisurely, luxurious fashion, in the garden at Laurent. The cost was astronomical, but this was a historic day, after all. The cold lobster and especially the Montrachet engaged my attention so completely I almost stopped worrying for a while.

On my way back to my office I passed Spaulding and Hobbs having an impromptu conference in the hall. Neither even glanced at me, but their whispered conversation ceased immediately until I was out of earshot. Snuffy looked drawn but calm again, so it was a good guess that by now he had an understanding with Washington.

I could have reconstructed with fair accuracy what was said between them the moment my office door closed behind me.

Spaulding: "*Do you think he knows?*"
Hobbs: "*Of course he knows.*"

2 4 5

A few minutes before eleven o'clock that night a woman unobtrusively clad in a gray pants suit, a green silk scarf over her head, and wearing large, heavy dark glasses debarked from a Pan American World Airways plane at Roissy airport and stood in line with other economy-class passengers while her oversized shoulder bag was passed through customs and her ordinary citizen's U.S. passport perfunctorily checked by an immigration clerk. Then she hailed a taxi and directed the driver to take her to 41 Rue du Faubourg St. Honoré.

Ambassador Mariana Hillman Otis, traveling incognita, had completed her six-thousand-mile journey from Paris to Washington and return.

She had been absent from her post for approximately thirty-one hours, having left the Residence after telling her butler she was going for a walk. At the corner of Avenue de Marigny she signaled a taxi and was driven to Roissy, where she proceeded to the Air France counter and picked up the economy ticket she had ordered by phone two hours earlier, showing the still valid passport issued three years previously when she was a private citizen. Her diplomatic passport, for use just in case, was securely tucked away in her purse.

No one recognized her either going or coming back.

The flight left Roissy at 5 P.M. and the ambassador reached Dulles International at eight o'clock Washington time, attracting no attention in the crowd of returning tourists. She taxied directly to her father's address on Connecticut Avenue. The house was locked and empty. After letting herself in she went immediately to the telephone and had the good luck to find Senator Bryce Halsted digesting his dinner at home and alone.

The chairman of the Foreign Relations Committee, startled but stimulated, agreed to receive her. Their discussion lasted nearly three hours, after which the ambassador returned home to Connecticut Avenue, called the White House switchboard, got through to the President, and obtained an appointment to breakfast with him at seven-thirty next morning.

That discussion, to which an astonished Secretary of State was summoned by the President, lasted exactly an hour. The ambassador then taxied back to Connecticut Avenue, booked her return flight, and took off shortly after 11 A.M.—late afternoon Paris time.

Now she sat facing me in the silence of midnight, a bottle of my scotch on the desk between us. Aside from a slight pallor and the shadow of fatigue under her eyes she seemed none the worse for her experience. She was smiling slightly, but there was no mistaking the grim set of her jaw, the almost fanatical determination behind that look.

"Courtailles was well informed," she was saying. "Pourparlers between Moscow and Washington have been in progress since April—in fact the major terms of the treaty have already taken shape and are due for discussion in New York next month—secretly—while the Secretary and the foreign ministers are at the U. N. Assembly. The British will be there, of course, and Nicollet's man, Bloire. The West Germans have been kept informed throughout, but not the Dutch, or the Italians, or the Belgians. The Secretary wants to have a fait accompli in hand before any announcement of the plan is made."

She paused and sipped her drink. I said, "He told you all this?"

"With the greatest reluctance and—I was going to say annoyance, but that wouldn't describe it. He was enraged, Tyler, and just barely holding it down. Only the presence of the man behind the desk in the Oval Office restrained him, and obliged him to answer questions from me that brought out, at last, the story of what's been going on."

Quietly, tiredly, she detailed the facts—the original West German démarche in Washington, in the first weeks of the administration, enthusiastic support by an ambitious new Secretary of State who proposed the plan to the President as a history-making move for world peace, the veiled preliminary soundings in London and Paris, which offered cautious encouragement, followed by the opening of top-secret talks with the Soviets, from whom the Secretary was hoping for final agreement during the forthcoming U.N. meeting.

"But wouldn't it have been the better course of action to bring it all into the open from the beginning?" I said. "Why has all the secrecy been necessary?"

"Because the Secretary trusts no one, and for fear that the people who believe as I do—there are millions of them—would be aroused and united in opposition. Not only Americans, but the people of free Europe and free opinion everywhere in the world. But if these people are confronted with an international understanding that could become the basis for a solemn treaty commitment, the Secretary is certain he can make his proposal stick."

"And the President?"

"He wanted to hear my view of it. He also wanted to be sure the Secretary heard it. That's why he called him in—burning with indignation, of course. Then he just let us fight it out between the two of us. It was more than I'd hoped for, having them both there together. Actually there was little I could add to what I said at the American Club, but I could ask questions. That's what I went to Washington for—that and to talk to Bryce Halsted."

"Halsted was a gamble."

"It was all a gamble, Tyler. I wasn't even sure Halsted would let me into his house. But he did. And listened patiently for at least half an hour before he began to ask questions of his own. He was stiff and grumpy at first. He made me feel like a trespasser, invading his privacy that way." She smiled again. "The black servant who answered the bell couldn't believe it when he saw a woman at the door. Neither could the gateman at the White House when he saw I was wearing pants."

"The Senator's probably still recovering from the shock."

"I think he was impressed, like the President, because I'd come all the way from Paris to see him. Once I was inside, he was a complete gentleman—insisted on giving me a drink, pressed food on me—but, mainly, he listened. It was all I needed. And I told him everything, Tyler—called it unconfirmed officially but said the reports had started spreading in Europe. My one fear was that the Secretary had taken him into his confidence and he knew about it already, although I doubted that very much—Halsted would have been on the Senate floor thundering his opposition as soon as he knew. And I was right."

Again she paused to sip her drink. "You must be exhausted, Mariana."

"From the neck down, yes. In a little while I'm going to put a note on my door not to disturb me until ten o'clock in the morning. Then I'm going to my bedroom and conk out like I've never done before. But I still want to know from you what went on here while I was away." Suddenly she made a face like a mischievous schoolgirl. "Do you realize I managed to outwit not only Spaulding but Ralph Hobbs and his whole damn CIA? Or did I?"

"You did."

"Shows how easy it is," she said, and added, "I don't care if they've bugged everything in the house again!"

"Snuffy was in a panic by last night. I told him I was ignorant of the whole thing, of course. This morning he was back at me—Washington was obviously giving him hell because he couldn't produce his ambassador. But when I came back from lunch he'd changed, and I knew then he'd had the word."

She nodded. "By that time I'd left the White House and the Secretary was back at State."

Another silence. I said, "Well, if I'm permitted to know—what's the conclusion from all this? The press is in an uproar, of course. I'll confess I was wondering last night if you'd still be the ambassador to France today."

"Perhaps by tomorrow I won't be," she said, "but neither the President nor the Secretary raised the question, so I did! I said I had no intention of resigning, though I would if the President thought it best. But I gave fair warning that if I did resign, I'd take the détente issue straight to the American people."

"What was their reaction to that?"

"No direct answer. The Secretary asked me to pledge in the presence of the President to make no further public statement about the situation without department clearance. I said I would obey—until further notice."

"And Halsted?"

Her tired little smile again. "I imagine the President—and the country—will be hearing from Senator Halsted, very soon."

We stood up together and I opened the study door. As she stepped into the hall she paused and turned back to me, speaking in a low voice. "Has Brad Lindley called?"

I shook my head.

She turned away again before I could see her expression. "Good night, Tyler" was all she said, and I watched her walk slowly down the corridor and into her apartment.

Returning to my own room, I saw Mitchell Remington's letter lying still unanswered on the escritoire. But I knew now I was no more able to write him the truth tonight than I had been to confess our deception to the ambassador.

Later I would have to face up to both, but not while Mariana's survival remained in doubt and there was anything I could do to help her.

There was one thing I could do right now.

A Paris concierge, more likely than not, has been roused from sleep for so many years by late night rings at the door that she, or he, never really wakens. It's reach up, press the button, and then roll over again, still dead to the world, leaving the supplicant free to find his own way, whether coming home without a key, making an unexpected visit, entering with intent to crime, or any one of many other motives.

The concierge at Number 11 Place Dauphine reacted true to form and I was the caller, but my motive was difficult to categorize, in fact I didn't quite understand it myself. Given my personal inclination, it was difficult, illogical, even senseless. I only knew I had to do what I was about to do, and felt it so urgently that I couldn't rest until I'd done it.

Once inside the apartment house I groped around until I found one of those two-minute lights for the stairway—no elevator in the four-story building. From then on it was simply a question of reading the brass nameplates, two on each landing, until I found Brad Lindley's apartment on the third floor.

The lights went out again while I was ringing his bell. Within, I could hear what sounded like a radio voice muffled by static. At least somebody was awake inside.

He came to the door himself, collarless and wearing a dressing gown.

"Tyler Paine, for God's sake."

"May I come in?"

He studied me a moment. "Sure. And have a drink."

It was a disheveled bachelor pad. The noise came from an elaborate shortwave radio receiver emitting sounds that identified a New York station. Lindley switched it off.

"Trying to pick up the latest," he said, "but interference is bad tonight." He nodded toward the liquor. "Help yourself."

I settled for some more scotch from an equally elaborate bar while my host filled a fresh pipe. Then he sat down near me with a quizzical stare. "You drunk or something, Tyler?"

"Do I look it?"

He laughed. "You look all right to me. But isn't it a bit eccentric to be arriving without notice at this time of night?"

"Conceded." I could have said, perhaps no more unusual than his night arrivals at the Residence, but I let it go.

"Anyway," he said, "it's always good when old friends get together, right?"

"Old friends" made it a little excessive but I reciprocated with a nod. "I'm glad I found you at home and not running around somewhere tracking down a story."

"Yeah." He blew a smoke ring. "This is a busy time. Matter of fact I just got back from watching a student mass meeting over at the Sorbonne."

"I thought things were pretty quiet in those parts."

"Not exactly."

"Anything I ought to know?"

He grinned, but without much humor. "Tomorrow's time enough. Meanwhile, I'm always looking for new angles. Got something for me, Tyler?"

"Not a news story, no."

He was watching me with shrewd, waiting eyes. "How's Yolande Vannier, by the way?"

"Not in Paris at the moment." Suddenly I laughed. "I hope you don't think I expected to find her here."

"I've had some luck in my time," he answered, "but I'm not *that* lucky." And after a moment, as if minding his manners, "I trust the ambassador is well?"

"Thriving. It's one hell of a political mess, isn't it?"

My turn to wait. But all he said, half chanting, was "The French they are a funny race. . . ."

"And so are the British, and the Germans, and the Russians, and the Americans," I finished for him.

"Did you come here to sing folk songs with me, is that it?" All at once he was exasperated. "Because if it's something like that I'd rather make it another night, if you don't mind. I'm tired and I want to catch some sleep."

"No, Brad. No folk songs."

"Or maybe you swilled a couple too many and took it into your head to come over here and tell me I was a shit to Mariana about that Courtailles dinner? If that was your idea you're a little slow getting it out, aren't you? A little scared, maybe? A little sorry now you came?"

"Nothing like that."

His anger suddenly filled the room. He was on his feet almost shouting. "Then just what the hell *is* this all about?"

In the abrupt silence I stood up with deliberation and faced him. It was very hard for me to say and I tried to say it quietly. "I think she wants you to come back, Brad. I think she needs you."

20

IT BEGAN AS something not really noticed—a faint, distant background noise that vaguely altered the accustomed hum of early afternoon traffic across the Place de la Concorde, heard almost subconsciously beyond the rim of office sounds in the Chancery.

I was sitting dejectedly at my desk, feeling the gray day in my veins and poring over the newspapers in dismay. Press reaction to the ambassador's talk was still clamorous. The Paris *Herald Tribune* was reporting an angry speech on the Senate floor by Bryce Halsted demanding that the Secretary of State either confirm or repudiate Mariana's warnings in her American Club speech. Failing a forthright comment from the Secretary, Halsted's Foreign Relations Committee wanted a statement from the White House itself. A separate article quoted influential editorials from coast to coast.

Figaro, astutely analyzing Halsted's address, called it the opening attack in a congressional offensive. I wanted to take the paper in to the ambassador but, in keeping with our custom, was waiting until summoned.

The French cartoonists were having a field day. Typical of left-wing reaction was a caricature of the ambassador as Marianne, symbol of France—the Stars and Stripes emblazoned on her headband—holding up a smoldering missile.

I was shaking my head over that one when I became aware of the sound again, this time unmistakably a faraway shouting and singing, confused with taxi horns and police whistles. Looking through my window, I saw nothing unusual, but the noise was coming steadily nearer. It was somewhere across the river, perhaps behind the Palais Bourbon, and then I saw the first faces, the head of a marching column with banners and waving signs tramping up the Boulevard St. Germain and out onto the quai toward the Concorde bridge. Police were moving along its flanks, watchful but evidently not interfering unless the marchers became disorderly.

Who were they and what was the purpose? Demonstrations are frequent in Paris but I hadn't heard anything about this one in advance. Suddenly I remembered Brad Lindley's offhand reference last night—the mass meeting at the Sorbonne. This crowd was coming from that direction, but still too far away for me to distinguish their age and dress. Whoever they were, there were a lot of them! The vanguard had reached the bridge and were starting across to the Right Bank, but the rear of their column was not yet in sight—a long, serpentine band of motley colors under the cloudy sky, pressing forward out of the boulevard's mouth.

A shrilling siren drew my gaze down to the Concorde itself. Police vans and patrol cars were moving simultaneously from the Rue de Rivoli, Rue Royale, and the *allées* alongside the Champs Elysées with synchronized precision and taking up tactical positions around the square. Within seconds, in a cacophony of protesting horns, massive traffic jams built up on all three main streets.

I looked back to the marchers again—the leaders were halfway across the bridge and the end of the column was still out of sight. I could see them clearly now, students all right, in shirts and blue jeans, at least a thousand of them already in view, though with all that long hair it was hard to distinguish males from females. I wondered if Cristy Otis and Yves Lannuc were among them. They were trooping forward ten or twelve abreast, arms locked, swaying placards held aloft as they came, voices in unison chanting that old refrain, *Ami go-home!*

And bound, of course, for the United States embassy, where marine sentries were just now swinging shut the high gates to the courtyard.

I dove for the door to the ambassador's office and opened it without knocking. She was standing at the central window looking down on the Concorde, Spaulding on one side of her, Ralph Hobbs on the other.

It was Hobbs who wheeled as I came in. He spoke harshly.

"Well, Paine, what is it?"

Mariana turned at his words and smiled at me.

"Can I be of any assistance, ma'am?"

"Yes, I want you here, Tyler."

Spaulding gave me a frown but neither man said anything more. I took my place just behind the ambassador where I could look over her shoulder at the crowds gathering behind police lines in the surrounding streets to watch the marchers stream onto the square and assemble in steadily growing numbers outside the Chancery gates. Tourists were gawking from the balconies of the Hotel Crillon next door. On the other side of the river the end of the column had emerged at last and the stragglers were hurrying to join their comrades on the bridge to swell the crowd before the embassy.

And just then the rain that had been threatening all morning began to fall. At first lightly, soon in a steady, heavy downpour, greeted by a roar of disappointment from the crowd.

Behind us a secretary said nervously, "Excuse me, sir, Mr. Hobbs, sir, a police commander asking for you at the side entrance. He wants you to call the marines inside, sir."

As he went out I saw clerks and secretaries standing in the hall and talking in whispers. They looked anxiously at Hobbs striding grimly past.

Below us the demonstrators were all assembled now. They filled the square as far across as the central fountains. At a signal from one of the leaders the hostile placards were hoisted high and a hoarse rhythmic shout went up through the rain—*Ot-is go-home! Ot-is go-home!*—accompanied by jeers and threatening gestures at the marine guards in the courtyard.

Spaulding stepped behind the ambassador, took her firmly by the shoulders, and drew her back into the room. "Better to stay out of sight, ma'am."

"On the contrary," she said. "I'm not going to take Nicollet's intimidation lying down."

Calmly she moved to the middle of her office, turned, and looked at us. When she spoke her voice was steady and clear.

"I'm going outside," she said quietly, "and if either of you—if *anybody* tries to stop me, it will have to be by force. I don't wish to be followed downstairs. Just stay here."

With deliberate steps she walked into the hall, nodded and smiled at the clerks and secretaries, and started down the stairs. I glanced at Spaulding. "*My God,*" he said softly, as if to himself, "*they'll kill her down there,*" and went hastily after her, mopping his face with his handkerchief.

I turned back to the window. The marines had disappeared. Outside the gates a line of riot police with clubs and helmets was taking up positions between the crowd and the courtyard, but I saw them turn as one man and look behind them when a long, astonished gasp came from the demonstrators, followed by sudden utter silence.

The American ambassador, coatless and hatless in the drenching rain, had walked into the center of the courtyard and stood facing them. I saw her lips move. She was saying something, calling out to them, in French, in those same clear tones I'd heard in the office moments ago. She was too far away for me to hear every word but I thought I caught the words *recevoir . . .* and *parler. . . .* As the demonstrators got the meaning of her statement a new storm of shouts swept through the crowd and drowned out her last words. It was a mixed reaction, part astonishment, part hostility, and to my own astonishment there were even a few isolated bravos and bursts of applause.

Something happened then that I'll always remember: the short, compact, black-clad figure of Mme. Hanotte, the housekeeper, bristling with defiance, hurrying out to join the ambassador as she stood there, and for a long moment they faced the crowd together, side by side.

Afterward, Mariana took the Frenchwoman's arm, they turned, and walked slowly back across the courtyard and into the Chancery.

Applause from the embassy staff followed the ambassador up the stairs and all the way back to her office. Mme. Hanotte walked proudly and protectively just behind, and after the housekeeper came Stuyvesant Spaulding, mopping his face again and motioning to the staff with his free hand to return to their work. One of Mariana's secretaries was weeping.

"The ambassador will receive a student delegation," I heard Spaulding say, sounding as if he'd arranged it himself. "Just keep calm. The situation is under control."

In the doorway Mariana held out her hand to Mme. Hanotte. The gesture said everything.

The housekeeper spoke, expressionless. "Mme. Ambassador will wish to serve refreshment to the delegation. I will see to it."

Stolid and sedate, she bowed slightly to Spaulding as she left.

"What was *she* doing in the Chancery?" he said irritably.

I reminded him that the housekeeper used the commissary and must have been in the building when the demonstration began.

Outside, the crowd was still babbling. They would be choosing a group of leaders to meet with the ambassador, who had already instructed Hobbs to urge the police to avoid violence.

I heard my phone ringing and went to my office. It was Yolande.

The delegation left shortly before four o'clock after nearly an hour's meeting with the ambassador. By that time, with the startling efficiency Parisians seem able to command in moments of crisis, if only then, traffic had been cunningly rerouted around the massed demonstrators. They received their returning leaders with cheers, heard a brief shouted message from a spokesman, then moved back in orderly ranks across the square and the bridge and down the Boulevard St. Germain on their way home to the Quarter.

Seven youths and two girls had been admitted at the Boissy d'Anglas entrance and had filed quietly into the ambassador's office. Yves Lannuc was not one of them. Spaulding stood at one side of Mariana's desk and I on the other. Once we were all seated the ambassador got up and moved to a small chair in front of her desk, facing the semicircle of tense faces. It was a nicety of welcome not lost on her visitors.

For after all they were not hoods or bums. These kids I was

257

translating simultaneously as they spoke knew what manners were, even if they rejected them. They remained unawed by the stately surroundings. Probably they all came from middle-class intellectual backgrounds, steeped in the European tradition of political passion and protest. Were they here only because Nicollet's agents put them up to it, as Mariana believed? Surely that wasn't the whole story. There was more to them than that. And as the dialogue proceeded I saw even Snuffy Spaulding's cold disdain begin to soften with relief, in grudging acknowledgement of the dignity these young people brought to the debate.

That's what it was—a restrained, reasoned debate on the issues their elders were now arguing in the press and would soon face in Parliament. They took their turns laying it out. No one seemed chief spokesman. They were solidly fortified, too, with the facts of past American actions—with Vietnam, Cambodia, munitions diplomacy. The cause Ambassador Otis was pleading, they told her to her face, would lead Europe eventually into global war.

Russia was to be trusted. *Bien sur* Russia was to be trusted! There was no longer any alternative. Trust had to begin somewhere, sometime, and the time was growing short. Détente would bring the end of the headlong arms race. It was the keystone of progress toward the final, the beautiful goal of worldwide peace under a truly united brotherhood of nations. How could it be denied?

They had had their say now. They awaited a final response to the incontrovertible logic of young idealists. They sat there courteous and cool, unyielding and secure in their faith, and stared back at the woman they wanted driven from their country for expressing her beliefs, while outside their followers stood patiently under the still falling rain, singing, cheering, laughing by turns, their clothes soaked through, their placards and banners dripping and drooping.

And Mariana just as patiently gave them her answer, in the same direct approach she'd used in the American Club speech, never condescending, never talking down from one generation to the next. If they would not accept it now, she said, on a day years from now they would remember what she'd said in this room today—that there is no peace without a guardian sword, that it would be supreme folly to place our trust in trust alone, that the priceless gift of freedom we have won with our blood will be lost again unless we keep the means to defend it.

The ambassador rose. The meeting was over. There was no last rebuttal, yet there had been no real meeting of minds. No one offered his or her hand in friendly *au revoir*. It had to be termed a standoff. But what had been created was a mutual respect that had not been there before. It was in Mariana's eyes and it was in their grave young faces when they filed out of the office to where Mme. Hanotte stood in the anteroom behind an improvised sideboard stocked with bottles of Coke and sandwiches. Her look was as nearly benevolent as I'd ever seen it. As the secretary closed the office door I wondered whether we might see it more often from now on.

Spaulding said, "I think the worst is over. I'd better check downstairs with Hobbs."

He left by way of my office. A moment later the secretary brought in an envelope containing a message just received from the code room. With a faint smile, Mariana showed it to me. It was from the President of the United States. It read:

HANG IN THERE.

I made it to the Rue de Bellechasse as soon as I could, which was a little after seven. By that time everything was back to normal—on the surface. Mariana had returned to the Residence, Spaulding was still busy reporting the day's events to Washington, and Yolande was waiting for me.

In the midst of the student demonstration, of all times, we'd had two minutes on the phone, just long enough for her to say she was back in Paris and for me to tell her how glad I was. She had been quiet and steady and sweet—not at all the emotional outpouring I would have expected. I said I'd join her as quickly as possible, and that was it.

As I left the Chancery the rain had finally stopped but the streets still glistened. A fragrant freshness from the Tuileries Gardens was in the air. Crossing the Concorde, I opened the taxi windows to the evening breeze and slumped back in my seat, relaxing for the first time in what seemed the longest day since the ambassador arrived in France. Sunset glinted on the river and filled the city with hazy light. The dome of the Invalides glowed in its rays. And everywhere around me a human music of voices and movement curled toward the sky like smoke.

A strange reunion, in a way. If I'd tried to describe it to myself in advance I'd have imagined something passionate, sensual, with tears and protestations on both sides. Instead it was like coming home to a wife who'd been off visiting her parents for a few days, no more dramatic than that—the demure kiss of greeting, my vermouth cassis ready for me in my big glass with the split of Perrier and the little ice bucket beside it on the tray, the curtain drawn over the studio window, everything known and lived in and comfortable in the dusky light. I was being waited on. I was being loved.

I didn't ask Yolande where she had been or what she did there, and she didn't tell me. Nor did I bring up the embassy, or Mariana, or the day just past. In fact for the first little while we hardly talked at all. I was puzzled, realizing I'd unconsciously steeled myself to endure a confrontation, until it occurred to me there would be no confrontation—for her the episode was finished and the hurt forgiven, not to be mentioned again. That thought, with our second drink, unlocked my tongue and bridged the unspoken rift between us. I took her in my arms then, and we gave each other what we both so badly needed of each other, together as we were meant to be.

But it was a new Yolande, more thoughtful, almost somber, who lay beside me later listening to my description of the student demonstration and Mariana's talk with their delegation.

"I thought Yves Lannuc might be one of the leaders, but he didn't appear."

She shook her head. "To Yves Lannuc's group this is only children's play. They are the true underground, Tyler. They don't demonstrate, they act. And when they act, it is danger for us all. They are afraid of nothing."

"The ambassador has been hoping Cristy will leave them and

come home, but she hasn't even answered her mother's letter. I can't understand her, Yolande. What's the attraction of that crowd for Cristy? She's erratic and undisciplined, yes, but there's no real evil in the kid. She's barely eighteen!"

"Perhaps she was looking for this discipline, and perhaps now she has found it. They are clever, these young revolutionaries! They have adult master guides who have taught the leaders to control the behavior of the followers. Together there are long meetings of self-criticism. And drugs, of course, to break the resistance, to color the mind. A child like Cristy, from her protected background, can be fascinated by this, yield to this. They break her down, they build her personality again. And *voilà*, she is converted! She is their prize—their hostage. They have done better even than to have taken her by kidnap."

"Maybe it *was* kidnapping." And I saw again the boy tightly holding Cristy's arm as they came down the staircase at the July Fourth reception. "But who are the adult guides who teach the techniques?"

She shrugged. "Communists, *sûrement*. Experts in guerrilla war. But what Communists?—Russians, French, East Europe, Chinese? Some perhaps members now of the *faculté*. I can tell you only what my friends in the Université have told me, and even they don't know the men, or the women! Or which underground group is which. They only know the results. Ah yes, they have seen the results!"

Once more she was silent, listening to the night sounds from the street, one slim hand lying lightly on my thigh, her head turned away, her eyes closed. She breathed slowly, softly, deeply. It was a moment like this that I'd dreamed of living again with Yolande, and I wanted to give myself to it completely, as she had done. But the day just past wouldn't leave me—its images crowded my mind, as hot and vivid as my first sight of that besieging mob on the Concorde, of Mariana with Mme. Hanotte standing alone in the courtyard facing its jeers and gestures, of Mariana's look when she handed me the President's message. It was still only mid-afternoon in Washington. . . .

I lifted my head and looked down at her in the dimness. "*Chérie,* I have to go back."

"I know." She spoke without rancor, her eyes still closed.

"But things look better. Something happened this afternoon that—well, it eased the situation for the ambassador quite a bit."

I saw her smile and felt her fingers squeezing my hand. "A secret of state," she said. "It's all right, Tyler. I will not reveal it."

"Not quite a secret of state. Anyway, with a little patience, the time will come when I can talk to you freely about what's been happening. It's been a lot more than I ever expected."

"A lot has happened to me, too."

"Lately I haven't been very good about you, Yolande. Not as good as you deserve."

"Better than I deserve." She reached up, pulled my head down, and kissed me. "Now leave, before I lock the door to keep you here!"

The weather had turned clear and cooler. A mellow three-quarter moon shed its light on the city, silhouetting towers and steeples against a cloudless sky, brightening the gloomy masses of the Louvre, lifting the heart. It was too beautiful to resist going back to the Residence on foot, and at the corner of Boulevard St. Germain I turned and slowly followed the route the student demonstrators had taken earlier in the day. Momentarily their shouts and cries made ghostly echo in my ears, then were drowned in the ceaseless rush of traffic—Paris was normal again, passing me swift and unheeding as it went about the business of pleasure.

Was it only two nights ago I'd fled the empty Residence to wander along this same street? Yolande still away, Mariana in Washington, and I alone with conscience, hating the part I played. Only two nights—it seemed a month, so much had come so quickly. And what a change in just these last few hours. . . . Yolande returned to Paris and to me, the President's message—so typically abrupt, so characteristically affectionate—that gave Mariana the confidence she needed to carry on. Tonight she could sleep in the sure knowledge he had *heard* her, and would watch and listen, whatever was yet to come.

I quickened my pace and broke into a brisk walk, feeling unaccountably buoyant and hopeful about the immediate future. I didn't really expect the ambassador to need her assistant for anything more tonight, she'd be far too tired even for a chat in the study, but it would hearten me just to be down the hall and on tap. For the first time in days I could be happy for her.

There was only my own dilemma nagging to be resolved, but it was easy to put it out of mind in my relaxed mood tonight. I could thank Yolande for that.

By the time I reached the Residence I was in high good humor, refreshed and renewed after the first decent exercise I'd had in a week. Even the security guard's surly nod in response to a cheerful good night failed to dampen my spirits. I mounted the stairs two at a time with a springy step and barely repressed an impulse to whistle as I strode down the corridor.

The door to the ambassador's apartment was just closing, and Brad Lindley strolled toward me.

It was an ugly jolt. The old quick jealousy swept over me. In my moonlit euphoria I'd forgotten Brad Lindley. Now our encounter during last night's brief and inconclusive visit to the Place Dauphine flashed before my eyes and instinctively I moved aside.

But a different Brad Lindley was blocking my way, smiling his easy smile, offering his hand.

I took it, God knows why.

He didn't say a word as he moved on. He didn't have to. His look told everything. In the moment I had a vision of Mariana's look, too—like Yolande's, soft, fulfilled, content.

And I knew that now I could answer the letter from Washington.

21

Embassy of the United States
Paris, France

Mr. Mitchell Remington
Department of State
Washington, D.C.

Dear Mr. Remington:

I have been remiss in not responding sooner, as I wished to do, to your letter of 16 August. The recent course of events, as you well know, has preoccupied us all. Still, even those pressures would not have prevented me from answering you if in the meantime I had been able to reach a decision which has confronted me virtually since my arrival in France with the ambassador.

You will recall, I think, that I accepted my current assignment after some hesitation. This was not in any way because I failed to appreciate the responsibility and trust with which the department has honored me. Rather, I had felt persistent anxiety that I might not prove, temperamentally, to be the right choice for this unusual job. My doubts were greatly increased by one additional mandate, stipulated on the very eve of our departure, which required me to furnish confidential reports to you on the ambassador's daily life in thought and action.

Nonetheless, upon considerable reflection, taking into account my duty to the Foreign Service and the many other desirable and useful functions I could perform, I set aside my reluctance and undertook the challenge. It was only after I actually put your special stipulation into practice that I began gradually to realize I might not be equal to its demands.

If any confirmation of my misgivings were needed, your letter of 16 August provided it. Very evidently I have not succeeded in furnishing the kind of information about the ambassador which you feel might have sounded warning of events to come and helped prepare you to deal with their consequences. I cannot account for this shortcoming on my part and can only offer you my profound regret.

At the same time I should make clear without equivocation that my failure to furnish such warning should not be attributed to any sense of political solidarity with the ambassador. The fact is that lately I have come to recognize, on the contrary, that my personal opinions on détente have never coincided with those of Mrs. Otis, not because I chose to follow department policy but simply because they are my own.

Let the record state also that the ambassador, for whom I feel both respect as an official and admiration as a person, knows nothing of the existence of this letter nor the motives which have impelled me to write it. I do not wish her to know and I trust she will never find out. No one has knowledge of my confidential correspondence with you unless they have been informed by some one other than myself.

Although I should be most reluctant to leave a mission where I have served with such gratification, I am sure you will agree that under the circumstances no other course lies open, and I herewith request transfer from my present duties.

Sincerely,

TYLER PAINE

The letter went off next morning, airmail, via the regular French postal service, the same route used by Remington's letter to me. There was every reason to suppose it would get through to him alone. The only distinguishing mark on the plain envelope was a *Personal* in the left-hand corner that would hardly excite the curiosity of anyone with a special interest in the undersecretary's official correspondence.

It was the hardest piece of writing I ever faced. I sat up until nearly three to do it, feeling a kind of anguish with every line, torn between my belief I was doing the right thing for myself and others, and a deep sense of loss I tried to but could not deny. In a word, I was miserable. Yet once it was done and sealed and mailed there was at least the relief of knowing I couldn't undo it now. I had set my own fate in motion. I had only to let it carry me where it would.

No summons to the study this morning. Our onetime normal routine had been swallowed up in the recent turmoil. I was sitting over breakfast when I heard the ambassador's step in the hall. She was humming softly as she passed my door, the first time I had ever heard it, and involuntarily I turned away.

Last night, walking home across Paris from the Rue de Bellechasse, I had wanted Mariana's happiness. Today, in spite of myself, because of Brad Lindley, I resented it. They were together once more. Even if I hadn't tried to bring that about, again in spite of myself, I'd always known it was inevitable. And strangely, knowing now Yolande had come back to me didn't help.

This was the way it was and the way it was going to be. The time for honesty had come, the time at last for all of us to be honest, with ourselves and with each other.

At my desk in the Chancery later the sense of déja vu was strong. People were busy and calm. Had yesterday's turbulent events really taken place? Whatever had happened, the ambassador had worthily upheld the national dignity and we could now return to the old official round of receptions and ceremonies, staff conferences, and efficiency reports. Through my half-open door I saw Abigail Spaulding bustling importantly through the corridor, happily preoccupied with her appointments schedule. Honora de Chapdelaine might well be closeted with the ambassador right now, consulting on prospects for the autumn social season, and any minute Beasley Turner would be dropping around with press gossip and an offhand alibi for his absence during the height of yesterday's disturbances.

I got up and closed the door, not that it would discourage him, and went back to my *Herald Trib.* In Washington the Secretary of State had somewhat haughtily agreed to go before the Senate Foreign Relations Committee, but in executive session only, to answer questions from Chairman Halsted and others about these presistent rumors concerning a secret deal with Russia involving the future of European security. Mariana must have already seen that, and been pleased that her endeavors were bearing fruit.

Methodically I checked through the French morningers, mostly hostile. Every paper had the embassy courtyard picture, some with the ambassador confronting the crowd alone, others of Mariana with Mme. Hanotte. The latter shot seemed to show the ambassador with a more defiant facial expression, so the Communist *Humanité* had used it after adroitly clipping out the housekeeper. Little doubt that Moscow had already laid down the line—*get Ambassador Otis.* Little doubt also that the U. S. Secretary of State had failed at least temporarily to achieve the same end and was even now contriving new means of doing so.

I've never liked the man, but as I reported to Mitchell Remington in my letter I felt sympathy for his aim to inaugurate a new era of trust between the superpowers. Too bad he had to go about it in such underhanded fashion. Of course politics, above all international diplomacy, is never simple. But the faith and dedication of those French students in the ambassador's office yesterday had gone a long way toward persuading me they were right to believe, and that Stoneface was using the wrong strategy to reach his goal.

As the morning wore on without a summons from Mariana I became aware that for the first time I was subconsciously dreading it. Somehow, after seeing Lindley in the hall last night, I just didn't want to face her. At the invitation of a garrulous but not particularly inquisitive Beasley Turner (for a change) I had lunch at the Crillon, where an AP correspondent mentioned that Auguste Nicollet had suddenly and unexpectedly called a full-dress news conference for seven o'clock. What for? The Premier hadn't specified. Beasley almost choked over his *tarte aux pommes* in excitement, scalded his throat with his demitasse, and bolted for the office, forgetfully leaving me the check.

The AP man noted the hasty departure and looked back inquiringly at me. "What's *he* got a red ass about?"

I shrugged. "He'll have to cover it tonight."

"Yeah. I guess Madam Ambassador would like to know what's on Nicollet's mind, eh? Or does she already know?"

"The ambassador doesn't always share her thoughts with me."

"Yeah." He showed buck teeth in a practiced homespun grin. "How much longer d'you think she'll last here, Paine?"

"Is there some question of that?"

He laughed and dropped a paw on my shoulder. "Just thought I'd try for your reaction."

"Any time," I said.

I may not have shown it, but I was troubled by the news, especially since Nicollet's last previous formal press conference had been held in April. It certainly looked as if the Premier, after months of secrecy, rumor, and backstage maneuvers, was ready to speak out at last, had been indeed forced to do so by the pressures of recent events. And as our friend from the AP pointed out, it was bound to involve the political status of the ambassador. It could mean as well, since the two questions were now inseparable, a government foreign policy statement on the eve of next week's National Assembly session which could encompass the whole issue of détente, relations with Washington and Moscow, and France's position on NATO.

Back in my office, again with this new feeling of reluctance to speak to Mariana unless spoken to, I left the news-bearing to the eager Beasley. But I was pretty sure he wouldn't be the earliest to get word to her—Brad Lindley would have reported in immediately. And it would be his second call of the day. After an occasion like last night, the first would have been a breakfast call.

Naturally.

It came to me with a jolt that I was thinking exactly like a jealous lover. With an effort, I put them both out of my mind—and in the same moment realized I myself had made no breakfast call or any other call to Yolande. Just as I reached guiltily for the phone the ambassador's extension rang.

"Yes, ma'am?"

"I thought we'd agreed to drop that ma'am long ago, Tyler." She sounded relaxed and easy and I could hear her smile in the words. "I'm sorry to give you such short notice, but I wonder if you're free to have dinner tonight—just the two of us at the Residence—and early, how about six? No duty—just fun. Can you make it?"

"With pleasure."

I tried not to show my surprise. But after we hung up I understood. I'd be filling in for a previous date with Brad Lindley, detained, of course, by the Nicollet press conference. And while Mariana waited for news of that crucial occasion, who better to hold her hand than faithful old Tyler, special assistant, trusted confidant, official consoler—and soon to be former all three.

It might just be the last such tête-à-tête we would have, but I didn't want to think about that.

I picked up the other phone. Yolande would have to wait.

Alone under the lofty ceiling in the upstairs dining room, we talked about everything except politics and Lindley, while the venerable Jacques served us with quiet perfection—reminiscing all the way back to our first wary meeting in Washington, smiling over the stuffy Social Usage briefings at the department, the captain's gala on the Atlantic crossing, Beasley Turner stuck with the welcoming bouquet at the Courtailles reception on the pier. Again we pondered the still unsolved bugging mystery, recalled the newly estimable Mme. Hanotte's fuss about Lafite-Rothschild '61, laughed at our champagne sousing in Rheims, reviewed Mariana's notorious stag dinner, the wild July Fourth rainstorm (but without reference to Cristy's disappearance), and, of course, the fashion show evening.

I didn't know whether the ambassador was thinking the same thing I was as the conversation finally dwindled. But looking back, that evening clearly marked the end of carefree times at the embassy. The era of Brad and Yolande began, yes, but from then on shadows loomed—Cristy unheard from in the Quarter, Mariana's deteriorating relationship with Spaulding, my own increasing difficulty with the reports to Remington. And over all hung the cloud of stealthy diplomacy in Washington and Moscow with its vital import for every Western capital.

Well, the bubble of secrecy had burst at last. Between them, Claude Courtailles and Ambassador Otis could take the credit. And as the story unfolded bit by reluctant bit, the latest chapter would be written tonight by the fine hand of Auguste Nicollet at the Palais Matignon, a short distance from where we sat.

I looked across the table at my hostess, youthful in a bright summer dress, hands demurely in her lap. "You have the gift of composure, Mariana. After what you've been through this summer, I can only marvel."

"Sometimes outward composure," she said, "but never inside."

"Right now that's hard to believe."

She gave me a charming little smile. "How keen you are! It's true that since—well, tonight I do feel really tranquil, Tyler. For the first time it doesn't seem to matter a damn what happens to me from now on. Do you ever have that feeling? I hope you do."

"When I'm with Yolande. But it never lasts."

With a swift impulsive movement she reached across and touched my hand. "Keep working at it, my dear. You'll find it happens more often."

"Have you found that?"

She hesitated for a moment and colored faintly. "I think so, yes."

"I saw Brad Lindley last night."

"He told me. He also told me you saw him the night before, in his apartment."

"I wish he hadn't."

Her voice was gentler. "Don't say that. It was the sweetest thing you ever did."

I don't know why, but suddenly I felt like a stranger. "Anyway, I'm glad you've made it up, for your sake," I said.

"Not for his sake, too?" And answering her own question, "I

know you thought he let me down badly when he broadcast about my seeing Courtailles."

"Everybody thought so."

"So did I. I remembered what he'd done in Marseille once before and decided I'd been terribly wrong in caring about him—he was just another journalist using me for his career. For quite a long time I expected never to speak to him again. But then, as it turned out, I saw he'd really helped me. It was Brad's broadcast that brought the whole détente question into the open and forced the issue for Courtailles, and for me." She paused. "Still, as long as he stayed away, I couldn't bring myself to be the one to speak first. I have you to thank for bringing him back, Tyler."

I shook my head. "It was only a matter of time while he got that temper of his under control before he'd be around knocking on your door."

She smiled. "However it happened, I'm grateful."

The cavernous quiet of the Residence closed around us again. I said after a moment, like another man speaking, "I wish you both well, Mariana."

"We had a long talk last night. Brad wants to retire—has he told you that? He's had the TV treadmill up to here. His head is full of book ideas and he wants to get down to his house in Sardinia and work on them."

"Do you see yourself in that house in Sardinia?"

Rapid footsteps in the hall forestalled her response. We both looked up to see Beasley Turner, white as a sheet, trotting toward us across the room, head bobbing up and down, eyes bulging.

"Madam Ambassador—." He was gasping a little.

"Yes, Beasley?"

"A shooting. Outside the Matignon. They tried—I think they were trying to get Nicollet. Blaise d'Archeval stepped in front of him—."

He stopped, totally out of breath, and grabbed the back of my chair. In the Faubourg St. Honoré an ambulance sounded its siren.

The night went very fast after that. By the time I got to the scene the Palais Matignon was already roped off to a distance of some three hundred yards, its gates were closed, the ambulance had departed, and heavy police forces were keeping the crowds moving.

My diplomatic ID got me nowhere with a gruff officer in charge. He had no information, period.

You could feel the tension in the streets and see it in the faces. I circled the police cordon and walked quickly on to the Chancery, but nobody was in the offices. The marine lieutenant on duty said, "They're all at the Residence, sir—Mr. Spaulding, Mr. Hobbs, and some security people."

It was nearly dark by the time I made it back, a muggy, oppressive evening threatening rain. I didn't see Spaulding but the guard told me he was with Mariana in her apartment. Hobbs had his command post set up in the study. He was on the phone to somebody at the Interior Ministry when I came in and gave me only a glance.

Beasley Turner got up from a chair and guided me back into the hall. He had his breath again and some of his color. "What did you find out, Tyler?"

"Less than nothing. I'm listening."

For once, he was telling me. He relayed what Hobbs knew so far. "There were at least two of them. Apparently one was caught. They missed the Premier because d'Archeval intercepted the shots. He's been taken to Beaujon Hospital. We don't know just how bad he is but they say he's pretty bad."

"Did this happen in Nicollet's office?"

"Outside the Palais. A little while before the news conference was supposed to start. Nicollet was coming back from the Elysée after seeing the President. D'Archeval and one or two other people were with him."

"Did you see it?"

He shook his head. "I'm glad I didn't. I was inside with about fifty reporters. We all ran out when we heard the shooting but the guards didn't let us see much. They rushed Nicollet upstairs and carried d'Archeval inside. By that time the guards had pushed us back into the street and the reporters were all running for phones.

Brad Lindley, too. The Residence was just up the street. I thought I'd better tell the ambassador right away."

"But *why*, Beasley? What's the motive?"

He shrugged. "Hobbs is trying to find out about that."

Down the hall the door to the ambassador's apartment opened and Stuyvesant Spaulding appeared. He looked shaken. All I got was a glacial stare as he walked past us and into the study.

I looked back at Beasley. "Have they identified the suspect?" I said.

"He's a student, that's all we've been told."

"A *student!* Why didn't you say so?"

He started to speak again but I brushed past him and went back into the study.

Hobbs had hung up and was facing Spaulding across the desk. "They know the group responsible for this. Right now they're throwing a dragnet over the whole Quarter. They'll bring in every damn kid that can move. Also, the ambassador is not to stir out of this building until further notice. Have the housekeeper make her stay clear of windows. They've put some people in the garden to watch the Avenue Gabriel side."

Spaulding nodded and went out again. I said, "Have there been threats against the ambassador?"

"A few crank calls so far. But we can't take chances on what they'll do." He moved around the desk and spoke sardonically. "It might help if *now* you'd give us Cristy's address."

"Hotel des Fosses," I said without hesitation.

"So you *do* know where she is!"

"I know where she was."

"What do you know about her friends?"

"The name of one of them. Yves Lannuc." I spelled it while he wrote it down.

"No other names?"

I shook my head.

"Political kid?"

"I'm not sure. He's a serious student."

"They're all serious students, Paine. Too goddamn serious, and this is where it gets them. I suppose Lannuc was in that demonstration yesterday."

"I didn't see him. But it doesn't make sense."

"What doesn't make sense?"

"I mean that demonstration was pro-détente, so it had to be pro-Nicollet, too. Why would any of those kids want to shoot Nicollet?"

He glared at me. "We're dealing with weirdos, Paine. Let the French figure it out."

"How's d'Archeval?"

"Critical. Chest wounds. Wouldn't have happened at all with proper security. Maybe they'll learn their lesson now." He picked up the phone. "I'll report your information. And stay around in case you're needed."

"Don't worry."

"Close the door behind you."

I went back into the hall. Turner wasn't visible but I could hear his excited babble echoing on the staircase. He was saying something to somebody in a pleading voice but I didn't catch the words. I'd taken half a dozen steps toward the stairway when Cristy Otis appeared on the top landing.

I had a single swift glance at her terror-stricken, tear-stained face as she ran past me down the hall to the ambassador's apartment, tore open the door, and vanished inside.

22

A T   P R E C I S E L Y   1 1   P . M ., a little over four hours after the assassination attempt at the Palais Matignon, Premier Auguste Nicollet appeared on France's television screens with his first statement. In solemn tones he announced that an extremist conspiracy designed to discredit his government's détente policy had been smashed and the plotters seized. He named them as members of the Guerre des Jeunes, Yves Lannuc's group. If it had not been for the heroic action of a government official, he said, the assassin's bullets would have pierced the body of the Premier himself. He asked the French people's prayers for the recovery of Blaise d'Archeval, now lying gravely wounded in a hospital. A sweeping investigation into the motive for the shooting and a possible international connection was still under way, he added, and its results would be made public as quickly as they became known. Meanwhile he wanted to give every assurance that the business of government was continuing without interruption in an atmosphere of complete calm. He concluded with the traditional Gaullist affirmation, *Vive la France!* and the screen went dark.

I watched Nicollet's TV appearance sitting in the ambassador's apartment, along with Mariana and the Spauldings. Cristy was in her old bedroom in the charge of Mme. Hanotte and under sedation administered by Holmes Anson, the embassy's favorite physician. On her arrival at the Residence in a semi-hysterical condition she had refused questioning by Hobbs but had told her mother she'd been caring for Yves Lannuc, who was in bed with a high fever, when word came of the assassination attempt. Despite her protestations the boy ordered her to leave at once and take refuge in the embassy.

What she still did not know, although Hobbs had since informed the ambassador, was that police raided the hotel shortly before ten o'clock, took Yves Lannuc from his bed, and lodged him in a cell at the Prefecture along with other prime suspects in the shooting.

Now Spaulding walked across the room, switched off the TV, and turned to the ambassador. He was gray-faced with fatigue. "I expect nothing more of substance tonight, ma'am. I suggest you try to get some much-needed rest. With your leave, Abigail and I will spend the night in one of the bedrooms downstairs."

"Please do call, Mariana, if there's anything at all we can do." Abigail gave the ambassador a stiff little peck on the cheek and left the room.

The deputy chief was staring impatiently at me. He wanted to talk about Nicollet's veiled reference to a foreign angle, of course, and this was no time for me to object to being excluded.

"I'll be in my room if needed," I said to the ambassador, and left.

In the hall I heard my outside line ringing insistently and hurried to answer it. Yolande said, "Tyler! Thank God. I have been worrying for you. Only police calls were allowed by the operator."

"There hasn't been a second to call you again since I phoned from the Chancery, darling."

"You have heard Nicollet on the television just now? Poor Blaise! Such a lovely man. But who were they who did this terrible thing?"

"A student group, the police say. Cristy got away and came here just before they arrested Yves Lannuc."

"Yves Lannuc!" There was a long silence. "Oh, Tyler! I told you how dangerous they are."

"Cristy says he's been sick in bed for two days."

"But what did Nicollet mean—'international connection'?"

I couldn't tell her. I wished I knew. But from the little I'd heard so far, it looked like a rough time ahead for Cristy, and her mother.

For the second night I had to tell Yolande I couldn't come to the Rue de Bellechasse.

"Not even *un petit moment, chéri?*"

"We're under orders here."

She sighed. "I will worry for you the whole night."

"Don't worry about me. Worry about the ambassador. It sounds as if they're going to try to connect her with all this."

"Perhaps," said Yolande, "they are right."

I didn't want to answer that and I didn't have to, because the conversation was ended abruptly by a discreet tapping at my door.

On the threshold, looking deferential, stood M. André Perpidan of the Sûreté.

"May I come in, M. Paine? I regret the necessity at this late hour, but M. Hobbs tells me that Her Excellency has already retired for the night."

I stood aside for him and watched him give the room a quick once-over before sitting down opposite me. "Your colleague has just informed me," he said gently, "that you are in perhaps the best position to answer my questions on this unfortunate occasion. I have reference, of course, to Her Excellency's daughter. She had been living with Yves Lannuc for some time?"

"She left the embassy July Fourth, but I don't know whether she has been living with Yves Lannuc or anyone. I know she has been living at the Hotel des Fosses because I visited her there, once. I've had no news of her since, none whatever. Except, of course, until she came home tonight. I haven't talked with her tonight."

"You are specific, M. Paine. I appreciate that. Would you tell me the substance of your conversation the last time you talked with her?"

"I delivered a letter from the ambassador. Miss Otis said she would reply later in writing."

"And the substance of the letter?"

"It was a personal letter. Naturally I didn't read it. I gathered it was a request to Miss Otis to return home, or at least to talk to her mother."

"The daughter said nothing further to you?"

"I don't recall her exact statement, but she conveyed the idea that she didn't want to come back to the embassy."

"The daughter made no reference to Yves Lannuc, or the nature of his activities?"

"None."

"Does Her Excellency know Yves Lannuc?"

"The ambassador? No, indeed."

"That is, to your knowledge."

"To my knowledge, of course. But I would undoubtedly—."

He held up a hand. "Has Her Excellency ever communicated with Yves Lannuc, or perhaps received communication from him?"

"I'm certain she has not."

"Again, to your knowledge."

"That is correct."

Why wasn't Spaulding or Hobbs in the room? I was being questioned by a French police official on extraterritorial soil in an extremely grave context.

"Nor have you personally had such communication with Yves Lannuc?"

"No." I stood up. "M. Perpidan, I don't object to answering your questions but this is a serious matter. Under the circumstances I think that at the very least an embassy witness should be present."

He nodded thoughtfully, still seated. "You are quite right, of course. I assumed that the embassy would be willing to co-operate with me, just as on a former occasion I co-operated with the embassy to investigate another matter on these premises."

"Let me ask you a question, M. Perpidan. Are you suggesting there is some relation between your two visits here?"

"It is not an impossibility. However, I am concerned just now with the events of today. As you know, my own bureau deals with problems of foreign affairs. But I have to remind you that there is a primary national aspect to the investigation as well."

"Which means?"

He shrugged. "It would be best if Mlle. Otis, the daughter, goes before an examining magistrate."

"I will see that the ambassador is informed of this conversation as soon as she's available in the morning."

He stood up now and extended his hand. "I thank you very much. You have been very kind to receive me."

At the door I said, "All of us here are mystified by what happened tonight at the Palais Matignon. The Premier spoke in his television statement of a possible international connection. Just what did he have in mind?"

For the first time I saw something like a smile begin at the edge of his lips.

"Did I question you about the ambassador's secret journey to America?"

"Not secret—merely incognita. A visit to her father."

"Ah?" he said, and shrugged again. "Good night, M. Paine."

He joined another man standing watchfully at the top of the staircase. I saw them out of sight and went to the study.

"I've been waiting for you." Ralph Hobbs swung his heels from my desk. "What did Perpidan say?"

"If you'd been with him, as I think you should have been, I wouldn't have to tell you."

"He wanted to see you alone, Paine."

"Is this regular practice between you two?"

"We've used it, yes."

"You have an understanding?"

"When it's a matter of mutual advantage."

"Like the bugging of the Residence?"

His face hardened. "What the hell do you mean by that?"

"Just confirming for my own satisfaction that CIA works with the French police."

"What's CIA got to do with this? The question is out of order. What did Perpidan say to you?"

"Why don't you ask him yourself? You work together."

"You keep this up and you're in trouble, Paine. What did he say?"

I told him and he seemed disappointed. "Is that all he said?"

"That's all he said. I'll tell the ambassador in the morning. Has Spaulding gone to bed yet?"

"Spaulding's work is just beginning. He's on the phone over at the Chancery, taking the heat from Washington. You better turn in now yourself. Tomorrow's a long day."

"Good night then."

"By the way—." He stopped me at the door. "Friend of yours was down at the gate a while ago asking to see you."

"To see me? Who was that?"

"Brad Lindley. I didn't let him in."

My alarm had been set for seven but it was the ambassador's call that woke me with ten minutes still to go. She sounded grave and steady. Would I escort her to the hospital to inquire as to the condition of Blaise d'Archeval?

At exactly seven-thirty I joined her in the limousine. On the front seat beside Pascal stood a basket of flowers the ambassador had picked in the garden on her way out. I noticed an extra detail of police discreetly nearby in the Faubourg St. Honoré. With the inevitable security car following close behind, we headed for Beaujon Hospital.

"You look as if you've had some rest, Mariana."

"Lying awake all night won't help."

"And Cristy?"

"I left her at breakfast with Mme. Hanotte. And for once, meek as a lamb. But that's all surface, of course. She's terribly worried about Yves."

"As well she might be." And I recounted my session with André Perpidan.

She heard me out, then said just as we pulled up before the hospital: "Tyler, Cristy swears their group had nothing to do with the shooting and I believe her."

More police here, keeping an eye on the small crowd gathered in vigil outside. Fortunately there were no reporters. We were watched in stony silence as we went in. It was a little early for the hospital staff, but we waited while word went upstairs and the *directeur* himself came down, hurriedly pulling on a white coat, a bearded man with the impassive doctor's look. He received us graciously and accepted the flowers for his patient.

"The count will be touched by your visit, Excellency. He is not now in condition to be informed. Yes, he is holding his own after emergency surgery. There is hope. There is always hope."

Workaday Paris was bustling awake on the return trip. Shop shutters were going up with a clang, bakeries busy with early customers. Hardly a glance at us whirling by, but then official cars were a common sight in this district. It could have been any eight o'clock of the week. I waited for Mariana to resume the conversation interrupted by our arrival at the hospital but she sat silent and motionless at my side.

It took an effort, but I said: "Brad Lindley came to the Residence late last night. Hobbs wouldn't let him in to see me. When Hobbs told me, I tried to reach him by phone but there was no answer. Hobbs was blocking all incoming calls, of course, except the ones he wanted, so there was no way for Lindley to get through."

Her expression didn't change. "Thank you for telling me, Tyler." It was all she said.

Stuyvesant Spaulding was waiting at the Residence entrance as we drove into the courtyard. He bowed stiffly, making no effort to conceal his profound annoyance, and opened fire at once.

"It was most unwise, ma'am, both politically and for your personal safety, to call at the hospital at this time. If you had bothered to let me know I could have warned you. A brief statement deploring the incident was required. I have already issued it to the press."

Her reply was curt. "I wanted to do it and I'm glad I did it."

He turned to me. "Henceforth I will be obliged, Mr. Paine, if you will keep me informed as to all unscheduled comings and goings."

"I didn't want to disturb you, sir. Mr. Hobbs had indicated you would have a very late night."

"Indeed," he said, as if that was none of my business, and turning back to the ambassador: "I have been in touch with Washington. At length. May I see you alone immediately?"

"Very well. Tyler, I won't be going to the Chancery today. Please stay here in the Residence in case I need you."

"I'll be in the study, ma'am."

I watched them go up the stairs together. Abigail Spaulding was just coming down. She stopped as if to speak to the ambassador, saw the expression on her husband's face, and decided to keep on going.

Whatever Washington had said to Spaulding wasn't going to be good news for its Paris ambassador, I was sure of that.

Hunched over the morning papers at my desk in the study, I shook my head in dismay. Yves Lannuc was squarely in the middle of it. The assassination attempt occupied most of the front pages, together with large head shots of Nicollet and d'Archeval. The best the photographers had been able to do on the arrested man was one quick view showing him from the rear, a defiant figure being shoved into a police car with his hands manacled behind his back. He was young, thin and dark, shaggy-haired and in shirt sleeves, wearing baggy trousers and what looked like espadrilles. His name was given as Charles Androuet, *sans adresse*, at least until recently a science student at Nanterre. No weapon had been found at the scene and Androuet was said to be denying all accusations. Lannuc's name was given among the seven or eight principal suspects in custody in addition to Androuet.

Dozens of arrests had been made during the night in the Latin Quarter. The winnowing process would go on all day at the Police Judiciaire. But despite their nightlong efforts, the papers had no more about the background of the shooting than I knew already. Evidently they were getting no help from the government on interpreting Premier Nicollet's reference to an international connection. They all had theories, involving everything from Albanian terrorism to the Corsican independence movement, none of which appeared to me to make sense in the détente situation. *Le Monde* reasonably suggested that perhaps pure anarchism lay behind the shooting, citing the number of arcane underground student groups with obscure and violent aims.

Among all these reactions only the leftist press raised the possibility of American involvement, but again as in the past it was individuals, "some of them connected with United States diplomatic missions abroad," who were held responsible, not the government in Washington. That was as near to saying CIA and Ambassador Mariana Hillman Otis as they got.

But it was near enough for the local edition of the New York *Herald Tribune,* which carried a compendium of French press comment and laid the leftist innuendos flatly on the doorstep of the Paris embassy. So both New York and Washington would be reading that comment when they woke up this morning.

And in Paris, Mariana's impulsive gesture of sympathy at the Beaujon Hospital would of course be seen as implying that she felt personal responsibility for the shooting.

I looked in vain for a quote from Claude Courtailles on the situation. Blaise d'Archeval, after all, until only recently had been his aide and his intimate. Maybe the ex-Foreign Minister was saving his reaction for the imminent session of Parliament.

My outside phone rang. The voice was solid and authoritative. "Tyler Paine? Marcus Feld. I'm at the airport. Your operator is not accepting calls for Ambassador Otis—is she all right?"

"Perfectly all right, Mr. Feld. She's in conference, I believe."

"Her father was upset when he couldn't get through to her last night after he heard what happened, so I arranged to fly over immediately. It looks as if she may need some advice, Mr. Paine. Will you inform her I'm here and at the Hotel Crillon as soon as I can get there?"

"I'll tell her."

One more complication. Now we had the importunate Marcus Feld to deal with. It reminded me that Brad Lindley hadn't called back this morning. If Hobbs was still putting a stop on calls to the ambassador then Lindley hadn't been able to reach her, either. I picked up the phone again and checked the network office. A bright female voice, very British: "Sorry, Mr. Paine, we don't know where to get in touch with him at the moment. He's frightfully busy, as you might suppose. I'll make sure he returns your call."

I'd hardly hung up before I heard steps in the hall and a respectful knock on the study door. I opened it to Mme. Hanotte, black-clad as always and very solemn. The ambassador would like to see me at once in her suite.

They were standing there in tense, expectant silence when I came in—Mariana, Spaulding, Ralph Hobbs, and a new addition in the person of Grant Farwell, the embassy legal attaché. A little apart from them stood Cristy Otis, wearing a dress, her face scrubbed, her hair neatly in place. I glanced at each in turn. Spaulding was obviously distressed and Hobbs wore his sourest look.

It was the ambassador who spoke, and I knew it was as much to the others as to me. "Tyler, I've decided to honor a request from the examining magistrate for Cristy's testimony. I will want you to accompany us."

Hobbs took a step forward. "You realize if you do this, Madam Ambassador, I can no longer assure your security."

Her answer was a slight smile of assent.

Spaulding made a despairing gesture. "I reiterate, ma'am—this will be the last straw! Your daughter is in no way obliged to go before a magistrate. More, I have told you Washington is adamantly opposed to you yourself becoming further involved in this ugly situation. By deliberately discarding the protection of your immunity, by appearing in public under these conditions, you are inviting fatal political consequences for the Paris mission. I can only warn you for the last time that Washington will know how to react to your defiance of its orders, finally and irrevocably."

"And I can only repeat to you," the ambassador said, "that for my part this is a simple matter of justice."

She looked at me. "We're ready, Tyler."

Again a silent ride through the city, like this morning, Pascal at the wheel, but with no security escort this time and now three passengers side by side in the back seat of the limousine, Mariana in the middle, Cristy staring expressionless at the river as we drove toward the Pont au Change. It was nearly noon. A faint scent of autumn lightened the sultry air. For a moment the majesty of Paris all around us seemed to overwhelm our human troubles. I glanced away from it at Mariana's profile, saw her serene and unafraid, and felt the old irresistible impulse to put my arms around her.

At the same time I had a feeling like premonition we would never ride together again.

We were crossing the bridge now in a maze of crowding, honking midday traffic, but instead of stopping at the Palais de Justice, Pascal turned sharp right and continued along the quai toward the Pont Neuf. I leaned forward to speak to him and felt Mariana restrain my arm.

"We're going to another address first," she murmured.

We drew up in front of Brad Lindley's apartment in the Place Dauphine.

23

THERE IS NO American law officer with duties exactly corresponding to those of a French *juge d'instruction* or examining magistrate, but district attorney is close enough. And like DA's offices in most old-fashioned public buildings, those in the Paris Palais de Justice have a shabby look, giving off long, gloomy halls leading to outer rooms with wooden benches worn and scarred by generations of unhappy people waiting to be questioned by the magistrate in his sanctum.

Such was the setting for Cristy's appearance before Monsieur le Juge Patrice Duparc.

At Brad Lindley's direction the three of us had managed to sneak into the Palais through a side door on the quai, so the ambassador wasn't recognized until we reached the judge's waiting room, where a knot of lounging reporters were checking the parade of witnesses in the Nicollet shooting case. You can imagine the effect of our unexpected arrival. But the *huissier* at the inner door, forewarned, had kept the secret and quickly ushered us through the swarming newsmen into a small antechamber.

I followed Cristy's anguished glance back at the row of prisoners waiting on the benches and saw Yves Lannuc among them. He looked feverish and gaunt but still defiant, a wisp of white scarf around his throat. It had to be the scarf ten-year-old Cristy Otis had knitted for her father. Then the door closed behind us and I could hear frustrated jabbering outside and the thud of feet racing for phones.

Whoever he was questioning at the moment, Judge Duparc cut it short and came in at once. He seemed young enough to be fresh out of the Sorbonne himself, but there was no mistaking the steel in his look. He murmured a brief formal greeting to the ambassador, bowed slightly to me, and without another word escorted Cristy into his office. She was a very scared girl but she kept her lips tight.

Her mother looked at her with pride in her glistening eyes.

The interrogation lasted nearly forty minutes. No sound penetrated the judge's padded door, but we could hear the rising tumult of anticipation in the waiting room. When at last we left, Cristy held securely between Mariana and me behind a protective phalanx of policemen summoned by the judge, we were pursued by shouted questions, popping flashbulbs and the whirr of film cameras into the hall, down the stairway and out to Pascal and the waiting car.

In the midst of it I was remembering the young judge's face as he delivered Cristy to her mother. He looked troubled.

Mme. Hanotte was waiting in the entrance hall when we returned to the Residence. No security men were visible, but as Maurice opened the car door I saw Beasley Turner standing nervously just behind the housekeeper. He waited while the ambassador gave instructions to Mme. Hanotte to accompany Cristy upstairs and order lunch for two in her room, then came forward.

"Mr. Spaulding has gone to the Chancery, ma'am, if you wish to speak with him. Washington was on the wire and he wanted to take it in his office. Also—." He flushed and hesitated.

"Yes, Beasley?"

"He told me to tell you the Foreign Ministry has asked him to call at the Quai d'Orsay tomorrow at ten to receive a communication."

I felt a sinking sensation but Mariana simply nodded without changing expression. "Is that all?"

"No, ma'am. Premier Nicollet talked to reporters as he was leaving the Matignon about an hour ago to see the President. My assistant was there—." He stopped again.

"Well, Beasley?"

"The Premier said the case is all wrapped up and Guerre des

Jeunes will be held individually and collectively responsible for the crime."

"He said guilt has been admitted?"

"No, ma'am. Apparently they're still denying it."

"Well, go on."

He spoke painfully. "The Premier mentioned a letter you wrote to your daughter. He said it contained information for one of the conspirators, Yves Lannuc."

"Nicollet has seen the letter?"

"He didn't say so."

The ambassador turned to me. "I suggest you go to the Chancery, Tyler. I want to spend a little time with Cristy just now. Keep in touch with me here. And you'd better let me know where you have lunch, just in case."

"I'll take him to the Crillon," Beasley said brightly.

"Oh, Lord!" I'd completely forgotten to tell her. "There was a message for you this morning, ma'am. Mr. Marcus Feld is at the Crillon. He talked with Mr. Hillman last night."

"I thought he might have" was all she said, and left us.

We walked to the hotel. Hard to believe it was just yesterday that I'd lunched there, it seemed more like a year since this nightmare began. Pattering along beside me, Beasley lost no time launching his monologue, the words gushing out in a cascade of relief after the effort of giving the ambassador her bad news.

"Well!" he said. "Well, well, well! Our leader has finally had it. Guess what Monsieur Blah is going to say tomorrow when he sees Stuyvie at the Quai. He's going to suggest very, very politely that Madam Ambassador be recalled to Washington, never to return, that's what he's going to say. Which will tickle old Stuyvie just about to death, because then he can go back to running the embassy all by his big masculine self, and Auntie Abigail can say 'I told you so from the very first.' As for Cristy babe, she'd better not set foot outside the Residence for one minute till the day she leaves with her mother for good, or they'll clap her into the pen along with her Left Bank buddies and not even a consul will get in to see her."

Why I didn't let him have it right there I'll never know. Maybe because I realized he was a little hysterical from shock and didn't really mean to be vindictive. So he just ran on and on through lunch while I sat facing him too sick at heart to listen anymore, making futile passes with a fork without putting anything in my mouth. Just once I thought of Yolande, poor girl, who'd probably been trying to reach me for hours, but the rest of it was all Mariana—the surprise session at Brad Lindley's, the endless silence between us as we waited for Cristy to come out of the magistrate's office, Mariana's face as she took the blows of Beasley's recital at the Residence.

"Nearly three p., old boy—shall we go?"

My host had stood up and was grinning down at me, full of food and drink and quite himself again, itching to get on with the gossip in greener fields.

On my way back to the office we stopped in the Public Affairs section to take a look at the teleprinters. Agence France-Presse already had the text of Nicollet's impromptu news conference and AP was filing a third lead on the sensation of Mariana's visit to the Palais de Justice.

"Hey—look at this!" Beasley called over from the incoming machine.

It was a UPI Washington dispatch with first details of Stoneface's appearance in closed hearing before the Foreign Relations Committee. The Senate hawks had sniffed him out. According to one of them, who asked to remain anonymous, the Secretary had confirmed Bryce Halsted's suspicion he'd made a recent secret visit to Russia without even letting his own ambassador in Moscow know he was meeting with the Soviet Premier and Foreign Minister at a site near the Finnish border.

"Wow!" Beasley chortled.

I could have said to him, "You think this is something? Stay tuned for Brad Lindley's report on tonight's network news."

But of course I didn't say it.

Don't let anybody tell you the European press can't be every bit as lurid as the most blatant American tabloid when it really gets a chance to sink its teeth into a juicy story—in this case a combination of crime, politics, and high-placed femininity. With the tallest headlines of the month, some in two colors, the Paris evening papers were outdoing their best previous efforts in recounting the latest sensational developments in *l'affaire Otis.* Walking back to the Residence by way of the Rue Boissy d'Anglas to pick up the final editions, I could hear newsboys shouting from a block away and saw lines at the kiosks around the Madeleine.

And there we were on the front pages, fighting our way down the halls of the Palais de Justice, Tyler Paine with bewilderment all over his face, Cristy clutching my arm for dear life, and Mariana on the other side as calm and assured as Princess Grace at a royal reception. Getting equal play in the opposite columns was Auguste Nicollet, wearing a smug look as he made his off-the-cuff remarks outside the Matignon earlier in the day. There had been more to these remarks than was carried on the news tickers. In at least one instance the Premier had allowed himself to be carried away a little too far—a lapse I was sure he'd soon be brushing off as a misquotation. According to this account, he'd replied to a reporter's question by saying, *"We have had means of monitoring the ambassador's private actions from day to day"*—as much of an admission of guilt in the bugging mystery as we were ever likely to get.

Less prominently displayed but still front-paged was the shooting story itself, surmounted by mug shots of Androuet, as well as Lannuc and other alleged leaders of the Guerre des Jeunes accused of carrying out the attempted assassination. Of course the editorial bias of each paper was clear from its opening paragraphs —the Left charging treason at home at the instigation of "foreign sources," the Right responding with cries of fabrication and frame-up. Blaise d'Archeval's perhaps fatal act of sacrifice was called noble by one side, foolhardy by the other.

I'd relayed all this to the Residence during the afternoon as fast as it came in, and the ambassador listened without comment. She did tell me Cristy had fallen into another exhausted sleep. She'd also talked reassuringly to her father in San Francisco and called Marcus Feld to say she was grateful for his sympathy but would not require his services at least for the present. Neither Spaulding nor Hobbs had been in touch with her.

Nor had they with me. Whatever was going on in this building outside the confines of my little office was their secret, although I had no doubt communications with Washington were frequent if not constant.

One thing I had time to accomplish, finally, was to call Yolande at the Chambre Syndicale before I left the Chancery.

"Tyler, *enfin!* You sound so very tired."

"I guess I am, at that."

"Have you news to tell me of—of her?"

"She's bearing up. You know she took Cristy to the *juge d'instruction?*"

"We have seen that on the papers." Unexpectedly she giggled like a little girl. "Oh, Tyler, the picture of you is funny!"

I agreed, and refrained from pointing out that the situation was no laughing matter for the ambassador.

"You saw what Nicollet said this morning?"

"Yes, that we have read also." As she spoke I thought I could hear whispers and movement in the background.

"Is somebody there with you, Yolande?"

"*Mais non, chéri!* I am alone in my office. When will I see you?"

"As soon as I can get away. Not tonight, I'm afraid."

"But, Tyler, this is so long . . ."

"The very minute I'm free, I'll come, you know that."

Hanging up, I had the sudden odd feeling I'd been talking to a stranger.

This is Brad Lindley in Paris, with a special report by TV satellite of a personal investigation into the attempt to assassinate Premier Auguste Nicollet.

At latest word the condition of Blaise d'Archeval, the government official who drew the would-be assassin's fire, remains stationary at critical. Doctors are giving the young, handsome, and popular Count d'Archeval a fifty-fifty chance to survive.

The first visitor to the hospital this morning was U. S. Ambassador Otis, who brought flowers she had gathered herself in the embassy garden. A surprise caller at the hospital this afternoon was former Foreign Minister Claude Courtailles, a deputy in the National Assembly and Premier Nicollet's political archenemy. The temperamental Courtailles broke off relations with his close friend and protégé d'Archeval when the count decided to remain with the Nicollet regime after Courtailles resigned, and today's gesture would appear to indicate a reconciliation. Besieged by reporters, the ex-Foreign Minister simply advised them to be on hand for his keynote speech at the Assembly session opening day after tomorrow.

The significance of that session for the future of Europe and our own country cannot be overestimated. The nations of the Western world as well as Russia and—never forget—the People's Republic of China, will be watching the outcome. For it is highly probable that this French Parliament will tip the balance in the fate of the Atlantic military alliance—will decide whether the armed truce between the superpowers will continue unabated or be succeeded by an era of mutual trust and true peace.

It is equally likely that this week's sensational events in Paris will have a crucial bearing on the Assembly's attitude, as Premier Nicollet has termed the shooting at the Palais Matignon a plot to terrorize supporters of his pro-détente policy on the eve of the Assembly meeting.

Nicollet's statements last night and this morning indicate that the government is satisfied that the underground activist organization called the Guerre des Jeunes—the War of the Young—is guilty of the crime. To this charge the Premier has appended a grave corollary: that the American ambassador to France was recently in communication with Yves Lannuc, an arrested leader of the Guerre des Jeunes and a friend and fellow student of the ambassador's daughter, Christine, at the University of Paris.

Lannuc and all other members of his group steadfastly deny any connection with the plot.

As you know, our attractive and dynamic envoy has been the object of controversy in the French press ever since her arrival last spring. The simple fact that a woman is occupying this eminent and sensitive position on the diplomatic roster here has been enough to excite public interest in everything she says and does. But the new ambassador proved to be more than a ceremonial figurehead, as her career colleagues in the embassy have learned—at times to their sharp displeasure. She early aroused official French irritation by her forthright attitude toward narcotics activity in Marseille, among other publicized moves.

A much more serious breach of diplomatic etiquette, in the French view, was the ambassador's unannounced private visit to the then Foreign Minister Courtailles at his Paris home amid reports of a political feud between Courtailles and his Premier. This act not only earned the ambassador a rebuke from her own Secretary of State, never made public, increasing earlier friction between them—it was also a factor leading to the resignation of Courtailles and his emergence as chief of a vocal anti-détente faction in Parliament which is about to be heard from in full volume.

Subsequent to the Courtailles incident there is reason to believe that the ambassador, resenting the reactions of her superiors in Washington, resolved to express her own views on what she regards as the threat in the trend toward détente. She did so in her now famous speech before the American Club of Paris, warning against dissolution of NATO and withdrawal of the U.S. nuclear arsenal in Europe. New demands were heard in the French press for the ambassador's recall, on grounds she was persistently interfering in France's internal affairs —demands culminating in the student demonstration on the Place de la Concorde, which the ambassador is known to believe was encouraged by persons within the Nicollet government.

But all this checkered ambassadorial history pales before the latest crisis over the assassination attempt and Premier Nicollet's charges linking the American ambassador to the conspiracy. In making those charges the Premier cites a letter the ambassador wrote to her daughter, then living like other Sorbonne students in a Left Bank hostel. The inference is that political information allegedly contained in the letter was to be passed on to Yves Lannuc.

Ambassador Otis has responded immediately to police inquiries into these matters, including questions about Christine's association with the Guerre des Jeunes group. Declining to take advantage of diplomatic immunity, the ambassador this morning escorted her daughter to the Palais de Justice and waited while Christine was interrogated at length by an examining magistrate. The substance of Christine's testimony I know to be as follows:

Her mother's letter, which she understandably discarded after reading it, was simply an affectionate note saying Christine was missed by all at the embassy Residence. It contained no other statements, personal or political.

Christine was on friendly terms with Yves Lannuc but never was a member of the Guerre des Jeunes.

All day yesterday until after the shooting occurred, Christine was at Yves Lannuc's bedside in the Hotel des Fosses, nursing him through an illness. She testifies to the fact that not only was young Lannuc not at the scene of the shooting, but the Guerre des Jeunes knew nothing of the plot to shoot Premier Nicollet until approximately three weeks ago, when Yves Lannuc was asked by a student of his acquaintance to attend a secret meeting of young Maoist extremists, among them Charles Androuet, at the home of Clément Marot, a Communist deputy in the National Assembly.

In presence of Marot, various alternatives were discussed as to ways of carrying out an act of violence to spotlight opposition to Nicollet's pro-détente policy. The Maoist group felt this policy must be thwarted at all costs, since if successful it would leave Russia free to prepare the conquest of Red China.

Within an hour after the meeting in Marot's apartment, Lannuc confided to Christine Otis that he had refused to associate the Guerre des Jeunes with the Maoist plans, although he had pledged not to reveal his knowledge the conspiracy existed.

Such are the main points of Christine's statement to the examining magistrate today.

Without prejudging the guilt or innocence of anyone else involved, it is this correspondent's inescapable conclusion that the Nicollet government's charge against the United States ambassador to France is a trumped-up effort to obtain her recall by reason of her adamant personal opposition to Nicollet's policy of détente.

This is Brad Lindley with a special report from Paris.

24

IT HAD BEEN no secret to Premier Auguste Nicollet that the news would break wide open. That was obvious by early afternoon, when Examining Magistrate Patrice Duparc made a somber and highly confidential telephone report to the Premier personally. Nicollet was simply waiting to learn when and how the story would come out. Meanwhile he had a few hours to consider his options.

Government TV technicians monitored Brad Lindley's satellite transmission as usual. Within minutes after the text was translated, copies were on the way to the Premier's office at the Matignon and the press chief at the Quai d'Orsay. Shortly afterward a late evening telephone conference between Nicollet and Foreign Minister Bloire decided on an overnight police roundup of all known Maoists and the expulsion of Brad Lindley from France within forty-eight hours.

Word of their decision was then passed to the Cabinet, from which the knowledge was leaked immediately to Clément Marot, giving him the opportunity to issue a blanket public denial in tones of outraged honor. The same statement contrived to make it appear Lindley had been expelled at Clément Marot's behest, but the latter effort misled nobody familiar with Auguste Nicollet's vindictiveness. In addition to getting Lindley for violating the secrecy of judiciary proceedings, the Premier had the satisfaction of settling earlier scores against a foreign correspondent who had repeatedly embarrassed his government.

Among those pleased would be Ralph Hobbs. I remembered Hobbs predicting that sooner or later Brad Lindley would be kicked out of France. I didn't want to think about Mariana's reaction. She didn't know yet. Mme. Hanotte had informed everyone the ambassador and Cristy were sleeping late this morning and not to be disturbed short of major emergency.

André Perpidan had been instructed to serve the government's expulsion order on Lindley after questioning him at his apartment as to the sources of his information. Actually, as soon became clear, there was no doubt in the minds of those concerned that the broadcast was accurate. Christine Otis did not invent her testimony. The chief problem for Nicollet now was finding a scapegoat to protect his own position. And he had to have him before tomorrow's opening of Parliament. The problem for Marot was surviving with his parliamentary immunity and political skin intact.

All this was evident, either directly or by sly suggestion, from the morning news reports. Listening fascinated to my bedside radio, I noted Marot had been called to a suddenly announced meeting of Communist chiefs later today, which undoubtedly presaged his official disgrace. Marot would do better, reported a Radio Luxembourg commentator with thinly disguised relish, to skip the summons and take refuge in the Chinese embassy before some pro-Kremlin fanatic in the party turned a gun on him.

To me the extraordinary facet of the plot was Marot's apparent belief he could get away with it.

Meanwhile the latest police dragnet had thrown up a prize catch of Maoists now facing interrogation by Judge Duparc. As a result of Christine's testimony it was not expected Yves Lannuc would continue to honor his pledge of silence, and identification of those attending the secret conference with Marot would soon follow.

I learned another highly interesting fact from Beasley Turner on arriving at the Chancery after breakfast. A remarkably early phone call from the Quai d'Orsay had informed the embassy Foreign Minister Bloire would be unable to receive M. Spaulding this morning as scheduled—which meant, of course, it was no longer feasible to request the ambassador's recall.

"You're a strange fellow," I said to Beasley. "You look almost disappointed."

"Me?" He professed astonishment. "Don't talk silly."

"Now you look guilty."

He blushed to his ears. "Come off it."

"I guess you just can't help yourself, Beasley. Think of all the excitement there would have been."

"Well—." He managed a laugh. "Don't you like excitement?"

There was plenty of it still around. Toward noon Nicollet appeared at the Elysée to report to the President. It was a long session from which the Premier emerged looking a little strained. But he had found his scapegoat. He told reporters he had informed the President that André Perpidan had just been relieved of his responsibilities as director of the conspiracy investigation "for reasons of greater efficiency"—in other words, for providing the government with inaccurate information.

Nicollet said the reason for the expulsion order against Brad Lindley was self-evident but declined to discuss Clément Marot's involvement in the plot on grounds he was too busy for further questions. He then hurried back to the Matignon.

At Beaujon Hospital, Blaise d'Archeval's condition was unchanged.

Yolande said, "Then she will not be recalled to America, *après tout*," and looked almost disappointed, like Beasley Turner in my office a few hours before.

"I didn't say that. I said the French can hardly request it, now. But in Washington the Secretary of State seems to want to get rid of her. He may still be able to clear it with the President."

We were lunching at a tiny place she knew near the Chambre Syndicale where the Quincy was a specialty. It was so good we'd already finished a bottle and started another. With the pressure easing off a little, at least for the moment, I could no longer refuse Yolande's insistence that we meet somewhere, anywhere, at any hour, just to see each other again. In the cool gloom of the restaurant she looked aloof, beautiful, and totally Parisienne, like any one of the fashion models sitting all around us, and once more I had that odd impression we had become strangers. As if the events of just these past few days—a separation that seemed like weeks—had somehow changed our relationship, in spite of ourselves, each of us cautiously, even fearfully now trying to recapture the way it was.

"But if she should go, Tyler. What will be your position then?"

"I don't know yet." I hadn't told Yolande about my letter to Mitchell Remington. Until I had a reply, I wasn't going to tell anyone. "Let's wait and see if it happens, first. Everything has been closing in so fast I can't see the forest for the trees anymore. And Mariana is unpredictable, as you must be aware by now. Who knows? Maybe she'll just resign."

"Is this possible?"

"Anything is possible in this situation." And I thought, with a little pang in my chest, of Brad Lindley. For Brad, wasn't she entirely capable of throwing up the whole thing and running off to Sardinia?

"The ambassador had much courage to go with her daughter to the *juge d'instruction*," Yolande was saying. "I think it has been good for her. People are changing their opinion of her, for that. At least the women."

I smiled. "Are you one of them? Are you glad for Mariana?"

Her little shrug as she drained her glass again. "She has been indiscreet, Tyler. As you have just said, she is unpredictable. I suppose that is feminine. She can't help it. But are these the qualities for an ambassador?"

"Dearest Yolande, being indiscreet is *not* only feminine. It can be masculine, too."

"*Les tapettes, oui!*" She laughed, then looked around guiltily. Two obviously effeminate men at a table across the little room had glanced up and frowned at the reference to homosexuals.

"You were overheard," I said.

"I know." She leaned forward and whispered. "One of them is chief designer for Frégaux. Here I must take more care."

"Anyway, don't let Mariana hear you talk this way. She's equal rights and equal abilities, you know."

"Mariana, Mariana!" The cool aloofness was suddenly gone, replaced by a dark intensity in her look. Her voice was edgy and the smile left her eyes. "Frankly, Tyler, shall we always speak of nothing but Mariana?"

"Wait a minute, darling—you're the one who's been asking about her."

"And why not, since you are the world's authority on Mariana? Since you spend your days and nights with Mariana. Since you give your life to Mariana!"

My turn to look around us. "I don't think you're aware that everybody's listening to you."

"No, they are listening to *you*. They recognize you, Tyler. You are my little celebrity! Anyway, I don't care what they listen to. We don't have to stay here. We can go now to Rue de Belle-chasse."

The wine was talking. I laughed. "It would be great, wouldn't it? But we both have jobs, remember?"

"Tyler—" her voice low and urgent. "Come back, now, to Rue de Bellechasse. This is very important to me."

"To me, too. But it's just not possible. Maybe tonight. I should be at the Chancery right now."

"Where she is waiting for you."

"No. She hasn't been there all morning. She may not come in at all."

"But you hope very much that she will be there now, yes?"

I felt the wave of exasperation rising. "Look—at a time like this, Yolande!"

"If she is in Paris there will be always a time like this."

"You know better than that. You know this is a time of crisis. There's nothing I can do about you and me till it passes. You're being unfair, *chérie*. Where's the Yolande I knew in the Sorbonne days . . . even a few weeks ago—."

"The Sorbonne days! Don't you understand yet? We cannot live in those days again. Not even of a few weeks ago. That Yolande is gone, Tyler. There is only today's Yolande, every day. You and I, we are *now*, not then!"

Helpless tears welled in her eyes and silence stood between us like a wall. I turned and made a sign to the waiter for the check.

Passing the ambassador's anteroom on the way back to my office, I hesitated a moment at sight of a nattily attired and vaguely familiar figure slumped dejectedly in a chair, several newspapers in his lap.

Marcus Feld recognized me first.

"Mr. Paine, isn't it?" He jumped up and intercepted me in the hall, black eyes somehow uneasy in the swarthy face. "I want to thank you for your courtesy when I called from the airport."

I shook the hand with all the rings on it. "I understand you talked with the ambassador."

"Oh yes. She called me. But I haven't seen her yet. I've been trying to reach her at the Residence but they say she's not available. So I thought I'd just try her office. I've been waiting an hour."

"Is she coming to the Chancery today?"

He gave a melancholy half-shrug. "The secretaries don't know. I thought you might know."

"I'm afraid I don't know, either."

There was an awkward pause. When he spoke again he was almost pleading. "Mr. Paine, let me be frank with you. I'm a busy man. I left Washington in the middle of a big case to come all the way over here to help Mariana and I find I can't even see her. Now, I know you're as close to her as anybody. She says she doesn't need any assistance. I'd like to hear—would you agree with that?"

"If that's what the ambassador told you, Mr. Feld, I'm sure she can handle whatever problems arise."

He glanced back at the newspapers on the floor in front of his chair. "She's got problems, all right. I can't make out much of that French, but the *Herald Tribune*'s got all the facts, haven't they?"

"Just about."

"It's a tough deal for Cristy. But she's a tough little girl." He said it without much affection.

"I think you'll find," I told him, "that Cristy Otis is going to come out of all this a changed young person—for the better."

"Yeah." I suspected he wanted to add, And about time, too. "Am I right in guessing they can both be grateful to Brad Lindley for that broadcast?"

"That would be my guess also, Mr. Feld."

"The paper indicates he's a good friend of Mariana's."

"I'd say so, yes."

Another pause. I felt sorry for him.

"Well," he said wistfully, "I suppose I'm keeping you from your work. I'll stick around here for as long as I can, but if she doesn't come in will you remind her I'll be waiting to hear in the hotel?"

"I certainly will."

"Even if it's just a phone call, Mr. Paine."

"I'll tell her."

"Quite a broadcast by Brad Lindley!" I heard him say as I went on to my office.

It was generous of him, considering they were both in love with the same woman.

The ambassador did not appear. Shortly before six, on my way over to make a final check on the news tickers, I saw the anteroom was empty. For our patient visitor's sake I hoped he'd been able to get in touch with Mariana again. But if I'd ever known a man with a lost cause it was Marcus Feld.

Beasley Turner was still hanging around the Public Affairs section when I stepped into the teleprinter room. He came out of his office to greet me and I looked at my watch.

"By this hour you should be on your third martini, Beasley."

"I've got a feeling," he said. "The Secretary's supposed to be addressing the National Press Club just about now."

And as if in telepathic answer to his words the bulletin bell on the UPI machine began to ring furiously.

Washington's National Press Club luncheons are the sounding board for anyone who will make news for the audience. The speaker can use them to push his campaign for whatever. In turn the club president can praise, tease, or roast the guest in his introduction, and when the speaker finishes he's fair game for questions from the floor.

I hadn't known Stoneface was scheduled to appear. In fact the date had been set up on short notice immediately after his hearing before Bryce Halsted's Foreign Relations Committee. Now we crowded the high-speed ticker side by side and watched the biggest story of the day come over, hardly believing our eyes.

BULLETIN FIRST LEAD

UNITED PRESS INTERNATIONAL

WASHINGTON, SEPT. 4: THE U. S. SECRETARY OF STATE WARNED TODAY THE TREND TOWARD DE-TENTE CAN BE IMPERILED IF NOT REVERSED IF ANY NATION SEEKS TO EXPLOIT IT TO WEAKEN AMER-ICA'S ALLIANCES.

IN REMARKS BEFORE THE NATIONAL PRESS CLUB BELIEVED DIRECTED NOT ONLY AT RUSSIA BUT ALL EUROPEAN COUNTRIES, THE SECRETARY LASHED OUT AT THOSE WHO WOULD "PERVERT THE BASIC AIMS OF COEXISTENCE."

HE SAID AT ONE POINT, "I AM AUTHORIZED BY THE PRESIDENT TO STATE THAT THE KEYSTONE OF AMERICAN POLICY IS RESPONSIBLE INTERNATIONAL CONDUCT AND WE EXPECT OTHERS TO RESPECT THE SAME STANDARD."

WE OPPOSE THE CONCEPT OF ANY NATION OR COMBINATION OF NATIONS ATTEMPTING TO WIN REGIONAL OR GLOBAL DOMINANCE, THE SECRE-TARY SAID.

HIS OUTSPOKEN SPEECH AND THE TONE OF HIS ANSWERS TO QUESTIONS TOOK ON ADDED SIGNIFI-CANCE ON THE EVE OF THE FRENCH PARLIAMEN-TARY SESSION OPENING IN PARIS, WHERE THE POLICY OF DETENTE HAS BECOME A PRIME IS-SUE SINCE THE ATTEMPT ON PREMIER AUGUSTE NICOLLET'S LIFE.

(MORE TEXTUAL COMING UP)

1257p Wash.

Beasley uttered a low "*Je-zus!*" and tore the paper off the machine. "I'll phone this to Spaulding at home right away." He handed me the second copy.

There was a phone at the nearest desk. I grabbed it and said to the night operator, "Give me the ambassador at the Residence."

Tonight Mariana would sleep the sleep of the just.

25

ARE THERE CERTAIN days in a lifetime when so much happens it's impossible for the mind to absorb it all at once? For me, for Mariana, and in varying degree for the others affected by the climactic events of these twenty-four hours, this was such a day.

At every level, step by step, like a catharsis decreed by destiny, questions that had gnawed for months at us all seemed to achieve their resolution: the Secretary's stunning about-face in surrendering his total détente policy to Senate and, as quickly became known, to presidential pressure as well; the astonished and disbelieving reaction from Moscow, which had been secretly assured by the Secretary of plain sailing ahead; the elation of relief that swept the Western capitals and free peoples everywhere; and in France, after a surprise disavowal of Premier Nicollet at just the right moment from the Elysée Palace, the inevitable consequences in the National Assembly, where Claude Courtailles' impassioned speech rode the momentum, party lines collapsed, and, late in the evening, the Government put the issue to a confidence vote and went down and out of office, overwhelmed by a solid majority.

Sitting in the diplomatic gallery, among the ambassadors of the NATO powers, of the Soviet Union, of China, Mariana Hillman Otis of the United States witnessed the victory she had done so much to make possible.

Her special assistant, not eligible to attend, sweated it out alone in his apartment at the Residence, hearing the verdict with decidedly mixed emotions—pride for his ambassador, but a feeling that once again, perhaps, the little man's longing for a real peace of brotherhood had been frustrated and a new arms buildup made certain.

Earlier in the evening I'd had to make the painful decision to decline an invitation to the Rue de Bellechasse, in favor of another invitation from Stuyvesant Spaulding to join Abigail and the senior officers of the mission in the Blue Room for a champagne party in Mariana's honor on her return from the Assembly.

Looking around at their beaming faces, I reflected that even though this was an all-in-the-embassy-family gathering, a place should have been made for one other guest. (Snuffy, of course, would have cried damned poor protocol.) I knew Brad Lindley had had a long private meeting with the ambassador before she left for the Palais Bourbon, but he deserved to share, if anyone did, in this public moment of her triumph.

Like all good diplomats, Stuyvesant Spaulding knew how to swallow his former words and switch tracks without a single twinge of conscience, as he now rather pompously toasted the sagacity of his chief, to the accompaniment of murmurs of "hear, hear!" and generous applause from the staff. And once again I found myself, as I had that long-ago first day on the pier at Le Havre, standing glass in hand next to the chief's daughter, demure in a freshly ironed dress and actually smiling a little, a new kind of smile for Cristy, since Ralph Hobbs had told her there was reason to believe her friend Yves Lannuc would be quietly released within the next few days. In the midst of all this pleasant noise there was even a moment when Cristy raised her glass in my direction and said in the warmest voice I'd ever heard from her, "Here's thanks, Tyler, for helping out. . . ."

I stared at her somewhat amazed, then raised my glass back. "I'm glad for all of us," I said. "Your mother's pleased you're home again."

But Cristy shook her head with all her old stubbornness. "I'm not staying, you know."

"Then it's back to the Hotel des Fosses?"

"I haven't told Mariana yet. I'm going to India with Yves."

"India!"

I was looking into the eyes of an adult. "We've been talking it over, Yves and I. The worst urban poverty anywhere in the world is in Calcutta. We can do a little something about it. Only a little, but something. I'm going to write to my grandfather, among some others."

I didn't really expect to see the ambassador again after the party, but soon after it ended and mother and daughter went upstairs to their suite the inside phone rang in my bedroom. Mariana said, "I thought you might have left to meet Yolande."

"Not tonight."

"Then if you're still decent, shall we meet in the study in ten minutes?"

She came in wearing a simple white *robe de chambre*, her hair up, looking almost as young as Cristy and smoking a cigarette. With that combination, I told her I hoped it was tobacco.

I had some good news for her. Just before I left my room the radio carried a late evening report from Beaujon Hospital. Blaise d'Archeval had been taken off the critical list and, if there were no complications, could be considered out of danger.

Mariana had some good news, too. "Marcus Feld flew back to Washington this afternoon, so he won't be pestering either of us anymore. And you'll be interested to know that Cristy and Yves plan to go to India to do some really worthwhile work."

"She told me. You approved?"

"Wholeheartedly. So will my father, I'm sure." She smiled with a hint of wistfulness. "Cristy's never going to be mother's girl. I think it's time I learned to live with that fact."

"Losing a daughter, and gaining a friend?"

With all the evening's festivities I hadn't had a chance to ask about the Assembly debate.

"It all went very fast, once the issue was joined," she said. "It was probably a tactical error of Nicollet's to force the vote, but you know how French impetuosity can take over. If he'd waited to let things cool down for a day or two the outcome possibly would have been different. The big blow to Nicollet was losing his President's support." She smiled. "Do you remember the day I presented my credentials? He told me then he'd have the final say."

"And will Courtailles form the new government?"

Her shrug was totally French. "That's up to Slyboots in the Elysée. The ministerial consultations may take days."

"Musical chairs? Here we go again."

"With a difference, Tyler. The air has been cleared. Sir Harold told me when we were leaving the Chamber tonight that Krubitsyn begged the President to wait until after the debate to make his views public. No dice. The French are definitely on the record now. The next Cabinet will come in bound to uphold NATO and American nuclear defense."

"Leading to another round in the arms race and a new increase in tension."

There was a silence. Afterward she said, "We disagree?"

"On détente, I'm afraid we do. Fundamentally."

"You've never said that before, Tyler."

"It isn't my place to try to influence you on high policy."

She was looking at me with a faint smile. "Brad Lindley said something very much like that this afternoon."

"I'm surprised. I should have thought he'd dictate your policy, high or low."

"You know him too well."

We both laughed and the momentary friction eased. I was glad to change the subject with a question I very much wanted to ask.

"Will Brad appeal his expulsion order now that Nicollet's gone?"

She shook her head. "He's leaving tomorrow. First to New York, to resign formally from the network, then to Sardinia. His decision is final. He says he actually feels grateful to Nicollet for dragging him out of his rut. From now on, every day is his own, free. What a wonderful thing to have, Tyler!"

I tried to keep the tremor out of my voice. "And you, Mariana —will you be off to Sardinia one of these days?"

"Brad wants me to join him. I'm sure you've guessed that. But I have no plans, except to stay on the job here."

I was swept by a sudden feeling of relief so intense I had to turn away for a moment.

"For that reason, and others," Mariana was saying, "I must ask you to withdraw your application for transfer. I'm going to need you with me—indefinitely."

I stared. "Mitchell Remington told you?"

There was a ghastly instant of trying to guess how much, until she said, "He wants my reaction before he answers your letter."

"For God's sake, is *nothing* to be secret in this department?"

It made her laugh, and after a moment I joined in. If Remington *had* told her about my double identity it hadn't mattered, Mariana still needed me. All at once, in my relief, I felt a kind of helplessness, as if everything that happened to me from now on would be out of my hands. I looked away again and took out my handkerchief to wipe my lips. Just minutes ago I'd sat here thinking the responsibility was all mine—to get out, to break with Paris, to make another start at another post in another country, leaving everything behind me, maybe even Yolande, partner in my effort to recapture the innocent past. Already Yolande knew better than I how vain that effort is. And now this beautiful, vital, dedicated woman who sat opposite was calling me back into the present from which none of us could escape, the future which all of us must face. There never had been any question I would follow her, I knew that now.

Or would she choose the future Brad Lindley offered? And if she didn't, how would Tyler Paine fit into her life? I tried to imagine Mariana's next mission. Moscow? They'd never have her now. Peking? Unlikely, with the Maoist plot in the background. The Cabinet in Washington—or would that be too dull? A woman Vice-President? It was coming, that was sure. The country would soon be ready for it.

As our eyes met once more, I had a strange feeling Mariana was thinking exactly the same thing.